The Piano Lover

The
Piano
Lover

The first novel of a trilogy by
William Karl Thomas
Copyright 2018

published by
MEDIA MAESTRO - BOOK DIVISION

Cover design by William Karl Thomas

ISBN 978-1-62768-005-9

Printed in the United States of America

This book is a work of fiction within which many real persons and/or events have been described. However, all of the dialogue, all of the non-historical persons, and many of the events, are a product of the author's imagination, making any resemblance of such characters to real people purely coincidental.

Published April 2018

Published by
MEDIA MAESTRO - BOOK DIVISION
P.O. Box 50672
Tucson, AZ 85703
http://www.mediamaestro.net

TABLE OF CONTENTS

Chapter One
LA LUNE

The first thing he noticed was the beauty of her somewhat narrow symmetrical smooth unblemished face, made all the fairer because it was framed by long slightly wavy jet black hair. The large wide set brown eyes narrowed, the nostrils of the aquiline nose flared, and the perfect red lips pouted in an expression of anger that matched her determined march across the street away from the La Lune nightclub. A short paunchy balding man in a beige business suit elbowed his way between tourists strolling down Bourbon Street as he chased after her shouting, "Aurora, wait, you misunderstood."

David Wales stopped and leaned against the black cast iron lamp post surmounted by a glass windowed enclosure containing a flame shaped bulb simulating the gas light of a prior century, like all the lamp posts in News Orleans' French Quarter. Bourbon street was filled with tourists visiting the night club district, and David marveled at how oblivious the pedestrians were to the couple's heated argument. He listened with curiosity as she spun around to face the man and responded angrily with the hint of a Spanish accent. "Whad did I misunderstood? You hand on my ass? You touching mi chi chi? You pigs breath when you say, 'Ohhhhh, all the girls do it. It's pard o' de job.' Well, no this girl! Vete a la chingada!"

David smiled as she countered the man's efforts to retain her employment with clever negotiations to increase her salary, peppered with a stream of Spanish language invectives. His eyes traveled down her long shiny black hair to her black velvet top that covered perky little bullet breasts and stopped

1

just short of her tightly fitted black satin pants deliciously contoured over her narrow hipped provocative buttocks and continuing down to her black Flamenco boots that made her shorter height equal that of the short man. As his eyes traveled with them back to the La Lune, the girl obviously having won a considerable raise in salary and respect from her employer, his eyes continued up to the marquee beneath the chartreuse green neon "La Lune" sign which proclaimed, "Appearing nightly, Aurora Alonzo, Classic & Folk Guitarist."

David pushed away from the lamp post and entered the corner bar which had been his initial destination. Bertolli's Bar was typical of Bourbon Street bars, its walls lined with Mardi Gras posters and masks and shiny mirrored beads in the green, purple, and yellow Mardi Gras theme, but distinctive in that it was one of only two bars in the French Quarter that had opera records on the juke box, the other being the Napoleon House which had a more Bohemian ambience. Bertolli's ambiance was predictable Italian food and a fifty-fifty mix of tourists and locals. Locals who worked in the quarter, mostly males, came here to hit on tourists looking for a spicy adventure to tell about when they got home. This might range from hardcore gigolos and female prostitutes to less mercenary souls just looking for a one night stand.

With his blonde wavy hair, strong square jawed face, and six foot square shouldered frame, David garnered his share of attention from the ladies, despite his effort to dress down by only wearing an off white pin stripe seersucker sport jacket instead of his black tuxedo on his way to work. He kept his tuxedo jacket and cumberbund at the nightclub where they were quick and easy to don and less likely to be soiled. The seersucker was actually cooler and, despite its incongruity with his tuxedo shirt and pants, did not keep the ladies from turning their heads as he passed by.

David, however, was more interested in the excellent 'spaghetti a la Caruso' and operatic juke box selections than in the tourists. He ordered his chicken livers in Marinara sauce over spaghetti at the end of the bar and then reviewed the selections on the Rock-O-La jukebox with its colored glass tubes of bubbling liquid.coursing up and down the front of its gothic shaped five foot high case. As much as he liked the Napoleon House and its juke box selection of classic Caruso and other artists recordings from the dawn of the recording industry, he had heard, from one of his fans at the club where he worked, that Bertolli's juke box had contemporary opera artists on it.

David had acquired his newfound appreciation of opera from customers at the nightclub where he worked who drifted in after operas performed at The Municipal Auditorium on Rampart Street a few blocks away. Some were opera fans and some were singers willing to perform in the background of the opera in exchange for a few complimentary tickets and because of the thrill of being dressed up in costume on stage. Once in a rare while an internationally famous opera star would show up in the club, but they were usually surrounded by a protective entourage preventing any opportunity to engage them. However, the opera fans and 'spear carriers,' which is what the underpaid background performers called themselves, were emboldened to engage David because of his limited repertoire of classical and semi-classic numbers sandwiched between Broadway show tunes and movie title songs.

Previously, David had only attended The Municipal Auditorium for piano concerts by Jose Iturbi, Carmen Cavalerro, and Oscar Levant, and, of course, when invited by female fans to major balls of the Mardi Gras season. Now the 'spear carriers' were providing him with tickets to *Carmen, La Boheme*, and *Aida*, and a whole new world of vocal performance and foreign culture had been opened to him.

Even though he didn't understand the languages, he liked the musicality of the French and Italian librettos, while Wagner's operas in German he appreciated more for the heroic music. He was particularly moved by the sound of the male bass voices, but a little concerned that might be interpreted as a homosexual trait. He had discovered basso profondo Jose Mardones old recordings on the Napoleon House juke box, but now discovered Ezio Pinza on Bertolli's juke box. The old die hards at the Napoleon House considered Pinza a 'sellout,' because he had done the Broadway musical *South Pacific*, but David was not swayed by such social bias and put his nickle in the slot of the Rock-O-La and pressed a Pinza selection.

As David retrieved his spaghetti a la Caruso from the end of the bar, one of the barkers from a strip club near David's club waved him over to his table. On the corners of Bourbon and St. Louis Streets were Louis Prima's 500 Club and Stormy's Casino Royal, clubs that featured ectadesiasts, exotic female dancers, who teased the largely male audience by disrobing slowly down to pasties and a G-string. Prima's was owned by the famous bandleader Louis Prima and, when not on the road or otherwise engaged, they'd actually perform there. The rest of the time most tourists never realized the band and bandleader on the stage were not the real thing. Most had come to see the ever changing lineup of nationally known 'strippers' such as Kalantan and Lili Christine the Cat Girl. Stormy's was owned by the locally famous and extroadinarily beautiful dancer, Stormy, who was married to a local columnist and who headlined her show. She shared the bill with local dancers such as Evangeline the Oyster Girl, who emerged from a giant plastic oyster shell like Persephone of Greek mythology, and Allouette and her famous tassles mounted on the front of her bra and activated to look like a twin engine prop plane in flight by her gyrations on stage.

Simmie, short for Simmons, was called a 'barker' because all the strip clubs in the first five blocks of Bourbon Street off of Canal Street had doormen dressed in ragtime style striped coats, bow ties, and straw hats who 'barked' out to potential male customers on the street the erotic features offered by the show inside. They calculated the cultural level of potential approaching males and varied their enticements from lines like, "Inside this carnal temple, young man, you'll find the goddesses of your dreams who will reveal to you the sweet mysteries of their alabaster silken bodies," to the more direct appeal of, "No need to hand surf yourself to sleep tonight, fellas, 'cause the voluptuous nurses inside are guaranteed to cure your blue balls and take every last wrinkle out of your pecker."

Simmie had a short roly poly figure, curly red hair, a little turned up Irish nose, and black beady eyes that darted everywhere but at the person he was talking to. His modestly attractive mother was a stripper in one of the lesser clubs at the lower end of Bourbon Street, but he remembered his childhood when she had been a prostitute in the workman's red light district around Lee Circle. Despite all this, he clung to dreams of a successful career in show business. At his age of twenty-two, he figured being a barker at Louis Prima's 500 club was a step up from his mother's past.

He squeezed his fried oyster 'po boy loaf sandwich together as he tried to get his teeth around it, making a loud crunching sound as David set his plate on the table and sat across from him. Simmie's eyes darted around the room as he talked with his mouth full. "I saw you grooving on that puta from La Lune while she was bitching out her boss. I'm not so sure about having a spik nightclub on Bourbon Street. Mebbe they should keep all those switchblades and syphilis in Los Marinos down on Decatur Street where they can slice each other up without scaring the tourists."

5

David put a bib on to protect his tuxedo shirt and bow tie. "I don't think La Lune's management is Hispanic, and I don't think a female musician is likely to hide switchblades in her classical guitar."

Simmie leered at him with almost enough courage to make eye contact. "And you don't think the complexion of her ass makes a damn bit of difference as long as it's as tight and juicy as hers."

David speared a chicken liver on his fork and waved it at Simmie. "That's the first accurate thing you've said since I sat down."

Simmie was eager to ingratiate himself with any and every entertainer in the French Quarter. "Hey, you wanna see a primo tight juicy ass, Kalantan is opening tomorrow night. Let me comp you into the early show before you go to work?"

David swallowed, closed his eyes, then looked at him. "Thanks, Simmie, that's very tempting, but we all know Kalantan's a lesbian. Why frustrate myself over something I can never have?"

Simmie's eyes bulged. "Yeah, but what a great fantasy, doing a lesbo in a threesome with that juicy older brunette that travels with her and pretends to be her aunt."

David rolled spaghetti onto his fork. "We have to give you credit for a fertile imagination, Simmie. I'd have thought that working on Bourbon Street for years would have made you jaded and cynical about sex."

Simmie waved his 'po boy sandwich at David, dropping an oyster out of it. "Hey, man, I'm still twenty-two. It's you old guys..... how old are you?"

David paused with a fork full of food at his mouth. "Twenty-nine."

Simmie's eyes bulged. "Wow, man, almost over the hill. It's you old guys who have wore your thingy out and given up on sex."

6

David swallowed. "Don't worry about me, Simmie. I plan to be doing right by my ladies when I'm a hundred."

Simmie laughed. "By then they will have bronzed your dick and it'll be in a glass case at the Cabildo."

David downed his last forkfull, smiled, then started to get up and remove his bib. "By then I suspect you'll be a tour guide there and tell them all you knew me when. I gotta go to work. Bye."

As David rounded the corner at Stormy's Casino Royal, he saw the man he knew to be the emcee at Stormy's step out of a doorway circled with blinking lights, above which a new sign had recently been installed announcing The Inn Between. The emcee was shorter than David, with black slicked back hair and a narrow face with slightly bulging eyes. He resembled the film actor Peter Lorre who was the one of the villains in *Casablanca, The Maltese Falcon* and other Bogart movies. However, his nasal Jewish accent sounded more like a New Yorker than a European. The emcee spied David and said, "Aren't you the kid who plays in the club two doors down?"

David slowed to a stop. "Yeah, I'm the cocktail pianist there. You emcee at Stormy's, right?"

As the emcee extended his hand, a taller older balding man exited the door and walked up to them. Both men were dressed in black suits with bow ties, indicating to David that they worked in the Quarter. The emcee smiled excessively, making David suspect he wanted something from him. Shaking David's hand vigorously, the shorter man said, "Yeah, yeah. I'm Bernie Brill. I just opened this little back bar, The Inn Between. It's between Casino Royal and Diamond Jim Moran's, get it? Kind'a like an after hours club, open from two in the morning, when most clubs close, 'till sunrise. So, you see, we aren't in competition with you guys."

7

David kept a straight face. "No, just the other club where you emcee."

Bernie's smile dimmed slightly and he blinked as he said, "Yeah, right. Hey, this here's Richard Rose, he's a Limey I just hired to tinkle the ivories in our new club. Being fellow pianistas, maybe you could take him in hand and show him the ropes. You know, introduce him to other entertainers, where the local eateries are, that kind of thing."

Richard looked embarrassed as David remained silent, his eyes darting from Bernie to Richard and back to Bernie.

Bernie said, "Yeah, well, what's your name again, kid?"

David remained placid. "I didn't say, but my name's David Wales."

Bernie's smile broadened. "Yeah, right, so you go by Dave or Davey?"

David's left eyebrow rose slightly. "No, just David."

Bernie looked down as he nodded affirmatively, then up as he grabbed both men's right hands and placed them together in an enforced handshake, saying "David Wales, this here's Richard Rose." As Bernie turned to leave, he looked at David and said, "Thanks, David. Come into The Inn Between or Stormy's soon and lemme buy you a drink." Then he disappeared into the blinking lights of the doorway.

Embarrassed, Richard shook David's hand once and let it go. "Well, my new boss is not the greatest ambassador in the world, but, for better or worse, he is my boss."

David smiled. "I never met Bernie before, but he's typical of management in the night club district. You just have to be careful about saying 'yes' to anything, because there's usually a hook that's added to the deal after you've said 'yes.'"

Robert smiled and nodded agreement. "I understand. It's more or less the same on the continent, I mean, Europe. You have your own continent, don't you? I've hosted shows on radio and telly in England and France, even played the

8

Palladium in London and the Follies Begere in Paris, and they all behave like George Raft in a 'B' gangster movie."

David raised his eyebrows, impressed with Richard's history. "Well, just make sure you're paid on time and in full. Unlike the Palladium or Follies Bergere, around here when things go bad they don't give notice, they just fold their tents and steal away in the night leaving all us little people holding the bag."

Richard furrowed his brow and nodded his head. "Duly noted, David, and thanks for the warning. And about that 'show me around' thing, you don't have to...."

David raised his hand to stop him. "No sweat, man, I'll be happy to, but it'll have to wait until after work....oh, but you don't get off 'til sunrise."

Richard smiled, closed his eyes, and shook his head negatively. "Really, that's all right."

David look at his watch and took a step forward. "I'm late, but let's have dinner at Felix's on Iberville tomorrow evening at six. Anyone can direct you there. Okay?"

Richard smiled and nodded affirmatively. "Jolly good, Roger that!"

David patted his shoulder and took off towards his club.

The club David worked at was named The Voodoo Room and was tucked away from the main tourist flow on a cross street named St. Louis between Bourbon and Dauphine. The principal illumination were the three foot high black candles that had grown from a single black candle in a Creme De Menthe bottle until years of wax build up turned them into huge abstract sculptures, one in each of the six long curves in the mahogany bar that ran down one side the full length of the club. The driftwood and moss adorned ceiling hid rubber spiders suspended by long black threads routed through eyelets to the rear end of the bar, one over each candle lit table which would be lowered onto the unsuspecting guests when their drinks were all finished and the house did not have to replace any spilled during their screaming reactions. Pete, the bearded tatooed bartender wore a horizontally striped tee shirt and red head scarf simulating a pirate, and was a fairly good prestadigitarian performing simple magic tricks during any lull in his work. The most novel feature of the club was a framed water faucet suspended behind the cash register by thin wires which, despite the fact that it had no visible plumbing attached, ran water continually into a funnel beneath it. If you asked for a water chaser for your shot of booze, Pete put ice cubes in a glass, then filled it from the suspended faucet to prove it was real water.

The fenced podium at the center of the wall opposite the bar supported a beautiful ebony full grand piano, an upgrade from the original battered baby grand which David had negotiated when he was first hired. David agreed to tune and maintain it himself as an inducement to the frugal minded management who choked on the cost of the new ebony grand. The low fence, made of three foot high turned mahogany balusters with a top rail too narrow to sit on, was to protect David from over-appreciative females and, sometimes, their jealous boyfriends. A small spotlight hidden in the ceiling highlighted David's blonde wavy hair, his blue eyes, and the satin lapels of his black tuxedo.

The Voodoo Room was on the ground floor of a three story building owned by Valentina Siciliana McGregor who lived alone on the second floor. Val's first names and dusky exotic beauty came from her Sicilian ancestry, and the 'McGregor' came from her former marriage to Mack, but she went by her maiden name. Valentina was fifty and still quite beautiful when David was first employed, and he thought to himself that if he had to sleep with her to get the job it would be no great sacrifice, indeed. But, despite the speculation of others who perceived a sexual tension between them, Val maintained a professional coolness around him and David reciprocated with a sincere respect for her design and management of her club. They would sometimes lock horns over issues like the piano upgrade or her insistence that he not discourage patrons from ordering drinks for him which increased the till, but they would compromise with him maintaining the piano and the bartender making extremely weak drinks which the waitress would scoop away after he toasted his benefactor and took one sip.

Val lived on the second floor and rented the third floor to Dimitri Lebedev, a Russian who had a marionette act at Aladdin's, one of the gay clubs on Bourbon Street. The act was bawdy, but extremely clever, and Dimitri kept innovating it with insightful sometimes dark story lines. It was Dimitri who had wired all the spiders in the ceiling, recruited the pirate cum magician bartender, and built the baffling faucet trick behind the register. Some regulars speculated that Val was a dominatrix and Dimitri was her slave, but the reality was a far more prosaic business relationship where Val gave Dimitri occasional rent discounts in proportion to his improvements in her club.

Dimitri had a crush on David, just as he had a crush on a dozen other handsome French Quarter entertainers in the past. Dimitri had told Val he would reward her financially if she could promote a relationship between David and him. Val had felt David out about his gender orientation, the conversation making David suspect that she might finally be giving him an invitation, but only resulting in leaving David puzzled and Dimitri depressed when Val informed Dimitri she thought it was never to be.

There was a narrow alley beside the building leading to two first floor patio apartments at the rear, one tenanted by Zoe, the head bar maid at the club, the other used for storage. David walked down the alley to enter the rear door of the club which Zoe had already opened to perform her earlier janitorial duties and receive tradesmen's deliveries. She was replacing burned out table candles in their little glass housings while Pete, the bartender, was filling the multiple stainless steel sinks with ice and plunging glass bottles of beer in them. Zoe had been with Val since before Val divorced Mack. Now in her late forties, nature had not been as kind to her as it had been to Val, and her matronly figure caused her to huff and puff as she lifted the tray of candles to replace them on the individual tables.

David walked over to his locker at the rear corner of the room near the end of the bar. Two additional lockers, on a short partition wall that hid them from the main room, held supplies. Beside the lockers was a board with all the wires leading to the table spiders and terminating in a pattern of nails in the wall arranged like the tables. He exchanged his seersucker sport coat for the black satin cumberbund and black tux coat, then looked at the nearby table against the rear wall where Val sat each night to survey the entire room from this secluded corner. Zoe had squarely placed the morning edition of *The Times Picayune* and the afternoon edition of *The New Orleans Item* on the table, and God help anyone who dared to touch them before Val had finished reading them by the end of the night. Beside the papers was a gooseneck desk lamp, a huge copper ash tray, a box of kitchen matches, and two unopened packages of the long cork tipped Russian cigarettes Dimitri provided to Val as part of his rent reduction scheme. On the wall between the table and the rear door leading to the rest rooms on the patio was a pay phone. On the wall at a lower level behind the table was an antique looking wall phone with a side crank for the ringer. Suddenly the antique phone rang.

Zoe hastened across the room to answer it with a simple, "Yes?" Then, "Yes, M'am." She hung up the phone to look at

David and Pete, then announced, "She's on her way down." Zoe took the box of kitchen matches and began to light the three foot high black candles on the bar as Pete went to unlock and spread open the front double doors and David turned on the spotlight over his piano. On her way back from the front end of the bar, Zoe lit a sporadic pattern of table candles until the entire room was dancing with flickering shadows cast only by candlelight. Everyone stood at attention as Val appeared at the rear door in her usual white blouse with black string tie, black skirt, black sweater, black silk hose, and black high heels. She took one step into the room, surveyed it slowly, then smiled at Zoe and said, "Let the games begin."

That was David's cue to be seated and begin playing something lively, usually a Scott Joplin tune that he would repeat endlessly until the first customers started arriving.

Chapter Two
THE USUAL SUSPECTS

David woke with a splitting headache. He viewed the opposite wall and, as sometimes happened with a hangover, he momentarily thought he was in Paris on the Champs Elysees approaching the Arc de Triomphe, instead of just viewing the floor to ceiling mural he had painted on the opposite wall, which, along with the skylight he had installed that allowed viewing stars from his bed at night, greatly disturbed his landlord.

His landlord had been reluctant to rent to a young man, much less an entertainer, her shrewd Cajun business sense telling her those were two strikes against him. But David had schmoozed the portly sixty year old Mrs. Saucier and, despite her tendency to frown most of the time when doing business, had succeeded in making her smile and rent him the loft above what had once been the stables of a rich man's townhouse on Rue de Nicholls. The loft was one humongous room with a tiny little bath and kitchenette retrofitted into one end and broad windows on the other end that looked out on the tiled and tin rooftops of the New Orleans French Quarter, the spires of St. Louis Cathedral dominating the distant center of the view.

As his headache subsided and his vision sharpened, he began to re-evaluate the brush strokes in the mural, noting where he might have done better and wanting to blame the imperfections on Julienne, the aristocratic creole girl his own age who had encouraged his idea to paint the mural and assisted him with her expertise as an artist. Now he remembered that Julienne had been in the club last night, teasing him about what details he might have put in the mural and which French master's techniques he might have imitated in it. Julienne was a long lean classic beauty with a long aquiline nose, long athletic legs, and a presence and wardrobe that bespoke class and wealth. David was inclined to believe that Julienne was interested in him, but her conservative demeanor and her family's wealth intimidated him from making any advances. He assumed that her frequent visits to the club were, in her mind, just 'slumming.'

Something stirred beside him and he turned to see glistening long black hair on a pillow and the contours of a shapely female derriere tightly encased by the white sheet beside him. For a moment he thought that, perhaps, Julienne had finally dropped her guard and came to his loft last night to do more than criticize his painting. The figure turned and the closed eyed sleepy face of a beautiful brunette appeared. Then it all came back to him in a flash.

****

Indeed, Julienne had come to The Voodoo Room the previous night, taking her favorite barstool at the end of the bar closest to the front door and flanked by the spear carriers who idolized her as their favorite 'culture vulture,' swapping their personal ratings on everything from the operas they appeared in and the current showings at The Delgado Museum to the work of the starving artists who displayed their paintings on the iron fence around Jackson Square. Julienne drank 'grasshoppers,' creme de menthe in milk, and kept ordering Cuttysark Scotch in milk for David because she was trying to save his stomach lining and convert him to some semblance of a healthy diet. David wrapped the glass with a napkin so no one would notice the milk, and used it to toast whoever ordered new drinks for him while Zoe's slight of hand would remove the new drink before he would have to touch it.

Lenny and Louie, two of the spear carriers in their twenties, were bosom buddies bonded by their close ages, their separate but similar rural Cajun backgrounds, and alcoholism. Julienne would tease them that their closeness made them suspect of being gay, even though she knew, from looking in the mirror behind the bar at the way they surveyed her figure longingly, that they were heterosexuals; shy and insecure around women, but definitely heterosexual.

Another spear carrier, Jules, was of questionable sexual orientation, because he lived with Armand and Justine in a menage a trois. Jules was a French Jew converted to Catholicism who played the organ at St. Louis Cathedral on Sunday mornings. Short and slim with a spoonful of straight black hair that barely covered the beginning of a bald spot, thirty-five year old Jules appeared more feminine than the twenty-nine year old Armand who was taller, more muscular, and had a full head of curly black hair. Armand was almost sullen, his silence marking his insecurity in the face of Jules greater intellect and talents, Jules carrying the conversation in a tone that puzzled everyone's estimation of his gender orientation.

Justine looked like a classic dominatrix, which is what everyone assumed her role was with the two young men. A Parisian in her early fifties, she closely resembled Val's dark beauty with her long shiny black hair and penchant for black clothing. Her cultured French accent was usually heard criticizing everything from American politics to the outlawing of absinth liqueur, but usually in humorous sarcasm. She appeared to have a strained relationship with Val, which indicated the two had some past history that remained a mystery to the younger people at the bar.

The previous night was the eve of Bastille Day celebrating the French Independence created July 14, 1789, when the revolutionists stormed the Bastille Fortress Prison in Paris and freed the political prisoners. At midnight David was obliged to accompany and lead the singing of the French national anthem, *Les Marseillaise,* in the original French lyrics, a performance that he had to repeat after The Voodoo Room closed and he, Julienne, and Dimitri, who had just finished his last show at Aladdin's, migrated to The Napoleon House a few blocks away. The two story century old residential corner building on Chartres and St. Louis was so-called because, in the previous century, it was intended to be the new residence of Napoleon once he had been rescued from the island of St. Elba, but he died before the rescue party arrived. The ground floor bistro was owned by Pete Impastato, who unplugged the jukebox and helped Julienne atop one of the round tables with marble inlaid chessboards as she, holding Pete and David's hands for balance, led all the loyal patrons in the stirring lyrics, "Allons enfant de la Patrie, la jour de gloire est arrive!"

After they had exhausted all of the many verses to the song that Julienne and David could remember, the crowd thinned and the noise abated. Pete plugged the jukebox in again and a scratchy Caruso recording belted forth his operatic basso voice. The trio sat at a corner table and debated where to go next. Julienne was warm to David, but only patronizing to Dimitri, hoping he would leave the two of them alone. When it became obvious Dimitri was not going to leave David's side, Julienne declined further bar-hopping with the explanation she had to get an early start on a new exhibition she was installing at the art gallery she owned, promising to return the next night to continue the Bastille Day celebrations. Upon entering the long DeSoto Limousine Yellow Cab, she kissed David on both cheeks, then cooly extended her hand to Dimitri who touched it self consciously.

18

As the long Yellow Cab pulled away, Dimitri's self conscious expression turned into a mischievous smile as he turned to David and said, "Let's go to Aladdin's. I have to pick up some marionettes that need repairs, and I can get us free drinks there."

David winced. "I don't think so, Dimitri. I know it's your gig and all that, but I avoid the gay bars. Straight males there are assumed to be interested, and I'm really not interested. No offense."

Dimitri's eyebrows raised as he shook his head negatively. "No, no. No offense taken. I completely understand."

David looked at his amazingly thin gold Patek Phillipe wristwatch, a gift from Julienne. "Maybe I should call it a night anyway. I promised to meet that new English pianist for dinner tomorrow."

Dimitri rolled his eyes as his mind searched for alternatives. It wasn't often he had an excuse like Bastille Day to tag along with David, much less have him all to himself. His eyes widened as he blurted out, "I know, let's go to the Gin Mill."

David's brow furrowed. "The Gin Mill? I never heard of it. It doesn't sound enticing."

Dimitri gestured for David to follow as he headed toward the river front. "Oh, come on. It'll be fun. It's one of those seaman hangouts on the waterfront."

David followed hesitantly. "Seaman's hangouts? You mean like Los Marino's where there's a stabbing or shooting at least once a month?"

Dimitri frowned and smiled at the same time. "No, no, no, no! This is a Greek sailor's hangout,. Very mellow. Very laid back. You'll see."

As David entered The Gin Mill on the very un-fashionable Canal end of Decatur Street, it appeared very conventional with dim red, orange, and yellow lighting, largely from neon beer signs that lined the walls and back bar. The only distinctive features were a crude panoramic mural of the Acropolis on the wall opposite the bar, and the fact that the juke box was blasting Greek music that sounded like dueling balalaikas. Formica topped tables surrounded a small dance floor with mostly men populating the bar and mostly amber bottles of Uzo wine populating the tables. All eyes turned to them and followed them as they approached the bar. Dimitri looked at David. "Cuttysark in milk, right?"

David surveyed all the eyes staring at them. "Yeah, right."

Dimitri smiled at the unsmiling bartender. "Cuttysark in milk over ice, and a Black Russian, please."

The bartender glared at him sullenly as he shook his head from side to side slowly.

Dimitri's smile faded. "What, you don't have milk?"

The bartender spoke as somberly as he looked. "No Cuttysark. No Kahlua. Just well Scotch and well vodka."

David noticed sporadic bottles of local beer on the tables, wrinkled his nose and said, "That's okay, Dimitri. I'll just have a bottle of Dixie beer."

Dimitri raised his eyebrows and held up two fingers to the bartender who retrieved two sweaty amber bottles of ice cold beer with their golden 'Dixie' labels, popping the caps and setting them noisily on the bartop.

As Dimitri handed him one of the bottles, David asked, "Why are they all staring at us?"

Dimitri tried to suppress his excitement as he pulled the beer bottle away from his lips and swallowed. "They don't see many Americans come in here."

David took a sip of beer and frowned at Dimitri. "Well, I assume they've seen you in here before, and why would they peg us as Americans and not Greek?"

Dimitri took a deep breath. "Not too many blonde Greeks, and not too many men as handsome as you come here."

20

Just then a small but well proportioned young man with very curly black hair and very tight fitting black pants and tee shirt walked up to David and extended his hand, then smiled and said what sounded like, "Zopono?"

David's frown deepend as he stared at the young man, but spoke to Dimitri. "What the hell is he saying? What the hell does he want?"

Dimitri was holding his breath and had to inhale deeply to reply. "He's asking you to dance with him."

David turned to Dimitri angrily. "Dimitri, I told you I didn't like to go to gay bars."

Dimitri shook his head negatively. "No, no. He's not gay. This isn't a gay bar. He's a Greek sailor. It's their custom for men to dance with each other."

David looked at the young man sternly and started to point his finger at him, but the sailor gripped his hand and pulled him out on the dance floor beside him, crossing his foot over in a dance step which, in an effort to keep his balance, David appeared to duplicate. A slightly older heavier man gripped David's other hand and pulled him in the opposite direction, both the Greek men crossing over their foot in the opposite direction as they maintained a line. The two sailors then pulled David backwards with them, then forwards with them, and David unconsciously began to mimic their steps.

When the audience began to clap their hands in time with the music, it occurred to David that this was a lot like square dancing, except the guitars were replaced with balalaikas and there were no women in the line. He noticed, however, that the few sullen faced women dressed in black were now smiling and clapping their hands. In fact, everyone was now smiling, even himself. The men released his hands as the older one stepped forward and did a solo with a Flamenco style pirouette, then the younger man stepped forward and repeated the same step, then the two looked to David

21

expectantly, and, despite the grimace on his face, he felt obliged to do the same. The two men gripped his hands as a fourth man joined the line which danced to the left and right and back and forth before the fourth man did his solo variation of the Flamenco step and each of the others repeated it. In time the line grew to sixteen men forming a circle completely around the dance floor, and David's grimace had evolved into a smile as he reluctantly admitted he was enjoying himself.

Dimitri remained at the bar, even after two separate men had invited him to join the line and Dimitri shook his head negatively. Then, as David danced left and right and forward and backward, he noticed another muscular man with a large black mustache approach Dimitri and invite him to dance. The man smiled mischievously as Dimitri declined, then the man slid his large hand down Dimitri's back to his buttocks and squeezed. Dimitri's eyes bulged as he shot three feet away from the man, who continued to leer at him. Dimitri's faced registered panic as he headed for the door, and David broke free of the dancing men and followed him out of the bar.

As the two walked rapidly in the direction of Jackson Square, David frowned at Dimitri. "What was that all about? I thought you said it wasn't a gay bar."

Dimitri's breathing slowed down until he caught his breath. "It's not, but that doesn't mean an occasional sailor might not try to live up to his Greek reputation, or down to it, if you prefer."

David looked away from Dimitri's obvious embarrassment. "Well, that little adventure had two unexpected surprises. You want to get some coffee at Café duMonde?"

Dimitri's normally pallid complexion was still blushed. "No thanks, I think I've had more than enough adventure for one night. I'll drop by the Voodoo Room tomorrow after my last show. Goodnight, David," and he headed down the iron fence on one side of Jackson Square.

David crossed Decatur to Café duMonde with its giant green and white striped canopy covering a huge patio surrounded by a low iron lace fence enclosing almost a hundred tables with iron bases and iron framed chairs. An elderly black man stepped forward from the cluster of black waiters uniformed in white shirts, black bow ties and pants, and long green and white striped aprons. At this early morning hour, Café duMonde was still populated by dwindling numbers of tourists and growing numbers of nightclub and restaurant staff getting off work. The elderly waiter greeted David familiarly with, "Evening, Mr. David."

David smiled at him warmly and said, "Evening, Alphonse. Is the corner table available?"

Alphonse's smile revealed two very noticeable gold incisors in the front of his mouth. "Sure is, Mr. David," and he escorted him to a corner table with the best view of Jackson Square across the street, its high black iron fence surrounding a full city block size park, its curvy pathways dotted with cannons and a central heroic size statue of General Andrew Jackson, hero of the 1815 Battle of New Orleans against the British, and later the 7th President of the United States. Behind the square could be seen the dramatically lighted St. Louis Cathedral flanked by the two multiple arched Cabildo buildings on either side, onetime government buildings from the Spanish Colonial period and now museums. On either side of Jackson Square were the block long identical three story Pontalba Buildings claiming to be the first apartment buildings ever built in North America. Their brick facades were festooned with iron lace balconies and their ground floor storefronts including the Vieux Carre (Old Quarter) District offices which mandated that the two century old architecture of the thirteen square block original city limits would be preserved by law. Viewed from the river front Café duMonde, the whole scene transported you to a centuries old era of opulence and elegance.

David ordered the only thing on their menu, café aulait and beignets, unless you wanted your coffee black, and surveyed the half filled patio. He recognized strippers and barkers from the Bourbon Street nightclubs, and singers and musicians from the bars with musical entertainment. As his gaze came to rest on the table nearest him, he was delighted to see the spitfire from La Lune that he had witnessed arguing with her boss at the beginning of the evening. She was in a heated discussion with a young man with long curly black hair that was shiny with grease.

"I done care eef ids a French town. I done care eef de French revolution was inspired by de American revolution. I done lake any song whad talks aboud 'impure blood,' 'q'uon sang impure.' Dad's racist to me." She was practically spitting the words at the young man.

The young man tried to sound reasonable. "But, Aurora, it was written two hundred years ago, it's a tradition, their tradition, and they're your audience, they pay your salary."

She squinted and glared at him at the same time. "Ramon, look around you. You see any black faces here?"

Ramon looked over his shoulder. "Yeah, every waiter here is black."

She shook her head negatively. "No! Add de tables. De customers. No one black face dere. Ramon, you live een a racist country. De Conquistadores talked aboud de impure blood of our Indian ancestors. De fair skinned oligarchs who rule Mehico today tink of you and mi as unworthy 'halfbreeds.' You wan me to reinforce fear and hatred by singing aboud 'impure blood.' No thees femenista!"

Ramon shrugged his shoulders and sighed. "Aurora, be realistic about the time and place to do battle. When you've

24

got a large enough fan base, you'll have enough power to pick and chose, to defy our employers and tradition. Right now you're just burning your bridges before you get to some basic goals. And those are bridges I still need to cross." Ramon stood up, retrieved his black case that housed a silver flute from under the table, threw some quarters on the tablecloth for a tip, and left. As he walked past David, Aurora's eyes followed him until they were focused on David.

Her slight frown of regret changed into a raised eyebrow of anger as the two stared at each other. "Whad you staring add, gringo?"

David's eyes circled her face and returned to her eyes, his expression almost passive with a closed mouth smile. "Pure beauty."

She leaned back with a look of disdain. "Is dad de bess line you can come up wid, gringo?"

David sipped his coffee and smiled. "It was true earlier this evening when I saw you giving your boss hell in front of La Lune, and it's still true."

Her eyes narrowed at him. "You were add La Lune tonide when id hoppon?"

David wasn't sure about her reference to 'it.' "I was on the street corner when you raked that fat bastard over the coals and apparently negotiated a raise before returning to La Lune. Then I had dinner at Bertolli's."

Her pursed lips relaxed and she blinked. "Bud you were nod dere add midnight when id hoppon?"

David's eyes lit up with interest. "I was working my piano gig at The Voodoo Room all night until we closed at two. When what happened?"

She bit her lip and looked at him suspiciously. "You a musician?"

David shifted in his chair and tilted his coffee cup to discover it was empty. "I play a cocktail single at The Voodoo

Room on St. Louis between Bourbon and Dumaine, just a few doors from Diamond Jim Moran's Restaurant."

She leaned forward and leaned both arms on the table. "De Voodoo Room. Dad's a gay bar, ride?"

David winced. "No, it's a...."

She shook her head positively. "Id's a tourist trap. I know."

David rolled his eyes. "No, actually, it's more like a local bar. Mostly Vieux Carre residents and some local media people, artsy craftsy types who like their music a little quieter and a little more cultured than Bourbon Street."

She scowled. "Bourgeois."

David smiled. "Yeah, maybe a little more upper middle class and a little more genuinely cultured." David gestured to Alphonse.

Her scowl turned into a sneer. "I bed you memorize every song dad was ever on *De Hid Parade.*"

David chuckled. "Would that my memory was that good, although I probably have every *Hit Parade* song that ever was in the fake books I sometimes resort to."

Alphonse arrived. "Yes, Mr. David?"

David gestured toward the table. "Another café au'lait, please, Alphonse." Then he looked at Aurora. "May I order you another coffee, Aurora, is it?"

She stood up and started to pass between David and Alphonse. "No, I tink I go."

David looked up at her. "Here I am trying to build a bridge, and all you can think to do is to burn it down."

She whirled around and glared at him angrily. "Id's muy impolite to eavesdrop on privade conversacion!"

Alphonse's eyes rolled toward the ceiling. David continued to smile at her and said, "It's hard to avoid overhearing someone who's as passionate about their prejudices as you are."

26

Aurora's eyes bulged, her face began to turn red, and her voice rose twenty decibels. "Prejudice?"

Alphonse leaned slightly toward her. "Coffee, Miss?"

She turned her face to him, distracted, and said, "Si, bud black." Then she sat at David's table in the seat opposite him, still glaring at him and demanding, "I'm prejudiced?"

David called to the retreating Alphonse. "And some more beignets, please, Alphonse." As Alphonse nodded and retreated, David turned back to her.

Aurora banged her fist on the table, making the powdered sugar in the empty saucer that had held the beignets jump in the air. Her neatly plucked jet black eyebrows rose in unison. "You have de audacity to call me prejudiced? You, you, capitalist pig, you!"

David looked off into space as if concentrating. "I've been called a wolf and a dog many times, and, on one memorable occasion, a stallion." Then he looked at her calmly. "But this is the first time I've been called a pig." He leaned back and smiled. "Would that I had a sufficient bank account to be called a capitalist. That would certainly be worth your disdain." He straightened up and set the dishes to the outside of the table. "But, alas, I'm afraid I am just one of the peons aspiring to become one of the bourgeois." Then he looked her in the eye. "And, yes, you're prejudiced. You're prejudiced against Americans because they were born into a world with more advantages than you were. You're prejudiced against the French because they cling blindly to traditions just as all older cultures do. And you're prejudiced against yourself because you don't think you deserve the good fortune to be headlining in a major nightclub with your name up in lights on the marquee. That's why you burn bridges behind you. That's why you quibble about the lyrics of a two hundred year old song. That's why you battle with anyone who holds a mirror up to your anger and self doubt."

27

Aurora's face was now scarlet as she raised her closed fist above her head, a fist with which she would surely have struck David had Alphonse not placed his full tray in front of her at that moment. She lowered her fist, closed her eyes, and inhaled deeply in an effort to control her anger. As David put too many sugar cubes in his coffee and stirred it, she opened her eyes and stared angrily at him. "So! Who are you? Siggy Freud's grandson?"

David sipped his coffee and smiled at her. "No. Like I told you, I'm just a fellow musician trying to make a living in a profession that explores and exploits people's emotions; new or old, good or bad, misguided or not."

Her eyes narrowed at him. "And you done tink id's racist to sing songs aboud 'impure blood'?"

David picked up one of the square beignet donuts and tapped the excess of powdered sugar off of it. "I think that every play Shakespear wrote, every opera Verde composed, and every song that ever made it to *The Hit Parade* probably offended someone somewhere for some obscure reason probably known only to them. If you're going to live your life looking for disagreement, then you wont have to look far, and you wont go very far."

She feigned a smile. "You nose muss ged muy brown from kissing so many tourista's boludos. You so agreeable you probably be de belle of de ball een jail." She became coquettish. "Ha' you ever been een jail, whad did he call you, Meester David?"

David smiled. "I've been to jail to bail out a lot of my friends. Would you like to take my number in case you need to call me from there? Or would I be presumptuous to consider you a friend?"

She thrust her head forward and narrowed her eyes again. "You are muy presumptuous, and pompous, and prejudiced, too. You done know wad ids lake to be a minority. You blonde hair, you blue eyes, dey open all doors fo' you."

David swallowed a mouthful of his beignet. "Aurora, you don't have to travel many miles from the heart of this city to find blue eyed blonde haired children who are hungry, whose blue eyed blonde haired fathers can't find jobs because they never finished highschool or were too hungry to concentrate when they were in highschool. Opportunity is equal parts of luck as well as talent and perseverance. You have the talent, and must've had some luck to get where you are. Maybe you need a little more perseverance to get across a few more bridges before you protest too much."

Aurora stared at her coffee and scraped her incisor teeth over her lower lip three times. Her anger seemingly abated, she nodded her head toward the row of black waiters and looked at David questioningly. "Why you call each udder by furse names, bud he call you 'Meester' David?"

David smiled. "We call each other by first names because, from our first meeting, we liked each other enough to introduce ourselves to each other by our first names. He addresses me as 'Mister' because he is at work and he is my waiter, and the manager would probably get on his case if he didn't address a customer as Mister or Sir or Ma'm."

She put one lump of sugar in her coffee and stirred it slowly, then looked up at him with that questioning look. "And whad ees a Ma'm?"

David pushed the dish of beignets toward her. "It's the English contraction of the French words Madame or Mademoiselle, comparable to the Spanish words Senora or Senorita."

She picked up a beignet and shook the powdered sugar off of it. "Somehow I tink you finish highschool." She took a bite of the doughnut and spoke with her mouth full. "No?"

29

David looked at a passing Yellow Cab on the now almost deserted street. "Yes, that and a little more." Then he looked at her chewing another mouthful of beignet. "But academic education cannot teach you some of the most important things in life, and you are living proof of that." He folded both arms on the table and leaned forward. "You've asked me some questions, now let me ask you some. What happened in La Lune at midnight?"

She finished her last bite of the donut, brushed her hands together to dust off the powdered sugar, then licked the final traces from her fingertips. "I tink you know. De people all wan me play *Les Marseilles*. I done lake dad song, dad line aboud 'impure blood.' Id's racist. I try, bud I stop add dad line. Dey all say, 'Why?' I try to explain, bud den I ged mad and de manager, he come up, and de people dey all fighting. Id was muy loco. I done know eef I still godda job."

He tilted his head slightly sideways. "You want me to talk to your manager?"

She looked at him suspiciously again. "You done know me. Why you do dad?"

He straightened his head and raised his eyebrows slightly. "Because pure beauty deserves a pedestal."

She narrowed her eyes at him. "Eef you serious, and eef dere no strings...."

He closed his eyes momentarily as he shook his head negatively. "No strings."

She spied a cab letting passengers out at the curb and sprung up to catch it. "Okay, meed me add La Lune an hour before de show, aboud eight," and she ran to catch the cab.

David stared as her velvet top trailed up behind her to reveal the tight black satin pants molding her buttocks. He sighed heavily as the yellow door slammed shut and the cab pulled away. He placed several dollars on the little bill tray, which included a generous tip, waved goodbye to Alphonse, and headed down Decatur Street in the direction of his loft.

A couple blocks away was The Morning Call coffee shop which had no large covered patio to attract tourists, but served the very same quality café aulait and beignets, only at a much lower price. It's interior marble counters were lined with longshoremen who unloaded the freighter's moored at the nearby docks, and truck farmers who had unloaded their greengroceries at the French Market attached to the rear of the triangular building spearheaded by The Morning Call. Between this building and Esplanade Boulevard were the poorest of the local bars and cafes where working class men ate, drank, and went up rickety stairwells with brassy looking girls from the bars.

David found himself walking behind a tall trim figured brunette fetchingly attired in a black velvet pants suit that seemed familiar to him. As he started to pass between her and the wall, he could sense her looking sideways at him. Suddenly she grabbed his sleeve and spun him around against the wall, stepping very close to him while she smiled mischievously and said, "Quel chance, mon ami. Oui! You'll do nicely."

The impact with the wall made David realize how much alcohol he had consumed that evening, as his head began to spin and his eyes tried to focus on Justine's face. "Do what nicely?" he asked.

"Do me," she said huskily as she pressed her body and her lips against his, and his nostrils inhaled the citrus odor of Benedictine Liquer mixed with Chanel Number Five cologne.

Ten seconds later, after her tongue had thoroughly explored his mouth, he caught his breath and asked, "And Jules and Armand? I thought you had a committed relationship with them?"

31

While her left hand brushed his tousled wavy blonde hair back from his forehead, her right hand snaked down the front of his pants and encircled his penis. "We had a fight. Besides, they have each other, and we have an open relationship," and again she pressed her lips to his while her right hand massaged him.

He pulled his lips away and squeezed his eyes shut, his left hand gently trying to restrain her right hand. "Justine, I don't know if I want to get in the middle of what's already a triangle."

Her left fingertips traced the contours of his ear and her lips rubbed against his as she spoke. "Your lips say no, but your dick says go! David, tonight you're going to learn the fullest meaning of why the word 'French' is an international sexual verb."

David groaned as his arms encircled her and his mouth opened to another tongue fest.

Chapter Three
IT'S A SMALL WORLD

Justine opened her eyes and looked up at the shocked expression on David's face. She smiled that same mischievous smile from the night before, and taunted him with the lines of a French children's story, *The Crow And The Fox*. "Ah, bonjour, Monsuier David. Que vous et jolie. Que vous mais semblez beau."

David realized his jaw was hanging open. He threw the rumpled white sheet off his body and jumped out of bed as if he'd been bitten by a bed bug. "I didn't realize I was that drunk last night." His eyes narrowed at her accusingly. "You took advantage of me."

Justine turned and rose up on one elbow facing him, the sheet falling away from her upper torso revealing a trim, pale, slightly full bosomed body. She continued the lines from the children's story as she stared at his groin. "San mantir, ce votre rammage est la meme a la votre plummage, vous est le phoenix des hotes de ce bois."

David looked around the floor, retrieved his blue striped boxer shorts, and tried to keep his balance as he put them on in a standing position. "Yeah, yeah, I know. You're the fox and I'm the crow you've conned."

With her free hand, she used one strand of her long shiny black hair to caress the dark turgid nipple of her breast. "Didn't I keep my promise to teach you the full meaning of the sexual verb, to French?"

David looked around for a cigarette, then remembered the pact he made with Julienne to stop smoking. At this moment he regretted their little ritual of flushing his last cigarettes down the toilet. Suddenly the thought of coffee was so strong he thought he could smell it, and he took the few short steps to the kitchenette at one end of the loft. "Really, Justine, the French did not invent fellatio." He ran water in a kettle, put it on the stove, and lit the gas burner with a large kitchen match.

"It was the Puritanical American soldiers coming back from France during World War One that coined that phrase in America." He poured the ground coffee from a can labeled 'Luzianne Coffee With Chickory' into the aluminum mid section of a drip coffee pot, snapped it into the bottom section, then snapped the top section on it before turning to face her as he leaned against the kitchen counter. "Although, I must admit, if you're any evidence, the French did improve it a hell of a lot." Then he turned to get two mugs from the overhead cabinet. "But you still took advantage of me."

Justine threw the sheet off of her, laid back, and stretched all four limbs provocatively. "Oh, David, I didn't have to try very hard to take advantage of you. A woman knows when a man is ready. Before I bumped into you, something turned you on so much you must have been stumbling over that thing between your legs."

David thought about watching Aurora get into the cab, then about the brassy girls in the lower Decateur district pulling their Johns up the rickety stairwells. He concluded that she was right, and it was definitely Aurora, not the brassy girls, who had made him vulnerable to Justine. He smiled at her. "Bullshit! I was innocently minding my own business, and you're the nymphomaniacal seducer of young men with a record to prove it."

She smiled lecherously. "David, I could not only tell that you were super horny last night, but I can tell you're in denial right now. Watch! All I have to do is spread my legs...," she spread her legs, "...open my labia...," she opened her labia, "...and play with myself...," she licked the long index finger of her right hand, placed it on her protruding clitoris, and slowly

34

stroked it up and down as David stared transfixed at the vertical motion of her crimson painted fingernail, "...and I can already see the bulge in those stupid looking underpants you're wearing."

He closed his eyes and shook his head to try to erase the image, turning toward the counter and surreptitiously running his hand down the front of his shorts to verify that she was, indeed, right. He placed the large black ceramic mugs on a silver tray with matching silver sugar and creamer, retrieved the milk from an antique looking refrigerator beside the sink counter, filled the creamer and returned the milk to the fridge. As he did this he said, "I hope you're going to finish that by yourself, because you'll get no further assistance from me."

Justine's head tilted back as the tempo of her finger slowly increased and her eyes slowly closed in a swoon. The water kettle started to whistle and her eyes opened abruptly. "Oh, I thought that was you giving me a wolf whistle."

David poured the boiling water in the top of the drip coffee pot and snapped the lid on it, setting it on a potholder he placed on the tray. As he turned to face her, he repressed a look of shock at discovering her continued masturbation, then frowned with impatience. "Stop it, Justine. I'm not going to continue the mistake I made last night. You're involved with two other men, you're a customer, and I think you're a friend of my boss. With all due respect to your beauty and bedroom talents, this has to stop."

Justine continued stroking herself and looked at him with a smirk. "Oh, I don't think Madame Valentina would ever consider me a friend. Bonne chance! Anything but! She'll probably hate me even more now that I've banged her boy toy."

David carried the tray to the bed, sitting on the farthest corner from Justine as he set the tray beside him and poured

35

two mugs of coffee, looking at her questioningly. "Boy toy? Who's her boy toy?"

She looked at him in disbelief. "Oh, come on, David. I've seen the way the two of you look at each other. Everyone checks out a good looking person's ass the first time they meet them, but when they're still doing it after knowing them a long time it's because they've got more than a passing interest."

David put milk and sugar in his mug, lifted it, then pushed the tray toward her with his free hand as if he were feeding a tiger in a cage. "Well, most men would find Val attractive, and I'll admit I've thought of it, even hoped she might give me a sign, but, no, we've never made that connection and I'm not her boy toy."

Justine looked at the tray and back at him with a slight frown, but without losing the rhythm of her stroking. "Well that kinda devalues my conquest of you last night."

David swallowed his coffee and smiled painfully. "Conquest? Was I part of the spoils of some war between the two of you?"

The mischievous smile returned to her face and her stroking increased imperceptibly. "You really don't know, do you? But I bet you'd like to."

David set his mug on the tray and swallowed the last of his coffee as the two stared at each other. "Okay. Yeah. What is it between you two? Why does she get that strange love-hate expression on her face each time she sees you or even just hears your laughter coming from the other end of the bar?"

Justine smiled a catlike smile. "I'll tell you...," then she paused.

David leaned slightly toward her, staring intently. "Yes?"

She removed her index finger and put it in her mouth, making a slight popping sound as she withdrew it from her pursed lips, "...if you'll take off those stupid underpants and come to bed."

****

When David tried to query Zoe about Justine's story, he discovered that Cajun lady could deliver 'the evil eye' with almost as much intensity as his Sicilian boss could. He stood paralyzed as she glared at him and said, "You're a nice boy, David, handsome and talented, but I guess you're not as smart as I thought if you'd think I'd verify anything that black hearted evil bitch said, much less betray Val. Compared to that vain piece of Eurotrash, Valentina Siciliana is a saint, and I'd take a bullet for her, if necessary. She saved me and that ungrateful French bitch from the streets of Storyville." Then she leaned forward and squinted her eyes at David. "For one, you better keep any gossip that evil bitch told you about Valentina Siciliana to yourself if you want to celebrate any more birthdays. And for two, you be very careful, young man, or that black widow will ensnarl you in her web, and you know what black widows do to their mates, don't you?" Then her eyes widened in an evil smile as she said, "They eat them alive!" and she left him standing as if he were in a trance.

****

Iberville Street ran parallel to Canal Street, New Orleans main thoroughfare. Named after the French explorer who laid France's claim to the Louisiana Territory, the West side of Iberville was a high wall of the backsides of mostly block long modern buildings fronting Canal Street. The East side of it marked the Western boundary of the Vieux Carre with smaller two story centuries old buildings mostly sporting iron lace balconies. A few doors South of Bourbon Street, an engraved wood sign hung from beneath a balcony and, in recessed gold letters on a green background, announced "Felix's Seafood."

David didn't see the tall balding Englishman among those surging through the doors of the restaurant in a rush to get an available stool at the counter on the right, or one of the tiny two seat tables on the left. His mind was still reeling from his encounter earlier that day with Justine, more from what she told him than from the intense sex he had prostituted himself to engage in as payment for her revelations. Not that it was a painful sacrifice, inasmuch as her expertise fulfilled her self proclaimed excellence and her body rivaled the healthiest of teenagers.

He decided to enter the restaurant for fear of not finding seating a few minutes later during the dinner rush hour. He elbowed his way almost to the back, when he saw Richard Rose at one of the rear tables waving to him. He sat on the Coca Cola designed wire backed chair and signaled to a nearby waiter that he was ready to order. Richard plucked the one page menu from the clip on the metal napkin holder. "So, David, what would you recommend?"

David smiled at him and said, "All of it. What kind of seafood do you like?"

Richard put the menu back in the clip and smiled at David. "All of it. Although, in the cold deep waters surrounding the British Isles, there's not all that much shellfish, and the stuff that's traveled in ice from the Mediterranean is often suspect."

David's eyes widened. "Well, the shelf of the Gulf Coast extends for miles before it gets deep enough to drown in, and that makes for some of the best oyster beds in the world." He reached out and caught a passing waiter by the sleeve. "Whoa, Pierre, those tourists can wait. I gotta get to work at The Voodoo Room on time, and Richard here's gotta start his new gig at Stormy's Casino Royal on time."

Pierre pulled his sleeve loose and scowled at him. "Yeah, and I gotta serve twenty tables at this end of the room and every one of them gotta be someplace on time. You know what you want or should I come back later?"

David responded instantly. "I want an order of soft shell crabs with rice, mustard greens, cornbread, and coffee." He turned to look at Richard. "Richard, you like oysters?"

Richard beamed. "That I do!"

David smiled. "Ever had Oysters Rockafellow?"

Richard licked his lips. "No, but it sounds decadent." He smiled at Pierre. "I'll have Oysters Rockafellow and coffee. Skip all the side dishes. I'm paunchy enough as it is."

Pierre looked at Richard's abdomen, raised one eyebrow, scribbled on his order pad, and left abruptly without saying a word.

Richard looked at David questioningly. "You do know that I work at The Inn Between, not Stormy's Casino Royal?"

David shrugged. "Yeah, but The Inn Between is so new Pierre probably never heard of it. So, Richard, you ever been to New Orleans before?"

Richard blinked. "No. Before the war, I took my new bride to New York on our honeymoon, but that was my only venture to the colonies."

David's brow furrowed. "Did your wife come with you this time?"

Richard looked at him hesitantly, then pulled a paper napkin from the dispenser and began wiping his knife and fork with it. "No. Actually, she died in the blitz. One of Adolf's buzz bombs caught her just as she reached the down stairs to the tube."

David bit his lower lip, looked down, and then up at Richard. "I'm sorry. I didn't know."

Richard rolled his eyes upward, then looked at David with a painful smile. "No, of course not. How could you? But tell me, David, how long have you worked in the French Quarter?"

David inhaled deeply. "Almost ten years, now. Ever since I got out of highschool. Some friends dragged me to The Voodoo Room on the same night the regular pianist decided to fight with Val over a pay raise and walked out. I offered to sub for him that night and Val offered me the job."

Richard leaned to one side as Pierre deposited two mugs of coffee from a full tray and continued to another table barely pausing in his movement. "Jolly good, being in the right place at the right time, I mean."

David added cream and sugar to his coffee. "I guess, for an unemployed teenager at the time, it was good luck. But, in the years since, I've only had three modest raises, and The Voodoo Room is a small local club with little or no chance of wider recognition or advancement." He stirred his coffee and looked around the room. "Some of the bigger clubs on Bourbon have spawned national recording stars like Louis Prima, Al Hirt, and Pete Fountain. But the only press The Voodoo Room gets is an occasional nod from local columnists or authors who've known Val for many years."

Richard sipped his black unsweetened coffee. "Val's your boss?"

David wrinkled his nose. "Yeah. Valentina Siciliano. The dark mistress of a mysterious dark past. I just learned more about her today than she would ever want anyone to know."

Richard leaned back in surprise as Pierre set their plates on the table wordlessly. "Good Lord, what the bloody hell is all this?" He stared at his platter of twelve stuffed oyster shells arranged in a circle on a bed of ice around a bowel of small round crackers, garnished with lemon wedges and a rim of salt.

David pointed to Richard's platter with his knife. "That's your Oysters Rockafellow. They saute minced oysters with whipped eggs and spinach, then stuff it back in the shell.

Some local chef invented it for a visiting politician and it's become a delicacy."

Richard looked at the oysters suspiciously and poked at one gingerly with his tiny fish fork. "I guess if I've eaten lamb's eyes and kush kush in Morocco, then I should be able to muddle through a plate of green oysters."

David made crunching sounds with his knife as he cut through the crisp breaded deep fried soft shell crabs on his plate. "Most people love Oysters Rockafellow. I like oysters any way you serve them, from raw on the half shell to deep fried oyster loaves on po' boy bread., I never met an oyster I didn't like, or eat."

Richard's suspicious frown mellowed to surprised delight as he began to wield his tiny fish fork more boldly. "I've learned that most of my bosses have dark secrets, and, as curious as I might be about your bosses past, the more important thing I've learned is that it is wisest and safest to guard your bosses secrets as carefully as they do. My boss not only looks like a New York gangster, he even played gangster roles in movies, and I'm sure he didn't learn everything about that character just from watching George Raft movies."

Now David's crunching sounds were muted as he chewed his food. "I don't know any more about Bernie than he told me yesterday when he introduced you. That was the first time I ever talked to the man, which is why I was surprised he approached me in the first place."

The Englishman talked as he chewed his food. "He really shouldn't have troubled you. I'd manage to stumble my way around in time."

David poured a little vinegar on his greens from the separate oil and vinegar salad dressing bottles on the table. "No, I don't mind. You've learned about Felix's today. If you like Chinese, there's Fongs's on Decatur next to Los Marinos, but stay out of Los Marinos, lots of Latino sailors and lots of

41

switchblades. Dominos for Italian, also on Decatur, or Galatoire's on Rampart. Tujague's for French, again on Decatur, but a little pricey as it's slowly becoming a tourist trap. And if you're really broke, the café behind The Morning Call if you don't mind eating with the longshoremen and the farmers operating the stalls at The French Market."

Richard had trouble trying to get the little crackers on his fork and finally resorted to using his fingers. "Do you know many of the entertainer's in the French Quarter, and are any of them Negro?"

David's fork paused on the way to his mouth. "I don't know the headliner's like Prima and Hirt, but they're rarely in town anyway. Some of the lesser ones I know, mostly pianists like Fats Pechon. He's black. Why do you want to meet blacks?"

Richard was scraping the last crusty residue from the interior of the oyster shells. "You Yanks may not realize it, taking jazz for granted because it originated here, but the Brits have a fascination with jazz, even the French. Josephine Baker was the biggest thing that ever hit The Follies Begere in Paris, and black American jazz musicians are all the rage in the London bistros."

David washed the last of his food down with the last of his coffee. "Well, the days of Louie Armstrong on Basin Street are long gone, and white jazz musicians like Al Hirt predominate on Bourbon Street, along with a lot of Dixieland jazz."

Richard frowned as he gestured to Pierre for the check. "Oh Gawd, I can't stand the sound of that cacaphony. Dixieland is a real bastardization of the original black jazz."

Now David frowned as Pierre handed Richard the check. "Actually, Richard, Dixieland is the original black jazz which black musicians still play at funerals and in black nightclubs where older black musicians who originated jazz still play. I

42

think what disturbs you are the straw hats and striped pants buffoonery of the commercialized white Dixieland bands. That, and the fact that the black jazz in your London bistros is an educated evolution of black jazz musicians who emulate the sophistication of people like Count Basie and Duke Ellington." He reached toward the check in Richard's hand. "Let me see what I owe."

Richard moved the check out of his reach and handed it back to Pierre with a large bill. "Please, David, let me thank you for your generosity in educating an emigree. After my boss and the crassness of most of the staff I've met so far, you're a refreshing bit of intelligence and culture in this touristy wasteland."

David pushed his chair back. "Well, it's not generosity if you're paying for it."

Richard retrieved his change from the little bill tray, leaving two quarters. "It's just a gesture, and just this once. We'll go Dutch hereafter, if you're kind enough to occasionally spare me the pleasure of your company and the treasure of your French Quarter wisdom."

David stood, wiped his mouth and hands with his napkin and dropped it on the table. "Sure, my pleasure. I'll drop by The Inn Between if I'm still up around sunset. Now, though, I've promised to meet someone before they go to work, and thanks for dinner."

Richard waved as David left, saying sadly, "Ta ta." Then he noticed Pierre staring glumly at the two quarters on the bill tray, and left.

****

The chartreuse neon sign at La Lune was already on when David arrived. He went to the end of the bar at the back of the thinly populated room and was almost hit by the swinging kitchen door as the short bald man in the same beige suit he wore the day before burst through it. David stepped back abruptly, made eye contact with the man, and asked, "Has Aurora arrived yet?"

The short man narrowed his eyes at him, pulled a cigar out of an inside pocket, and proceeded to clip the tip off the cigar with a gold cigar cutter attached to a gold watch chain. He lit the cigar with an engraved gold cigarette lighter and blew a puff of smoke toward David, looking at him with a menacing smile. "Stugats, you jamook. Headliners don't see customers before or after work in my establishment, not unless they're hosting a large table with several bottles of very expensive champagne."

David was surprised that he enjoyed inhaling the second hand smoke of an expensive cigar that was obviously intended as an insult. He kept a poker face as he said, "I'm the pianist at The Voodoo Room, and I was helping her with some music."

The short man narrowed his eyes even more. "You her compare? You don't look like no spik."

David did not rise to the man's baiting. "I was helping her with the French lyrics to *Les Marseilles*."

The short man's eyes bulged as he removed the cigar and blew another cloud of smoke at David. "That greaseball lavaccia almost caused a riot with the frogs in here last night. I'm thinking of canning her lime licking ass."

David maintained his poker face. "Well, sir, you know what you can do with those bitter limes?"

The short man sneered at him and spoke sarcastically. "No, what do you do with bitter limes? Tell me, jibone."

David looked down, and then back up. "You add a little sugar and make some profitable limeade."

The short man's sneer melted into interest. "Yeah, what kind of sugar?"

David rolled his eyes toward the ceiling. "How about, maybe, a mention in Tommy Griffith's column, *Laginappe*, headlined 'La Lune Latina learns Liberte?'"

The short man returned the cigar to his mouth where he chewed on it while his eyes rolled from side to side. Then he looked at David and spoke through his cigar clenched teeth. "You got an in at *The New Orleans Item*?"

David allowed a slight smile to appear on his face. "Mr. Griffith is a fan of mine."

The glimmer of a smile appeared on the short man's face. "He give you any press before?"

David's smile grew ever so slightly. "From time to time."

The short man shifted the cigar to the other side of his mouth without touching it, allowing his smile to broaden. "You write that line of poetry, or did she."

David closed and opened his eyes. "Let's just say she inspired me to write that line of illiteration."

The short man raised one eyebrow questioningly. "You one of those blonde haired Italians from Northern Italy? Your family from Milan?"

David raised one eyebrow. "Let's just say I'm a fan of Caruso and Enzio Pinza."

Aurora appeared at the end of the bar carrying her guitar case, then froze as she saw the two men together.

The short man stepped toward David and patted his chest twice with his open palm. "Okay, let's just say you get me press and you're my compare, too." Then he took two steps toward Aurora and put his face close to hers with a lecherous smile. "Be nice to my compare, here. He just saved your ass." Then he walked toward the front of the bar smiling and puffing on his cigar.

Aurora glared at David. "Whad did you say to him?"

David stepped forward and reached toward the guitar case. "Let me carry that for you."

45

Aurora stepped back, pulling the case out of his reach and raising her voice "Whad did you say to him?"

David took a deep breath. "I told him I'd get La Lune a mention in a popular local column."

Aurora continued to glare at him. "Whad kine o' mention?"

David put his hands in his pockets and looked off into space. "Just a little blurb about you learning *Le Marseilles* with the headline 'La Lune Latina Learns Liberte.'"

Aurora's glare turned into wide eyed infuriation. She uttered a string of Spanish invectives so loud and fast David couldn't understand a single word, with his very limited Spanish vocabulary, until she slowed down enough to say, "Ah, chingado,tu Cabron, tu idiota, Wha'd make you tink I wanna learn anyt'ing French?"

David shrugged and continued to look off into space. "Maybe the fact that he has ninety-nine customers who speak French to every one that speaks Spanish. Maybe the fact that if the entertainers whose salaries he pays don't bring in customers, then he doesn't have any money to pay those entertainers." Then he took his hands out of his pockets and extended them slightly toward her, looking her in the eye. "Maybe the fact that he was going to fire you until I convinced him that your obstinance could be turned into an asset!"

Her eyes narrowed and she punctuated her words with her index finger pointed at him. "I done need you!"

He stared at her in silence for ten seconds, then hitched his belt up with both hands and said, "Yes you do. We all need each other from time to time. If you don't want to cooperate with me to get you both publicity, then go find out what else he might accept from you to give you your job back." He inhaled deeply, looked down at his Cordovan leather plain toe shoes, then back up into her eyes with a slightly furrowed brow and a pained smile. "In the meantime, I'm going to work. If you want to know the full details of my idea, meet me at Café duMonde after work, because the columnist will probably be at The Voodoo Room tomorrow on his usual night." David walked around her as she stood like an angry statue staring into space until he was completely out the front door.

Chapter Four
THE WEBS WE WEAVE

For the first time, David sensed anxiety when Val announced, "Let the games begin," and Zoe opened the front double doors of The Voodoo Room. Early in his employment he had learned that one of the rules of the 'game' was to try to avoid sleeping with customers. Women he met outside of the club, who knew nothing about the club, would mostly respect his workplace as his 'home turf.' When he had differences with them, they were far less likely to show up at The Voodo Room and make scenes.

He remembered the first time a beautiful young girl threw herself at him in the club. After the girl had spent an hour flirting and staring lovingly at him, Zoe told him that Val wanted to see him on his break. When he approached Val at her rear corner table, she indicated he should sit at the chair opposite her. He sat obediently and asked, "Yes, Val?"

She tapped the ash off her long Russian cigarette and looked at him sternly. "A smart bird doesn't foul its own nest."

At first David didn't get the message. His mind flashed to bird's nests he had found as a child and he seemed to remember they were frequently littered with feces. Maybe those were just the chicks, and the adults knew better."

She saw his confusion and asked him, "David, how many women have you slept with?"

He tried not to look shocked. "I really haven't kept count."

She raised one eyebrow. "Any of them give you trouble when you broke up with them?"

He still wasn't sure where this was going. "Nothing I couldn't handle."

Val squashed her cigarette stub out forcefully and, without looking at him, said, "Well don't try to handle any of your relationship troubles in my club." She looked him in the eye. "It's not good for business." Then she turned, picked up her copy of *The Times Picayune*, and shook it open noisily as she started to read, indicating that he had been dismissed.

A few weeks later David understood better when the beautiful little blonde who had thrown herself at him got drunk in The Voodoo Room and threw a hysterical scene that included announcing to all the sordid details of their affair, his inability to commit to her expectations, and threats of suicide. After she had climbed over the railing of the little fence that surrounded his piano and he had escaped to the other side where Zoe barred the girl's access to him, the girl turned to the women seated closest to the piano and appealed to them. "Is it that he doesn't understand that I love him, or that he doesn't understand what love is? Isn't it love when I told him I'd go anywhere with him, I'd do anything for him? Isn't it love when I gave him my virginity, performed sexual acts I never knew existed, even offered everything I owned and every cent I had and my eternal devotion for the rest of my life? But, other than my body, all he seemed to want was his 'space.'" As the older women tried to console her, David saw Val glaring at him from the corner of the room.

Later that night, when closing up, that last thing she said, in an angry tone and without looking at him, was, "Make damn sure that's the last time you ever shit in my nest," and she slammed the patio door behind her as she exited.

When Justine walked through the door, David had a momentary flash of the love struck little blonde, which was dissipated by seeing Jules and Armand trail behind Justine. While he anticipated she would possibly taunt him with innuendos about their encounter the preious night, he doubted she would create a four way confrontation in public. Of course, there was the possibility that her taunting might extend to Val, in which case David could face the unexpected consequences of a quarter century of animosity between the two women. As Pete served the trio drinks at the end of the bar, they all raised their glasses to him with a smile, and David's anxiety subsided somewhat.

When Julienne arrived, David's anxiety returned with a possibility he had not considered. Justine probably assumed that Julienne was either intimate with him or was enamored of him, in which case her taunting might include Julienne. Zoe brought the Cuttysark and milk drink Julienne always bought for him at the beginning of the evening. When he had told her she really didn't need to buy him drinks, she had said, "David, it's just like throwing a rose to a performer on stage, plus, I want you to have a safer drink handy to save your stomach lining. I know you don't drink the hundred or so drinks your fans compliment you with each night, and that Zoe secrets them away for you. I just want you to know we appreciate that you give the place a little class and we enjoy your company." As David lifted the glass to her, he also reasoned that, in addition to the fact that she owned an art gallery, her Creole family was stinking rich.

Justine approached the piano with two drinks, her own and one for David. She placed the drink beside the covered one from Julienne and said, "I'm bringing this drink so Zoe can't play any shell games with it. When you drink it, and I want you to really drink it, I want you to do so with the awareness and acknowledgment and appreciation of all the bodily fluids I ingested for you last night." David smiled painfully as he lifted the glass toward her in toast. She mimicked his painful smile, her eyebrows raising, and said, "Don't look so paranoid, David. I'm not going to advertise our little secret to all your adoring fans. Now let me see if you like my drink as much as I liked yours last night."

51

David's eyes closed as he barely sipped the drink, and when he opened his eyes he saw Justine's eyes widen and her devilish smile broaden. She raised her glass to him, said, "Cheers," and returned to the bar. He noticed Julienne's eyes follow Justine back to the bar, then look at him briefly without expression, then turn back to the conversation in progress there. He looked toward the corner table and noticed Val staring at him without expression, then turn her gaze back to what she was reading. He made a mental note that he should go over to Val on his break and be nonchalant in hopes of minimizing any suspicions.

Suddenly there was a commotion at the front end of the bar as Lenny and Louie arrived, Louie carrying a milk crate filled with stoppered quart milk bottles filled with an amber liquid which he began distributing to select women. Louie was the shorter, balder, and more retiring of the two, his thick black rimmed glasses and breast pocket row of pens in a plastic pen holder marking him as the more academic and pedantic of the two. His chemistry degree got him his job working at a testing laboratory on St. Charles Avenue that had the Government contract to test all products entering the international seaport in seagoing tankers, the five gallon cans of product to be tested being filled from holds that contained as much as a million gallons of product. Lenny and Louie ran their cars on the fuel products that were frequently tested, Louie tweaking the formula of the diesel or alcohol products to work in their gasoline driven engines.

Louie gave Zoe two bottles, one of which Zoe relayed to Val. He handed Justine and Julienne both a bottle, their wide eyed expressions exhibiting surprise and appreciation. Julienne brought the amber quart milk bottle over to David excitedly, holding it up to his nose and saying, "Smell." David took a whiff and moved his head back swiftly as his nostrils were filled with a familiar perfumed scent. Julienne smiled ecstatically and said, "Louie was running a test from a French tanker filled with Channel Number Five perfume, and, to celebrate Bastielle Day, he just gave each of us a thirty-two ounce bottle of it." She blinked and said, "Do you realize that, at fifty dollars an ounce, he just gave each of us a sixteen hundred dollar bottle of perfume?"

David looked at the bottle and raised one eyebrow. "Yeah, and in such a fancy bottle, too."

Julienne put the stopper back in the bottle and said, "Hell, if it's Channel Number Five, I don't care if it's in a chamber pot. That little four eyed Cajun has my most sincere and profound gratitude. I think I'm going to go plant a big kiss on him," and she headed back to the bar to wait her turn as Justine, Zoe, and a number of regular female customers were lavishing their appreciation on the blushing little man.

Val set the amber milk bottle on her table, looked at it for quite a few seconds as a smile grew on her face, then did something unusual for her. She got up and walked the length of the bar toward Louie, everyone making a path for her. She took Louie's already lipstick smeared face in her hands and planted yet another kiss on his receding hairline. Then, looking Louie in the eye, she said loudly, "Pete, serve a round of drinks on the house so we can all toast our thanks to Louie, here, for making this such a memorable Bastielle Day." A cheer went up throughout the room as Val chuckled huskily, then released Louie's face. As she turned to retrace her steps to the other end of the bar, David saw her exchange cool glances with Justine.

Hoping the incident with Louie had put Val in good spirits, David took his break and walked over to Val's table. He looked at the milk bottle on the table and said, "Wow! That was a grand gesture Louie made, wasn't it? And you, too, spreading the joy with a round on the house."

Val was still smiling at the milk bottle, then lifted her smile to him, then looked behind him as her smile faded. Justine was passing behind David, presumably on her way to the rest rooms outside the rear door to the patio. She stopped momentarily behind him, reached under his tuxedo coat tail to pat his bottom three times, then said sexily, "Sweetie, I hope you liked the drink I brought you as much as I liked the one you gave me last night," then she retreated through the rear door.

David was speechless as Val raised one eyebrow and said, "Maybe this would be a good time for you to return to the piano and help maximize the joy I just spread around, 'Sweetie.'" He nodded his head affirmatively without looking at her, and returned to the piano with the same dread anxiety he had felt just before the doors opened earlier. As a group of women moved Louie toward the piano, David found himself fulfilling yet another request for *Les Marseilles*.

As the evening wore on, he became increasingly aware that his life was being complicated by secrets. He was now responsible for keeping secrets about Val he had learned from Justine. He was now attempting to keep his one night stand with Justine from Val and Jules and Armand and, well, everyone. And he really wanted to go to Café duMonde after work to see if Aurora would show up, but he didn't want to share what may or may not be a new friendship with everyone else, particularly Julienne. His mind searched desperately for excuses to avoid going bar hopping with everyone after work.

When Dimitri arrived at the end of the evening, a posse had gathered around Louie as the hero of the evening. Everyone wanted to fete him with food and drink and, as Zoe pushed the swarm of almost ten people out the front doors and shut them, David saw his chance to escape. "You guys go on, I'll catch up with you later. I have to talk to the new English pianist at The Inn Between.

Julienne stood in front of him, opened her milk bottle, and dabbed a fingertip of Channel Number Five behind each of his ears. "That's fine. We'll all go with you and meet the new 'English' pianist."

As the rest of the group chorused agreement, David waved his hands in protest. "No, no, no! This is not a social call. It's about business. You guys go ahead. I'll look for you at The Napoleon House, and, if you're not there, tell Pete where you're headed and I'll follow you. Go, go! Have fun! I'll see you later."

The group headed toward the waterfront, Julienne clutching her milk bottle to her chest and looking over her shoulder at him with a reluctant smile. He walked a short ways behind them until he was standing at the door to The Inn Between, then, because some of them kept looking back toward him, he entered the door surmounted by a blinking lights marquee.

The Inn Between club was very tiny. It had actually been the back bar to Stormy's Casino Royal, but Bernie Levine had negotiated with Stormy's management to give him a lease on it as part of his long term contract to be emcee for the show in the main room..

The lighting was low and mostly red, the carpet was very thick, and the half dozen tiny round tables took up half the room balanced by the tiny bar and a spinet piano in the other half. A tiny piano bartop overhung the top of the spinet with five barstools clustered around it. David sat at one of the barstools as Richard nodded at him without stopping his soft jazz rendition of *A Foggy Day In London Town*. When Richard finished the number, he stopped long enough to light a cigarette and say, "Didn't think I'd see you so soon. I haven't finished digesting those green oysters. Lem'me buy you a drink."

55

David shook his head. "No, thanks. I'm just using you as an excuse to shake some of my friends."

Richard sucked on his cigarette and placed it on the ashtray next to the 'kitty,' a giant brandy snifter with several silver dollars and a variety of paper money deliberately composed in it to encourage generous patrons. "How flattering. The only friend I've made uses me as an excuse to escape his multitude of friends."

David's brow furrowed. "No, I didn't mean it like that. I meant I'll spend more time some other night, just not tonight."

Richard accompanied himself as he sang a children's song titled *Playmate.*

David inhaled the second hand smoke from Richard's cigarette in the ash tray. "Well, Playmate, don't know if I want to share my dollies with you, and, New Orleans being below sea level, we don't have any cellars with or without doors here." He stood up and pulled down the sleeves of his seersucker sport coat he had put on at the end of the evening. "But I'll spend some 'jolly' good times with you some night when I don't have other appointments."

Richard continued keyboard variations of the *Playmate* tune. "Hot date?"

David drummed his fingers on the piano bartop. "I don't know about hot in the sense you mean, but she is a spitfire, and she may not even show up."

Richard took a puff from his cigarette. "The flattery never ends. He uses me as an excuse to dump his friends, then he dumps me for a girl who may very well dump him."

David slid his hand off the bar top and headed for the door. "Well, I've never claimed to be able to predict women, and I have doubts about any man who makes such a claim. See you another time, Richard," and he exited as Richard began playing *Thanks For The Memories.*

****

Alphonse replaced David's cup with his fifth café au lait as he ate the last of his second order of beignets. He regretted not having gone to Fong's or the French Market Café for more solid food than half a dozen beignets, inasmuch as Aurora hadn't appeared in the hour since they both got off work. In a small way he felt relieved at not having to ask a favor of the columnist, but the disappointment at not seeing her was greater.

The columnist was a long time friend of Val's, as were a multitude of local authors, artists, entertainers, media types, and people who were movers and shakers, but unseen and on the underside of the overt political system. He wasn't sure of the columnist's sexual orientation or what the columnist might expect of him in exchange for the infrequent blurbs about him and The Voodoo Room he put in his column. The only time the columnist had come in with a woman was with an aging but famous movie star who was appearing in a play at the St. Charles Theater. The columnist took him out to the patio, put a fifty dollar bill in his pocket, and told him he was leaving the female star in David's company so he could take her through the quarter after work and "show her a good time." When David had finished a two hour tour of the more conservative sights the Quarter had to offer after two in the morning, he delivered her to her hotel room at The St. Charles Hotel, and was promptly pulled into her room by his tie as if it were a dog's leash. For a woman in her fifties, she was as fit and sexually adept as Justine, but slightly more zoftic and less controlling. Despite the dog leash entrance, she really wanted a man to take control and David to be her 'walk on the wild side,' and he did his best to deliver her fantasy. He felt he owed it to the columnist, not that it wasn't a pleasant duty to fulfill.

His reverie was interrupted by the arrival of Aurora who wore a dead pan expression as Alphonse pulled the chair out for her and she said, "Café negre, por favor, Alphonse."

David leaned forward in his chair as Alphonse retreated. "I was about to leave because I thought you weren't coming."

She averted his eyes as she looked at the square across the street. "I din plan to come. Bud, when I tole Ramon and de bass player aboud you offer, dey convince me I should."

David surveyed the patio and, as expected, seated off in an opposite corner were the flutist and a big beefy Latino who he guessed was the bassist. "Well, I hope you realize you're perfectly safe with me and don't really need to bring your posse."

Her eyes narrowed slightly as she looked him in the eye. "I done never feel safe since I cross de border years ago. No even before."

He looked at her compassionately. "Maybe that helps explain why, with all your beauty and talent, you are still driven by insecurities."

She leaned back as Alphonse delivered her coffee. "Gracias, Alphonse." She put one cube of sugar in her coffee and stared at it as she stirred it slowly with her spoon. "Done worry aboud my insecurities, jus' tell me how I keep my job," then she looked at him, "wid'oud strings."

David inhaled deeply. "Well, the columnist usually comes at nine when the doors open. Tell your boss you're going to be an hour late in order to do the interview, and he's so happy to get the publicity he'll readily agree. Meet me at The Voodoo Room at nine, you know where it is on St. Louis just North of Bourbon. I know he'll like the tag line and theme I'm providing, but you'll have to go along with it. The theme is that I'm teaching you French lyrics like *Les Marseilles* and *Le Mer*, and you're teaching me Spanish lyrics like *Poinciana* and *Besame Mucho*."

She frowned. "Bud, I already know dose French songs."

He grimaced. "And I already know those Spanish songs, but the theme is cute, and it explains away any concern about your declining to sing *Les Marseilles* last night. And, most of all, it's an excuse to get your name and your club's name in the papers." He watched her eyes dart around to avoid eye contact. "It's called publicity, Aurora, and it's the life's blood of any entertainer, and their employers. Ask anyone. Ask your friend Ramon." He leaned back. "And, incidentally, don't bring your posse tomorrow night."

Suddenly David was aware of people just outside the low iron lace fence that bordered the patio. He looked up to see the group that had left The Voodoo Room with him all staring at him in surprise. Justine leaned on the low railing of the fence and stared at Aurora with a sarcastic smile. "Damn, David, that's the best looking Englishman I've ever seen!"

Aurora stared resentfully back at Justine. David kept his cool and said, "This is Aurora Alonzo. She's appearing at La Lune."

Aurora turned her resentful frown toward him and said, "I godda go. I'll be you club add nine," and she rose to leave.

David called after her, "And bring an eight by ten glossy for Tommy, and a bio if you have one."

Julienne stepped up to the fence beside Justine, smiling politely. "She's quite beautiful. I hope we're not interrupting anything."

His brow wrinkled as he simultaneously smiled. "No, no, no. We were just going over some foreign songs. Please, all of you, join me. We'll pull some tables together." As the group went around the open end of the fence and approached his table, to which Alphonse was already adding more tables, David gestured to Julienne. "Please, Julienne, come sit across from me."

Julienne sat, still smiling politely. "So, what happened to your Englishman?"

He smiled nonchalantly as Justine sat beside Julienne. "We got through our business early and I decided I'd get a jump ahead of you guys by coming to Café duMonde."

Justine sat beside Julienne and teased David. "Where you just happened to run into Aurora, the most beautiful girl in the place."

He blinked. "No, Julienne is the most beautiful girl in Café duMonde, because she is as beautiful as you were at her age."

Justine frowned slightly. "That's not the greatest save I've ever heard from your bag of platitudes, but I'll settle for it."

Julienne leaned back as Alphonse set their coffees in front of them. "Well I think the only reason he can get away with that line is because Aurora is no longer here."

He inhaled deeply. "Enough about the vanities of women. Tell me where you've been, what adventures you've had!"

Jules sat down next to Justine and set her quart bottle on the table. His voice occasionally slid off into a falsetto when he was a little high, as he was that evening. "Would you believe, Just like Val, Pete ordered a round of drinks for everyone on the house after Louie gave him a quart of the Channel Number Five for his wife." He smiled superciliously, "I shouldn't have had three glasses of wine with dinner, I think I'm getting a little tipsy at this point."

Armand sat next to him and moved the quart bottle to the middle of the table, out of harm's way, and spoke without smiling. "Yes you are, and it's not a pretty sight."

Jules looked at Armand as a smile broadened on his face and he tried to suppress a giggle. "Armand, you look so serious. Life's short, so lighten up and live a little, Sweetie."

Justine stared at David. "Yes, Armand. Take a lesson from David. Surround yourself with beautiful women and make love while the sun shines, or the moon shines, or anything shines."

Julienne held a beignet with one hand and flicked it with the finger of the other hand to get the excess powdered sugar off of it. "Is that you philosophy, David, to be a rampant hedonist?"

David looked at the group of faces that turned to hear his answer. "There are worse things than being a hedonist; being an arsonist, a sadist, a fascist. But I think Justine speaks more for herself than for anyone else. She's the only woman I know who practices defacto polyandry."

Armand looked at Justine and furrowed his brow questioningly. "Is that what they call a menage a'trois in America? Polyandry?"

Justine raised her eyebrow as she stared at David. "When its two men and one woman, Armand. When it's two women and one man, they call it polygamy."

Julienne washed her bite of beignet down with her coffee. "Somehow, we've gone from female vanity to male vanity."

Jules looked from Justine to Armand, then back to Justine. "Anything in the pursuit of love is not in vain."

Lenny, who rarely had much to say, smiled at Jules. "Well said, Jules." Then he looked at Julienne who returned his smile with a condescending one, causing him to turn his gaze to the nodding Louie beside him.

Partly to cover Lenny's self conscious embarrassment, David announced, "Well, I'm not as wealthy as Val or Pete, but, in this setting, let me offer you all a round of drinks on me. So, since I'm picking up the tab, stuff your faces with beignets and gorge yourself on café au lait's until you're so caffeinated you wont be able to sleep until noon!"

Julienne raised her coffee cup in toast. "Three cheers for our big spender, David!"

Then Justine raised her coffee cup and said, "And three bigger cheers for our bigger spender, Louie, who gave all us ladies a fortune in Channel Number Five." They all raised their coffee cups and turned to Louie, who was snoring.

Chapter Five
WHAT WE DO FOR LOVE

Justine was about to follow Armand and Jules through the paint chipped door and up the creaky stairs, then turned to say to Julienne, "A girl like you shouldn't be in this lower end of Decatur Street, and definitely not at this late hour."

Julienne smiled politely. "I wouldn't be here if David hadn't agreed to Lenny's request to accompany him while he delivered the last bottle of Channel to his friend. Besides, it can't be all that bad if you three live here."

Justine shook her head from side to side. "It's not by choice, child. I spent the early part of my life down here, the wasted part. I only returned to follow these two spoiled children who insist on defying their wealthy parents by living in poverty in a menage a trois. Don't defy your parents by acquiring any kinky tastes down here, because this is the very womb of kinkiness."

Julienne wrinkled her nose. "We'll only be here long enough for Lenny to deliver his gift."

Justine called to David, who stood nearby. "David, tell her about Lenny's girlfriend, and about that place across the street where she works. And stay by her side, don't leave her for a second." Then Justine shut the door abruptly as David linked his arm in Julienne's and guided her across the street.

The three story building was typical of this part of the quarter, the upper floors with iron lace balconies and the ground floor with folding doors that opened almost the entire front so, instead of display windows, the entire store was displayed. Originally a merchant would have the side and rear walls covered with shelves displaying merchandise, which was protected by a counter in front of all three walls. Only a few

63

barrels or boxes of merchandise might be displayed in the center floor area. That was before the days of merchants funneling ingress and egress through a single door monitored by a cashier and electronic sensors detecting stolen merchandise on its way out or guns on their way in. The current merchant followed the old traditional pattern, one side and rear wall lined with deep wooden un-upholstered booths, and the third wall with a bar surmounted by a huge pink neon sign that declared, "Betty's Bar." Betty herself sat like an empress before the cash register at the outside end of the bar, her young but obese figure, brassy blonde hair, and overly made up face with its perpetual cupie doll smile looking somewhat like the fat lady in the circus. A half dozen tables and chairs filled the center of the open room, but they and the booths were mostly empty at this very late hour. Next to the exterior folding doors was a small exterior door to the upstairs stairway.

Julienne looked at the garish pink, red, and purple neon signs over the bar. "So, tell me about Lenny's girlfriend and Betty's Bar."

As Lenny made a beeline for a girl seated alone at a back booth, the quart bottle of Channel in his hand, Louie dove into the empty booth next to her, closed his eyes as he leaned into the corner, and immediately began snoring. David pulled out a chair for Julienne, as far from the girl's corner booth as possible and as far from Betty as possible. "You probably noted the density of bars in this area which, given the overall density of bars in the French Quarter, might make you wonder how this modest one could survive."

She sat down. "The density of bars in the French Quarter survives because of millions of tourists who are lured there by millions of dollars in advertising." Then she surveyed the almost empty bar. "But I don't think this establishment falls into that category."

64

He remained standing. "And you'd be right. I'm having a beer. What would you like?"

She looked toward the bar and said, "I'll just have a beer, too. They probably don't have Bohemia, so just a Jax or Dixie or whatever."

He ordered the beers at the bar and brought them back, setting a frosty golden labeled bottle of Dixie in front of her. He inspected the two empty glasses he had brought and set the one he considered the cleanest next to her beer. She re-inspected the glass, then filled it half full of beer. "So, how does Betty's Bar survive?"

He re-inspected his glass, pushed it aside, and took a long drink from the bottle. "By selling something more addictive than liquor."

Julienne frowned. "They sell drugs?"

He set his bottle back down. "No, that's next door at the so-called Chinese restaurant whose nameless sign simply says, 'Chinese Food.'"

She looked surprised. "I noticed it when we were crossing the street. That dinky little place next door with nothing but a small counter, five or six barstools, and two customers in it?"

He blinked and smiled broadly at her. "That female customer is a call girl, that male Chinese customer is her pimp who books her appointments through the pay phone on the wall, and that curtained doorway at the end of the counter leads to a mah jong game room with a lot of heavy duty money on the game table."

Her brow furrowed questioningly. "And the drugs."

He took another tug at his bottle and said, "There's a guy at a small table next to a stairwell at the rear corner of the game room. You can get little nickle or dime bags of horse or snow to go, or go up the stairs where an old Chinese lady will pack and light an opium pipe for you and lead you to an empty bunk bed where you can enjoy your 'pipe dreams.'"

She looked puzzled. "Nickle bags, dime bags, horse, snow?"

He made a little inch size square frame with his hands. "Five or ten dollar tiny envelopes of heroin or cocaine. A big nickle is fifty dollars, a big dime is a hundred dollars."

She chuckled. "Why the cryptic double talk? Why not just say what it is?"

He shrugged. "It's carney talk. Carnival people really got it from the gypsies, a secret language so the customers wouldn't know what they're talking about. If they're cheating at cards, then it helps to be able to say to your shil, your partner in crime posing as a fellow card player, when to play a certain card, or when to create a distraction for the pick pocket to better do his job. If you're selling drugs, it's better to use code words for them and for sums of money that would reveal a transaction is occurring."

She took a sip from her glass. "Does the city know or care?"

David held his drink up to look at the neon sign through the lens created by the beer filled amber bottle. "The police know, but don't care as long as they get their cut. The city knows, but leave it to police, unless a tourist gets rolled or murdered or disappears. Then they go through the motions of 'cracking down' and 'cleaning up.' But it's only for show and only temporary."

They began to hear Lenny and the girl's voices raised in argument. Julienne's brow wrinkled in concern for Lenny. "Justine said to tell me about Lenny's girlfriend."

David looked toward the corner booth, then down at his bottle on the table. "You never learned how Betty's Bar survives." They looked at each other. "It survives by being a bordello more than a bar, and Lenny's girlfriend is one of its hapless employees who's paid with little nickle and dime bags she's hooked on, which motivates her to go up those stairs outside with any man who give's Betty the proper amount to put in that register in front of her."

Julienne peered into the rear booth bathed in the pink and purple glow of the neon sign. "She has a beautiful face and figure, but that hair is almost green from the peroxide and those dark circles under her eyes make her face look decades older than her body."

He took a deep breath. "She must be good at what she does, because Lenny became smitten months ago during the St. Patrick's day party at the trio's pad across the street, and he's been trying to save her soul ever since."

Julienne looked at him suspiciously. "St. Patrick's day party? I don't recall that. Why wasn't I invited?"

He shrugged. "Maybe they thought it was too rough for you. Maybe Justine considered you too much competition. As I recall, it seemed to happen on the spur of the moment after you'd gone home."

She looked across the street. "I've never been in their apartment. What's it like?"

He chuckled. "It's like a set from the opera *La Boheme*." He pointed to the second floor balcony of the narrow three story building across the street. "It's behind those windows on the second floor. That balcony's where they hung him."

Julienne looked horrified. "They hung someone?"

He waved his hands from side to side and leaned forward smiling. "No, no, no! Not like that. What happened was, Louie had been testing some dyes in his lab, five gallon samples taken from ocean tankers in port. He took some green dye to Tony's Italian on Bourbon and had them make a few green pizzas which he brought to The Voodoo Room."

Her face brightened. "I remember that! It was fun. I thought it would taste funny, but it didn't."

He nodded assent. "Right. After The Voodoo Room closed, we all hit a couple of spots in this general direction, and I think you left when we were at Café duMonde or Morning Call."

Julienne emptied her bottle into her glass. "I don't remember, but that's usually the case. I consider coffee as the termination of the alcohol."

David winced. "After that's when we ended up in that apartment."

She looked up at the balcony. "What's it like inside?"

He chuckled again. "A mess, but a sort of stage managed artistic mess. Half finished paintings lying askew everywhere, nail kegs and crates used as end tables with huge candles on them, sort'a like the built-up candles on the bar in the club, but not all that big. I think they periodically have their electricity turned off for non-payment. There are old sofas and small mattresses throughout the apartment with old blankets thrown over them to hide their worn condition. And the place smells like a winery."

She look disapproving. "Sounds like the setting for an orgy."

He blinked. "Probably has been, but not that night, at least not as I remember. I fell asleep on one of the sofas, then woke up to go to the bathroom. While I was peeing, I noticed the bathtub was green up to the high level mark. As I walked back towards the balcony, stepping over sleeping bodies and empty bottles, I saw something green on the balcony that I couldn't make out. As I stepped on the balcony, I saw Betty and all the whores staring up at the balcony, then turned to one side and saw Armand's naked body draped over the railing like laundry hung out to dry. They had dyed him green from head to toe to celebrate St. Patricks day."

Julienne looked horrified again. "Oh, poor baby! And he's not even Irish. Did it have any toxic effects?"

He chuckled again. "None other than to passers by who saw his green face framed by a turned down hat brim and turned up collar as he slinked through the streets at night for about a month."

She looked inquisitive. "And that's the night Lenny met his girlfriend at Betty's?"

David looked toward the corner booth and sighed. "Yeah, I saw him from the balcony standing with Betty and the girls. They had wanted to dye him green because, although he's Cajun, they said he looked the most Irish, and he had retreated to Betty's Bar for safety."

She looked toward the booth. "He might have been more safe to be dyed green than to fall in love with a hopeless case."

He turned and looked her in the eye. "Would you give up as readily on one of us if we acquired a disability?"

She wrinkled her nose. "If you acquired a disability by accident, no, I wouldn't give up on you. If you acquired a self destructive behavior by choice, probably I would." Then she narrowed her eyes at him. "Are you trying to tell me something, David? Do you buy nickle and dime bags, or sleep in the old Chinese ladies bunk beds?"

He closed his eyes as he shook his head negatively, then opened them and looked her in the eye. "No, never fear. I'm addicted to music, caffine, and the company of beautiful women. Those are enough vices for me. I love my life far too much to mess it up with drugs or alcohol."

She raised one eyebrow. "I don't know about the alcohol. I've seen you travel that road beyond the borders of 'happy land' a few times."

David tilted his beer bottle up and spied through its neck to its empty interior. "Only because of the peer pressure of friends and fans. I tend to fall asleep before I can consume dangerous amounts."

Suddenly there was shouting from the corner booth as the girl could be seen running to the front of the bar clutching the milk bottle. Lenny slid out of the booth and fell to his knees as he attempted to run. David ran over and assisted him to his feet as Lenny squealed, "Stop her. She's going to sell the Channel."

David looked at him sternly. "Well, what did you expect, Lenny?"

Lenny wobbled in David's arms and stared at him wide eyed. "You go next door and see if she's buying anything. I'll go upstairs to her room and she if she's there."

David shook his head. "I can't do that, Lenny. I've got Julienne here."

Julienne had moved to Lenny's other side to help hold him up. "That's okay, David. I'll go with you."

Lenny found his balance and began to work his way to the front of the bar, holding on to chair backs along the way. He spoke in a pleading tone. "Please, David, go next door and just let me know if she's there. I'll be upstairs."

David frowned at Lenny. "I can't leave Julienne with Louie. He's sound asleep."

Julienne pulled David toward the front of the bar by his hand. "I'm not about to stay here without you, David. Come on, we'll go together, see if she's there, and report back to Lenny."

When they reached the sidewalk, David grabbed Julienne's forearm and stopped her. "You wanted this since the instant I mentioned it, to go sight-seeing in that game room."

She gave him a pained smile as she grabbed the front of his shirt with the arm he held and pulled him toward the door. "The girl, David! She's what's important now!"

As they entered the door, the skinny Chinese pimp in the striped seersucker suit barred their passage through the curtain and glared at Julienne. David made eye contact with him and nodded his head up and down positively. The pimp looked back at Julienne, then stepped aside and held the curtain open for them.

Julienne held her breath as she surveyed thed dark smoke filled room. She sensed the odor of expensive cigars and exotic Egyptian and Russian cigarettes. The darkened room was dominated by a huge central round table illuminated by a single overhead lamp with a leaded Tiffany glass shade. The eight or more men around the table were an international collection of Asian, Latin, Carribean, and swarthy Europeans, the two well dressed Americans looking ghostly white amid the group. The perimeter of the table was lined with a semi-circles of mah jong tiles made of laminated ivory and bamboo, their ivory faces engraved with Chinese symbols and conge, each semi-circle with the inscribed ivory facing the individual player. Two large piles filled the center of the table, one of tiles with their faces down, the other with a small fortune in silver dollars, Mexican gold fifty dollar pieces worth far more than their face value, and an assortment of twenty, fifty, and one hundred dollar bills.

As Julienne's vision adjusted to the darkness, she suddenly gasped. Seated on the stool at the rear of the table was an obese man in a police uniform, replete with visored cap, badge, sidearm, and truncheon. She whispered to David, "Did you see that cop?"

David responded calmly and softly. "That's Vinny, the patrolman on this beat. He comes in here at this hour to stay warm, and probably because it's safer than being on the street."

Her brow furrowed. "I guess that means the good news is that no tourist has been rolled, murdered, or disappeared."

A small elderly Chinese man in a waiter's uniform came up to David and said, "Velly solly, pardon sir, but him," and he nodded at a well dressed older Latin man on the other side

71

of the table who made eye contact with David, "Him speakee, how much fo' girly?" Only he pronounced it 'ger-ree.'

David and Julienne looked at each other with repressed smiles, then at the Latin man with more restraint. His beige suit matched his tanned face which made his wavy white hair and perfect teeth appear all the whiter. In the collar of his yellow silk shirt, he wore a bolo necktie with a heavy gold buckle which framed an immense convincingly genuine emerald whose facets flashed sparkles of green light with every movement he made. Beside the tiles before him were a half dozen tall stacks of Mexican fifty dollar gold pieces. His brown eyes flicked back and forth between David and Julienne, stopping long enough to survey her figure, then return to her eyes as his smile increased.

Julienne stepped closer to David and put her arm through his. He looked at the waiter and said, "Tell him the lady is not a working girl and is not for sale. Tell him she is the guest of the musician."

The waiter bowed repeatedly as he backed away, saying, "Velly solly, sir. Velly solly," and he scurried away.

Julienne grimaced at David. "So much for my haute coiture wardrobe from Maison Blanche, if I'm taken for a hooker on Decatur Street."

The waiter reappeared, bowing even lower. "Velly solly, a hundred pardons, sir. Him speakee, how much fo' musician?"

Julienne put her hand to her mouth to hide her uncontrolled giggle. David forced his lips to remain closed as he repressed a chuckle. Then he looked at the concerned waiter and said, "Tell him the musician is not for sale, either."

The waiter didn't leave, but looked frightened as he looked to the Latin man, then back to David. "Velly velly solly, sir, a thousand pardons, but him speakee, you say no, he speakee he pay fo' times as much for ger-ree and musician togedder."

David's expression changed to exasperation as he said forcefully, "Tell him, NO...thank...you!" Then David escorted Julienne to a position where the cop's immense body blocked any view between them and the Latin man.

Julienne gave David a pained smile. "Well, at least I'm not the only one who looks like a slut." She surveyed the room looking for the girl, her gaze coming to rest on the man in a pin striped suit seated at a small table beside the rear stairwell. "Let's go ask the guy by the stairs if he's seen her or if she went upstairs."

David gripped her arm and restrained her. "I'll go ask him. You go stand beside the cop, not close enough for him to touch you, but within his line of vision. You'll be safe there. Just, whatever you do, do not stand behind any player close enough to see their tiles. If they thought you were signaling other players, it could get very nasty. Now go!" And he pushed her gently toward the police officer.

Julienne reluctantly sidled up to slightly more than an arms length distance from the officer, carefully avoiding eye contact with the Latin man. The cop looked to be in his early forties, around three hundred pounds, and, based on his name and appearance, probably Italian. She noted the sweat stains under his arms and on his back, and, in addition to the mixture of tobacco odors, she could smell his body odor. Only a couple players took note of her presence, only momentarily checking her distance from the player's nearest her, and with no seeming recognition that she was the only female in the room. However, when the officer turned and smiled at her, revealing a gold front tooth on one side and a missing front tooth on the other side, his survey and obvious approval of her figure made Julienne's skin begin to crawl and she fought the urge to run.

Suddenly David was standing between her and the officer, whose lecherous smile dissolved into disappointment at his arrival. "According to the pusher, she's not here, but he

73

wouldn't tell me if she was, anyhow. So I think we'd best get out of here and see if we can find Lenny."

Just then the pimp came through the curtain and spread his arms wide barring traffic through that passageway and shouting what sounded like hysterical gibberish in Chinese. Everyone started stuffing their money in their pockets and heading for the rear stairwell as the Chinese waiter folded up the two halves of the large round table toward the center and all the tiles and remaining money fell noisily through the center seam into the boxed pedestal under the table. When the empty table was flat again, the Chinese waiter spread a tablecloth and placed a flowered centerpiece and several place settings on it. The officer awkwardly dismounted his stool, removed his sidearm and truncheon holding them both pointed toward the ceiling, and announced, "Okay, folks, this is a raid!" He then turned to Julienne and, with a big smile, winked at her.

David pulled Julienne toward the rear stairs where they joined the last of the escaping players. Hearing a crashing sound, she looked around to see several police knock the pimp flat on the floor and trample over him as they flooded into the room. The pusher pushed her violently into the stairwell before joining her and bolting the door behind him. With David in front of her pulling her up the stairs, and the pusher behind her with both hands on her buttocks urging her forward, they reached the second floor where she smelled the acrid tarry odor of the opium pipes and saw the sleeping bodies in the bunk beds. As much as she wanted to see it all and drink it all in, David and the pusher kept dragging her forward until they were exiting onto a balcony and descending exterior stairs with an iron lace railing into a beautiful patio. The collection of players began to disperse through different doorways, the Latin man stopping before one doorway and gesturing for David and Julienne to follow him and looking disappointed when they passed him by. The players all disappeared until she was alone with David exiting through a wrought iron gate held open by the pusher who closed and locked it behind them as they slowed down to walk peacefully on a quiet cross street close to David's loft.

By the time they reached the door that led to his residence, the sun was rising and pedestrian and auto traffic had begun a new day. He turned to her and took her hands in his. "That was not what I intended when I invited you to accompany me and Lenny. I really should have let the evening end with coffee and beignets."

She smiled and frowned at the same time as she stepped closer to him. "Oh, no, I wouldn't have missed this evening for the world. And, perhaps, it's not entirely over."

David looked over her shoulder, then raised his hand to flag a passing taxi. As the Yellow Cab stopped and the rear passenger door popped open, Julienne said, "Well, I guess that answers that."

David looked at her. "Answers what?"

She smiled wistfully. "Oh, nothing." She kissed him on both cheeks. "Thank you, David, for a memorable evening. I wish you and Lenny good luck in finding the girl, preferably the right girl," and she ducked into the cab and closed the door.

David looked puzzled as the long cab sped off into the growing morning traffic.

Chapter Six
SO SHALL YE SOW, SO SHALL YE REAP

As he approached the gate to the alley beside The Voodoo Club, David saw Aurora waiting across the street. She crossed the street to join him as he opened the gate for her and they walked to the patio where Zoe was emptying a dustpan into the garbage cans below the stairs to Val's apartment. "Zoe, this is Aurora. Aurora, Zoe, the left brain of this operation. Val, my boss, is the right brain, and I'm somewhere South of both of them."

The women exchanged smiles and nods and the three entered the club's open rear door, David leading Aurora to a table near the piano where they both set down the briefcases they were carrying, his a brown leather and hers a paisley printed canvas. He pulled out and handed her some piano music arrangements of French songs, his printed biography, and his glossy eight by ten mug shot. She pulled out and handed him a book of Spanish songs for the guitar, a biography handwritten on ruled paper, and a glossy eight by ten photo of her singing with a country western band. The two looked over each others paperwork.

David read her biography and asked, "Did you write this?"

She looked at him with a hint of anger, then back at his own biography as she spoke. "I had some help. My English is no perfect and I no ha typewriter."

He looked at her photo. "I didn't know you sang with Jake Yocum's band. How'd you hook up with a top country western recording artist who, to my knowledge, never did any Latin songs?"

She didn't look up as she shuffled through his musical arrangements. "Es mucho you no know aboud me. You knowledge may nod be as grande as you tink."

He looked at her. "So enlighten me. How, when, and where did you meet Jake Yocum?"

She sat back, looked at him, took a deep breath, then looked past him in the general direction of the piano. "I meed heem in Mehico. He hear me play guitar, ged me green card to play and sing wi' hees band."

He looked back at the photo. "So why would you ever leave his band? If you stayed with him long enough, you'd probably be on a dozen records by now."

She stacked all his paperwork and shoved it back toward him. "Cause he wan someone younger."

He looked astonished. "Someone younger? Are you kidding? You can't be much over twenty, and I suspect you're even younger than you look."

She leaned back and folded her arms and spoke angrily. "He wan more dan me canta et guitarra. He wan more dan I can gib."

David sensed he should ease up. "Okay, but Mr. Griffith might ask you about working with Yocum, so just say you left him because you wanted to try a single." He stood up and took both his and her music to the piano. "Here's what I suggest we do when he gets here. You'll go over the song *Poinciana* with me, I could probably use some help on some of the Spanish pronunciation. And I'll go over the first stanza of *Les Marseilles* with you, and don't get testy about the fact that you already know it. Just play along with the coaching theme. Remember, it's going to benefit you and your employer to have both your names in the paper, and that's worth bending the truth a little here."

Aurora was about to respond when they heard the old wall phone ring. Zoe picked it up, then announced that Val was on her way down, and the candle lighting door opening ritual began and ended with Val making her entrance with, "Let the games begin!"

David played one song, then stopped and took Aurora over to Val's table. "Val, this is Aurora Alonzo. Aurora, this is my esteemed boss lady, Valentina Siciliana. Aurora's appearing at La Lune and we've been helping each other with some lyrics to French and Spanish songs we both play, but could probably sing better with a little coaching from each other. If Tommy Griffith arrives early enough tonight, would it be okay if I pitched a blurb for his column about our mutual coaching? Might get both clubs a little press."

Val had a suspicious grin on her face as she looked from one to the other, watching them squirm for a few seconds before she replied. "Sounds fine to me, but it's Tommy's call. I'll send him over to you if and when he arrives." The suspicious grim returned to her face as she flicked her newspaper open, signaling to the two young people that they were dismissed.

David made room for Aurora on his piano bench and said, "Let me sing *Poinciana* through once without your comments, then I'll repeat it phrase by phrase and you correct any mis-pronunciation I make." As he sang, Aurora's cold uncomfortable expression began to relax into a slightly surprised, but still slightly reserved smile.

The columnist arrived on schedule at nine fifteen and headed straight for Val's table. Zoe served him his usual martini with a twist of lemon and left. Val folded her paper and the two old friends started catching up since their previous weekly encounter, Val appearing more animated than in the relatively few conversations she conducted at her table in the course of a week. He was of average height and looks for a forty-ish Frenchman who looked more like a math teacher or accountant than a witty columnist whose column commented on cultural events, customs, and trivia with an occasional spicy dash of gossip. It was obvious when Val mentioned David's blurb idea and the two started looking toward the two young people on the piano bench. The columnist walked over to the railing around the piano, smiled, and said, "Don't let me interrupt. Go ahead with what you were doing and just let me observe for a little while."

Ten minutes later they were all at Val's table where the columnist said, "I think it's a cute bit, but I don't think the 'Liberte' in the heading you suggested is sufficiently identifiable with *Les Marseilles.* I think I'll title it 'Voodoo Vocalist Coaches Gorgeous Guitarist.'"

David suddenly felt desperate knowing that, without La Lune in the heading, Aurora's boss would not be as happy as he'd like. He and Aurora looked at each other awkwardly, then he countered, "How about, 'Voodoo Vocalist Coaches La Lune Lovely?'"

The columnist turned to look at Val, who was glaring at David. After an awkward five seconds, Val nodded her head almost imperceptibly, and the columnist smiled at the young people and said, "Sounds great. I'll probably have the piece in just before the weekend and, hopefully, you'll see some results Saturday and Sunday."

As David escorted Aurora to the front door, she sneered at him and said, "La Lune Lovely? You hadda make a sex object oudda me?"

David raised one eyebrow. "I had to keep your boss from being pissed with both of us. You try coming up with a headline in ten seconds or less that satisfies both our bosses."

She sighed heavily. "Que sera, sera."

He handed her the canvas briefcase. "How about dinner at Fong's Chinese Café on Decatur after work? I could help you improve that bio, get it typed up and copied for you."

Her eyes narrowed. "I say 'no strings.'"

He looked surprised. "There are no strings in their House Lo Mein, only shrimp and chicken and beef and...."

She headed out the door with a reluctant smile. "Okay, okay! Around tree, eef I can make id."

He continued to tease her as she walked away. "...and pork and mushrooms and water chestnuts and green onions and...," and he walked back to the piano with a smile.

****

As David was about to enter Fong's Restaurant, he spied Aurora talking to some young men he presumed to be Latino sailors at the corner doorway to Los Marino's Bar. She was smiling and apparently joking with them, but they seemed to be pulling her by her arm into the bar and, despite her smile, he sensed her reluctance and wondered if she was being coerced. When she disappeared through the doorway, David walked swiftly to follow her.

The music from the four piece Mariachi band was deafening, their instruments not really needing the electronic amplification that made ripples appear in the drinks on the tables. The red, white, and green lighting was barely bright enough to light the pathway through the tightly packed tables to the tiny dance floor where the young men were pulling Aurora. The tallest of the young men held her by both wrists, trying to get her to sway her body in synchronization with his shoulder and hip dance moves. Though she still smiled, her brow was furrowed with reluctance.

David stepped beside her and placed his hand higher on her wrist above the young man's hand, smiling at her and ignoring him. "Hi, Aurora. I was entering Fong's when I saw you and wondered if you'd forgotten our meeting, unless, of course, you want to cancel."

The young man pulled her wrist forcefully away from his hand and stepped between David and Aurora, sneering at him. "Aye, gringo, 'dis is no place for college boys. Tenga usted una puta en la calle Decatur. Venga su culo muy pronto, et viva mas anos." Which prompted a tittering of laughter among bystanders.

Aurora wrenched her wrist out of the young man's grasp and stepped away from him. David quickly stepping between her and the young man. She appeared angry at the young man and exasperated with David. David responded, "Okay, I know when I'm not welcome. We'll be going now."

The young man appeared to be folding his arms, but was actually retrieving a 'dirk' knife from the leather sheath strapped to his left forearm under his shirt sleeve. He pointed the knife within inches of David's chest, glaring at David and threatening, "Venga en solo, a venga en el feretro!"

David looked at the knife point, then at the unsmiling faces around him as the bystanders fell silent, the mariachi music still blaring in the background. He understood the first part of the threat commanded him to leave alone, but looked confused about the latter part, which stated the alternative was to go in a 'box;' i.e., a coffin. He felt his body being pulled backward as Aurora gripped the back of his coat, stepping in front of him so close to the tip of the knife that it almost touched her cleavage. Her eyes bulged as she glared infuriated at the young man, screaming at him. "Basta, Francisco! Que loco usted? Et tu demente? El es mi pianista. Escuche mi cantas Frances." She stared at the point of the knife almost touching her skin, then back into his eyes as he lowered it to his side. "Deseo tu a arresto? Aficion a viven en prision?" She started to turn, stopped, narrowed her eyes at him, then snorted and said, "Idioto," then completed her turn and pushed David toward the door. Now she focused her anger on David. "Et tu tambien un idioto! Que pensamiento, tu?"

She continued to berate him in broken Spanish until they were a block away from Los Marinos Bar on St. Louis Street. Looking over her shoulder to insure they had not been followed, she stopped, placed her hand on his chest, and spoke in a remorseful tone with an apologetic frown on her face. "Oh, David, I am mucho sorry. Es verdad! I jus' wan' ged you oudda dere safely. Forgive me, por favor."

David smiled at her. "Okay, I forgive you for saving my life." He continued to smile at her, her frown melting into a smile as she placed her other hand on his chest, closed her eyes, and bowed her head to touch her hands. He put his hands on her shoulders and felt her body shaking almost imperceptively. He pushed her back slightly as her eyes rose to meet his, then said, "I don't think we should go back to Fong's, too close to Los Marinos. Do you like Italian?"

Her smile broadened and her eyes widened. "I love Italian."

He blinked. "Good. We're only a block from Tortorich's. We can sit by the window and watch the tourists going into Antoine's across the street and paying ten times as much as we are."

They sat in the back room whose walls were lined with glazed tile in turn of the century patterns. Across the street the lines of tourists had disappeared and the front doors of world famous Antoine's Restaurant were closed, but the lights inside the leaded cut glass windows still blazed and danced with moving shadows as private parties continued into the night. The aproned waiter set their plates in front of them, his with linguini and beef daub, hers with a single calzone. David pointed at her plate with his fork. "Is that going to be enough for you?"

Aurora positioned the calzone carefully on her plate as if it was a little animal about to be slaughtered. "Yes, I lake dem. Dey remind me o' Mexican empenadas."

He twirled the linguini expertly on his fork. "So, how did you meet Francisco?"

She set her knife and fork down and looked at him as if she were about to get huffy again, then changed her mind, began to slice the calzone, and said, "Some Mexican sailors come to de club 'cause I guess I lake a celebrity to dem. Dey were mucho enthusiastico and make a scene and god tossed out. Dey always wan' me go a Los Marinos, bud I too scared. Mexican men tegan mucho machismo. Pero Francisco mi mira sur la calle, jus' be friendly, buy me drink. He nodding to me."

He paused with a fork full of beef and asked, "And Ramon?"

She set her knife and fork down again and put her hands in her lap. "Ramon es mi amigo. Mi gay amigo." She tilted her head to one side and narrowed her eyes slightly as she stared at him. "David, por que you wanna know mi estado civil, wan we say 'no strings'?"

He chewed and swallowed a bite of beef, then looked her in the eye. "Aurora, I'm not some macho idiot who's going to drag you anyplace you don't want to go, but I'm also not gay. I'd like to help you and become your friend in the process, but I'd also like to know how many of your other friends carry knives or lay any special claims on you."

She straightened her head, narrowed her eyes further, and spoke in an angry husky whisper. "Nadie reclamar a mi! Nadi poseedor a mi! Solamente mi! Mi! Mi! Mi!."

His eyes widened as he leaned back in his chair. "Okay! I got the message. You are passionate about your independence. I admire that. I applaud that. Now, one last question on this subject, are you gay?"

She looked at him smugly. "You din' know si Ramon gay, why you tink mi gay?"

He swallowed the last of his meal and said, "I don't know. That's why I'm asking. Are you gay?"

She smiled mischievously. "How dey say en Los Estados Unidos, tha's fo' mi to know and you to fine oud."

He put his napkin on the table and smiled at her. "I look forward to that challenge." He signaled the waiter for the check and said, "Now, I suggest that we go to my place where there's a typewriter and some privacy, I'll ask you a few questions that you'll refrain from getting angry at, and we'll compose you a new professional looking bio and resume worthy of having printed."

Her mischievous smile returned to a suspicious frown and she turned and stared through the window as the lights in Antoine's began to go out one room at a time. She looked back at him and said, "No strings."

He smiled benevolently and said, "No strings. The typewriter uses little levers and springs. No strings."

Her suspicious frown melted into a reluctant smile.

****

Davids' old Underwood portable typewriter smelled of the kerosine he would sometimes squirt into its dusty mechanism to free things up, but it still had a sticky letter 'Q' key. David reasoned that, next to the 'Z' key, the 'Q' was the least used key on the keyboard. He was a good touch typist, having figured out in high school that being the only boy brave enough to take a typing class would maximize his exposure to girls, be more useful, and be less embarrassing than taking a home economics class and learn how to operate a sewing machine. His typing was efficient enough to sometimes sound like a machine gun. Rat-a-tat-tat!

Aurora sat in one of the two straight backed wood chairs at David's wood kitchen table and watched his eyes focus on the white pages as he typed. She had somewhat enjoyed the game of making him struggle to get answers to his questions, as he described it, "like pulling teeth." While it was true she was reluctant to give him honest answers to some of his questions, she was more than willing to give him the fictional answers she knew would compose the kind of documents that served the best interests of her career. Still, it was fun making him 'pull teeth' to get the fictional information out of her, and her way of testing the sincerity of his interest in helping her. If he was only interested in seducing her, he would have posed less questions and not probed them so deeply in his effort to get accurate answers.

As the typewriter continued to 'rat-a-tat-tat,' she got up and strolled along the long wall with the mural he said he had painted. She touched her fingers on the Arc de Triomphe as if she might feel the dimensional texture of its base relief images. She noted the cars in the traffic did not look American and had names like Renault and Panhard and Citroen. At the outer edges of the mural she noted the people seated at outdoor cafes reading papers like Le Journal, Paris Match, and suddenly she caught her breath, The Times Picayune. She looked closer at that table to see the reader was a lone young man who resembled David. She looked over her shoulder at him as he continued to type, realizing he was a person committed to detail, accuracy, and the truth, even if the truth was an aspiration rather than a reality.

She walked over, stood behind his chair, and placed both hands on his shoulders, massaging the muscles at the base of his neck, hearing the zipper like sound as he pulled the last sheet of paper out of the typewriter, stacked it with the other sheets, and turned toward her. She removed her hands and looked down at his face as she heard him say, "Not that it was easy, but I now think we have some useful tools to promote you bookings to club owners, agents, and any other

86

opportunities that come up." He looked from the papers up to her face as he shook the stack of papers in his hand, "Now we need to get a good mug shot of you to put on these before we print them."

Aurora made a decision. She said, "Stand up, David." He looked confused, then stood up. She knelt before him and, in one continuous motion, opened and pulled down his pants and shorts simultaneously, then pushed him back to be seated in the chair. She looked at his shocked face and said, "Dis my way say muchos gracias, bud remember, no strings." Then she placed both hands on his knees, spread them apart, and started to lower her head.

David dropped the stack of papers, which scattered to the floor, as he placed both hands on her shoulders to restrain her. His shocked expression turned into a pained smile. "Whoa, Aurora, I didn't ask you for anything in exchange."

She lowered her hands to clasp them in front of her and leaned her head to one side. "I know. Le agradezco su ayuda. You save my job. You teach me cantos. You escriba mi fomento. My way say t'ank you."

He picked up the papers and placed them on the table as he said, "But what if I want more?"

She sat back on her heels, placed her fingertips on the floor on either side, and straightened her head as her brow furrowed and she said, "Dis no anytime t'ing I do. Dis, how you say, one time token of mi appreciacion."

His brow furrowed also. "No, I mean...." Then he looked at his lap, stood up, raised his shorts and pants, and closed them. "I mean, what if I want..." He pulled the other chair closer to his, lifted her by her shoulders, and gently pushed her onto the chair, looking into her eyes. "What if I want a relationship? What if I want.......strings?"

She looked down at her hands and shook her head sideways. "You no wan' mi, David." She looked at the stack of papers, put her hand on them, and tapped them three times with her fingers. "Dis.....dis all lies. You no know mi viva. You know verdad, you no wan' mi nunca."

His brow smoothed and he looked at her with compassion. "That's for me to decide."

She stared at him with an expression somewhere between anger and shame, one which he could only interpret as pained. "You wan' know why I angry, why I no truss, why I a freak? I tell you! I tell you mi whole dirdy story!"

He looked at the veins bulging in her temples. "That's okay, Aurora, I wasn't accusing you of anything. I'm not asking for any confessions."

She stared at the floor. "No, I godda tell you, 'cause you remind mi."

David looked confused. "Remind you? Of what?"

Her eyes began to glisten. "You de tured man who really try to help me. Mi padre, El Gato, et tu."

His brow furrowed deeper with confusion. "I remind you of your father? And who is El Gato, the cat?"

She looked off into space as if she were hypnotized. "Mi madre es muerte a mi tres anos." She looked at him briefly, then back into space. " Mi madre die when I was tree. Mi padre es un bracero, uno migrand worker, leave me con el hermana cuando he pick cotton et peas por el gringos del Norte. He no know he sister do drugs. Elle mi vende a la puta calle. She turned me out when I was eleven, trading my body for drugs to dealers in her casa. When I was turdteen, she sold me outride to a bordello."

David spoke softly. "Aurora, you don't have to do this."

She looked at him. "Yes, I do," then back into space. "You ask about El Gato. He was a gringo who came to de bordello, sometimes a week at a time. He pick me soon after I arrive, keep me in he room sometimes a week or more. Furse I tink he mucho viejo, he beard and he belly, bud I done know

88

he famous country western star, make mucho dinero. You know heem por el nombre Jacob Yocum. After mi padre, he furse man tread me kind, like a lady, buy me pretty clothes and jewelry I tho'd was diamonds and gold, bud really costume jewelry. His amigos call him 'Cat' all'a time, so we name him 'El Gato.' He teach me many tings, good and bad."

David closed his eyes. "Aurora, don't."

She ignored him. "He teach me how to dress 'cause I no god mucho clothes before. He teach me how to ead in cantina 'cause I no ead in restaurand befo'; which fork fo beans o salad o fish, which spoon fo café o sopa o fruitas, which knife fo bread o steak o butter. And bess of all, when I curious aboud he big shiny guitar, he teach me how to play id; how to toughen mi fingertips so de strings no cud, how to pluck melody o chord o otra ritmos, how to use de body like a conga drum." She sighed heavily. "Bud he also teach me how I be la mas gran puta."

David shook his head from side to side. "That's enough, Aurora."

She took a deep breath. "You need to know. I need to tell you." She looked down at her open hands, then back up into space. "El Gato teach me how to use eye contack and smiles to take control when I give him blow job, how to use my hair to tease and my hands to stroke, and dad way udder men no choke me like before. He teach me positions to take and tings to do and words to say so men canna go too deep and hurd me inside. He teach me to give myself enema and use my finger to stretch and relax mi culo so he ting no hurd me dere."

As tears appeared in her open eyes, tears also squeezed from David's closed eyelids as he spoke a single word, "Please...."

The tears traveled slowly down her cheek. "El Gato, he proud o' me, how good I play guitar. For two, tree year, he so happy to see me and I so happy to see him. Then he gone almos a year, and when he come back I grow taller, mi chichi mas grande, I tink he be happy I become a real woman." Her brow furrowed and her face began to show the beginnings of sadness. "Bud he no pick me. Instead he pick anudder tiny liddle girl. Den I remember wad he say when he look down at my small body benead him. He say, 'You remine me o' my sister.' I think of he sister lake she an old woman lake he an old man. Den I remember when he fok mi culo and say, 'Dis way you no ged pregnand and mom no know.'" She took a deep breath. "Suddenly I realize, dis ole man I love, when he a boy, he seduce, maybe rape, he liddle sister. He pick liddle girl like me because he wanna relive commid incest."

David opened his tear stained eyes and yelled at her. "Stop it, Aurora, stop!"

She turned and looked at him. "David, you should know, before I see you tonide, for de furse time een muchos anos, I gib myself enema jus in case you wann'a fok mi dere, because you de furse man I care aboud like I cared aboud El Gato o mi padre."

David shook his head slightly side to side. "Aurora, I'm not your father, and I'm not El Gato."

Now she shook her head slightly side to side. "Dads de problem. You a beautiful young man like on de cover of one of dose cheap novelas I used to learn to read, and you kind to me in de nurturing way like mi padre et El Gato." New tears began to flow down her cheeks. "Dough you seem to lake me, I scared to dead dad any minnid you gonna go pick peas in California or pick some skinny liddle girl who look like you liddle sister."

David slid to his knees before the chair she was seated in, and embraced her tightly, saying softly, "I don't have a little sister, and I wouldn't last ten minutes picking peas in a field. So you have nothing to worry about." Then he kissed her lips gently and they looked into each other's eyes.

She smiled through her tears. "Oh, David. I know you a young man wid lods o ladies and no interess een commitmend, bud will I be safe eef I try to hold on to dis novela dream for jus a liddle while?"

He hugged her tightly again, saying, "You are safe, and my love's not a dream, it's reality." As the words left his lips, his eyes popped open and an alarm went off in his head. He heard an inner voice saying to him, "Okay, David, you never lied to chicks before, but did you just hear yourself saying the 'L' word?" He took a deep breath, feeling her perky breasts pressing against his chest in the process, and thought to himself, "Okay, maybe that's the way it happens!"

Chapter Seven
BRAVE NEW WORLD

Aurora smelled coffee. With her eyes still closed, she lowered the rumpled sheet that covered her head and inhaled deeply, a satisfied smile spreading across her face. The night before had been a catharsis for her and a revelation to both of them. It wasn't the first time in her life that she had a beautiful young man or a tender lover, but it was the first time in her life that she had a tender lover who was a beautiful young man. Older men were more inclined to be tender and generous in their lovemaking, but younger men placed more value on what they perceived as their assets; looks, strength, and aggressiveness, and seemed to take her assets for granted, particularly if they were paying for them. Older men who were as callous as younger men were, in her opinion, simply proving their immaturity.

David had apparently learned that generosity begat generosity, and he could read female signals with the same skill he displayed with the English language, sensing when she wanted aggressiveness, and when to surrender to her lead. She was glad that the explicit language she had used the night before to deliberately shock him had not inhibited him from exploring every part of her body. The fact that he explored every part with his fingers and his mouth, in addition to his penis, told her that she was with a man who was both experienced and void of hangups or reservations about the scope and beauty of sex.

Her past experience had led her to realize how impossible and unlikely were the expectations of the cheap romance novellas she had read in Mexico, and still sometimes bought at American news stands that stocked Spanish language publications,. Still she shared the dream of most women that she could somehow meet a man with all the virtues of a novella hero. Although David was materially wealthy only in comparison to her childhood poverty, she realized he was not wealthy by American standards and unlikely to be a fabulously rich prince in disguise like some character in a novella. But her experience also told her that his talent, his generosity, and his skill as a lover were a rare combination that she was most fortunate in attracting, and she should savor it for as long as it lasted, and not destroy it with the fear of eventually losing him.

She felt the bed sag as he sat on the edge and opened her eyes to see him set the coffee tray between them, smiling at her with what a novella would describe as "the burning light of love in his eyes." He could not possibly realize that her smile was partly her amusement at remembering such romantic lines from a novella, and partly her joy in marveling that she was actually experiencing such a moment. Her smile broadened as she looked at the silver tray and sugar and creamer, still realizing that he was not a prince in disguise, but enjoying that his taste included such princely accessories. She raised up on one elbow and put a single spoon of sugar in the modest black mug while he added excessive sugar and cream to his, raising her cup and closing her eyes as she inhaled the rich aroma. She opened her eyes and sipped the coffee, then closed her eyes again with a smile on her face, thinking it should not surprise her that a man who is such a good lover can also brew a good cup of coffee. She opened her eyes, still smiling, and asked, "Do you do windows, too?"

His bare chest shook with unspoken laughter as he looked at her with a confused smile. "Windows? What the hell are you talking about?"

She shook her head sideways as she set the coffee mug down and said, "Nada. Por que tengan usted talento en todo?

You so smot. Por musica, por escriba, you even make la mas bueno café." Then she reached up and rumpled his wavy blonde hair and leered at him. "And you fok lake an angel!"

He smoothed his rumpled hair back with his hand. "I didn't know that was a pre-requisite for an angel."

She sipped her coffee and shrugged one shoulder. "Well, eef I ever med one, I'd expect heem to fok as good as you."

He set his mug on the tray, leaned on one elbow, and gripped her foot that was exposed below the bottom of the sheet. While his thumb kneaded the sole of her foot, he raised it to his mouth, playfully bit her toes, then kissed the arched instep. "Well, based on that criteria, you definitely qualify as an angel."

She set her coffee mug on the tray and smiled with suppressed laughter. "Good! Den you forgod all aboud lass nide."

He could not stop smiling at her. "Last night was the beginning of one of the world's great romances."

She reached down and stroked the side of his face. "Tu es mi primero romance verdad. Mi primero amore voluntario, amore perfecto."

He looked in her eyes, extended his tongue and began to lick a trail up her instep and calf, his hands lifting the sheet as his head disappeared beneath it. She laughed uncontrollably as she gripped his head through the sheets and pressed it to her, her laughter turning to heavy breathing, grunts, and eventually high pitched screams that she attempted to stifle. Within minutes they became a twisted ball of rumpled sheet and human flesh, a kaleidoscope image of linen and limbs and lips in which it was impossible to distinguish an individual torso, a Daliesque painting of two angels in heat.

****

95

That evening, at The Voodoo Room, Justine, Armand, and Jules arrived wearing new shiny black leather tight fitting pants and colored suede coats; Armand's tan, Jule's gray, and Justine's wine colored. When Julienne and the others admired them, Justine explained, "Armand's father negotiated with him to finish his studies at Loyola in exchange for giving him his allowance retroactive for the past fifteen months. Now he can quit his job as a busboy at Arnaud's Restaurant."

Armand rolled his eyes. "I was about to be fired, anyway."

Justine leaned toward Julienne and spoke in a hoarse whisper. "He's so spoiled. He's never held a job for more than three months."

Jules spoke in a nervous squeaky falsetto. "Wha'd'ya mean. I've held my job at the cathedral for five years!"

Justine smiled artificially at him. "I wasn't speaking of you, Sweetie. Besides, being paid for one day a week, give or take a few weddings and funerals, is not exactly a full time job. But you are consistent and reliable, and we love you for it." Justine turned back to Julienne and spoke in a quieter whisper. "God! It's like raising two children."

Julienne sipped her grasshopper and smiled. "I'm assuming the fringe benefits are worth it."

Justine lifted her drink and said, "God, I hope so. I'll just have to live long enough for one of them to outlive their parents and inherit their fortune."

Julienne rolled her eyes and turned to look toward David at the piano. "David seems to be in good spirits. He's been playing all my favorite love songs like *All The Things You Are* and *This Is My Beloved*."

Justine turned to peer at David, noticing that he was smiling more than usual. Then she stared at Julienne who was staring at David, studying her face as if she was looking for something. "Did you and David get it on the other night after you dropped us off?"

Julienne turned to her and blinked, a shocked expression on her face. "Well, frankly, I don't kiss and tell." She looked back at David. "But we did have a wild adventure in that gambling and opium den across from you when the police raided it."

Justine scowled toward David, her voice hoarse and accusatory. "No! Really? After I told him to protect you, he fed you drugs?"

Julienne frowned and smiled simultaneously at her. "No, we didn't do any drugs. We were chasing after Lenny's girlfriend. But there was a South American guy who wanted to buy me, and then both of us, before the police arrived and we all escaped through the opium den to another street." She looked back at David. "It was the most exciting night I've ever had."

Justine returned to her drink. "Then I take it you and he didn't do it." Julienne looked at her inquisitively as Justine signaled the bartender who stopped rolling a silver dollar back and forth across his knuckles to amuse nearby customers and approached her, wiping the bar in front of her with his towel. "Pete, gimme a Cuttysark in milk."

Pete smiled. "You want Zoe to take it up to him?"

Justine looked at David and smiled. "No, give it to me. I wanna' take it up myself."

Julienne's brow furrowed. "I think he still has the one I ordered."

Justine continued to stare at David. "That's all right, I'm not trying to get him drunk and seduce him. I just wanna' talk." She took the drink out of Pete's hand and walked slowly up to the piano, the males at adjacent tables admiring her leather clad buttocks as she passed by.

David smiled at her as she approached, executing a series of arpeggios as a segue until he began the next song. "Hello

Justine." Then he looked at the drink in her hand. "No need for that, I already have one."

She set the drink next to one wrapped in a napkin. "One never has too much tribute, David. Besides, I have a request."

His brow furrowed slightly. "I'm really not a request artist, but, if I know it, I'll try to please."

She placed one hand over the other on the corner of the piano and rested her chin on them. "Oh, you know this one. It was written for you. And I want you to sing it to me."

His brow furrowed deeper. "Now you're really taxing my talents. You know I don't like to sing in front of all these opera fans."

She smiled like a cat. "Oh, this doesn't require an operatic voice, just that earthy kind of recitation you cabaret singers are so good at."

He gave her a pained smile. "Okay, what is it?"

Her smile broadened. *"Just A Gigolo."*

The corners of his mouth turned down and one eyebrow went up.

Her eyes narrowed at him as she whispered, "Who'd you sleep with, David? I know it wasn't Julienne, because she's still in that adoration from afar mode. I doubt that it's Val, because that wouldn't have put that supercilious grin on your face and inspired all those syrupy love songs. Who'd you fuck, David? Tell me!"

David sat straight up, stared straight ahead, and started a Scott Joplin tune. "I'm sorry, M'am, I don't know that one."

Justine reached into her cleavage and pulled out a fifty dollar bill, dropping it into the giant brandy snifter kitty with a flourish, saying imperiously, "Sing the song, David!"

His tempo slowed ever so slightly as he stared at the kitty. "Take that back, Justine. You guys can't afford to waste money like that."

She glared at him and spoke in a stage whisper. "Don't worry, we came into a lot of cash. Either tell me who you fucked, or sing the song, David!"

David stopped so abruptly, several people turned to look at him. He looked down, then raised his head with a dazzling professional smile and sang the melancholy song, *Just a Gigolo.*

Justine turned to the tables closest to her and, fanning her face with her hand as she headed back to the bar, mimicked the voice of a Southern Belle. "I do declare, he is the very image of a romantic gentleman. I do believe he has given me the vapors!" Her performance was greeted with a smattering of laughter.

David exited the piano and headed toward the rear patio door. As he passed Val, she frowned and said, "It's kinda early for your break." David frowned without looking at her and said gruffly, "No it isn't." The door flapped back and forth as he bolted through it.

The patio was bathed in the blue light of an almost full moon. The air felt cool on his forehead as he stood in the center of the flagstone floor, his eyes closed, one hand on his hip, the other touching his forehead. The door flapped noisily behind him. He put both hands at his sides and braced himself, assuming it was either Justine continuing her taunting or Val complaining he took a break too soon.

Julienne's voice sounded solicitous. "Are you alright, David?" He turned and looked at her apologetically. Her brow was wrinkled with concern. "I don't mean to pry, but what was all that about?"

He tried to smile without complete success. "Just Justine being Justine. Sometimes people with tragic lives like company in their misery. Why? What did she say to you?"

She looked sideways at the banana tree and palmetto landscaping. "Just that she wasn't trying to seduce you,

99

although, sandwiched between two young men half her age, I don't see why she would still be on the prowl."

He inhaled deeply. "Some people's hunger is never abated. But, no, she wasn't prowling, just enjoying taunting me."

She sighed. "Again, not that it's any of my business, but what would she have to taunt you about?"

He put his hand on her shoulder. "Nothing of profound consequence, and certainly nothing as dark or as tragic as her own secrets."

The door flapped again, and Zoe was standing at their side with a dour expression on her face. "Val says, your break is over."

David avoided eye contact with Val who glared at him as he resumed his seat at the piano. His eyes followed Julienne returning to the end of the bar and the discovery that Justine and the two young men were gone. Julienne did not sit down, but finished her drink while standing. She looked at him, blew him a kiss, and exited the front door. He mused that the evening, which had started for him on such a high note, had devolved into a mild depression. His mind searched for some positive straw to clutch at. He put his fingers on the keyboard and started to play *Put On A Happy Face*.

Later that evening, about an hour before closing, Richard Rose came in and sat at the rear end of the bar near Val's table and near the witch doll on the back bar which Dimitri had wired invisibly to remote controls. Dimitri also came in before closing, having finished his last show early, and had brought with him his show's headliner, a beautiful drag queen who went by the name of Princess Pocahontas. Princess Pocahontas was actually a full blooded American Indian, but of local Choctaw descent, not Algonquin as was the original Pocahontas. Princess, though petite, was beautiful in face and figure, and, though in feminine street clothes, was amazingly convincing in full drag. Princess and Dimitri sat at the very end of the bar between Richard Rose and Val's table, so Dimitri could converse with Val.

They had never seen Richard before and his English accent led them to assume he was a tourist. Richard, not knowing Princess was a drag queen, was obviously smitten and looked like he wanted to strike up an introduction. For these reasons, Dimitri decided to play his puppet game on him. Hiding in the corner where the doll's remote controls were, and speaking into a funnel attached to rubber tubing that terminated in a black parabolic reflector behind the witch doll, Dimitri whispered hoarsely into the funnel. "Hey, Limey!" Richard looked perplexed. "Yeah, you, the one about to fall off your stool ogling that pretty girl next to you. Look at me. I'm over here behind the bar." As Richard stared in confusion at the seemingly uninhabited backbar, Dimitri slowly made the witch doll wave her hand and lean slightly forward and to one side. Richard almost did fall off his stool as he perceived the dolls motions, his eyes bulging and his cheeks puffing up with an unspoken exclamation. Dimitri continued with the cackling witch's voice. "Don't waste your fish and chips on that one, Ducky, she's out of your league." Richard's jaw dropped and he began to smile in amazement at the doll, realizing he was being tricked, but unable to figure how. "You should hook up with me, Snookums, and I'll show you where to put your bangers and eggs. Besides, I'm closer to your age, a mere three hundred years old."

Richard put both hands on either side of his face and burst out laughing, looking from David at the piano to Princess, Val, and Dimitri, who had come out of the corner, all smiling at him. Richard looked at the doll, who still waved at him as Dimitri operated the string behind his back, then looked back at them. He spoke breathlessly. "My Gawd, how the bloody hell do you do that?" Dimitri moved the string from behind

101

his back to his front, moving it back and forth in synchronization with the witch's waving hand. Richard looked from Dimitri to the witch and back again. "How bloody ingenious can you be. You really had me going there for a minute." Then he downed the rest of his Scotch and water in one big swallow, banged the glass down loudly on the bar, and turned back to them with a huge smile.

With his smile reassuring them he was not offended, they all laughed. Dimitri parked the string on the pegboard in the corner and said, "Just one of the many features at The Voodo Room, a story to tell your friends in England about the freaky Americans you met on your visit."

Richard interrupted his adoring gaze at Princess to look at Dimitri and say, "Oh, I'm not a tourist. I just started working at The Inn Between a couple doors down." He turned to look at David walking toward them. "Actually, I came in to say hello to David who has befriended me and is helping me find my way, a stranger in a strange land."

Uncharacteristically, Val spoke up, a forced smile on her face. "And it got a little stranger tonight. Pete, give this gentleman another of whatever he's having for being such a good sport about Dimitri's little trick, and to welcome him to The Quarter."

Richard smiled at Val. "Why, thank ye kindly." Then he turned his gaze back to Princess. "It is indeed a strange, exotic, and beautiful place."

David gestured to each individual as he spoke. "Richard Rose, this is Ms. Valentina Siciliana, my esteemed boss; Ms. Zoe Sellier, her second in command; Dimitri Lebedev, according to him the world's greatest puppeteer appearing nightly at Aladdin's; Pete Cermak, a master presdigitarian and alchemist bartender; and this alluring creature you keep staring at is Princess Pocahontas, the headliner at Aladdin's."

As Pete set a drink in front of him, Richard pulled his eyes off of Princess and surveyed the group with a smile. "Greetings, one and all, and I look forward to a long and lucrative stay in your strange but beautiful land." His eyes turned to Princess again. "Would that I were John Smith, and you could save me from the savages."

Princess looked at him with a pained smile and spoke in a husky breathy voice. "Actually, I am one of the savages. I'm pure Choctaw Indian." She sighed. "And, in case it makes me even more strange and savage in your eyes, I'm a performer in a female impersonators club."

As Richard bit his lip and began to blush, Dimitri changed the subject abruptly. "David, I brought Princess over because she needs some new special material to update her act. I thought, inasmuch as her current main number is *I Enjoy Being A Girl* from *South Pacific*, maybe you could write her a parody of another number from that same musical score, or something completely different, but preferably within the theme of being American Indian or interracial or transsexual."

David smiled at Princess, whose pained smile grew warmer. "Sure! Why don't I come review your act, and I'll see you in a day or two after that with some ideas."

Dimitri clapped his hands and smiled at Princess. "Oh, goody, Princess! You've got the best in the business creating your new act." Then he narrowed his eyes at David. "And, David, when you bill her, keep in mind she gets the family discount."

David chuckled. "Don't worry, I'm very affordable, and extremely vulnerable to pretty girls."

Dimitri extended his hand towards Princess. "Come on upstairs, Princess, and I'll show you that costume I'm making for you."

Princess's smile had grown to a seductive one as she slid down from her barstool. "Of course, I know I'm in good hands with you, David. Thank you, thank you, sweetie." Then she stood on tiptoe in her spiked heels in order to kiss David on the cheek before exiting to the patio with Dimitri.

Val turned her attention to her newspaper as David sat on the stool beside Richard, who asked, "Buy you a drink?"

David shook his head negatively. "No thanks. What brings you here?"

Richard smiled. "I could say I just ducked in to dump my multitude of friends, but that wouldn't be true. No real reason, other than to check out your club's ambience and your piano style."

David snickered. "Well, I hope the club impresses you, but my style is a long way from your experience and keyboard abilities."

Richard took a sip and smacked his lips. "Actually, you're not bad. Rather reminiscent of early Broadway and turn of the century operettas, heavy on the Jerome Kern and George Gershwin, light on the contemporary Broadway scene. You are definitely a romantic, even your semi-classics are sweet and light as opposed to the ponderous thunder and lightening stuff."

David noted Val beginning to stare at him, indicating he had exceeded his normal break time again and motivating him to get off the barstool. "Right, probably because the thunder and lightening stuff is just too hard for me to play. Gotta go dish out some more syrupy romantic stuff now."

Richard touched his sleeve to detain him. "David, do you think Princess Pocahontas or you would mind if I tagged along when you review her act?"

David continued toward the piano. "Not if you're buying the drinks."

****

When David approached La Lune, the neon sign and marquee lights were off and the front doors shut. He looked around for Aurora and saw her peeking out of the front door of Bertoli's Bar which stayed open until sunrise. They approached each other with big smiles and gripped each others hands, hesitant to embrace in public. They turned towards his loft, still holding hands between them which swung as they walked. They couldn't resist turning towards each other with that same big childish smile every few steps. Half teasing, half asking, she said, "I nod sure you coming. I thod mebbe you come to you senses and say you self, 'Uh oh, beeeeg mistake.'"

He chuckled. "No such luck. Maybe I'm your beeeeg mistake, but I'm not letting you get away that easily," and he lifted her hand to kiss it and link her arm through his as she looked around to see if anyone was watching before placing her other hand on their linked arms and leaning her head on his shoulder.

She rolled her eyes up to him and asked, "So, wod hoppon tonide I had one guy try and ged up on stage wi' me and my fad boss grab he ear and drag heem oudda da place."

He laughed. "Well, my tormentors weren't so physical, One made me sing *Just A Gigolo*, hinting that I was a gigolo. Reminded me of someone who recently said my nose was getting brown from kissing too many tourist's asses."

She punched his bicep playfully. "So, are you a, how you say, gigolo? A male puta, ride?"

He shook his head once. "Sort of. If I am, I'm the poorest and dumbest one around because I never asked for anything. Then Richard Rose, another pianist, came to visit and, oh yes, one of the female impersonator acts from that club across from yours, she asked me to write some new material for her."

She raised her eyes. "Dey pay you?"

105

He shook his head positively. "Yeah, I don't charge them much, a few hundred dollars at most. My problem is that I have to ask Val if I can come in early to use the piano."

Aurora's smile brightened and she spoke eagerly. "Eef you lake, I bring mi guitarra et help you add you place. I be you piano and you teach me por escriba la musica."

David's eyes widened and his smile broadened. "Ohhhh, I like that. You be my piano and I'll run my fingers up and down you and, together, we'll make sweet music!"

She stepped in front of him, put her arms under his seersucker sport coat, and embraced him tightly as she tilted her face up to receive his kiss.

Chapter Eight
INTERNATIONAL AFFAIRS

David Wales and Richard Rose were conspicuously conservatively dressed as they squeezed into the pink and purple nougahyde upholstered booth closest to the stage at Aladdin's. The sea of young men that stared at them were mostly dressed in tight fitting pants and mesh or gossamer tops. There was the occasional long haired or bearded slightly older patron in faded or torn jeans whose only hint of the bizarre was a collection of tattoos or a gold pierced earring. The low level lighting was mostly pink and purple, the odors a mixture of alcohol and sweat, and the intermission music a recording of Edith Piaf whose French lyrics few could translate, but whose soulful sound all felt they understood.

Richard looked at David with a questioning frown. "Why aren't they dark on Monday nights like most clubs?"

David ignored the young men seated closest to them who were trying to make eye contact with him. "The largest clubs run seven nights a week, some even twenty four hours a day, because of the endless supply of tourists. They just rotate the entertainers so the headliners can have a few nights off each week. Fortunately, Princess is off tomorrow night and we're off tonight, otherwise we'd have no opportunity to catch her act."

Richard looked around the room cautiously, noticing with slight irritation that everyone was looking at David and not at him. "Will Princess be having a drink with us after her performance?"

David's response was interrupted by the appearance of the waiter dressed in nothing but a gold thong, pink see through harem pants, and gold sequined slippers with curled up toes.

Despite his tall handsome appearance, he wore women's makeup and spoke in a falsetto voice. "Hello, my name is Alexis and I'll be your waitress tonight."

Richard frowned as David asked, "Cuttysark and water, right, Richard?" Richard nodded agreement. "And Cuttysark and milk."

The waiter's eyes widened and his lips pursed. "Ohhhhhh! You must be David. Dimitri said you'd be at the first show." The waiter held the order pad close to his face and pointed to Richard with his pencil. "And you brought your father. How sweet!"

Richard frowned at the waiter. "You're a cheeky bugger, aren't you?"

The waiter made goo-goo eyes at him . "And wouldn't you just love to bugger my cheeks, you old fart. Now then, would you like any sandwiches or a cheese basket with those Scotches?"

David leaned forward to block Richard's angry stare at the waiter. "No, just the Scotches. And could you ask Princess and Dimitri..."

The waiter finished his request. "To join you after their performance. Of course, Sweetie. They'd be delighted. I'd be delighted! We'd all be delighted!"

David raised both eyebrows while trying to keep a smile. "I think the four of us is all this booth will accommodate."

The waiter pursed his lips and made a smacking kissing sound. "Maybe next time, Sweetie," and he left.

Richard's anger simmered. "Cheeky faggot. I've a good mind...."

David sighed heavily and interrupted him. "Not the time and place, and certainly not in Princess's domain."

Richard's anger fizzeled into a glum expression. "Right you are, laddie. Why can't they all be like Princess? A real lady, she is. A beautiful lady."

They watched as Dimitri's marionette stage was rolled onto the tiny dance floor preparatory to the show. The waiter arrived with their drinks, blinking in a flirty fashion as he served David's, rolling his eyes in exasperation as he served Richards, then minced away quickly without saying a word.

David looked at Richard as he glared at the retreating waiter. "I don't know how familiar you are with the gay community, Richard, but it's been my experience that it is as varied as the heterosexual community and you shouldn't take anything for granted. That said, gays and straights both have a tendency to be disinterested in anyone twice their age, unless the older one is rich and/or famous."

Richard lifted his glass and stared at it as he gently moved it to make the ice rotate in lazy circles. "Roger that, laddie. I came close to being both rich and famous, and never had a problem with booze that would have prevented it ...," he set the glass down and still stared at it with a slight frown, "...until the war." He stared into space and bit his lower lip. "Then Beth got blown into itty bitty pieces by the bloody huns, and my world got blown into itty bitty pieces along with her." He looked at David with a pained smile. "And that's when I fell off the wagon the first time, and straight down to the bottom of the bottle."

David looked from Richard's eyes to his glass and back to his eyes. "If you're a recovering alcoholic, why are you drinking, and why are you working in a whole district dedicated to drinking?"

Richard picked up his glass and stared at it again. "I drink because I'm one of those bloody fools who thinks he can do so moderately, and I work in this cesspool because I was sacked from my highly successful radio show in London for continuing to rant against the Germans after the war."

David sipped his drink. "So Paris, Morocco, all those places....?"

Richard blinked. "Steps down the ladder, one by one."

David frowned slightly. "And you consider the French Quarter the bottom of the ladder?"

Richard waved his glass in a circle as he surveyed the room. "Look around ye laddie. It ain't exactly the Waldorf Astoria."

The strident sounds of trumpeted fanfare blared forth from a scratchy record that had been played a few hundred times too often. Dimitri's voice followed as he imitated a circus ringmaster with a French accent, slightly tinged with a Russian accent. "Mesdames et monsieurs, and all you queers out there who can't figure out what you are!" A round of laughter, applause, whistles, and catcalls resounded in response. "Presenting the world famous, internationally renowned, world's greatest marionette artist... God I can't get enough of this guy... Dimitri Lebedev!" More applause and whistles, followed by a somber recording of the first few bars of *The Volga Boatman* as the curtains of the chest high marionette stage opened and a spotlight made a bright circle on the left side of the marionette stage. A twenty inch high doll, dressed as a jester and with an old sad looking face that resembled Dimitri, walked laboriously on stage, each step followed by another four bar repetition of the opening strains of *The Volga Boatman*. The Jester stopped at the middle of the stage, looked up, and his eyes bulged open and his jaw dropped in a startled expression. Then he spoke in a whining sad sack voice. "Oieeee! You came."

During the next round of laughter and applause, one eager fan yelled out, "We love you, Dimitri."

The Jester's shuffling movements and speech pattern began to resemble an old Jewish man. "Yeh, yeh, I love you too. I love all you faggots." A self conscious smattering of laughter. "You know what a faggot is, don't you? It's this thing that's impaled on the end of a stick...." Raucous laughter

110

interrupted the Jester's line, his head and eye movements registering somewhere between fear and confusion. "...and you light it and it glows with a brilliant warm flame..." More applause and cheers. "...lighting up the darkness....right into the deepest corners of the closet." The Jester took a surprised step backward at the resulting increase of volume in applause and cheers.

As the audience quieted, the Jester stepped forward and said, "Folks, tonight we have the rare honor of being visited by another, other than myself, internationally famous, world renowned, world's most famous Englishman...."

David and Richard turned to hear a nearby patron say to his companions, "Oh goody! This is new. I never heard this routine before." David and Richard turned to look at each other, then back to the stage.

"...that nemesis of the Nazi hordes, that bulldog of Britain..." David's brow knit and Richard's jaw dropped. "...the one, the only..." The Jester then gestured to the right of the marionette stage. "...lets hear a big round of applause folks for...Sir Winston Churchill!"

As a twenty inch high marionette caricature of Churchill appeared on stage right, replete with a smoking cigar in one hand, the crowd roared, and David and Richard both heaved a sigh of relief. Churchill turned to the audience and raised his other hand with index and middle finger forming his famous 'V' for victory sign, resulting in another wave of applause. Churchill looked at his hand forming the 'V', then back at the audience and said, in an imitation of the famous man's gravelly voice, "That stands for 'vagina'. I don't play on your team." The resulting laughter was mixed with a few good natured boos and hisses. Then Churchill did a double take of the Jester. He waved his cigar at him. "Hey, you!"

The Jester touched both hands to his chest and looked from Churchill to the audience and back at Churchill. "Who, me?"

Churchill's eyebrows moved into a frown. "Yeah, you in the Communist uniform. Weren't you standing behind Stalin at the Malta Conference?"

Waiting for the laugh response, the Jester said indignantly, "This isn't a Communist uniform! I'm a jester!"

Churchill tapped his cigar and wiggled his eyebrows like Groucho Marx. "That's an oxymoron. All Communists are jesters."

The Jester's eyebrows shot up and his eyes bulged. "Aha! But all jesters are not Communists."

Churchill did another double take of the Jester. "You're right. That outfit makes you look more like a bloody pimp." As the Jester frowned and the audience laughed, Churchill walked over to the Jester and spoke in a confidential tone. "So, laddie, if I were in the market for a little slap and tickle, think you could find me a pretty lady, hopefully one prettier than Eleanor Roosevelt. You know, one that could help me shiver me timber, so to speak, bounce me bollocks, if you know what I mean."

The Jester looked down and shook his head side to side sadly. "Oh, God, I really wish I didn't know what you meant."

Churchill held his hand up to shield his mouth and spoke in a loud stage whisper. "Inasmuch as I'm here in the colonies, don't you Yanks have some exotic options, you know, perhaps one of those wild and wooly redskin savages?" Then Churchill closed his eyes, clenched his fists in front of himself, shook his body and grunted with excitement.

The Jester raised his hands in protest. "Wait, wait, hold on there, cool down, Winnie, old boy." The Jester sighed deeply and shook his head negatively as Churchill stared at him. "How in the hell did you ever become Prime Minister, you horny old Brit?" Churchill opened his mouth to speak and the Jester raised his hand to stop him. "Don't, no, no, that was a rhetorical question. Mr. Prime Minister, it just so happens that here, on this very stage, we have one of the most beautiful representatives of the ancient and proud Chocktaw nation." The Jester put his hand to his mouth as he called out. "Oh Princess! Princess Pocahontas!"

Loud applause and whistles greeted Princess as she walked around the proscenium in a skin tight mini-skirted sheath made of shiny pink Indian beads with matching beaded spiked heels. Her lightly oiled tawny skin glowed, her large almond eyes were accented by stage makeup, and her full exquisitely shaped lips relaxed into a sensual pucker when she wasn't speaking. She stood at the right side of the stage where her hormone induced natural bullet breasts were level with and immediately adjacent to the marionette stage floor, her low neck line and cleavage revealing a heaving sea of flesh. Blinking her eyes as she surveyed the audience, her wandering gaze turned to the Jester as she spoke in a breathy young girl's voice. "Yes, Dimitri, did you call me?"

Churchill waddled over to her, almost stepping onto her breast, his eyes bulging as he stared at her cleavage while muttering almost incoherently a litany of lust that sounded something like, "Oh my...oh Gawd...Whudd'a you, whudd'a you...Jeeeeez....I gotta...Oh Jeeez..lemme see...oh Gawd...lemme touch...Oh my Gaaaaaaawd?"

The Jester rushed to his side and pulled Churchill back, saying, "Princess Pocahontas, representative of the Chocktaw nation, meet Sir Winston Churchill, one time Prime Minister and representative of the British nation."

Princess closed her eyes and nodded her head demurely. "Pleased to meet you, Sir Winston Churchill."

Churchill stood flabbergasted, still muttering, "Hubbadah, hubbadah, gimme, gimme, I gotta, I gotta...!"

The Jester rolled hi eyes. "The Prime Minister says he's pleased to meet you, too, Princess. Perhaps you'd like to discuss some trade deals between your nations. "

113

Princess's eyebrows rose as she said, "Yes, Mr. Prime Minister, I have a beautiful Indian headdress with genuine eagle feathers that trail all the way down...," and she turned to show her shiny beaded beautifully sculpted buttocks, "...my back to the floor. Tell your Queen that I have a trade deal, I'll trade my headdress for that sparkly thing she wears on her head."

The Jester winced. "You mean her crown?"

Princess smiled. "Yes, that's it. Her sparkly crown."

The Jester jutted his head forward slightly as he winced. "You mean the one with the 28 carat Khoorinoor diamond in the front?"

Princess smiled and nodded her head affirmatively. "Yes, that's it. The one with the big sparkly thing in front."

Churchill was now hypnotized by her buttocks, still mumbling, "My Gawwwd...whatever...big sparkly...beautiful bottom...gimme...gimme...gotta have!"

The Jester shook Churchill by the sleeve and spoke in a stage whisper. "Winnie, snap out of it. Behave yourself!"

Churchill stood erect, shook himself, and blinked. "Yes, er, trade, er, let's go somewhere and have breakfast while we discuss this." Churchill paused, then leered at her and leaned forward as he spoke suggestively. "How do you feel about 'bangers?' I mean, I have this sausage and eggs I'd like to give you."

Princess leaned slightly forward and, still smiling, spoke sternly. "Actually, Mr. Prime Minister, I have my own sausage and eggs, thanks just the same."

Churchill's jaw dropped as his shoulders and torso shrunk down into a dejected heap. The Jester stepped forward, spread his hands out, shrugged, and said, "Well, folks, so much for foreign affairs." As a background recording for the song, *I Enjoy Being A Girl*, began, the Jester continued. "To entertain our visiting dignitary, and all you gender confused homos out there, here's a girl who has no doubts about her gender, regardless of her plumbing, our one and only, the fabulous Princess Pocahontas!"

Applause greeted Princess as the marionette stage rolled back and she stepped center stage to be joined by three dancing waiters on both sides. Despite the tiny stage, which led some of the dancing waiters to have to sit on the laps of ringside patrons momentarily before their next dance cue, the troupe, led by Princess, executed a polished vocal and choreographic performance that would have made Broadway proud. David and Richard overheard nearby patrons surprised reactions, one saying, "Okay, now this is the regular show," and another, "Yeah, the Churchill bit was cute, but what was that all about?"

David looked at Richard pensively. A glum Richard said, "Never mind. I know what it was all about. I wonder if that bloody Ruskie put her up to that. I'll bet he is a bloody Communist!" Richard finished his drink in one gulp and smacked his lips as he set the empty glass down with a bang.

David looked anxious. "Richard, I was just kidding about you buying the drinks. If you want to go now, I'll make your excuses and cover the tab."

Richard stared at the enticing figure of Princess sitting on the knee of and being tossed around like a baton by the half dozen chorus boys. "No. If she wants me to piss off, she'll have to tell me her bloody self. Plus, I want to hear that sniveling Ruskie faggot explain trashing the man who held the free world together while Stalin waffled and Hitler plotted world domination." He turned his empty glass upside down and tapped three times impatiently. "Where the bloody hell is that bloody faggot waiter?"

David nodded toward the stage. "I think he's dancing with the object of your affection. Would you like us to move to the bar so you could get a drink?"

Richard rubbed his nose vigorously with one hand as his anger subsided. "No. I'm okay, David. Don't worry. I wont make a scene."

As the routine ended with the chorus boys holding Princess aloft so high that she had to put one hand over her head to avoid hitting the low ceiling, the recording began to make a scratchy looping hiss before the sound system was turned off. Dimitri appeared in a tight fitting suit, silk shirt, and string tie just in time to grab Princess's hand as the chorus boys set her down to thunderous applause and she made her bows holding his hand. When the applause finally died down, the two of them headed for the booth as all eyes followed them. Dimitri was about to slide into the booth next to Richard, but Richard vacated the booth and gestured for Princess to be seated between him and David, Dimitri being left to sit on the outer part of the booth next to Richard.

Dimitri spoke very diplomatically, looking at Richard. "I hope you don't mind our borrowing from our little surprise meeting the other night. I like to spice up the act with little experiments like that from time to time."

It was obvious Richard was making an effort to control his anger. "Well, when I covered the ceremony of Sir Winston Churchill being knighted by the Queen, I didn't recall his acting like an idiotic sex pervert."

Princess reached across to touch Dimitri's hand, her arm touching Richard's chest and her face and tone expressing concern. "See, I told you he might be offended."

Richard closed his eyes, feeling titillated by the pressure of her arm against his chest. "No, no. That's alright, Princess. After all, this is a nightclub and it was all in good fun." He opened his eyes and smiled at her. She smiled, blinked, removed her hand from Dimitri's and patted Richard's hand twice before folding her hands in her lap.

Dimitri spread his hands. "Well, the least I can do to make amends is to order us all drinks and pick up the tab for this table tonight. You guys having more of the same? Perhaps some food, anyone?" David and Richard raised their glasses and shook them to indicate another round. Dimitri signaled for their waiter.

David was eager to change the subject. "Princess, you have a fabulous routine there. Even if I could come up with new material, I couldn't choreograph anything as professional as that."

Dimitri smiled eagerly. "We already have a choreographer, Alex. He's your waiter." Richard frowned before Dimitri continued. "He was a gypsy on Broadway about to get his first show as a choreographer when his mother in New Orleans got ill and he came home to take care of her. Broadway's loss, our gain. He's great, isn't he?"

Richard looked into his empty glass. "Better hoofer than he is a waiter, I'd say."

David was eager to cut Richard short. "Yes! That takes care of the choreography. I can just block any storyline I come up with so he can fill in the dance blocks. Dimitri, those instrumental background recordings you use, do you have the whole score to *South Pacific*?"

Dimitri's eyes popped a little every time he discussed something that interested him. "Yes! Isn't it delicious? That and a dozen other Broadway musicals I've borrowed from. It's a little record company in New York called 'Valentino.' They do background and sound effect records for the entertainment industry."

David feigned interest. "Do you have the records here at the club?"

Dimitri's eyes grew larger. "Just the *South Pacific* one." He started to move to the outer edge of the seat. "Would you like to see it? The jacket it came in is bound with the entire musical score. I could bring it to you."

David started to rise at the same time as Dimitri. "That's okay. I'll go backstage with you to look at it." David touched Dimitri's elbow as he headed back stage.

Dimitri suddenly realized what was happening. "Oh, I see what you're doing, David. You're..." David started pulling Dimitri along with him, Dimitri obviously torn between leaving Princess alone with Richard, yet enjoying the opportunity to be alone with David.

When they were gone, Princess wiggled to one side to make space between her and Richard. He looked at her sadly. "That's okay, Princess. You don't have to stay here, or I can go, if you wish."

She looked at him quizzically. "No, stay. I just moved over so I could look you in the eye when I talk to you. I don't trust people who don't want to look me in the eye when they talk to me. It's like they're in denial that I really exist."

He slowly smiled. "Roger that, little lady. I know, in the past, when I used to blather on about the Nazis or the Ruskies after it had become politically incorrect to do so, people used to talk over my head as if I wasn't there and I hadn't said what I had said. Obviously I was a thorn in the side of their altered reality, and they jolly well wished I didn't exist, or at the very least do them a favor and go away. Which I did."

She tilted her head as she looked at him. "Did they look at you that way when you were young because you were gay?"

He looked surprised. "No. I was never gay. Good Lord, I was married almost twenty years. Why would you think I'm gay?"

Her eyes bulged and she leaned back a little. "Richard! It is Richard, isn't it? My God, you look at me like a starving tiger looks at a gazelle."

His eyebrows rose. "Of course I do. You're one of the most beautiful creatures I have ever seen."

She straightened up and sighed heavily. "Man, you do realize that under this beaded dress I really do have my own sausage and eggs, don't you?"

His head bobbed up and down a couple times as he bit his lips and said, "Yes, I understand your confusion. Please, let me explain." He sighed. "I loved my wife dearly. After she died in the war, I could never seem to relate to another woman. I wanted to blame the Germans, or someone, and in doing so my career went to pot. I could only get work abroad where people hadn't heard that I had gone crazy. I finally ended up in Morocco, a place where morality was unheard of."

She suddenly showed a spark of interest. "Ohhhh! I loved *Casablanca*. Did you play piano in a place like Rick's Café?"

He smiled. "As a matter of fact, I did. I also discovered another bar, one only frequented by males."

She asked, "A gay bar?"

His brow furrowed. "Not exactly. The customers were adult males, and the entertainer's were all males of a very young age."

Now her brow furrowed. "How young?"

He winced. "Too young, certainly by English or American standards, but not by Moroccan." He sighed again. "In the center of this bar there was a large curved polished log with polished pegs protruding from the top of it. As the flutes began playing Arabian music, these beautiful naked young boys would come out and do a little dance before they sat on one of the pegs, kinda dancing up to it and easing themselves onto it. Each boy held a tin cup and men would go up and place money in the cup. If it was not enough money to please the boy, he would empty the cup back into the man's hand, an embarrassment to the man, which would induce the man to keep adding money to the cup to avoid embarrassment. If it

119

was enough money, the boy would offer him his other hand and accompany him to one of the upstairs rooms."

A frown had grown on Princess's face. "This is your explanation? That you learned pederasty in Morocco is the reason you're attracted to me?"

He looked at her imploringly. "You inferred that you weren't judgmental. Please let me finish." When she didn't reply, he continued. "I had never had an experience like that before, neither homosexual nor like that, with a young boy. I was drinking heavily in those days. And, yes, I was turned on by the sexual spectacle and oddity of it all. I went upstairs with a boy, quite a beautiful boy, and, for the first time in almost a decade, I was not only turned on, but I found myself in a relationship, a physical, sexual, and loving relationship."

She looked at him disapprovingly. "You paid a boy for sex and you thought he loved you?"

His face was stern. "I paid a boy for sex because that was how he survived, because that was the only way I had access to him. And, yes, he loved me because I was a kind, gentle, and generous lover, and a provider, and a protector to him. And yes, although I could never look at another woman in bed without being consumed with the feeling of loss over my wife's death, somehow, with that boy, I was able to love again. And yes, I know what a farce a psycho analyst would make of my sad tale, but that's the way my life evolved. That boy was the last person I could love, that I could ever think of loving, until I saw you in The Voodoo Room the other night."

The waiter arrived with drinks Dimitri had ordered on his way to the back stage. The waiter sensed a moment between Richard and Princess and left silently. Princess wrapped her small pink fingernailed hand around the stem of the large Shirley Temple pseudo cocktail and stared at it. "I'm too young to know much about the war. I don't think about people

120

as Nazis or Ruskies, as civilized or savage." She looked him in the eye. "That hurt me when you called me a savage."

Richard looked remorseful. "I am so very very sorry, Princess. I apologize profoundly. I never meant to refer to you as a savage. I was simply quoting a line from the only book I ever read about Pocahontas. You are the farthest thing from savage in my mind. You are the epitome of culture and beauty and all that any man could desire. Please please forgive my that one brief indiscretion."

Princess lifted her glass to him with a questioning expression. "I'll forgive you, if you'll forgive me...and Dimitri...for the Churchill skit."

Richard smiled with relief. "Done." And they clinked their glasses together.

Chapter Nine
THREE'S COMPANY

David exited the stall shower drying his hair with a towel. He looked toward Aurora who sat cross legged and totally naked in the middle of the bed stringing her guitar. She squinted as she guided the little brass eyelet over the tailpiece, then threaded the string across the bridge and nut, and into the hole of the key axel, turning the key to take up the slack. Her brow furrowed and her lips puckered in concentration as she tightened and plucked the string repeatedly to tune it. David smiled. "You are the total image of a musician's wet dream."

She giggled. "I tho'd dad would be a girl holding a clarinet while giving head."

His eyebrows raised. "That works, too." He walked to the table, draped the towel over the chair, and sat down before the typewriter surrounded by typed pages and music scores. "You guys have given me an impossible challenge to create Princess's new routine."

She put her feet on the floor, positioned her guitar, and played a series of chords to insure the new string was properly tuned. "How so?"

He wrinkled his nose. "Dimitri only wants the theme song to come from *South Pacific.* but the choreographer wants it to be *There Is Nothing Like A Dame* because that's an all male dance number. You want it to be *You've Got To Be Carefully Taught* because you're fixated on prejudice. Princess wants it to be *Younger Than Springtime* because she's considering a May/December romance with Richard. And I want it to be *Some Enchanted Evening* because it's the biggest hit in the show, the word 'enchanted' relates to gayness, and it'll allow

Princess to make the audience love her better than any of these other songs."

Now Aurora wrinkled her nose. "Yeah, bud, *You Gotta Be Carefully Taught* is aboud de whirl being prejudiced against gays. And dad's a gay club, ride?"

He stared at the papers before him. "It's more about racism than being homophobic, but it's a downer, either way. I really think I should go with *Some Enchanted Evening*."

She played a riff on the guitar, lingering on the newly installed string and making it slide slightly above and below its true note by riding it sideways across the fret. "David, you smo't an you fair. You do wad you tink bess fo Princess, and I know everyone will lake it."

He smiled at her in surprise. "Why, thank you, sweetheart. You just made it a lot easier to get started." He searched through the papers. "Now, where is that first draft of the parody to *Some Enchanted Evening* I wrote earlier?"

She picked up a typewritten page beside her. "Here id is, I was looking add id. Id's good, bud id's only fo men. Done dey have gay girls en dis place?"

He took the paper from her. "Other than tourists, they're practically no women. Just drag queens and a few bull dykes who are so butch they look like rough trade males. You'd think that mid twentieth century American society would be as willing to accept lesbians having their own bars as much as Paris and Berlin do, but it doesn't."

She began to strum the melody to *Some Enchanted Evening*. "Wid juss goes to prove dad Los Estados Unidos ees nod only prejudice against race, bud also against gender. Id's a racist patriarchal society."

He watched her fingers strumming the strings and concentrated on the melody. "America is not unique for racism or having a male dominated society. I've traveled a little bit of the world and found both those flaws in every

124

society I've seen. Even societies that have a ninety-nine percent black population have a color caste system that is racist, and countries with fundamentalist theocracies are worst for subjugating women."

She stopped playing and frowned at him. "Okay, meester smo't man, wad ees 'funny mental theo crazies' mean?"

He frowned. "Don't stop. I was timing the parody lyrics to the melody."

She shook her head from side to side. "No! We godda deal. I you piano, you teach me tings. Wad ees 'funny mental theo crazies' mean?"

He chuckled. "Your pronunciation is wrong, but your metaphoric image is right on."

Her nose wrinkled as her frown increased. "Meta who?"

He closed his eyes and sighed. "Okay. One thing at a time. Fundamentalist means people who believe so strongly in basics that they can't consider any other point of view. And theocracies are governments that are based on religious beliefs and religious laws, such as most Moslem countries."

She shook her head up and down. "Los pais del Catolica tambien. La Popa, los Cardenal, los Obispo, los Sacerdote, todos los hombres, ninguna mujers. Solamente monja, el mas bajo en la Iglesia. Monjas probres. Dose poor nuns."

He waggled his jaw from side to side. "Okay, it is true that it's a 'man's world.' But all men are not misogynists."

She laid her guitar down and waved her hands. "Wade, back up. Primero, wad ees una 'meta whore'?"

He refrained from laughing. "It's 'meta-phor.' It means words or images that represent and try to explain something else. For instance, when I say I see something in 'my mind's eye,' we know my brain doesn't have eyes inside it. The phrase 'mind's eye' is a metaphor for how my brain works when I imagine something that doesn't exist yet in reality."

Her brow furrowed. "So, when I tink of una melody por a new song I wan' to ride, de metaphor ees 'in my mind's ear'?"

He smiled with surprise. "That's very good, and absolutely right!"

She smiled proudly. "Okay. So whad ees a 'miso genius'?"

He bit his lower lip. "The pronunciation is mi-sodge-jen-nist. It means a person, usually a man, who hates women. And remember what I said, not all men are misogynists. In fact, most men are not."

She looked questioning. "So, wad you call a man who no hade women?"

He wiggled his eyebrows. "Most of them all called David."

She threw her guitar pick at him and it bounced on the table. "No, really."

He shrugged. "Because they are the majority, there's no specific term for them. Men who are fairest to women we refer to as being 'sensitive men.'"

She moved toward him swiftly and sat on his lap facing him, her legs straddling his hips, her arms loosely around his neck. "Tu es mi persona sensible, David. Sentir para tu. Te sientes por mi. Es verdad, si?"

David hesitated as he felt himself getting excited. He swallowed hard and looked up into her eyes and whispered, "Si."

She undulated her hips slightly, then smiled and said. "Ooooh! I tink I feel you sensitivity muy bueno," and she reached down and inserted him into her.

****

Justine frowned at Louie. "Of all the beautiful songs in *South Pacific*, why is your favorite song *Bloody Mary*?"

When Louie hesitated, Lenny interjected with a suggestive smile on his face. "Cause he's getting it on with the nigger cleaning lady at his lab, and she has a gold tooth in front that reminds him of Bloody Mary's beetle juice stain."

Now Justine frowned at Lenny more fiercely. "Pray tell, who taught you to use that word in reference to a Negro?"

Louie asserted himself. "Yeah, Lenny, they prefer to be called 'colored.'"

Justine shook her head sideways. "No, Louie, the term is Negro, the Spanish word for black. That word Lenny used is just a bastardization of the Spanish word and, Lenny, it's considered derogatory. If your mother didn't wash your mouth out with Octagon soap for using that word, I will if you ever use it in my presence again."

Lenny smiled sheepishly. "Actually, my mother used to say ni...."

Justine glared as she interrupted him. "Lenny! You like the taste of Octagon soap?"

Louie blinked and avoided eye contact with Justine. "Actually, Justine, they really prefer the term colored, as in the National Association for the Advancement of Colored People, or NAACP as they're better known."

Justine frowned. "That just doesn't make sense. Asian's are colored yellow. Indians are colored red. South Americans are colored tan. Negro, which means black, is their true color, and that's how they're known in Europe. In France we say 'le jazz noir,' which means black jazz."

Jules sipped his drink and looked at her sheepishly. "Everyone sees themselves in a particular niche, Justine. Just like you don't want to be called French, but rather Parisian."

Justine looked confused. "Yes, but 'colored' is just so ambiguous."

Louie shook his empty beer bottle and signaled Pete for another. "Maybe the NAACP is an all encompassing agency acting as advocates for all non-whites."

Lenny snorted. "Yeah, maybe they advocate for the Tonkinese in the South Pacific, too."

Louie glared at Lenny. "At least my lady friend earns her living legally and is paid in cash, not heroin."

Lenny frowned ferociously at Louie. "You don't have to spread my business out on the street, Louie!"

Louie responded angrily. "Yeah, well you spread mine out there. Besides, after that fiasco at Betty's Bar the other night, everyone already knows your business!"

Pete banged a beer down in front of Louie and spoke sternly. "Behave, you two. If Val hears you mixing it up in here, she'll ban you for a month."

Julienne came through the front door and Jules and Armand moved down one barstool to make room for her to sit next to Justine. "What's all the fuss about?"

Justine looked sullenly at Lenny, then looked toward David at the piano. "We were just remarking about how David's been playing the score to *South Pacific* so often recently."

Jules waved his drink at Justine. "I told you, he said he's writing some special material for an act at Aladdin's and he only has a guitar at home to work with, so he's going over the score on the piano here where he works. Besides, I like *South Pacific*!"

Julienne nodded her head positively toward Pete who was holding up a grasshopper cocktail glass. "We all like *South Pacific*. So what's the fuss about?"

Justine glared at Lenny again, then turned to Julienne. "Just a fussy misunderstanding, a potato pototto thing, much ado about nothing. What's new in your world?"

128

Julienne looked toward David at the piano. "I've just been out shopping to get David some little thank you gift for the adventure we had down on Decatur Street the other night."

Justine looked at Julienne's face trying to read her feelings. "What'd you get?"

Julienne looked at the grasshopper cocktail Pete set in front of her and frowned slightly. "Nothing. He's so hard to shop for. I couldn't give him a cigarette case or lighter because I've been trying to get him to stop smoking. It's pointless to give him booze or decanters or a cellarette because he never drinks except when he's out or here."

Justine raised one eyebrow. "You do know those are B-drinks Zoe takes up to him, practically no booze in them, and he never drinks them anyhow?"

Julienne wrinkled her nose. "Of course, I know that. I just send that occasional Scotch and milk up to him so he'll have something to line his stomach with to protect him from whatever alcohol he actually does consume."

Justine smiled. "And to remind him that you're here."

Julienne looked down embarrassed. "Yes, and to remind him that I'm here." She looked up and at Justine. "Although he seems to notice that without too much prodding."

Justine shrugged. "Give him a toiletry kit or a manicure kit or some cologne."

Julienne chuckled. "He gets tons of that stuff from other female customers." She nodded toward Lenny and Louie. "Sometimes he brings bags of that excess stuff like care packages to these two."

Justine smiled slyly. "You seem to know a lot about him. You begin to sound like an old married couple. Is there something about your relationship I don't know?"

Julienne sipped her drink without looking at Justine. "I told you I don't kiss and tell." She set her drink down and stared at it. "Not that there's that much to tell at this point."

129

Justine raised one eyebrow again. "But, perhaps?"

Julienne looked toward David at the piano again. "But, perhaps, we should see if we can get him to play something from another Broadway musical other than *South Pacific*." She looked at the row of regulars beside her. "What would you guys like to hear?"

Justine chuckled. "I don't think I should make any requests after he got upset with the one I made the other night."

Lenny looked at Louie and smiled facetiously. "How about *Dark Town Strutter's Ball*?"

Jules eyes began to bulge. "Ohhhh, ohhh, I know. How about switching from *South Pacific* to *Carousel*!"

Julienne's eyes widened with delight. "Oh, yes, *If I Loved You*!"

Jules blinked. "And *You'll Never Walk Alone*!"

Julienne smiled and began to dig in her purse. "Perfect! Good idea, Jules." She pulled out a five dollar bill and proffered it to Jules. "Here, put this in his kitty."

Justine pushed Julienne's hand with the five back. "Put your money away, mon cherie. Jules and Armand have an allowance of discretionary money of their own for things like this now."

Jules looked at Julienne, pursed his lips and rolled his eyes in jest, then fished in his pocket for some tip money as he strolled up to the piano.

Julienne blinked at Justine. "Oh, you mean Armand's father....."

Justine closed her eyes as she nodded her head affirmatively. "Exactly."

Julienne sipped her drink. "You better make sure he attends classes and keeps up with his homework."

Justine shifted her hips on the barstool. "Don't worry. I give him the proper incentives."

130

****

Mrs. Saucier narrowed her eyes at Julienne, then at the two men standing beside the delivery van, then back at Julienne. "Yes, I know you're his friend. I've seen you come and go from his apartment, sometimes at hours I wouldn't want my daughter to keep. And aren't you the one that helped him paint that mural? You know, I'll have to charge him for repainting that wall if he ever moves out. It'll come out of his security deposit, assuming there's enough left to cover the painting."

The two men looked impatiently at Julienne who smiled painfully at the landlady. "Please, Mrs. Saucier, I just want to deliver a gift."

Mrs. Saucier frowned. "But he's not there now, and I can't let you into his apartment without his permission."

Julienne pleaded. "But it's supposed to be a surprise for him. How can I surprise him if he knows you let me in?" Julienne reached into her purse and pulled out her driver's license and business card. "Here, take my information, and if there's any problem, you'll know how to contact me, and I'll satisfy any complaints."

Mrs. Saucier squinted at the cards. "Your last name is the same as that banks."

Julienne retrieved her driver's license. "Yes, well, that's because it's my father's bank."

Mrs. Saucier's eyes narrowed again. "That bank turned me down for a building improvement loan."

Julienne's eyes widened innocently and her mouth betrayed the hint of a smile. "Oh, well, perhaps I could talk to my father about that."

Ten minutes later Julienne pulled the door to David's apartment wide open as the two men struggled to maneuver the baby grand piano up the narrow stairs and into the area

Julienne indicated by the window with a view of St. Louis Cathedral in the background.

Mrs. Saucier watched enviously as Julienne tipped the two men generously. Mrs. Saucier moved toward the door and waited there expectantly for Julienne to exit with her. Julienne stood resolutely by the piano, smiled sweetly at the landlady, and said, "I'll lock up when I leave, and I'll have my father's bank manager call you about your new loan application." Mrs. Saucier hesitated, looked toward the staircase thoughtfully, then nodded and pulled the door to as she descended the staircase.

Julienne set her wicker basket down on the small kitchen counter, retrieved David's silver tray, and removed the bottle of Mumm's Champagne and two crystal champagne glasses from the basket. She surveyed the room thoughtfully, trying to decide if she should move the table and chairs closer to the piano before putting the wine tray on it. She snorted with the thought of how many times she had wanted to bring better furnishings to his apartment, but didn't to avoid appearing to be a 'nest building' female and a threat to his independence. Of course, the piano might be considered a furnishing, but she now had the rationalization that he needed it for his work, so it shouldn't be considered invasive. Setting the tray on the table, she noticed the plastic guitar pick and inspected it questioningly before replacing it in its exact location.

She wore a fitted black lace cocktail dress with a short hem than revealed a lot of her well toned thighs whose complexion matched the silk slip beneath the lace. Her only jewelry was a medium size strand of genuine pearls and small pearl cluster earrings. Her black stiletto heels were the highest she owned, but not as high as the dancers on Bourbon Street. Her only other preparation was the diaphragm she had inserted so carefully, just as she had done so many times before, feeling

132

disappointed or foolish or both each time she removed it later, unsoiled and unnecessary.

She decided it would be best to move the table and chairs closer to the piano, that way he would see her seated there when he opened the door, and she would be closer to him if he ended up playing the piano while they drank the champagne. She positioned her chair at the best angle for him to see her upon entering, trying a cross legged pose, then uncrossed. She repositioned the wine bottle and glasses several times, then remembered she had forgotten the corkscrew. Just as she was about to get up for the corkscrew, the door opened.

Julienne sat back in the chair and tried to change her startled expression into an anxious smile as David entered, his eyes darting from Julienne to the piano and back to Julienne, then widening with total surprise. Julienne's eyes searched his for a clue of some happiness in his expression, then she noticed movement behind him, and her smile started to crumble as she focused on Aurora entering the door. Like David, Aurora's mouth hung open as she looked from Julienne to the piano and to David.

David blinked. "Well! Here are two beautiful things I didn't expect to see when I walked in. Julienne! What have we here?" as he looked from Julienne to the piano.

Julienne's eyes darted from David to Aurora and back to David. "Perhaps an awkward moment. I don't know. You tell me."

David walked over and touched the corner of the piano. "First, you tell me what this is doing here?"

Julienne picked up the silver tray and turned toward the kitchenette. "I heard you had trouble working on some routines for want of a piano, so I thought I'd help you by providing one." She looked at Aurora as she set the tray on the sink counter. "It's also a thank you gift for sharing the adventure we experienced at Betty's Bar and the Chinese

133

gambling den the other night." She put the two crystal glasses in her wicker bag.

David looked at the bottle on the tray. "And what's that?"

Julienne picked up the champagne and looked at it. "It was to toast your new piano, but I didn't bring enough glasses." She set the bottle down and turned to Aurora. "I remember you from Café duMonde. I'm sorry, I don't recall your name."

David moved to the kitchen counter and removed three plain water glasses from the cabinet. "Julienne, this is Aurora Alonzo. She's appearing at La Lune and has been helping me work on the routine with her guitar."

Aurora was admiring the piano, running her hand over the glossy black curve on its side. She turned to Julienne and mimicked Julienne's pained smile. "I am...," she looked at the piano again, "I was hees piano, juss anodder piece of furniture een hees life." She looked at David, who frowned at her. "Tanks to you, he done have to seddle for juss six strings, now dad he hab over a hundred."

David removed the foil and inserted the corkscrew in the bottle, pulling it out with a popping sound accompanied by the sound of bubbles as he filled the three glasses. "Aurora has helped with more than the music. She's provided some good advice about the nature of the material."

Julienne accepted one of the glasses he proffered to both women. "I have no doubt she's provided you an invaluable service." She smiled reluctantly at Aurora. "I only hope my gesture in no way intrudes upon her service."

David rolled his eyes. "Gesture? My God, Julienne, that beautiful thing is overwhelming. But, seriously, I can't accept such an extravagant gift. I doubt that your father would approve."

Julienne frowned at him. "My father didn't pay for it. I did!" She looked at the piano and began to smile. "In fact, it

134

looks so good there, I think I'll get one for my place.." She turned and looked at him. "So, David, how much would you charge me for piano lessons?"

David's eyes widened again. "Hell, Julienne, this piano would buy you a lifetime of lessons."

Julienne tilted her head to one side and smiled broadly. "Done, then. I'll accept a lifetime of piano lessons in exchange for this piano."

David inhaled deeply. "Well, that's not exactly.....I mean...."

Aurora touched the piano again and smiled at David. "David, I hoppy for you. You fran' ees muy generoso." She walked over to Julienne and struck a hands on hip pose. "And you fran' ees muy bonita." She looked into Julienne's eyes boldly. "I lake you."

Julienne looked a little confused. "Well, thank you." She hesitated a moment before adding, "I appreciate beauty and talent, and, I guess, unsolicited compliments. Surely that's enough reason to like you, too."

David joined them and raised his glass. "To the four of us."

Julienne looked perplexed. "Four?"

David smiled. "Two beautiful ladies, one fabulously lucky man..."

Aurora clinked her glass to the other two. "An' wan muy bonita piano negre!"

Thirty minutes later, David opened the Yellow Cab door as Julienne ducked her head and entered, turning to look at him with a disappointed smile. He swallowed deeply before saying, "I really wish you'd stay. I haven't even had the chance to play something for you on your unbelievably generous gift. And you didn't have to insist Aurora stay when she offered to go. She really does have her own place, you know."

135

She looked down at her wicker basket and back up into his eyes. "Well, thanks for that reassurance. I didn't really know. But, if your offer to give me a recital... a private recital, is sincere, and your offer of lessons is sincere, I'll enjoy spending some time alone with you soon."

He took her hand and kissed the back of it. "I look forward to that...soon." He shut the cab door and watched it disappear down Rue Governor Nicholls as twilight descended on the skyline.

As he entered his loft, Aurora was seated at the piano with her hands in her lap. "Done worry, David, I no touch you muy bonito piano nuevo. Id still cherry for you."

David sighed and raised his eyebrows as he looked at her. "I don't know what to say. She was embarrassed. I was embarrassed. You! You were the only one that didn't seem embarrassed."

Aurora shrugged. "Por que mi tiene embarrass? 'Cause you fok someone before you med mi?" She laughed. "I no tink you cherry, David , no way!"

David wrinkled his brow. "Actually, I've never slept with Julienne. I've known her a year and she's been up here a number of times. She even helped me paint that mural. But, somehow, we never got around to sex. I've never been sure she was interested."

Aurora's eyebrows shot up, her eyes widened, and her mouth made an 'O' shape. "Ohhhh, she interested! Muy interested!" Then her brow wrinkled. "Es verdad, David, you never fok her? She gorgeous. Mon Dios, I fok her myself."

David looked at her puzzled. "I thought you said you weren't gay?"

Aurora got up and sat at the table, tilting the champagne bottle to verify it was empty. "Oh, David, en la casa de putas I fok liddle boys and old men, liddle girls and old men's espousas. I even see udder girls fok perros et caballos." She shut her eyes and shook her head from side to side. "I done know wad es straid o' gay, bueno o' mal, okay o' loco."

David smiled at her sadly. "Aurora, did you ever live with a woman?"

She opened her eyes and looked at him dispassionately. "I lib wid ocho otra putas."

He waggled his head side to side. "I mean, other than in the bordello, did you ever have a female lover for any length of time?"

She tilted her head to one side and raised her eyebrows. "Why, David? Would dad change you feelings por mi?"

David collected the glasses off the table and put them in the sink. "Not really. It might change my fantasies when I dream of you."

Her eyes widened as she smiled. "Tegan sus duermes con mi, David? I lake dad! Now I tell you I lake fok you fran, you duerme sus menage con los trios. Verdad?"

David winced. "Si, yes, of course. It would be futile of any man to deny such a fantasy."

Then Aurora winced. "No fantasmismo! You wan,' we tegan una menage."

David ran water and started washing the glasses. "As eager as you sound, and as eagerly as I might wish it, I don't think Julienne is ready for a menage a' troi. I wasn't even sure she was ready for me."

Aurora brought the champagne bottle and tray over to the sink. "You fok her fiurse, den you suggess una menage. She wan you mucho, David. She do anyting fo you. I do anyting fo you." He turned and looked at her warmly as he took the tray and washed it. Her mouth curled into a wiley smile. "You lake dad. You wan' dad. Es verdad, si?"

David set the tray on the drainboard with the glasses and looked at her with a guilty smile. "Si."

Chapter Ten
ENCHANTED EVENING

Aurora, Julienne, Richard, and David squeezed into the pink naugahyde booth closest to the tiny dance floor in Aladdin's, David seated between the two ladies and Richard on the end next to Julienne. Julienne asked David, "Why do you look so concerned? The last I heard, you were happy with what you'd written for Princess."

David winced. "It's not what I've written, but Dimitri's restaging of the routine."

Aurora frowned. "He should no mess wit you worts!"

David gave a pained smile. "He didn't change my words, but he reassigned the roles and sequence of numbers. After all, he's the producer of the show and he paid for the material, so he can do anything he wants with it."

Richard snorted. "Well, despite my differences with that 'nancy' Russian, I have to admit he's talented at staging and satire, and I've come to appreciate that he truly has Princess's best interests at heart." He leaned past Julienne to look at David. "I'm sure he's done well by your material, David."

The waiter appeared, a different young man, smaller and slighter than their previous visit, but still attired only in a gold thong, pink gossamer see-thru harem pants, and gold curled toe slippers. "Hi, I'm Fifi. I'll be your waitress tonight. Your regular waitress is in the show, but told me to give a special welcome to David and his father and their lovely guests."

Richard frowned angrily as Julienne winced and looked at David. "Does that mean that I am Richard's guest, or yours?"

Aurora's eyebrows raised as she blinked. "Noooo! I tink it means we a menage a catre."

Julienne looked at David questioningly. David rolled his

eyes and said, "It means nothing. The choreographer is just taunting Richard."

Richard growled under his breath, "Cheeky faggot!"

David's brow furrowed. "Let's not feed them any straight lines, Richard. Satire is the theme of this place and the psyche of many of its employees."

The waiter bit the top of his order pad and feigned innocence. "Oh my! Did I say something? Should I just leave and come back when all the fur has flown?"

David stared at the waiter. "I'll have a...."

The waiter interrupted him as he wrote on his pad. "Cuttysark and milk. Right?"

David answered, "Right," and looked at Julienne.

"Grasshopper, please," and Julienne looked at Aurora.

"I have a beeeg Margarita. Comprende, beeeg?"

The waiter blinked and mimicked her. "Si, beeeeeeeeg!"

Richard scowled at the waiter. "And I'll have a double Cuttysark, straight, with a water and ice chaser."

The waiter smiled. "Si, a beeeeeeg Cuttysark for daddy." He dotted his pad with his pencil aggressively, then blinked several times as he asked, "Anything else? Snackypoos? Dueling pistols? Arsenic?"

Richard spoke menacingly. "I think we have had quite enough, and you have more than fulfilled your role as a rude sarcastic pitiful excuse of a waiter."

The waiter blinked three times, said, "Whatever big daddy says," and minced away.

David sighed. "Richard, the more you let them push your buttons, the more they'll delight in doing so. If you'll go with the flow, just laugh with them, then they can't laugh at you."

Aurora nodded. "Si, Ricardo, he dish you, you dish heem. He say 'daddy,' you say 'you call me daddy, dan you mus' be mi bastard son of thad bag lady I bag twenny years ago.'"

David and Julienne laughed involuntarily. Julienne smiled

140

at Aurora, then looked at Richard. "They're right, Richard. Most female impersonators feel they have to be larger than life, and they often mimic the worst in women, the catty sarcasms and bitchiness that, let's face it, many women are capable of. That's why the French call it 'traveste,' they create a travesty of the female image."

David smiled at Julienne. "Well put, Julienne. I didn't know you knew much about effeminate gay males, much less such in depth analysis."

Julienne raised one eyebrow. "Are you kidding? I own an art gallery where the majority of the artists are gay males." She shrugged. "Granted, they aren't all effeminate or female impersonators, but I'm pretty familiar with a wide spectrum of the gay community."

Aurora poked David with her elbow. "Mira, David! I tole you she much braver dan you tink."

Julienne's brow furrowed as she looked at Aurora. "Thank you, Aurora." Then she looked at David questioningly. "You've known me over a year, watched me keep my cool in the gambling den and when we were running from the police, and you don't think I have courage?"

David sighed. "I think, when Aurora used the word 'courage,' she meant to say 'experience.' I would never doubt the courage of anyone who could stand on a chess table in The Napoleon House and sing *Les Marseilles*."

The waiter set the drinks down and left. Richard tossed his double Scotch back, then his water chaser, and smacked his lips. "Ahhhh, I remember the last time I sang *Les Marseilles*. It was when I was playing the piano in Morocco and the crew of a German ship sat at the table next to the piano. When it got to the line 'quon sang impure,' I glared at them with all the hatred I could muster." He sighed and looked into his empty glass. "But they didn't understand I was speaking of them, and they applauded my performance as a dramatic reading, never realizing I related it to them."

David turned to Aurora. "See what I mean. Lyrics like that are perceived by each listener based on where the listener is coming from."

Aurora frowned. "I steel tink id's racist!"

Before David could respond, the scratchy hissing sound of the public address system blared forth with the overture from *South Pacific* as the puppet stage rolled onto the dance floor. The six chorus boys leaped and twirled across the stage attired in tight fitting khaki short shorts and tight fitting khaki short sleeved shirts unbuttoned to the waist line. Nobody seemed to question the incongruity of their black ballet shoes. By the end of the overture, they were all posed around the perimeter of the dance floor in dramatic postures reminiscent of *Swan Lake*, all except the choreographer, Alex AKA Alexis their former waiter, who was spot lighted on one side of the stage looking masculine and aloof.

As the music to *Some Enchanted Evening* began, a second spotlight followed Princess's entrance on the other side of the stage. She wore a skin tight chartreuse mini-skirted sheath emblazoned with sequined palm leaves that spiraled up her torso, with matching sequined spike heels and aquamarine and chartreuse facial and hair makeup that also shimmered and sparkled. She sang the original Broadway lyrics of the song, only the gender changed, as in, "You may hear him call you across the crowded room. Then fly to his side, and make him your own..." These were sung to Alex, who played hard to get, leading Princess on a circular chase around the dance floor before finally enveloping her in his arms at the end of the song.

The chorus boys exited both sides of the puppet stage, Alex blowing Princess a kiss as she waved goodbye to him, and the spotlight followed her to the side of the stage whose khaki curtain had a center seam. The loud sound of a zipper opening was heard, the seam folded to one side to reveal a zipper that opened from the top enough to let the Jester puppet stick his head through, the zipper effect and the Jester eliciting a two staged level of laughter and applause. Once again, a voice in the background was heard saying, "We love you, Dimitri!"

Richard looked around the room with a frown, saying, "Who is that?" Several people on both sides of their booth frowned at him and whispered, "Shhhhhhhhhh's."

The Jester looked both ways with a surprised expression. "Oh, you came." More applause and catcalls.

Princess rolled her eyes. "Almost!" More laughter and applause. "Did you see him? Isn't he dreamy?" She swooned, clasped her hands, and looked skyward. "I never dreamed I'd find someone so strong and handsome!"

The zipper sound effect accompanied the final opening of the curtain as the Jester stepped out and raised his finger. "And young! Thank God! I was afraid you'd end up with Enzio Pinza. He's twice your age, you know, old enough to be your father, for God's sake!"

Richard scowled. David raised his eyebrows and whispered, "We admire satirical talent, remember?" Again, nearby patrons frowned and "Shusssed" them.

Princess stomped her heel and pouted. "Oh, Dimitri! Why can't you be happy for me?" She smiled and looked off into space again. "I found someone who loves me, with all my imperfections."

The Jester winced. "With all your sausage and eggs."

Princess closed her eyes dreamily. "With all my...." Then she opened them and scowled at the Jester. "I'm not going to let you rain on my...my...my enchanted evening." Then she wrinkled her nose at him. "You're just jealous!"

The Jester's expression melted into sadness. He looked down and away from her. With closed eyes, his shoulders shook once with a silent sob of grief.

Princess looked remorseful. "Oh, Dimitri, I'm sorry. I didn't mean to hurt you."

The Jester waved one hand at her and replied without looking at her. "No. That's okay." He turned to look at her sadly. "You're right. I am jealous of you....you, my alter ego."

Julienne stifled a chuckle and spoke under her breath, "Tell me something I didn't know," followed by "Shusssssh" from the nearby patrons.

The Jester shrugged and turned his palms up. "You have all the beauty, and I have all..."

Princess put her hands on her hips and scowled at him. "All?"

The Jester rolled his eyes and stared off into space. "Most...a majority share...maybe a tad more in the brain department." He blinked his eyes and smiled at her innocently.

Princess relaxed her pose and rolled her eyes. "Uh huh."

The Jester turned and looked at her soulfully. "And I'm truly happy for you, Princess, really I am. To have found love regardless; for richer or for poorer, in sickness and in....nebriated, in May or December, in New Orleans or Catmandu, for..."

Princess held up both metallic chartreuse fingernailed hands to stop him. "Okay! I get it. You're happy for me." Then she turned her palms up. "But you have no need to be jealous. After all, you've got...," and her jaw hung as she looked off into space.

The Jester looked at her hopefully. "Yes?"

She put one hand on her hip, gestured with the other, and looked off into space in the opposite direction. "I mean, there's....."

The Jester took an eager step toward her. "Uh huh!"

Princess closed her eyes tightly and held her hands up in front as before, then opened her eyes to stare at him and again gesture towards him with palms up. "After all, you have so much talent."

The same voice in the background yelled, "Second that!"

Richard raised his head and looked around the room. "I think it's that damn Ruskie stroking himself!"

Now half the room turned towards him with a resounding, "Ssssssshhhhhhhhhrrrrrrrrrrr!"

As the Jester spoke, the spotlight on Princess started to slowly fade. He looked down and sighed heavily, then looked up with a forlorn expression. "Yes, that's true. Can't deny that. But, is that all? I would trade it all for just..."

As Princess' spot was totally extinguished, a small spot lit the other side of the stage where another doll stepped around the curtain. Its muscle builder figure was clothed in the khaki short shorts and open shirt, and its head and hair closely resembled David, but its eyes were those flat round rag doll's eyes with a white background, a clear front window, and a black disk for an iris that moved loosely inside with each movement of the doll, sometimes appearing wall eyed or cross eyed or rocking back and forth when the doll came to a stop.

Richard leaned toward David with a smile. "Oh, we do love that satirical talent, don't we?" As the surrounding patrons glared at Richard, a big man closest to him said emphatically, "Shut the hell up!"

The Jester suddenly noticed the other doll and, as the music to *Some Enchanted Evening* swelled over the speakers, began to sing in a comic falsetto operatic voice. At the end of each phrase, the Jester struck a coy or flirtatious pose, while the David doll went through a series of body building poses and ballet moves. The Jester sang David's parody.

145

Some enchanted evening
you may see a strange one
you may meet a strange one
across a crowded room
and somehow you know
this strangest of men
will try to impale you
again and again.

Who can explain it
and why should they try
why sit in closets
and cry and cry and cry.

Some enchanted evening
if you should be so lucky
to find someone so plucky
to love you as you are
Then fly to his fly
and make it your home
or all through your life
you'll orgasm alone.

Colored stage lights came up as the six chorus boys ushered Princess back on stage and performed a variation of their earlier routine to the instrumental second chorus of *Some Enchanted Evening.* As the last stanza came to a close, Princess ended up beside the Jester, putting her head next to his, and Alex ended up next to the David doll, putting his head next to the doll. They all sang the last line in unison, "Or all through your life you'll orgasm alone."

Then the chorus boys began dancing to the *South Pacific* overture, each taking a center stage bow to audience applause, ending with Princess and Alex taking their bow while the

Jester and the David doll locked arms, entered the khaki curtains, which zipped closed behind them and the zipper sound effect coming over the closing bars of the overture.

The audience went wild, giving the performers a standing ovation as the chorus boys came out and bowed in unison, followed by Princess and Alex, and Dimitri who came out to take another bow. As the applause died down, Princess and Dimitri headed toward the center booth as everyone made room so Princess could sit next to Richard with Dimitri again on the outer edge.

Dimitri smiled at David eagerly. "Well, David, what do you think? Do you approve of my little tweaks to your material?"

Everyone turned to look at David with repressed laughter twisting their mouths. David scanned everyone's eyes, looked down as if he was going into a trance, then looked up with his best professional smile. "I thought it was amazing, Dimitri. Your talent constantly astounds me." He looked at Princess. "And you, Princess, you made us all proud," he looked at Richard, "And some of us more than a little excited."

Aurora's eyes widened as she smiled at Princess. "Ees verdad, Preencess. You de hottest girl-boy I evah see. Hot! Hot! Hot!"

Princess looked demure as she smiled at each in turn. She spoke in a little girl's voice. "Thank you. I just feel so fortunate to be the beneficiary of so many people's talent. David, Dimitri, and Alex, our very talented choreographer."

The waiter brought a round of drinks for everyone and left. Richard lifted his glass. "It's a team effort, my beautiful Princess. You are all fortunate to have each other, and we, the audience, are the greatest beneficiaries of your combined talents. Here's to talent!" Everyone leaned forward to clink their glasses together.

147

****

David chuckled to himself as he walked down Royal Street with Julienne on one arm and Aurora on the other. Julienne smiled at him questioningly. "What's so funny?"

David looked from one to the other. "I was just thinking, would either of you find me attractive if I looked like that doll Dimitri created, minus the rag doll eyes, of course?"

Julienne shook her head from side to side. "Not me. I think it's a natural equation, the more muscle, the less brain."

Aurora looked at Julienne. "You right! Las mas macho, las menos eschuche. De stronger dey are, de more stupido, more brutale," she looked at David, "more miso-genius."

Julienne looked at her questioningly. David interpreted. "The more misogynistic. Well, that makes me feel better about not being musclebound. Now, if I could just get my eyes to work right," and he crossed his eyes and turned to look at each of them, prompting their laughter.

When her laughter subsided, Julienne gripped his biceps with her free hand. "No, you have just the right balance of brain and brawn, even though there are a few things you haven't figured out, yet."

Suddenly Aurora let go of David's arm and stood still, smiling at them as they turned to look at her in surprise. David asked, "What's wrong?"

She continued to smile. "Nada. No'ting wrong. This my turn, I live a la Calle Dauphine."

David steered Julienne toward Aurora. "Okay, then we'll walk you home."

Still smiling, Aurora held up her hand. "No. No necessito. I'm okay." She looked at Julienne who stared at her with a perplexed expression. "Go play dad piano bonito fo' her. She deserve to hear how id sound."

Julienne stood with her mouth slightly open, holding on to David's arm with both hands.. She tilted her head to one side and asked Aurora, "Are you sure? You're welcome to join us."

Aurora smiled at Julienne. "Nod tonide." Then she looked at David. "Maybe some nide soon. I lake dad."

David stared at Aurora intensely. "Are you sure?"

Aurora closed her eyes and nodded affirmatively. "Si. Mucho sure." Then she turned and left, saying, "Have fun!"

Julienne looked at David as he stared intently at Aurora's retreating figure. She asked, "Are you okay?"

David broke his stare and turned to smile weakly at her. "Yes, yes. I'm okay. I just didn't want to offend her."

As they headed for his loft, she asked, "Are you okay serenading me solo on your new piano?"

He smiled at her. "I would love to serenade you, but it's your piano, not mine. I can't accept such an expensive gift, but I'll let you lend it to me until you want it back, or sell it, or whatever."

She smiled and shook her head negatively. "Oh no! You can't welch on our deal. That piano is yours in exchange for a lifetime of piano lessons. Aurora is my witness, and you can't wiggle out of it."

David chuckled. "Well, let's just see how serious a student you are."

In the courtyard leading to David's loft, they had to walk around the construction materials for Mrs. Saucier's new building improvements as a result of her newly approved bank loan. They saw Mrs. Saucier peeking through her curtains on the ground floor as they ascended the stairs.

David turned on the lamp he had put on one side of the piano's music rack. It had a vase shaped metal base supported by a cast iron dragon on each side, its garnet colored glass shade casting a warm pool of light in the immediate area of the piano. As Julienne dragged one of the chairs close to the piano bench, David sat on the bench and opened the keyboard cover. He looked toward the door and said, "The landlady never complained about Aurora's guitar, but I don't know how she'll take to the sound of a grand piano at this hour."

Julienne helped him remove his coat, which she hung on the back of the chair, then placed her hands on both his shoulders and massaged his muscles as he rolled up his shirt sleeves. "Oh, I think Mrs. Saucier will cut us a little slack, at least until she's spent all of her bank loan."

David looked perplexed. "Her what?"

Julienne ignored his question and sat in the chair. "Play something for me."

David played the plaintive strains of a classical number. Julienne smiled and closed her eyes as she said, "Ah, *Clair deLune*, Claude Debussey, I love that."

He looked at her as he played. "I've always been drawn to music about the moon. The first thing I ever learned to play was Beethoven's *Moonlight Sonata*."

Julienne opened her eyes. "Then you should be playing at La Lune. But, then, you've come close in befriending Aurora who does play there."

David didn't hear her because he had reached the faster center movement of the piece filled with arpeggios. He closed his eyes and his body swayed slowly to the music's tempo. Julienne was aware that her body was leaning toward him as if he were a magnet. She watched the muscles of his forearms and biceps flex as the music began to reach a crescendo. She closed her eyes and held her breath for the few seconds before the crescendo peaked. As the softer sounds of the final movement echoed the first movement, she started breathing again and opened her eyes, aware that she sensed a visceral feeling in her body and the same feeling of longing she had experienced watching David at the Voodoo Room. But now, they were not at the Voodoo Room, and they were alone.

As David finished the last three almost silent doublets in the closing, Julienne applauded and smiled enthusiastically. "That was beautiful, David!" Then she turned and looked toward the kitchen. "Is there any ice in that antique refrigerator of yours?"

David turned toward her. "Yes, but I'm afraid I might have nothing to drink. Perhaps some old Chianti I keep in case I bring home Italian. But I never finish it and end up using it to cook with."

She got up and headed for the kitchen. "That's okay. I just want an ice cube to rub on my forehead. I brought some Mumm's for us, but we can drink that at room temperature." She saw him start to rise and held up her hand. "Don't get up! Keep playing, and I'll bring the wine to the piano."

He sat down and began to play a Jerome Kern medley beginning with *The Last Time I Saw Paris*. She popped the cork expertly and carried the silver tray with the bottle and crystal glasses she had brought, setting it on the empty side of the music rack and filling the two glasses. She lifted hers and started to dance in twirls around the mural of Paris, stopping and miming beside each image referred to in the song. With the last line, she ended up sitting on the bench beside him, leaning slightly to allow his arm to reach the top end of keyboard.

She set her glass down and picked up the melting ice cube in a handkerchief which she rubbed alternately on her forehead, neck, and breastbone. David began another Jerome Kern tune, *Long Ago And Far Away*, and she began to hum the melody and sing some of the lines, "...I dreamed a dream one day," she turned and looked at him, "and now that dream is here beside me."

Because she had stopped singing, David began singing the second stanza, thinking she forgot the lyrics. Just before the

151

final line, she looked at him and sang, "Just one look and then I knew, that all I longed for long ago was you."

The two stared intently at each other, then, to break the tension, David began playing *All The Things You Are*. Julienne asked, "Would you sing it for me, David?"

He stopped, looked down at the keyboard, then started again, singing the song to her. As he started the last eight bar phrase, she placed her hand on his thigh and looked into his eyes as he sang, "Some day my happy arms will hold you, and some day I'll know that moment divine, when all the things you are are mine." The instant his hands left the keyboard, the two embraced tightly and hungrily devoured each other's mouths with tongue probing and lip chewing that sounded like a hungry dog that just stole a steak off the kitchen table.

Suddenly David released her and, gripping both her shoulders and holding her a few inches away from him, his brow furrowed and he said, "Julienne, is this really what you want?"

She looked at him incredulously and, standing and pulling him by both his hands toward the bed, she said, "Are you kidding? Didn't you hear me singing to you just now? I've waited for this for over a year!" and she swung him onto the bed where he landed on his back before she straddled him, pulling her skirt up to her hips in the process. She lowered her face to his and kissed him again as she unbuttoned his shirt.

When she rose to grip her dress and pull it over her head, revealing she wore no underwear, his brow wrinkled and he said, "It's just that, I don't want to take advantage or lie to you."

She began to unbuckle his pants. "Listen, David, I'm not that eighteen year old blonde they told me about who embarrassed you at the Voodoo Room. Neither of us are virgins and neither of us have expressed any commitments."

His eyes widened. "So you're sure?"

She smiled at him. "I don't need to ask you if you want me, because I can feel the answer to that growing beneath me as we speak. So just shut up, David, and help me get your pants off."

Chapter Eleven
CHANGING OF THE GUARD

Richard watched David put his thumbnail under the flap on the belly of the cold boiled crab and peel it back until the body of the crab broke away from the back shell, revealing the interior white crab meat. David looked at Richard expectantly until Richard imitated the action, pulling the tab back until the crab popped open and emitted a spray of water that sprinkled his face. Richard froze. "Oh, my God. I think I got it in my eye!"

David consoled him. "That's okay. It's just water. It's harmless."

Richard wiped his eye with his knuckle. "But it's salty and a little peppery. It burns a little."

David was less consoling. "Just blink a few times and it'll go away. Now watch, we scrape this part away, it's called 'dead man's meat,' it's the lungs. Then we break the body in two like this, and see, it forces the white meat of the leg muscles to protrude a little." He picked up a tiny fork with three tines. "Then we take the fish fork, they really should call it a crab fork because it's just the right size to get into the muscle compartment for each leg, and pull the meat out like this." He extracted a large clump of white crab meat and dipped it in the little bowl of melted garlic butter before popping it into his mouth.

Richard looked around the white tiled walls of Medina's Seafood Restaurant on the upper end of rue Chartres near Canal Street. "A Greek name, with Italian decor, in a former French colony. I must say, your French Quarter is quite international."

155

David spoke between bites of buttery crab meat. "I think of The Quarter as being more eclectic than international. It has to do with being free spirited, accepting people's differences."

Richard began to smile slightly as he tasted the buttered crab meat. "I guess that's why they call it 'The Big Easy.'"

David removed a bit of crab shell from his lip. "I think that comes more from the Storyville red light district on Esplanade during the turn of the century. I think the je ne sais quai I'm talking about comes from the integration of multi-national Europeans with the local Indian and emancipated black populations. New Orleans is probably more of a melting pot than any other American city, and that's what produced jazz, a unique world class cuisine, and a flavor I've never experienced in any other metropolitan area in the United States."

Richard wiped butter dripping off his chin. "Well, the French Quarter reminds me more of the older parts of Paris than any other city I've been in, and I've been in most major European, Middle Eastern, and North African cities." He picked up a crab claw and stared at it. "It also shares a joie de vivre which is more typically Parisian than what I'd call French. Some of those clods in Provence can be quite sullen."

David touched Richard's hand with a nut cracker to get his attention, then demonstrated how to crack the big crab claw and extract the large white and pink muscle within. "We have a similar distinction you'll see if you visit areas outside of the city. Cajuns are more influenced by their environment than their genetic mixture of local Chocktaw Indian and the Acadian French from Nova Scotia and Quebec who were forced South during the French Indian wars ending in 1763. Cajuns closer to the seashore can be quite jolly, while the farmers inland can be very pedantic and narrow minded."

Richard cracked his crab claw which squirted water on David's shirt front. "What the bloody hell? Sorry about that, old boy!"

David wiped his tux shirt front with his napkin. "No problem. I keep an extra shirt in the locker at the club just in case."

Richard tried the nut cracker on the smaller crab legs. "Speaking of multiple shirts and multi-national and such...."

David inspected the spot on his shirt. "Yes?"

Richard continued to pick at the crab legs as he spoke. "How'd it go with your multiple multi-national ladies the other night after the show?"

David set down his napkin and took a sip of his beer. "Okay. It went okay." Then he picked up his tiny fork and continued eating.

Richard looked at him. "Okay? That's all you can say? Forgive me if I'm prying, but I originally got the impression you had a thing with that Mexican spitfire, but the way Julienne was talking and looking at you the other night, and you left with one on each arm, it does inspire the imagination."

David held the fork full of crabmeat in front of his face and said, "You're forgiven," then popped the morsel into his mouth.

Richard looked perplexed. "Forgiven? For what?"

David wiped his mouth with his napkin and pushed his chair back. "For prying."

Richard frowned. "I make you privy to the darkest secrets of my dissolute life, and all you can tell me about yours is I'm prying?"

David stood up and opened his wallet. "No. You asked forgiveness for prying. I just said you're forgiven." and he tucked a large bill under the edge of his plate before he turned to leave.

Richard smiled mischievously and yelled at David's retreating figure. "Well, that just tells me it was more decadently delicious than I ever imagined."

****

David shut his eyelids tightly and pulled the sheet over his head. "What are you doing? The sun has barely begun to rise, the hour when all good night owls begin to sleep."

Julienne stood up to let the silken sheath ripple down her body where she smoothed the last few wrinkles over her narrow hips and well shaped buttocks. "You're the night owl. I'm the poor slave who must open an art gallery and smile at tourists and art patrons for eight hours before you even wake for your first meal of the day." She stepped into her high heels and tapped them on the floor to insure a snug fit.

David groaned and his words were muffled by the sheet over his head. "If you're looking for sympathy, you'll get none from me. You've sapped the last ounce of strength from my body, and now you're tap dancing like you're in a Busby Berkly musical just to keep me from sleeping."

Julienne eyed the thin sheet molded to his body, smiled mischievously, then reached out and stroked the bulge at his crotch several times, feeling it quiver beneath her hand. "Ohhhh, poor baby. Did I wake you from your sweet dreams. You go back to sleep and see if you can recapture whatever it was that made this thing dance like its doing now."

David's voice growled. "Get out of here now, before I tear that silk sheath off of you and the art gallery will have to report you missing!" He smiled under the sheet as he heard her retreating laughter and her heels echoing with a hollow wood sound on the stairs down to the courtyard. He took several long deep breaths, and reflected on the week of lovemaking with Julienne since the show at Aladdin's.

158

Suddenly he heard footsteps ascending the stairs and he inhaled deeply to feign irritation as he said, "What the hell did you forget now?" He felt the side of the bed sag and then a hand once again caressing the bulge at his crotch which had just begun to subside. Despite his exhaustion, he felt flattered, and feigned irritation in his voice again as he said, "Good God, Julienne, haven't you had enough?" And he pulled the sheet down to find Aurora smiling down at him.

"No, David, I have no, nod fo a week. Wad you try to do, kill dad girl wid you ting?"

David's face registered confusion and shock. "Aurora! Oh, God! I'm so sorry. I should have contacted you."

Aurora continued to smile as she shook her head side to side. "Dad's all right, David, I unnerstan. She strange new pussy fo you." And she pulled the sheet down, lowered her head, and licked the length of his semi tumescent organ, looking up at him again with a smile. "I can tase her. She juice, id still on you."

David rose up on his elbows. "Aurora, how did you get in here?"

She lay her face on his crotch, her cheek touching his organ as her hand began to caress his abdomen. "I wade fo tree morning till she leave de courtyard door unlatch, den I run across de streed befo la port cerrado."

His brow furrowed. "Did she see you?"

She hesitated. "No, nod yed." Her hand traveled up to his nipple where her index finger flicked back and forth across it rapidly. Then she turned her head, rested her chin on his penis, and stared at him. "Did you ask her?"

He blinked. "Ask her what?"

As she spoke, her chin bounced his penis up and down. "Aboud us. De tree of us. Aboud de treesome."

159

David's body was aroused and he found it hard to concentrate. He closed his eyes and said, "I don't know if she's ready."

She raised her chin and lifted his penis up before her. Holding it by the base, she gently tapped it against her nose, saying, "You never know less you ask." Then she held it to one side and asked, "You still wan treesome, David?"

With eyes still closed, he nodded affirmatively.

She gripped the base of his penis tighter. "You still wan me, David?"

Again, he nodded affirmatively, opened his eyes, and began to smile at her.

She looked at his penis in her hand. "You wan dis ting speak fo you, David?"

His smile increased as he looked at her intently. "I think it already has."

She smiled as his penis grew in her hand, then said, "Muy bueno." She closed her eyes, opened her mouth, and inserted the head of his penis into it.

****

David pulled the sleeve down on his one and only black coat, other than his three black tuxedos. He rarely wore it or the one and only slim Jim black tie pinned to his everyday white collared shirt with a black pearl stickpin. The suit had probably shrunk since the last time he wore it years ago, the sleeves riding up over his black pearl cufflinks and the coat feeling a little snug in the shoulders. He shifted his weight to the other foot as he stood at the curb before the exterior doors to his residence on Governor Nicholls Street, then looked up at the early morning overcast sky, wondering if they'd get rained out on the procession to the cemetery.

The rear door of the long Yellow Cab limousine opened

160

before it came to a stop in front of him. Richard sat on the back seat in a grey suit with a black armband on his upper left sleeve, Julienne and Aurora on either side of him. Dimitri sat on one of the two fold out backward facing jump seats, and Princess vacated the other one to sit on Richard's lap and free the jump seat for David. Dimitri and all three ladies were dressed in black, although Princess kept trying to pull the hem of her short skirt down, surveying all with an apologetic smile as she said, "I'm sorry. I don't own any dresses with long skirts. Do you think Alex will mind?"

Richard supported her back with one hand and patted her shiny black hose encased thigh with the other, saying, "Of course he wont mind, Duckey. He'll just be so grateful you're there."

Dimitri stared at Richard's hand on Princess's thigh, then looked up as he made eye contact surveying everyone. "I want to thank you all for coming to support Alex in his hour of grief. I know most of you didn't know his mother, but I can tell you she was a wonderful woman. As a single mother, she scrubbed floors and made many sacrifices to send him to dance school. And when he came out, she was very supportive of him. That's why he sacrificed his Broadway career to come home and help her when her cancer progressed enough to require personal assistance."

Julienne smoothed her black hose down her leg as she said, "I met her once, when Alex brought his paintings to the gallery. They were all excellent watercolors of dancers and stage set designs. I don't remember her name...."

Dimitri interjected. "Rosalie Pienas. Her parents were from the Caribbean."

Julienne smiled at him. "Yes, Rosalie, tall, beautiful, a café au lait color. I presume his father was white."

Dimitri looked somber. "He never knew his father, but he was probably white."

Aurora sounded a little testy. "Whad, black, café au lait! Me vale verga! Who cares? Rosalie sound lake una madre maravillosa! Alex estan uno hijo talentoso! No importa el color!"

David frowned slightly at Aurora. "No judgements here. Just observations, speculations. We all admire Alex's talent and his mother's sacrifices. If we didn't, we wouldn't be here."

Richard tilted his head to one side. "I, for one, look forward to seeing a real jazz funeral."

Julienne smiled at him condescendingly. "The preferred term is funeral with music. And you might be interested that the church is in the historic Treme district North of The French Quarter. The procession will terminate at the St. Louis Cemetery, another historic landmark with above ground crypts because of New Orleans below sea level water table. The headstones and marble sculptures and carving on the crypts are quite artistic, also somewhat colorful in some of the inscriptions."

Dimitri winced. "Oh yes. I remember one that started 'The illegitimate child of,' and another 'The Unfaithful wife of.' Reminds me of the time I visited the cemetery in Tombstone, Arizona, that had headstones that said 'Cattle rustler,' 'Card cheat,' and 'Hanged on Boot Hill.'"

Aurora still had that testy sound in her voice. "Sound lake de French, dey have mucho prejudice."

Julienne gave Aurora a pained smile. "Tombstone, Arizona, was not French territory, Aurora, and the tombstones and crypts in St. Louis Cemetery are one and two hundred years old. Every culture evolves from a less democratic and more prejudiced past to a more democratic and liberal future."

Aurora looked sideways past Richard and Princess to make eye contact with Julienne. "Bud do dey have to carry de prejudice forward in de music and language?"

162

Julienne tilted her head sideways and smiled at David. "Good point, Aurora. Hopefully there's room for improvement in all of us."

The cab arrived at the white wood frame church where mourners were ascending the wooden steps and filing past Alex and a short portly dark skinned man at the door who greeted them with sad smiles and mumbled "Thank you"s for condolences expressed. Dimitri paid the cabbie and declined David's offer to contribute, while the others ascended the steps toward Alex.

Alex's smile brightened as they approached him, extending both hands to grasp both Dimitri's and David's hands and shake them, pulling them over to the man beside him. "Dimitri, David, I want you to meet Gabriel Jackson, my mother's partner and de-facto widower."

Gabriel shook their hands enthusiastically and spoke with a gravelly voice which, together with his short body and dark round face, was like a Louis Armstrong impersonation. "Pleased to meet 'cha. Really, I 'yam. Alex 'as spoke so highly of you'se. I wanna tank you fo' all you done fo' 'im."

The group all shared introductions as Alex explained to them, "Gabriel is a fabulous cornet player and will be leading the procession to the cemetery. He has his own marching band called The Treme Troubadours. You have a treat in store for you when you hear them play."

They made their way to the front two rows of bare wooden benches with bare wooden backs, cordoned off with a satin ribbon labeled "Aladdin's." There they joined some of the waiter's from the club who were already seated together with a half dozen other people from an expensively dressed elderly white couple to singles with varying skin tones and colorful attire. The coffin before the central pulpit was closed and flanked by many floral wreaths and a large sepia-toned photographic portrait of Rosalie on an easel. Aurora created

163

a murmur among the Baptist mourners when she knelt and crossed herself before the coffin in Catholic tradition before joining the others on the bench.

The minister was very tall, very dark, and very handsome. He obviously loved the sound of his own sonorous bass voice and having a captive audience, most of whom were receptive and responsive to his dramatic intonation and theatrical gestures. In eulogizing Rosalie, he partly recapped the history of The Great Depression; her gratitude to Franklin and Eleanor Roosevelt for receiving the first toilet ever installed in her home, her employment in the W.P.A. (Work Projects Administration) cleaning U.S.O. (United Service Organization) Clubs during World War II for the magnificent sum of twenty-five dollars a month, and his own depression era employment in the C.C.C. (Civilian Conservation Corps) as a laborer building roads and upgrading state parks for subsistence wages. He lauded Alex for his theatrical accomplishments, but challenged all of Alex's generation to not only appreciate the challenges that were overcome to pave the way for them, but also feel an obligation to fulfill the social and economic options that were made available to them "so that Rosalie's sacrifices will not have been made in vain."

Most in the front row felt obliged to echo the chorus of "Amen"s and "Hallelujah"s that followed the Minister's eulogy. Alex walked up to the podium, paused, looked down for ten seconds, then looked up and surveyed the congregation, making eye contact with almost every individual in turn as he spoke. "I thank Reverend Brown for praising my mother, and I thank him for challenging me and my generation to fulfill the opportunities that she, and so many of our parents, have sacrificed to create for us." He closed his eyes and shook his head sideways. "I am so very grateful that I had the opportunity to spend her last years on earth with her."

Dimitri whispered under his breath, "He gave up a promising career to do that."

Alex opened his eyes and looked up at the rear ceiling of the church. "I had known from a very early age that she had sacrificed a lot to make opportunities for me. But witnessing her physical pain in these last years, sharing her stories of details and events I had not known before, these gave me a profound understanding of the depth of that sacrifice, and the resolve to resume my career and fulfill her dreams for me." The congregation murmured approval. Alex looked at Dimitri, then David, then the elderly white couple who had not joined in the Amens and Hallelujahs. "So, with the help of God and some very good friends, I plan to return to New York and make my mother proud."

At this point the choirmaster prompted the robed choir to commence the old spiritual, *Amazing Grace,* as the Minister opened the casket and the congregation began to form a line for the final viewing. Julienne looked toward the elderly couple and whispered to David, "I bet they're Rosalie's last employers."

Gabriel stood next to her and said under his breath, "And you'd be right. Bud dey also Alex's grandparents. After dere son pass away, dey look her up, wan to help Alex. Dey hire her, pay her well, and pay his tuition. Bud de cancer demon got hold of her by then, and de money did'n take away de pain."

David asked Gabriel softly. "Does Alex know?"

Gabriel looked toward Alex standing beside the coffin accepting condolences as mourners passed by. "She tole him right before she die. Dey weren't happy wit' his lifestyle, bud dey sincere about helpin' him."

Outside the church, Gabriel changed into a military coat and hat with much gold braid and brass buttons. His marching band formed behind him, the bass drum imprinted with "The

Treme Troubadours." They began to move with a slow paced sliding step, playing a dirge in a minor key. This followed the tradition of sad music to the cemetery, followed by happy music on the return trip to Rosalie's house where plenty of good food and happy thoughts were expected.

Dimitri's group marched behind Alex and beside the others from the front two rows, with the exception of the elderly couple who left in a car and waited at the cemetery for the procession. Others marched behind them, and Aurora spotted Alphonse from Café duMonde among them. Linking her arm around his, she pulled him into the front ranks. David noticed him and said, "Hello, Alphonse."

Alphonse smiled self consciously and responded, "Hello, Mister David."

With her arm still linked with Alphonse, Aurora smirked and began to swagger. "Hello, Meester David. How are you Meester David?"

David's chest shook with repressed laughter, then said, "I'm fine, Miss Aurora."

En route, David and Richard exchanged glances noting their admiration for Gabriel's musical talent. Richard raised his hand to shield his voice as he whispered to David, "He's the right age. Dare we ask him if he's Armstrong's illegitimate brother?"

David smiled, bit his lip, and repressed a chuckle as he shook his head negatively.

Back at Rosalie's house, Dimitri and David sought Alex out and Dimitri said, "Tell us your schedule, when you might be leaving. Aside from having to replace you, we want to throw you a 'bon voyage' party.

Alex's eyes were still red from crying at the cemetery. He had to take a deep breath before he talked to keep from breaking up again. "Oh, Dimitri, don't start planning some extravaganza. I will be leaving the club sooner than the city."

He looked questioningly at the elderly couple looking very uncomfortable across the room. "I'm supposed to spend some time with my newfound grandparents, and, aside from monetary considerations, I admit I'm curious about my father and his family's history. Being white, it's hard for you to understand how it is for us 'betwixt and betweeners.' We get prejudiced dumped on us from both sides. For being as black as he is, Gabriel has been the most understanding of anyone other than my mom. I guess being that close to her helped make him aware of what I was going through."

David looked across the room at Gabriel talking to the elderly couple. "I can believe he can be compassionate. I'd like to believe that compassion would come naturally to someone with his musical talent, someone who can play sad music as profoundly as he did today, and still have the joi de vivre to lift our spirits on the return trip."

Richard had joined them just in time to hear David's remark, then added, "It's a shame a talent like his is not recognized outside of the community. Maybe looking and sounding so much like Armstrong is a handicap. Maybe they think he's a caricature."

Alex closed his eyes, sighed, then opened them to look at Gabriel. "Well, if I have any success in New York, Gabriel will be the first person I pull up the ladder."

Dimitri raised his nose and peered down it at Alex. "And who, pray tell, will be the second?"

David laughed. "Don't worry, Dimitri. He'll be pulling and we'll be pushing. Just hope you don't get trampled by all those chorus boy waiters from Aladdin's."

****

Aurora knelt naked on the bed and stared at David seriously. "David, I wan you do someting fo me."

167

David closed his eyes and pulled the sheet over his head. "Aurora, have pity on me. I play the piano for five hours. Julienne exhausts me for the next five hours. Then you arrive with the sun and drain whatever fluids remain in my body for another five hours. I am going to crumble into a pile of dust and blow away soon."

Aurora raised her eyebrows and shook her head negatively. "No, no! Nod sex. You do dad fine fo me. I 'preciate you save some o you fluids fo me." She straddled his body with her hands and knees, holding her body above his as she smiled down at his face hidden under the sheet. "No. I wan' you ride some musica por me. No! Nod musica, ride worts por la musica."

His eyes still closed, David lowered the sheet from his face. "Write words? For what music?"

Still smiling, she squatted on his hips and said, "Dere's dis musica, una canta por los toreros, dey play id before de bullfide."

David frowned at her hips resting on his groin. He looked at her pleadingly and whined, "Please?"

Her eyebrows rose and her mouth made a surprised 'O' circle. "Oh, sorry!" She dismounted his hips and lay on her side beside him, her face close to his. "Dis musica, id no tengan no worts, bud id famous fo de bullfide. I tink, you ride de English worts for me, dis musica become a, how you say, crossover song for bode los gringos an los chicanos."

David opened one eye and looked at her. "What music?"

She leaned on her elbow and rested her face on her hand, smiling down at him. "Manana, I bring me guitarra an play fo you. You escribir la musica, den you escribir las worts ingles. You lake! Id's muy classico!"

David opened his other eye. "If we do this tomorrow, transcribe the music and write lyrics to it, I hope you don't expect to have sex, too."

168

Her eyebrows rose again and she brushed her palm across the blonde hairs on his chest. "Mebbe, tomorrow you escribir la musica, an de day after you escribi las worts. Dad way we still hab liddle sex, si?"

David closed his eyes and covered his face with the sheet. "Muy liddle Muy muy liddle. El mas pequeno sex en todo del mondo."

She laughed. "You habla espanol ees terrible, pero su sexo ees grande!" And she kissed his lips through the sheet.

Chapter Twelve
THE NIGHT WAS MADE FOR LOVE

David wrote the last few words on the music manuscript with a pencil, frowned at them slightly, erased and rewrote one of the words, then leaned back from the piano keyboard and smiled. Seeing his smile, Aurora set down her guitar and moved to the piano bench, kneeling beside it and placing her hands on his thigh as she looked up eagerly at him. "So, is finish? Si? You canta por mi, por favor."

He turned to her with a doubtful smile. "I don't know. I can sing love songs, because I love women. But bullfighting is not my cup of tea."

She scoffed at him as she reached for the manuscript, but he held it in place on the music rack with both hands. She rested back on her heels and frowned playfully at him. "Done be silly. Id's nod lake a macho ting. Torreros are lake nancy boys, dey prance around een tide fidding embroidered pantaloons. Tu canta 'e mi canta, id make no differencia."

He took a deep breath and said, "Okay. Here it goes." He played the introductory interlude and thereafter played only chords with interludes between the phrasing.

There once was a great
Matador
who was known near and far
so they say.

But behind his bravo
there lay something hallowed
revealed in his words
as he prayed. - and so he prayed:

I come to you now
as the hour grows late,
for I soon play with fate,
in the arena.

That which others may find so bold,
has a meaning which is not often told,
only you may know the fear that I hold,
and if I am consoled,
it's through La Macarena.

For yours is the heart
that sees my tears
and feels my fears
as I pray.

And now as I leave
wont you bless all my pleas
in your name
La Macarena.

David took his hands off the keyboard and turned to Aurora, who sat open mouthed, her eyes glistening. He frowned at her. "Well, what do you think?"

Aurora inhaled deeply and said, "Por Dios mio, I tink you a fokking genius! You hid de bull on de head, ride between de eyes!"

David continued to frown and tilted his head to one side. "You like it?"

Aurora sat beside him and stared at the manuscript. "You bedder fokking believe I lake id!" She put both hands on the music, tracing the lyrics with her finger. "Wid dis I have all de chicanos crying in dere Margaritas and all de gringos buying bullfide tickets." She lifted the manuscript off the music rack with both hands and shook it. "Wid dis I ged record contract, I make de big time, I tell El Gato he keeees mi culo!" Suddenly she became serious and looked David in the eye. "David, you know how I ged record company listen to me?"

David looked down at the keyboard and bit his lower lip, then said, "Let me ask Richard, or maybe his boss, Bernie Brill. They've got East and West coast connections." He reached for the manuscript, but Aurora pulled it away.

Aurora smiled at him pleadingly. "Lemme keep it fo now, David. I wanna practice id, okay?"

David turned his palms up and shrugged. "Well, maybe I should make us copies of it so the original doesn't get lost."

Aurora hugged the manuscript to her chest. "Okay, you copy later. Fo now, lemme practice id a liddle."

David shrugged again and stared at the empty music rack. "Okay, I guess."

Aurora quickly put her guitar and the manuscript in her guitar case, then returned and knelt by the bench, laying her head on his thigh, her hands caressing his inner thigh. "You so good fo' me, David." She put her chin on his thigh and looked up at him as her hand reached his crotch and stroked him through his clothing. "I love you, David. I do anything fo' you, anything you wan'. Wad do you wan', David?"

David smiled at her and stroked her long shiny black hair with his hand. "As much as I'd like to do so many wonderfully obscene things to you and with you, I'm afraid I'd probably fall asleep in the process."

Aurora's eyebrows raised in surprise, then she stood up and, dragging him to the bed by one hand, she pushed him down and began to undress him. He laughed and said, "Maybe you didn't understand me, but..."

She put her finger to his lips to quiet him. "Noooooo! I unnerstan'. Dad's okay, David," and she pulled his pants off, tossing them on a chair. "I fix you fo bed, to sleep, an een sus

173

duermes, I wan you dream of fokking me, and mebbe fokking Julienne an me togedder." He closed his eyes as she pulled the sheet up to his chin, then stroked his crotch through the sheet with her hand. "Remember? You wan dad. You promise me."

David opened his eyes to see her smiling at him as she picked up her guitar case and headed for the stairs. He answered sleepily, "Yes, I remember."

****

Justine walked up to the piano, then rolled up the twenty dollar bill and used it like a tiny spyglass to look at David as he returned her gaze. The customer background noise in the Vooddo Room masked her low voice as she said, "I'm spying on you, David, and, sooner or later, I'm going to find out who you're fucking," She dropped the rolled up bill in the brandy snifter kitty. "I'm guessing it might be either Julienne or that little Mexican alleycat, but Julienne's really too good for you, and, if it's that alleycat, I hope she doesn't give you some disease that I don't want to catch."

David smiled professionally at Justine. "Don't worry, Justine. You wont catch anything from me, because I'll never again give you the opportunity to do so."

Justine smiled at him maliciously. "Don't forget, David, I can really mess things up between you and Val, not to mention with all your fans and friends here."

David finished a number at the keyboard and reached for his drink. "For a lady who lives with two men, one of whom has rich parents who are not happy about that situation, you're in an awfully fragile glass house and should not be threatening anyone with a rock fight."

Justine smirked. "Oh, you'll be back to sample more of this after your latest piece of fluff finds out you're hopelessly

174

committed to bachelorhood," and she turned and wiggled her derriere as she retreated to the group at the front end of the bar, a gauntlet of admiring males at nearby tables eyeing her tightly clad pants as she passed.

As if in shifts, Julienne slid off her barstool and, giving disapproving stares to the same males in the gauntlet who now admired her silk sheath molded figure as she made her way up to the piano, she turned her smile on David. "Well, at least I saw you give Justine your best customer quality smile, so I guess she must not have been harassing you too much."

David was playing Duke Ellington's *Satin Doll*, which had become an occasional theme song when Julienne entered the club or approached the piano wearing one of her trademark satin sheaths that draped so well on her lithe figure. "Justine's like a cat challenging a dog, more screetch than scratch."

Julienne opened her little bejeweled clutch purse and withdrew a twenty dollar bill. "Well, I saw her put something in the kitty, so I'm not to be outdone by her." As her hand extended toward the brandy snifter, her eyes narrowed and she looked at him warmly. "Please play *My Secret Love* for me."

David stopped playing and covered the top of the brandy snifter with his hand, saying abruptly, "No!"

Julienne blinked in surprise. "No, you wont play my request, or no, you don't want me to put this in the tip jar?"

David smiled at her painfully. "Both. No, I don't want you to continue tipping me because, regardless of what some people think, I am not a gigolo. And no, I don't want to play that song for you in front of everyone, because, as I thought we had agreed, I don't want to advertise our little secret to everyone here."

Julienne's brow furrowed as she bit her lower lip. "Don't you think it would look stranger for them to see you refuse my request?"

175

David looked at the end of the bar where everyone was staring at them with perplexed expressions. He removed his hand. She dropped the bill in the kitty and said, "Play anything." David began to play the song, *I Apologize,* and the pained expression on her face melted into a grateful smile.

As Julienne returned to the bar, Justine narrowed her eyes and asked, "What was that all about?"

Julienne remounted her barstool and sipped her grasshopper. "Oh, he didn't want to take my tip because he didn't know my request."

Justine pressed further. "He knows more show tunes than all of us put together. What in the world did you request?"

Julienne swallowed, licked her lips, and inhaled deeply before staring down the length of the bar. "Er, Chopin's Etude Number Twenty-Seven."

Jules looked at her in consternation. "Chopin never wrote an Etude Number Twenty-Seven."

Julienne downed the last of her grasshopper, shrugged, and said, "No wonder he didn't know it." Then she slid off her barstool and headed for the patio restrooms.

As she paced the courtyard flagstones beneath the starry night sky, she almost regretted that she had given up smoking a few years prior. She heard the swish of the door to the courtyard and sensed Justine's presence beside her.

Justine spoke slowly and sarcastically. "Chopin's Etude Number Twenty-Seven? I seriously doubt a classy young lady like you could make that mistake."

Julienne inhaled deeply and looked up at the stars. "You'd be surprised the kinds of mistakes a classy young lady like me can make."

Justine continued sarcastically. "Hmmmm. You mean like fucking a honky tonk pianist with no future or marriage plans?"

176

Julienne whirled around and stared at Justine so angrily Justine's eyebrows rose. "I've been of legal age for more than a few years, and who I fuck is nobody's business but my own! Not my parents business, and certainly not yours!" Then Julienne raised one eyebrow. "And I don't think Valentina Siciliana would take kindly to your calling her nightclub a honky tonk."

Justine chuckled. "Valentina Siciliana doesn't take kindly to anything I say."

Julienne maintained her angry stare. "And now you're trying to add me to that club?"

Justine sucked her lips in, looked down, then up again. "No. Not really. Despite the fact that I'm envious and jealous of rich people, for some reason I like you."

Julienne sighed. "Then I suggest you retract your claws and keep your insulting questions to yourself," and she re-entered the rear door to the club as Justine stared at the flagstones where Julienne had stood.

David saw Julienne return from the patio obviously agitated. She picked up her clutch purse from the end of the bar and approached him with an irritated look on her face. "I'm going to leave early, David, but I wanted you to know it has nothing to do with our earlier conversation."

David finished the number he was playing with an arpeggio. "What happened? I saw Justine following you." And his eyes followed Justine as she returned from the patio and joined the group at the end of the bar.

Julienne sighed and said, "Oh, nothing important. I'll tell you tomorrow night at your place." She turned to go, hesitated, and turned back to him with a questioning look. "I'm sorry, I shouldn't assume you'll see me on your night off. Did you want me to come over?"

David started to extend his hand to her, looked toward the bar, then rested his hand on the railing of the low fence around

177

the piano. "Of course I do. I still have to play your request for you."

She smiled, "Thank you."

David licked his lips. "Do you mind if Aurora joins us? I wrote some lyrics for one of her numbers, and she'd like to perform it for you and get your opinion."

Julienne blinked. "Sure. If that's what you want."

David smiled with relief. "Okay then, it's a date."

With slightly raised eyebrows, Julienne said, "Okay. Good night, David," and left, avoiding the group at the end of the bar.

****

Bernie Brill looked from Richard's eyes to David's eyes as Richard looked up from his piano keyboard. Bernie frowned questioningly. "I don't get it. Didn't that spik chick work with Jacob Yocum? Why can't he connect her with his record producer?"

David and Bernie sat on the two bar stools in front of Richards tiny spinet piano bar. David looked from Richard to Bernie. "She left Yocum's band several years ago and that's no longer an option."

Richard played the intro to *There's No Business Like Show Business*. "I told David you had worked for Julian Hoffman on that TV series, *N.O.P.D.*, and that Julian is not only a film producer, but also has a record label."

Bernie blinked and rolled his eyes. "Oh yeah! I forgot. I think it's called Bluetunes or something like that."

David pushed a Kraft envelope across the bartop toward Bernie. "We cut an acetate demo of her performing a song I wrote for her. Any chance you could get your friend, Julian, to listen to it?"

Bernie picked up the envelope and looked at it suspiciously. "I dunno. That son of a bitch still owes me money from the TV series." He looked at David. "So, I do this and who owes me? You or the chick?"

Richard had a facetious smile on his face. "Actually, I figured you'd be happy for the opportunity to return David's favor of showing me around the French Quarter, being's as how you were too busy at the time."

Bernie gave Richard a dirty look. "Oh yeah. I forgot about that." Bernie looked at David with a phoney smile. "Thank you for that, Mr. Wales. I'd be happy to bump your spik chick to the head of the line of all those kids waiting in a record producer's office for a break." Then his eyes narrowed as he smiled facetiously at David. "We even now?"

David smiled and sighed. "Most definitely, and I thank you profoundly on behalf of myself and the young lady."

Bernie gave Richard another dirty look as he slid off the barstool and carried the envelope through the swinging doors that separated The Inn Between from Stormy's Casino Royal, mocking Richard as he said, "Ta ta, ducky."

****

Aurora finished the song with a spectacular classical finish of Flamenco plucking and percussive techniques. David and Julienne both inhaled deeply and simultaneously applauded in genuine response to Aurora's performance. David nodded his head affirmatively. "You know, Aurora, aside from your fabulous guitar arrangement, your accent gives the English lyrics the right authenticity. I think it'll be a show stopper that you should put at the very end of your performance, because you're not going to be able to top that afterward."

Aurora's eyes widened with delight. "Es verdad. Por la performance, I wear a modern feminista version de la traje de

179

luces, de torero's 'sude o' lights.' Mebbe I even wear de sword on de side, or open mi guitar case and take de sword out furse befo de guitarra." She turned to look at Julienne seriously. "Did you lake id? Tell me de trude. I wan to know."

Julienne closed and opened her eyes as she nodded her smiling face up and down. "Aurora, you are beautiful, you are an immensely talented musician, and, with that song by David, you have an exceptional and timely performance number. I really think you should try to record it."

Aurora smiled excitedly at David. "Dad's next. David god a Hollywood agent to leesten to mi demo. We, how you say, 'cut' a acetate een de studio on Basin Streed wha he fran Gabrielle know. Eef de agent lake, dey record me een Hollywood."

Julienne smiled with surprise at David. "That's fabulous! When did all this happen, David? You must be a busier little bee than I ever imagined."

Aurora opened the tiny refrigerator and removed the champagne bucket with three champagne glasses tucked in the ice around the bottle. "Oh, he very busy bee, bud done worry, he save all he honey por tu." She proffered the bottle and corkscrew to David for him to open. "Add lease mos o id."

David rolled his eyes as he inserted the corkscrew in the bottle cork and Aurora handed Julienne a chilled glass. David popped the cork and said, "The important thing is that this could be a breakthrough for Aurora. Most recording careers begin with a single hit, and this might be hers."

Julienne raised her glass. "And this may be the breakthrough for David as a composer and lyricist. Let's not forget that." As David finished filling all three glasses, Julienne raised hers and said, "To success!"

David raised his glass. "To friendship!"

Aurora raised hers while she smiled warmly at Julienne. "To Amor! To love!"

David set his glass on a small silver tray on one side of the piano music rack as he sat on the piano bench and began to noodle on the keyboard. Julienne added her glass next to his and sat beside him. Aurora gripped the remaining end of the bench and ordered, "Stan up!" As David and Julienne raised slightly, Aurora pulled the bench toward her so there was enough room for all three to sit together with Julienne wedged tightly in the middle.

Julienne's eyes widened as she looked toward David. "Play some more Jerome Kern. I love Jerome Kern."

Aurora smiled at David. "Si, David. Teach me una canta de Jerome Kern."

David closed his eyes in thought while both women sipped their drinks, then began singing the song, *I've Told Ever Little Star*, focusing every other line on each of the two women.

When he had finished, he continued to play an accompaniment and nodded to Aurora who began singing directly to Julienne.

I tole every estellar
just how sweed I tink you are,
Why have no I tole you.

I tole ripples in de brook
just how grade I tink you look,
Why have no I tole you.

Frans eschuche si mi amore,
Siempre diga 'Si,'
Quieres reconocer,
Quieres confesar,

Possible tu desconomo
pero resabemos,
Por que no diga mi.

Aurora stared at Julienne with what appeared to be adoration, while Julienne broke eye contact long enough to take a deep sip of her drink. Then she looked at Aurora with an expression both perplexed and pleased, finally saying, "My God, Aurora, my Spanish isn't all that good, but, if you were a man, that would have definitely convinced me."

Aurora smiled at David. "Okay, David, we godda convince her. Teach me anodder Jerome Kern song."

David raised one eyebrow as he glanced between the two women, then began to accompany himself singing *We Could Make Believe.* After finishing it, he again nodded to Aurora who began to sing the refrain, putting her arm around Julienne's shoulder and slowly pulling the two of them together as she sang.

We could made believe I love you,
Only made believe dad you love me.
Otras find peace o mind in pretending;
Could no you? Could no I? Could no we?
Made believe our lips she's blending
En un besamos or two, or tree?
Mide as well made believe I love you,
Fo to tell de trude, I do.

With their lips only inches apart, Aurora kissed Julienne long and tenderly. Julienne did not flinch, but, instead, closed her eyes until, when their lips parted, she continued to stare into Aurora's eyes. Then she set her glass on the tray, closed her eyes, and shrugged her shoulders, saying, "My God it's getting warm, being squeezed so tightly in here."

Aurora stood up, gripped both Julienne's hands and pulled her to her feet and towards her. "David, play some mo' Jerome Kern while I dans wid Julienne."

David rose and turned on the sound system, saying, "I think this album has some Jerome Kern. I'm going to put it on and lie down for a little bit. As the music began to flow from the speakers, David lay down on one side of the bed.

Julienne looked slightly confused. "I don't know if I can lead."

Aurora placed her hand in the small of Julienne's back. "Dad's okay. I god de pants on. I lead."

Julienne's brow furrowed. "But I'm taller?"

Aurora smiled. "So, take dose stiletto heels off."

Julienne balanced herself leaning on Aurora's shoulder. "Good idea, particularly after all that champagne. What sadistic man invented stiletto heels?"

Aurora's gaze surveyed Julienne's torso up to her eyes. "De one who loves how grade you legs look in dem." As the music began, Aurora pulled Julienne closer and stared into her eyes as the male vocalist sang through the speakers the song, *The Night Was Made For Love.*

As they danced, Aurora held Julienne close enough that the contact of their breasts and pelvis' began to excite Julienne. She tried to gently separate their bodies with a slight pressure on Aurora's shoulder, but Aurora would not release the contact. When Aurora began to kiss her neck, Julienne's hand moved to the back of Aurora's neck intending to retrain her. Instead, to her surprise, her fingers spread through Aurora's glistening black hair and pulled her head closer, Julienne's eyes closing in momentary surrender to the feeling. In a final effort to repress her own feelings, Julienne tore herself away from Aurora, spinning in a complete circle and landing in the middle of the bed as she said, "My God, is it true, champagne is an aphrodisiac?"

183

Aurora lay down on the left side of her, facing her with her leg over Julienne's leg and her hand holding Julienne's chin. "Id's trude! Id's de bubbles, an' de boddle, id's a phallic symbol, no?" She kissed Julienne tenderly."

Julienne turned a Mona Lisa smile to David. "David, aren't you going to do something? This woman is trying to seduce me. Aren't you going to defend me?"

David turned to her, placing his leg over her right leg and his hand casually across her silk clad flat abdomen. "Do you want to be defended?"

Julienne closed her eyes as she felt blood rushing to her pubic area as a result of his hand on her abdomen. Then she felt Aurora's hand leave her chin and casually caress her left breast on its way to rest beside David's. Both her nipples suddenly became turgid and she felt an instinct to reach both her hands towards the groins of the people on either side of her. She fought the temptation, inhaled deeply, and opened her eyes to stare at the stars seen through the skylight above her head. Her lips felt dry and she licked them before asking, "David, is this what you want?"

Julienne felt Aurora's breast press against hers as Aurora emitted a single chuckle. "Id's verdad! Ees uno hombre. Done you lake wan two people love you, wan two people wan express dad love fo you. Id's de greatest ting een del monde."

Julienne closed her eyes again. "David?"

David moved his head forward and kissed her neck. "It's your call, Julienne."

A dove landed on the edge of the skylight and looked down at the three humans as the one in the middle moved her hands out to cover the groins of the outer ones, and the man moved one hand up to cup a breast, and the other woman moved her hand down to disappear into the delta below.

The Matador Song

words by William Karl Thomas

from the trilogy "The Piano Lover"

public domain folk music

Emin / F / Dmin / Amin

In Mex - i - co there lived a great ma-ta-dor who was known near and far so they say But

Emin / F / Dmin / Amin

be - hind hi bra - vo there lay some thing hal - lowed re - vealed in his words as he prayed and so he

Amin / C / Dmin / Amin

prayed I come to you now as the ho - ur grows late for I soon play with fate in the a -

G / Bdim

ren - a but this which o-thers may fi - nd so bold has a mean ing which is

C / F / G

not of - ten told on - ly you may know the fear that I hold and if I am consoled it's through La

C / G / C / D / E / Dmin / G

Maca ren-a For yours is the heart that se - es my tears and fe - els my fear as I pray And

C / Caug / Dmin / D / Dmin / G7 / C

now as I leave wont you bless all my pleas in your name La-Ma-ca-ren - a

Chapter Thirteen
THE SWEETNESS OF YOUTH

Julienne looked at Aurora's smaller naked body lying at right angles to hers, the back of Aurora's head resting on Julienne's abdomen with her eyes closed and the fingertips of both hands lightly flicking across her cherrystone nipples. Julienne's fingers lifted the shiny tresses of Aurora's long silky hair and let them fall like a black waterfall down to Julienne's abdomen. Julienne spoke to no one in particular. "I never thought I'd ever feel like this for a woman."

Aurora opened her eyes and looked up at her with a smile. "You mean have de hots fo a woman?"

Julienne blinked and continued to fondle Aurora's hair. "Yes, that too. To find a woman's body desirable, do things to her I could only imagine a man doing." Just then they heard David turn on the stall shower and both looked off to the corner of the loft simultaneously, then back to each other. "But, also, to feel tenderness. To enjoy watching her sleep, to blow cold air on her nipples and watch her hug herself for warmth."

Aurora giggled. "Dad was you? I tink, dere's no win een here."

Julienne caressed Aurora's shoulder and upper arm. "I guess this isn't new to you, but it's all strange and mysterious to me."

Aurora turned her head and stared intently at Julienne. "Why you scare to call id love? You brunette, he blonde, bud you love heem. You French, mi Chicana, bud you can no love me because I no have a prick?" She turned on her stomach, put one arm underneath Julienne's thighs and gripped her hip, then buried her chin in Julienne's mons veneris. "I love you, I even canta mi love por tu. Wid dis same tongue and lips, I kees every pard o' you body and make you cry out fo God over and over. Bud still, you can no love mi?"

Julienne touched Aurora's cheek tenderly and looked at her anxiously. "Until now, I've only experienced love with a man. We've had different pasts, different experiences. But, I guess what I feel` for you could be called love. Perhaps different from what I feel for David, but with much of the same tenderness, gratitude, and desire."

Aurora rose to her knees, placed her tongue just above Julienne's mons veneris, and licked a line up to her mouth before straddling her pelvis, hovering inches above her on hands and knees. She spoke in a husky whisper. "Say id!" They stared at each other intently. "Say you love me!"

Julienne closed her eyes, then opened them with an almost angry stare. "I'm afraid."

Aurora raised her head in surprise, resting her buttocks on Julienne's pelvis. "'Fraid o whad?"

Julienne stared at Aurora's perky breasts. "I guess I'm afraid there wouldn't be enough love to go around. That one of us would become possessive. That one of us might get jealous."

Aurora repressed a laugh. "I no jealous o you. You can no be jealous o mi."

Julienne raised her eyes to Aurora's. "Why not?"

Aurora looked at her in utter surprise. "David no love mi. He love you!"

Julienne looked at her in confusion. "How can you say he doesn't love you? It didn't look that way thirty minutes ago when he was pounding your butt so powerfully I thought your face was going to end up in my womb!"

Aurora placed both hands on either side of Julienne's face. "Mi Amor, David, he lust por mi. Pero, lo sentimiento solamento tengan por me ees, how you say, pity. He can no love la nina probre que abuso sexual. David, he love to fok mi, pero, he no love mi." She lowered her head to Julienne, kissed her mouth passionately, then held her face inches away. "He love you. Solamente tu." Aurora sat up, her hands still on Julienne's face, one finger tracing the full lips. "Ees possible, I de only wan who love you boat. He pity me. You...."

Julienne pulled Aurora's face down to her own. "I love you, Aurora. I truly do love you." And she kissed her again passionately.

As their lips parted, Aurora turned to lay beside her as Julienne's hand raised to caress Aurora's breast. Aurora closed her eyes and said, "Bud you only love mi mout." Then she opened her eyes and looked at Julienne's hand on her breast. "And mebbe mi chi chi."

Julienne tweaked the hard nipple between two fingers. "What do you mean?"

Aurora looked at her with a smile. "You scart o mi pussy."

Julienne cupped the perky breast lovingly. "Why do you say that?"

Aurora chuckled. "Each time you face ged near mi pussy, you look lake id gonna bide you." Aurora raised her eyebrows. "Mi pussy tase good. Ask David."

David approached the bed naked, drying his hair with a towel. "Ask David what?"

Julienne frowned at him. "Nothing that concerns you. Go away! You're interrupting a beautiful moment of discovery."

David turned toward the kitchenette. "Well, if nobody needs me, I guess I'll make some coffee."

Aurora reversed her position so their pelvis' were adjacent to each other's face. She ran her fingers through Julienne's soft pubic hair "I already discover you pussy. You wan discover mine?"

Julienne ran her fingers through Aurora's tightly curled pubic hair. "Ohhhhhh! Soixante neuf! Okay!"

Aurora looked perplexed. "Soixante neuf?"

Julienne turned her face to Aurora's. "That's French for sixty-nine."

A smile spread across Aurora's face. "Ahhhhhh! Si! Sixty-nine. I love id!"

Aurora raised and moved one leg behind her, causing her labia to part. Julienne's eyes widened and she made a sudden intake of air. Aurora asked, "Que passe?"

Julienne spoke with awe. "Your labia. It's edged with black."

Aurora giggled. "Dad's de Indian."

Julienne turned her face toward Aurora's. "I only saw mine with a mirror once. Does it have a black edge? I'm pure Creole, French and Spanish. Maybe there's some darker Spanish pigmentation."

Julienne made another sharp intake of air as Aurora's fingers parted Julienne's labia. Aurora suppressed another giggle. "No, bud lods o passionate pink an a few red hair." Aurora looked towards Julienne with a smile. "I tink wan o you ancestors was a wedback."

Julienne's eyebrows rose. "A Mexican?"

Aurora shook her head. "Nooooooo. He no swim de Rio Grande. He probably swim de English Channel."

Julienne chuckled. "So where'd you get your degree in anthropology?"

Julienne sucked in air abruptly as Aurora's finger traced a circle around Julienne's labia. Aurora answered smugly, "I won tell you where I god dem, bud I spend mauchos anos gedding two degrees, one in pussiology and one in penisology."

Julienne began to breath heavily as her fingers parted Aurora's labia wider and she lowered her head, her words beginning to sound muffled.. "And I bet you were the Valedictorian of your class."

David spooned coffee into the mid-section of the drip coffee pot, then sneaked a peek over his shoulder at the two women exploring each other. He inhaled deeply and heaved a sigh of relief.

****

Bernie Brill came through the swinging doors that connected Stormy's Casino Royal nightclub to The Inn Between, his little after hours back bar. He slapped one hand down on the tiny bar top on Richard Rose's piano, startling Richard who stopped playing abruptly and turned to him questioningly. "What?"

Bernie smiled smugly. "Good news for your Voodoo Hoodoo pianista friend. His spik girlfriend scored with that demo. Julian wants to fly her to Hollywood to record it. He thinks all the wetbacks in California will eat it up."

Richard smiled broadly, revealing a few discolored molars. "That's great! Do you want to tell him, or can I?"

Bernie closed his eyes momentarily and waved his hand distractedly. "You tell 'em. You're the one who hooked him up with me." Bernie eyed the figure of one of the strippers from the club being escorted to the piano bar by a male customer. "The news oughta help him score with her, and if she wants to thank me in person, she's welcome." Bernie wiggled his eyebrows suggestively at Richard.

Richard raised his eyebrows. "I'll be sure to relay that message to him." Then he turned to the couple who sat at his bar as he started playing.

Bernie patted the piano bar top lightly, then walked over to the main bar and leaned over it to whisper to Vito, the bartender. "Is Rose running a tab? I smell booze on him."

191

Vito leaned closer as he continued drying the glass in his hand. "He don't run no tab. He keeps a pint in his pocket and walks across the street on his break for a few blasts."

Bernie frowned, bit his lips, then said, "Lemme know if he drinks on the premises or if he gets sloshed."

Vito nodded affirmatively. "You got it, Boss."

Bernie straightened up. "Gotta go usher some more cooze onto the stage," then exited through the connecting door to Casino Royal.

Richard glanced back and forth between Bernie and Vito with concern.

****

Alex placed both hands on the checkered tablecloth and smiled as David and Dimitri pulled their chairs up to the table and admired the centerpiece of an artfully arranged bowl of fruit and vegetables. David asked, "Is that real or wax?"

Alex nodded affirmative. "It's real. Help yourself. A lot of it compliments the dishes on the menu."

Dimitri stared around the room as black women in 'mammy' costumes served a collection of affluent looking tourists. "Why is it you seem to love these 'kitchy' touristy places? I'd think those mammy costumes would offend you."

Alex picked up his artistically folded napkin and stared at it. "Actually, my mother worked here as one of those mammys. These fleur delis designed folded napkins were one of her contributions to the ambience. The white woman who opened this place thought of it as an opportunity for black women to make money, and she paid them well and allowed them to contribute everything from decor touches to recipes."

David respectfully opened his napkin. "I guess all that looks touristy is not necessarily guilty of crass commercialism."

192

Dimitri looked glum. "Well, most of it is. When tourists come in Aladdin's, I delight in shocking them."

David smiled. "And that's your trademark and why the management loves you, because the tourists love to be shocked."

Alex gestured with both hands. "Just like this place has a trademark of genteel elegance and great food. The eggs benedict are to die for. They make their own Hollandaise sauce from scratch."

David smiled inquisitively at Alex. "And to what do I owe the honor of being treated to a classy breakfast?"

Dimitri leaned toward Alex expectantly. "You're about to marry some rich old fart producer who's going to keep you in a life of luxury." After three seconds of silence, he countered, "You're about to marry some gorgeous young coke head who's going to keep you in the poor house the rest of your life." After another three seconds of the other two staring at him in silence, he frowned and concluded, "Don't tell me you're marrying some rich old female patron of the arts who thinks you're straight. You traitorous sellout, you."

Alex looked at David and the two chuckled, then he smiled at Dimitri. "No, but what I have to say does involve four old farts, or, at least, three old farts and a fartress."

Dimitri feigned distress. "Oh, my God. You've become a geriatric gang-banger."

Alex shook his head sideways. "No. Rather, I want to make the two of you a proposition."

Dimitri's face lit up. "Ohhhh! Finally, I get to be in a threesome with David."

David frowned at Dimitri.

Alex looked sternly at Dimitri. "Shut up, Dimitri. You're making David uncomfortable and making this more difficult than necessary." Alex inhaled deeply, then stared at the centerpiece. "As you both know, before I came home to help

193

my mom, I had some good press about my dancing career, and I was the choreographer in two successful musicals. The four elderly producers of those two shows like me and...."

Dimitri leaned forward and David raised his hand to restrain him, saying, "Shut up, Dimitri."

Alex blinked and continued. "The four elderly producers like me enough to trust my judgement, and, since my return to Broadway, they've said they'd look at any musical project I thought worthy enough to present to them."

David looked puzzled. "So what's your project, and what does it have to do with us?"

Dimitri looked at Alex anxiously. "You're not talking about the marionette extravaganza I told you about. You're not thinking of taking that to Broadway, are you?"

Alex tilted his head to one side and looked from one man to the other. "Not exactly. I'm talking about creating a musical based partly on the book for your extravaganza, with David as the composer and lyricist to turn it into a musical instead of a marionette show."

Dimitri looked somber. "There would be no marionettes in the show. I would simply be the writer of the book for your musical?"

Alex looked at Dimitri cautiously. "You would be the principal writer working from your original idea for your extravaganza, but I think David would have some useful input for the book, and I know I have some definite ideas to inject."

Dimitri looked crestfallen. "That sounds like something a long way away from my original idea."

Alex looked sympathetic. "Dimitri, you know you could never find a venue, much less funding, for your original idea. This is an opportunity for the core of your ideas to be realized, and in the grandest venue you could aspire to, Broadway."

Dimitri closed his eyes. "I dunno. Maybe you're right."

Alex looked at David. "David, I realize you don't know Dimitri's story line, but I can tell you that it involves a modern social fantasy, both gay and heterosexual and black and white characters, and it would probably be considered blasphemous by most Christian religions. Given that, and any complications of working with Dimitri and myself, would you consider working on such a project?"

David looked at Dimitri with a reluctant smile. "Well, I confess I do admire Dimitri's considerable talent, including his talent for satire and sarcasm." He looked at Alex. "And I have no reluctance to tell the truth no matter who it might offend. So, yeah, if Dimitri thinks he can work with me, I'm in."

"Okay, over breakfast, let's discuss a projected schedule for completion of the book outline and three to six of the key songs necessary for a presentation. But I'll leave Dimitri's explanation of his original idea for a later discussion between the two of you. Too many cooks can spoil the pot and I'm sure Dimitri will have enough stress dealing with the transition of a marionette show to a Broadway cast." Alex opened the menu, then closed it again. "I don't need that. I'm having the eggs Benedict." He tossed the menu in front of David. "If you don't care for eggs Benedict, they have an excellent quiche Lorraine."

****

Julienne gripped Aurora's hair on both sides of her head and pulled her face out of Julienne's crotch until Aurora's body slid across their mutual sweat and their lips met in a long tongue searching kiss. Aurora's face backed away with a mischievous smile. "See, I tole you. You pussy tase good!"

195

Julienne blinked and her tongue ran around her lips. "I didn't think about that. I was thinking how good your mouth tasted."

Aurora beamed with a smile. "Dad's you pussy. Id tase goooooooooood!"

Julienne's brow furrowed as her hands left Aurora's hair and traveled across her shoulders to cup both her perky breasts. "It's not fair. You seduce me into this threesome and, just when I'm getting addicted to it, you run away to Hollywood.."

Aurora kneeled between Julienne's legs. "Done worry. I be back soon. Until den, David lake de way you tase, too." Aurora turned toward David as he set the silver tray with coffee and three mugs on the bed and tied the sash of his seersucker robe "Done you, David?"

He sat on the edge of the bed and began putting milk and sugar in his coffee. "Don't I what?"

Aurora began to rub Julienne's mons veneris. "Lake de way her pussy tase."

Julienne covered Aurora's hand with her own to stop its movement. "Oh God, don't do that. I'm too exhausted to come again."

David smiled and sipped his coffee as he looked from one woman to the other. "The two of you are a carnal feast I never dreamed of tasting. To feast my eyes on your bodies, to smell the natural scent of your skin and hair, to hear your moans and sighs and praises to God, and to taste your sweat and the sweet essence of your orgasms. Oh yes, the two of you taste heavenly, and I am blessed among men."

Aurora stared at him entranced. "Aiiiiii chihuahua. You talk like a angel, like a fokking horny angel. I hope you nod too tired to come." She looked around until her eyes settled on a half empty champagne bottle on the table, then looked at him. "Eef I pour champagne en id, will you drink champagne from mi pussy?"

He smiled at her with raised eyebrows. "That sounds great, but, could I finish my coffee first. I need it for stamina?"

Aurora leaned forward and cupped both Julienne's breasts in her hands, smiling excitedly as she asked, "Hey, you wan me drink café from you pussy?"

Julienne winced. "My God, Aurora, I think that would be too hot."

Aurora shook her head negatively. "No, lemme show you," and she took a gulp of coffee and lowered her head to Julienne's crotch, sealing her coffee filled lips around Julienne's clitoris.

Julienne placed both hands on Aurora's head intending to push her away. She looked at David with an expression cross between surprise and panic. Then her eyes started to wander, her fingers began to stroke Aurora's hair, and a dreamy expression came over her face.

David set his cup on the tray and lifted the tray off the bed and onto the floor. "Are you okay, Julienne?"

Julienne started to breath deeply and her eyes opened wide as she looked at him. "My God, David! It's soooooo goooood! It's like liquid gold on my clit." She moved one hand toward him and clutched at the sleeve of his robe. In a husky pleading voice she said, "Please, take that robe off." She moved her hand to her mouth and closed her eyes as she began to lick her finger tips. "Come to me, give me your fingers, your tongue, your cock. Please, David, NOW!"

****

197

Alphonse set the coffees and beignets in front of David and Dimitri, then left. Dimitri picked up a beignet, tapped the powdered sugar off it, and set it uneaten on his plate. He wiped the powdered sugar from his fingers and nervously rubbed his hands together. "It all started a few months ago with a joke Richard Rose told in front of us all. He always likes to illustrate how unsophisticated Americans are."

David put cream and sugar in his coffee. "What was the joke?"

Dimitri looked skyward. "This Texan is trying to impress a Frenchman with how sophisticated Americans have become and he says that this best selling American book, *Lolita*, is about an adult male having a sexual affair with a thirteen year old." Dimitri wrinkled his nose and looked at David. "Which doesn't really make sense when you realize *Lolita* was written by a Russian."

David reached for a beignet. "True, but the story's laid in America and written for an American audience. But, go on, finish the joke, or is that it?"

Dimitri closed his eyes and gestured with both hands. "So the Frenchman looks down his nose at the Texan and asks, 'A thirteen year old....female,.....or male?' Which leaves the Texan wandering off muttering to himself 'How'd I let a fucking pervert frog top me?'"

David finished a bite of beignet, wiped powdered sugar from his lip, and said, "Sounds like Richard's droll humor, but how did that incite your story line? Don't tell me you created a story line about pedophilia?"

Dimitri squeezed his eyes shut. "No, no, no!" He opened his eyes and tilted his head. "It made me think about the gender twist in the punch line, that unexpected option that the answer to a question might be an unexpected gender. Aside from the fact that Nabakov wrote about pedophilia, I took the idea of the unexpected gender choice and applied it to other issues. It's certainly a theme that comes up a lot in the gay world. A gay male having to explain to a potential female partner that it's not her, it's him. A drag queen having to explain to a male who's attracted to her that she also just happens to have some male genitalia."

David washed a mouthful of beignet down with some coffee. "Okay, so how did you apply the gender twist?"

Dimitri winced. "Well, before I get to that, lemme give you the premise of it all. After you hear this you may just pass on the whole thing, anyhow. This is a story about a French Quarter nightclub pianist who's in love with two girls, one who's cultured and one who's from a counter culture."

David's brow furrowed. "My, what a strange premise, how unique, how unusual. That couldn't possibly have been drawn from the life of anyone we know."

Dimitri held up both his hands in front of him defensively. "Now, before you get angry, just remember that it was you who decided to get involved with a high class American girl and, at the same time, a foreign immigrant with a sordid past and a confused gender identity."

David raised one eyebrow. "And just how many people have been keeping tabs on this oversexed piano player?"

Dimitri rubbed the side of his nose without making eye contact. "Not that many, really. Just his employer, his employer's waitress, and a stalker who lives on the third floor."

David closed his eyes, sighed, then looked at Dimitri sternly. "Unnnh hunnnh. So, tell me more about this torrid twisted trio."

Dimitri sipped his coffee daintily, then set the cup down. "Well, the young man faces more of a challenge than you might think, because the immigrant girl he loves is not really a girl, but a transexual performer in the gay club where he works."

199

David gave a pained smile. "Well, it's nice to know you used a little imagination, but very little."

Dimitri looked at David inquisitively. "Weren't you the least bit attracted to Princess? I mean, I practically threw her at you and you just let that disgusting old limey pervert steal her away."

David looked concerned. "Dimitri, does Princess know you're using her as your avatar?"

Dimitri leaned his head on one hand and stirred his coffee abstractedly. "I guess your term is right, she is my avatar. I kept hoping you'd screw her, maybe she could lure you to my apartment while I hid behind a peep hole and watched, or, after you screwed her I could seduce her and somehow share that vicarious experience." He pushed his coffee cup forward, folded both his arms on the table, and buried his face in them, his words muffled as he whimpered, "Ohhhhh. I am so totally fucked up!"

David looked at nearby customers who stared and Alphonse who discreetly looked away. "Oh, come on, Dimitri. The mind police are not going to arrest you for having fantasies. We all have them."

Dimitri raised his face, sniffling as he dabbed the tears from his eyes with his napkin. "Only yours are more socially acceptable and realistically attainable." He threw out his hands in despair. "I, on the other hand, have to fall for the straightest guy there is in a French Quarter full of gorgeous gay men. How's that for self fulfilling defeatism?" He set the napkin down. "And, no! Princess may have guessed I was attracted to you, but she didn't know I was trying to hook you up with her." He looked at David again. "But, really David, didn't you feel anything for her. She is so irresistibly juicy."

David threw his hands out in despair and rolled his eyes. "I don't know, Dimitri. Yes, she is gorgeous, and no straight man could look at that ass without momentary visions of lust.

But, I've been very busy recently, not to mention frequently sexually sated and exhausted." He closed his eyes and tilted his head from side to side. "I dunno. Maybe at another time, under other circumstances."

Dimitri shrugged his shoulders. "Well, thank you for that. At least I don't have to think I was fantasizing something totally impossible."

David caught Alphonse's eye and pointed to his and Dimitri's cups. "Okay. If you're through crying in your café au lait, can we get back to the book plot? Horney pianist digs sexy transexual and beautiful straight girl. What next?"

Dimitri took a piece of paper from his coat pocket and unfolded it. "Alex wrote down a few 'must haves.' For starters, he insists on one role casting. He wants Gabriel as a principal in the show, and he wants him cast as the angel."

David almost did a spit take with his coffee. "The angel?"

Dimitri smiled for the first time since they sat down. "Yeah! Originally I cast the angel as this Nancy little queen with a squeaky voice like Tinker Bell. But Alex sees the angel like Louis Armstrong, and nobody looks more like Louis Armstrong than Gabriel. And get this, the angel's name is The Angel Gabriel, and he shows up in the club looking for work with his horn."

David frowned. "You mean like one of those old mile long horns?"

Dimitri shook his head sideways as his eyes popped open. "No, no! It's a beat up old cornet, and he's a jazz player."

A smile began to spread across David's face. "I like it. I like it."

Chapter Fourteen
A CRISIS OF FAITH

Zoe hung up the hand crank on the wall phone and said, "She's on her way down," then began to light table candles. Pete went to open the front doors and David stepped through the little fence gate to sit at the baby grand piano on the dias. Val stepped through the patio doors into the room and was about to speak, until her eyes fell on David at the piano. She said, "Oh, David. You're here." Zoe finished lighting the three foot high black bar candles and stood looking at Val in surprise. Val looked at her as if remembering something she had forgotten, then said, "Let the games begin!"

David began playing *Twelfth Street Rag* and Val did something unusual. Instead of sitting at her table immediately, she walked a few feet toward David and said, "David, stop playing. Come over to my table." She turned towards the table and stopped, sensing that David was frozen with surprise. She looked at him over her shoulder, saying, "Now," then approached and sat at her rear corner table. David arrived and stood at attention a few feet from her. Val was obviously trying to appear non-threatening, even though Zoe staring at her from ten feet away did not help. "Sit down, David. I want to talk to you."

David sat with a concerned expression. "Is everything okay, Val?"

Val tapped the package of Russian cigarettes with the long blood red fingernail of her left index finger as she stared at the Cyrillic lettering on its red and gold label   "Well, yes, everything's alright, at least here at the club, that is." Then she looked at him cooly as she folded her hands on the table. "David, do you like your job here?"   She blinked and continued before he could answer. "I mean, did you plan to stay here indefinitely, or did you have some ambitious future plans?" Again she continued before he could answer. "I mean, I left you a little something in my will, but the bulk of my estate goes to the church and this building goes to Zoe. You need to think of your future, and where you might want to spend it."

David swallowed hard. "Val, am I being fired?"

Val's eyes widened. "Oh, no, David! I'm sorry, I didn't mean to frighten you." She closed her eyes briefly and bit her lip, then looked at him seriously. "It's just that, there's someone in the patio who wants to talk to you. When you talk to them, I want you to consider what they say seriously. They will offer you choices, and the choice you make may be a great opportunity....or something you'll regret the rest of your life."

David looked scared. "Who's in the patio?"

Zoe scowled at him and spoke angrily. "Shut up, David. This lady could have you whimpering on your knees begging for mercy, but, instead, she's offering you choices. Shut up and be grateful!"

Val gave Zoe a pained smile, closed her eyes and nodded her head once, which caused Zoe to fold her arms, bite her lip, and look up at the ceiling. Val looked David in the eye and spoke more compassionately than he had ever heard her. "Go talk to them, David, and, whatever you decide, I will pray for your happiness and good fortune." David hesitated. Val picked up the Russian cigarettes with one hand and waved him away with the other. "Go. Now! Talk to them."

The patio was lit more by moonlight than the few coach style lanterns under the overhang of the patio apartments. The white hair of the man in the business suit shone bluish in the moonlight, his back to David, the sheen of his sharkskin suit bespoke wealth. Although two inches shorter than David, the man turned to face him with strength and confidence, the hesitation before extending his hand a signal to be on guard. The man spoke with a deliberate cadence to his voice, obviously measuring his words carefully, like an adversarial lawyer in court or a man carefully controlling his anger. His handshake was strong, twice vigorously, and a hesitation before release. "David Wales, correct?"

David felt like he was in some Western cowboy gunfight and wondered if he should be looking at surrounding balconies for snipers targeting him. "Yes, sir. And who, may I ask, are you?"

The man maintained an unblinking eye contact with David. "I'm Rene DeVille, Julienne's father," and he stared at David searching for meaning in David's reaction.

But David remained calm and allowed the corners of his mouth to hint at a smile and his head to nod ever so slightly. "Then, it is a pleasure to meet you, sir."

DeVille made his words sound like a challenge. "Is that so?"

David looked up at the moon, then back into DeVille's eyes. "Yes, sir. I, along with everyone here at The Voodoo Room, am very fond of Julienne."

DeVille looked at him from head to toe, then back into his eyes. "Very fond, you say. Would that fondness include caring about what's in Julienne's best interest?"

David looked at DeVille from head to toe and back into his eyes, nodding his head slowly in the affirmative. "I most certainly care about what I consider to be in Julienne's best interest."

DeVille's eyes never left David's. "Well, I would consider it in Julienne's best interest if you would listen to and accept an offer I'm making you. Let's call it an offer of employment at a Miami radio station I own. You'd make four times what you make here, twice what anyone at that station makes, and have a two year contract with two more two year options with raises. You could chose from a half dozen job titles, or you could create a radio show of your own, possibly a program of piano music. That is your principal talent, isn't it, playing the piano in nightclubs?"

David understood DeVille's offer, but felt compelled to challenge him. "I didn't know my musical talents were so well known or appreciated, but I fail to see how your offer would benefit Julienne. She appreciates my musical talents and I'm sure she would regret the loss of them were I to leave."

DeVille raised one eyebrow and stared at David intensely. "Your acceptance of my offer would benefit my daughter because you'd be accepting an agreement to neither see her again nor tell her who made the offer." DeVille smiled smugly. "And as for missing your talents, those are replaceable from people with far greater credentials and who are far more appropriate company for my daughter."

David looked up at the moon again, and back into DeVille's eyes. "For one, I can neither accept your offer nor the conditions that accompany it. For two, your daughter and I are both of legal age and free agents regarding whose company we keep. And for three, I would invite you to get to know me better before judging me so harshly, because I truly have your daughter's best interests at heart."

DeVille's eyes narrowed as he glared at David. "I have inquired and know enough about you to be convinced my daughter would be far better off without you in her life. Be forewarned, young man, I will not allow my daughter to fritter away her inheritance on expensive gifts like grand pianos, gold watches, and silver tea services. You'd be far wiser and richer to accept my offer in Miami than to think you can fleece Julienne of her money."

David sighed and looked at DeVille with a sad smile. "The only silver tea service I own I inherited from my mother, and Julienne loaned me her grand piano temporarily in exchange for piano lessons, the kind of pastime a proper young lady acquires when she's keeping the appropriate company of intelligent and cultured people. If you have no faith in me, sir, then have a little more faith in your daughter's taste and choices."

DeVille inhaled deeply and his throat rumbled as he exhaled. "It's your choice to decline my offer that we both will regret, just as Julienne will regret ever knowing you." DeVille turned and started to exit toward the alley beside the building leading to the street. "Good day to you, sir."

David watched him disappear down the alley, then entered the swinging doors to the club to see Val and Zoe staring at him expectantly. Zoe spoke hopefully. "Miami?"

David shook his head negatively. Zoe sucked air into her lungs in surprise, and Val slouched back into her chair with a concerned expression. Zoe spoke angrily. "You stupid, David!"

Val leaned forward and slapped her hand on the table, glaring at Zoe, then looked at David with a steely eyed expression. "Okay, David. You made your choice, but accept the responsibility that goes with it." Val shook her head negatively. "Don't hurt anyone." Then she shook her head positively. "Do the right thing and I will pray for your protection."

Suddenly David began to feel the weight of DeVille's words, and the responsibility of his decision.

Val picked up her *New Orleans Times Picayune* and snapped it open noisily. "Now get your ass up on that piano bench and lure some customers in here," and she focused her attention on the paper.

****

207

As the two couples entered the slate roofed ancient looking one story building at Bourbon and St. Phillip Streets, Richard Rose asked David in a hoarse whisper, as if there were ghosts within who might hear him, "Did the pirate Jean LaFitte really own this blacksmith shop?"

David selected an empty table near the coal burning open forge at the center of the room and pulled out a chair for Julienne. "Well, like most French Quarter history, that story is long on legend and short on specifics, but the building pre-dates the American Revolution and would have been the kind of central location out of which La Fitte fenced his pirate's booty."

Richard pulled out a chair for Princess who looked around with a doubtful expression and asked, "Why is it so dark in here?"

Julienne's eyebrows raised as she looked at David, who said, "I'm told it's because there's no electricity in here and the only lighting is the forge and the table candles."

Now Princess's eyebrows raised. "No electricity?"

An older man, slightly stout and slightly bald, walked from behind the bar to stand beside David as David sat at the table. David looked up at him and said, "I'm told that there's no electricity because Harold Bartle, the owner here, had his electricity cut off for non-payment, then decided to leave it off and precipitate a feud with the electric company."

Harold smiled down at David. "That's sorta correct." Then he looked at the others. "But, you gotta admit, it does kinda enhance the authentic atmosphere."

David gave Harold a pained smile. "And it also helps to hide any undesirable details."

Harold squinted and wrinkled his nose. "Don't worry, the undesirable details don't usually show up until after two A.M. when most of the bars close and the die hard drunks arrive."

David's gaze circled the group. "Harold, this is Julienne deVille, Princess Pocahontas..."

Harold blinked at Princess. "I know Princess. Hello sweetheart." Harold pursed his lips, put his hand on David's shoulder, and squeezed it. "So, David, you finally decided to join our team."

David sighed. "Princess is here with Richard. Richard Rose, this is Harold Bartle, owner of this historically dark establishment."

Harold chuckled. "At least 'til the end of the month when the next mortgage payment is due." Then he looked at Richard and his smile dropped. "You're old!"

Richard blinked and his eyes widened. "Well, sir, I do think you have a few more years than me."

Harold's eyes widened. "I have more hair than you, too, but that's not enough to get someone as beautiful as Princess."

Richard's jaw dropped, and he was about to speak again when David interrupted, looking up at Harold and saying, "Harold, why don't you go back to the bar and send one of your polite well mannered young waiters to take our order?"

Harold looked from David to Richard, then back to David, who leaned slightly towards him and said, "Now!"

Harold looked at the table candle in it's ruby red glass jar and nodded his head affirmatively. "Yes, yes. Why don"t I do that? In fact, I will." And he turned and returned to the bar.

Richard's eyes, still wide with surprise, circled the table. "Why, why, the nerve of that cheeky old faggot!"

Princess dismissed him with a wave of her hand. "Oh, he's just like that. He comes into Aladdin's from time to time."

Richard looked at her with concern. "He comes on to you?"

Princess wrinkled her nose. "He dishes with all the drag queens, but you can tell he really wants to hook up with the

209

butch waiter boys. I feel sorry for him. He's just a lonely old man."

Richard looked around the room. "A RICH lonely old man."

David tilted his head to the side. "Maybe, once upon a time. He's related to the Claibornes, one of the black sheep of the family, and he's talented, plays the piano fairly well and has had several successful bars and restaurants, but alcohol and other vices keep him from ever holding onto the fortunes he's made."

Julienne looked at David. "My father financed some of his early ventures, but, after a few foreclosures, he began to treat him like a leper."

The waiter came, took their orders, and left. David put his hands on the table and looked at Richard. "So, Richard, knowing that I don't like to waste my night off drinking alcohol, why did you insist we come here tonight?"

Richard managed a smile. "First, I kept hearing about this place and wanted to see it." He looked around the room. "And now that I've seen it and been insulted by the owner, I am thoroughly unimpressed." Everyone laughed. "And second, I brought us here so we could make a toast."

Julienne's brow furrowed questioningly. "And what are we toasting?"

Richard smiled broadly as he reached into his coat pocket and pulled out a tan Kraft envelope. "This!"

Princess looked at the envelope curiously. "What is it?"

Richard waved the envelope slowly as he stared at David. "Well, I haven't opened it, yet, but I held it up to the light and can see what's in it. Besides, Bernie Brill, who gave it to me to give to David, told me what it is."

David gave Richard a pained smile. "Okay, enough with the buildup. Gimme that!" And he snatched the envelope from Richard's hand. He peeled back the flap and dumped the contents into his opened hand. Out came a single 45rpm record with a blue label.

Julienne gasped. "Is that Aurora's record with David's song on it?"

Richard smiled at her and nodded affirmatively. "Bernie Brill said that Julian Hoffman said it's selling great in California, it's already listed in the trades among the top 100, and he thinks it'll be on The Hit Parade radio show within the month." He smiled at David. "How's it feel to see your name on a record label, David?"

They all watched David's face as he stared at the record initially with a smile, but the smile slowly faded to a frown. Julienne asked, "What's wrong, David?"

David bit his lip and set the record on the checkered table cloth. "Yes, it would be nice to see my name on a record label. But it's not there."

Julienne snatched up the little single and stared at the label. "What? That's impossible. Lemme see. Here it is." And she held the record closer as she read the small print. "*The Torero's Prayer*, performed by Aurora Alonzo, English lyrics by......Aurora Alonzo."

Julienne leaned back and the three stared in shock at David, who stared at the ruby red table candle. Richard was wide eyed again. "That bloody little bitch! How could she? She ripped you off, David!"

David sighed, then looked at Julienne and spoke softly. "Yes, I guess she did."

The waiter arrived and set their drinks in front of them, then left. Richard wrapped his hand around his Cuttysark on the rocks and looked up at David. "Well, then, what should we toast? To plagiarism? To theft? To betrayal?"

David looked at his drink and shook his head negatively. "Nooooo. Maybe we should toast to life's bitter lessons."

Julienne stared at the candle and waggled her jaw sideways before saying, "I don't know. I think I'd rather vote for betrayal."

Princess looked like she was on the verge of tears, then she tapped the base of her Shirley Temple cocktail glass on the table and looked up resolutely. "Oh come on, folks. Let's not cry over spilt talents. David lost his first record label byline, but Aurora lost something far greater. She lost the best damn songwriter she could ever hope to have, and she'll never be able to top the first song that David wrote for her. But David's got a lot more great songs in him. So let's toast David's future songs, future record label bylines, and future success."

Richard smiled warmly at Princess. "That's the spirit, sweeties. My sweet Princess can appreciate the cup half full, the dark cloud's silver lining, the..."

Julienne gave a pained smile as she interrupted him. "Okay, okay, Richard, we get the positive picture here." She raised her glass. "To David's future success!"

They all clinked their glasses together over the candle and chorused, "To future success!"

****

Julienne hesitated before the cut glass framed door of the palatial mansion while the street cars clanged their way through the wide neutral ground of the St. Charles Avenue Garden District. She was about to lift the huge brass knocker below the cut glass window in the center of the door, then spied Nettie through the glass approaching. She felt somewhat relieved that Nettie, rather than her mother, was answering the door. Nettie's impeccably neat black and white maids uniform and the gentleness of her mature black smiling face beneath the white lace cap somehow carried Julienne back to her less complicated childhood. As Nettie opened the door and spoke,

212

her soft warm voice was reassuring and calming to Julienne. "I see you through the glass, Miss Julienne. Yo' father's waiting for you in the study." Nettie shut the door behind Julienne and retreated down the carpeted hallway.

As Julienne entered the book lined study, she didn't see her father, despite the brilliance of the massive crystal chandelier. Then she saw a plume of smoke rise from a maroon leather chair facing the garden seen through leaded glass windows. She asked questioningly, "Daddy?"

Rene deVille rose, Cuban cigar in hand, and looked at his daughter with a concerned almost doubtful expression. Julienne inhaled deeply and tried to calm her voice. "Daddy, thank you for seeing me. I have a few questions, if you don't mind."

DeVille leaned toward an end table beside the chair and tapped the ash off his cigar into a huge copper ash tray. Without looking at her, he asked, "Concerning?"

Julienne was surprised that he had not moved toward her, not smiled, and not embraced her. Her apprehension increased as she moved toward the two sofas facing each other before the fireplace. "A number of things." She leaned against the mantlepiece with the portrait of deVille's menacing looking father in law above it, and turned her head sideways to look at her father. "I've seen our family tree on the wall in your office, but the names and birthplaces are all French and Spanish. Weren't any of our ancestors from above the English Channel?"

He picked up the copper ashtray and tapped his cigar against its rim again. "No, Julienne, you are pure Creole, a mixture of French and Spanish aristocracy. Something of which you should feel very proud. Why do you ask?"

Julienne opened her mouth to speak, but thought better of it. She pushed away from the mantlepiece and turned toward the sofa. "It's not important." She turned her head to look at

213

him again. "Another thing I wanted to ask you about is David Wales."

DeVille carried the copper ashtray with him toward the fireplace, gestured for her to sit on one sofa, then sat on the opposite one. "And what about your David Wales?"

She clasped her hands and learned forward as her eyes narrowed slightly. "David says you threatened him."

DeVille looked at the cigar as he rolled the lit end around the bowl of the copper ashtray in his other hand. "Not so. I never threatened him."

She looked at her hands, then up at him. "Perhaps I phrased that incorrectly. David said you sounded threatening. Maybe you were threatening me."

DeVille looked at her with a hurt expression. "No, child. I would never threaten you."

Julienne chuckled. "Well, that's a bald faced lie. You used to threaten me concerning every major purchase I made and every boy I ever dated."

DeVille squeezed his eyes shut and shook his head sideways. "That was different. That was discipline, and before you were of age."

She straightened up and leaned against the back of the sofa. "That's right. I did come of age. I earned my Ph'd in art. Despite the loans and extensions on the loans you made to my gallery, I did pay them off completely. And, concerning my desire to be independent, I made a success of my gallery. The artists I've promoted and invested in, despite your concern that they were from modest origins or gay or prone to vices, have become known internationally and earned me substantial profits." She leaned slightly forward. "I appreciate all you've done for me, but I am of age, I am independent, I am successful, and no one, yourself included, should presume to discipline me, or David, or dictate our choices."

214

He puffed on the cigar, then blew a smoke ring and watched it rise in the air. "Of course neither I nor anyone else has any right to dictate your choices, Julienne, but I too am of age, independent, and at least as successful as you, and I have the right to question the wisdom of your choices, and to refrain from supporting them if I think they're not in your best interests."

Julienne glared at him. "Indeed, you are AT LEAST as successful as me. I've heard you be facetious in doing business with others, but this is the first time I recall you being so with me." She looked down, took a deep breath, and raised her eyes to again glare at him. "And what support have I asked for which you'd rather withhold?"

He ripped the cigar from his mouth and returned her angry stare. "Don't play innocent with me, Julienne. There's that building loan to his landlord, that outrageously expensive piano and watch you bought him, and I'm told you're constantly giving him cash in front of everyone in that Voodoo Room nightclub."

She leaned forward and narrowed her eyes at him. "That building loan was my idea, and Mrs. Saucier has made all her payments on time. That watch was just like the one I gave you at the same time. That piano was so he could give me lessons, but he refused to accept ownership of it and regards it as my property. " She leaned back and looked up at the chandelier. "And he even asked me to stop putting cash tips in the kitty on his piano so people wouldn't think he's a gigolo."

DeVille stubbed out his cigar in the ashtray and stood up abruptly. "Well I think he's a gigolo, and I keep waiting for the other shoe to drop, for him to get you to buy him his own nightclub or an expensive car or pay his gambling debts which may or may not really exist."

Julienne stood up and raised her hands toward her father. "Good Lord, daddy. David has never asked me for anything. He doesn't gamble. He barely drinks, and he has no vices."

DeVille looked down, then up at her with almost pity. "Oh yes he does. He is a womanizer of the worst kind. I've heard about women throwing scenes over him in that club." He looked down, sighed, then up at her again. "Did you know he keeps the company of that horrible old Parisian whore, Justine?" He took a step toward her and extended his hands. "I worry about you, baby. Not just your money, but your reputation, your safety, disease. You know, it's just as easy to fall in love with a rich man as with a poor one. There are plenty of my banker friends with handsome educated sons who have no need to steal your money."

Julienne stepped back, pressing her hands against her sides. Now she looked at him with pity. "You forget, daddy, that I've met many of your banker friend's sons, and if you're concerned about young men who are womanizers, gamblers, and vice ridden, you don't have to look any further than that lot. Next to them, David is a prince among men."

DeVille lowered his hands and clenched them into fists. "A prince of thieves, perhaps."

Julienne reached down to the sofa to retrieve her purse. "Tell me, daddy, how is it you know so much about David, and Justine, and my social life in the French Quarter? Do you have me followed?"

DeVille unclenched his fists and looked at her almost pleadingly. "Oh baby, you know I own dozens of banks and corporations across five states. Surely you realize I couldn't have acquired all that without a vast information network."

Julienne tapped her thigh with her purse as she turned toward the door. "A spy network, and to spy on your own daughter."

216

He shrugged. "Especially my own daughter. Julienne, you're worth more to me than all those banks and corporations. Naturally I want to protect my most valued possession."

She bit her lip, then looked at him over her shoulder. "Well, daddy, to refresh your memory, I am of age, independent, and no one's possession. If you value my happiness and future contact with me, please respect my privacy, my freedom of choice, and my relationship with David Wales. He may be a prince of thieves to you, but the only thing he's stolen is my heart."

DeVille's eyes glistened. "And if he breaks it?"

Julienne raised one eyebrow. "Don't worry. If he breaks it, you wont have to do anything. I'll kick him in the balls myself."

DeVille smiled through his tears as she walked through the study door, down the hall, and out the cut glass windowed front door.

Chapter Fifteen
DOORS OPEN, DOORS CLOSE

When Julienne entered The Voodoo Room, Justine was already ensconced at the front end of the bar, flanked by her two young paramours. Julienne waved Armand aside to make room so she could sit next to Justine, then flopped her purse noisily on the bar and turned to face Justine. "Justine, do you know my father, Rene deVille?"

Justine was caught off guard. "I know OF your father. But I don't move in such rarified social circles."

Pete caught Julienne's eye as he shook a grasshopper cocktail glass questioningly. Julienne nodded positively, bit her lip, then asked Justine, "Would you know if Valentina Sciciliana knows my father?" Justine looked pensive as she remained silent, but Julienne persisted. "Well, does she?"

Justine closed her eyes, raised her head as if in thought, and said, "Valentina Sciciliana knows a lot of important people. It is possible that they were acquainted a long time ago."

Julienne looked at her hopefully. "In what capacity."

Justine opened her eyes and turned to look at Julienne. "The other night you asked me to respect your privacy. Not that any love is wasted between Val and me, but, in this case, I have to respect her privacy."

Julienne's brow furrowed. "Not even if it involves my father?"

Justine turned back to her drink. "Especially if it involves your father. You'll have to ask Val that one yourself."

Julienne picked up her drink as fast as Pete set it down. "I don't think I'm that brave. I heard Zoe say she could make a dog whimper with her evil eye. I'm not superstitious, but I don't want to get on her bad side for a lot of reasons."

Justine turned to Julienne. "Well, I'm trying very hard to respect your privacy." Then she raised her eyebrows and smiled broadly. "But if you'd like to elaborate on those reasons, I'm all ears."

Julienne sat up straight and held one hand in front of her mouth. "You speak no evil, I speak no evil."

To Julienne's surprise, she heard Aurora's happy giggling voice. She turned to see Aurora placing her own hands on her eyes, then ears, then mouth. "See no evil, hear no evil, spik no evil. Yes! I god dose monkys on mi boo-shelf." Aurora threw her arms around Julienne's waist so hard, Julienne slid off the stool to stand in Aurora's embrace. "Aiii, chihuahua, mi amour, I meees you so much," and Aurora proceeded to hold Julienne's face in both hands and kiss each cheek.

Justine sat up straight and stared at the two women. "Well, who needs to speak. Actions speak louder than words."

Julienne placed her hands on Aurora's shoulders and gently extricated herself from Aurora's embrace. "Aurora, I think you need to talk to David."

The two looked toward David who had spotted them and was leaving the piano headed for the patio doors. Aurora turned to Julienne with an effusive smile. "Yes, I go talk wid heem now, bud later we all go celebrade, mi treed, anywhere you lake. An I tell you all aboud Hollywood. Eeees mucho glamoroso." And she headed for the patio doors.

David stood in the patio and heard the swinging doors whisper closed behind him, then turned to face Aurora. As their eyes met, hers widened along with her ecstatic smile, his narrowed beneath a questioning brow. She flew to him and, wrapping her arms around him, exclaimed, "Mio Dios! David, id's sooooo good to see you. I meees you tanto mucho." Her eyes were closed as she hugged him tightly, then she opened them as she moved away just far enough to grip both his hands and smile up at him.

David's expression was bland with only one eyebrow slightly raised. "Aurora."

Her smile softened as her eyebrows began to question. "So, you heard? Our song ees la ultima! Id top de chards!"

David's eyebrow rose higher. "Our song? I seem to recall that I wrote the lyrics and somebody else wrote the original music, but the only name I see as composer and lyricist on the records and sheet music is yours."

She shrugged, frowned, closed her eyes and shook her head sideways. "Ohhhh, David. Dad's jus' Julian. He did dad." Her eyes opened as she looked at him apologetically. "He say id bedder fo' de marquee. Besides, de musica, she's in, how he say, 'publico domain.'"

David frowned. "I don't recall writing those lyrics fifty-nine years ago, which is the time the copyright laws require to declare something to be in public domain."

She squeezed his hands and shook them slightly. "Ohhhh, David, why you care aboud dese tings? I'm back. We togedder. You take care por mi, I take care por tu. Eees verdad?"

David released her hands and folded his in front of him. "I think taking care of me requires putting my name as lyricist on all media, and returning any royalties collected as lyricist to me."

She turned her palms up and shrugged. "Julian won do dad. He say I godda lock dis song in fo de Aurora image. He say, after all, id was mi idea to ride de worts."

David glared at her questioningly. "So, if Julian asks me to write another song for you, say words and music, then that song belongs to Julian because it was his idea?"

She turned her hands over and shook them side to side as she winced. "No, no! I no say dad. I know ees your worts."

221

David raised one eyebrow again. "So, this is all Julian's fault. He has the power to make you lie, to make you steal?"

Aurora pressed her palms on her thighs, looked down, and bit her lower lip. "Id's in de paper I sign wid heem. Heee's mi managerio. He say all tings por la musica, records, radio, TV, even por la cinema." She looked up at him imploringly as her hands moved towards his.

David moved his hands behind him and locked two fingers together. His eyebrow lowered and he looked at her regretfully. "You were once owned by a madam. Then you were owned by El Gato. Now you're owned by Julian. And all of them made you screw someone. This time you're screwing me, but not in a nice way."

She put her hands together with locked fingers and looked up at him with a pained expression. "Please, David. Once I tole you aboud my pass, and you say 'please done.' Now I beg you, David, please done."

David closed and opened his eyes. "As I recall, you insisted on telling me the truth. As painful as it was to hear, I ultimately appreciated your doing so. As painful as it may be for you to hear now, there is no 'you and I' as long as Julian is in control with the power to make you plagiarize and steal from me."

Tears welled in Aurora's eyes. "I done know all you say, David, bud I done wanna hurd you and I done wanna lose you. I done wanna lose my novella dream."

David looked down sadly. "All novellas have an end, and some closest to reality have a sad ending." He turned and walked toward the patio doors.

The tears streamed down Aurora's face as her hands raised pleadingly. "Please, David, done go. Please!"

As the patio doors closed, Aurora closed her eyes and lowered her hands to her sides. The only sound in the patio was her sobbing which, along with her tears, slowly ebbed until she turned and headed for the alleyway that led to the street.

****

Julienne's spike heels echoed throughout the vast emptiness of St. Louis Cathedral as she and David arrived at the front pew before the gold plated alter to stand beside Richard Rose, Justine, and Armand. She leaned closer to whisper in David's ear, "I realize that Armand and Justine don't take their Catholicism or fear of ex-communication that seriously, but couldn't Jules lose his job as organist if he was caught doing this?"

David whispered out of the corner of his mouth. "Unquestionably. The bishop would probably re-instate the inquisition and put all three of them on the rack if he knew. After all, this is the Roman Catholic Archdiocese of New Orleans. But Dimitri is paying Jules handsomely for the risk of using his organ practice time for this ceremony."

She tried to suppress a giggle. "I bet this is the first time a gay wedding was ever held in this building."

David had to suppress a chuckle. "The first church was built on this site almost 240 years ago, and I doubt that this is the first time a gay union was celebrated one way or another here."

Richard whispered angrily as he glared at Julienne. "How many times do I have to tell you, I am not gay?"

She looked at him questioningly. "Richard, you're a male, you're marrying a male."

Richard closed his eyes and shook her head sideways. "Princess is not a male, she is my lady fair."

Julienne looked at David for agreement. David shrugged. "Potato, pototto. A rose by any other name. Let sleeping dogs lie together, be they gay or straight, British or Choctaw."

She smiled at him. "Is this the first time you've been the best man at a gay wedding?"

He raised his eyebrows and tilted his head to one side. "Yes, as a matter of fact. Nice to know I still have some firsts to look forward to in my life."

She looked around her in both directions. "My father would be shitting gold doubloons if he knew I was here."

David had a hard time suppressing his laughter. "God, I love that image. Clink....clink clink clink!"

Richard whispered again angrily. "Will the two of you please bloody well behave!"

Julienne bit her lip and looked contrite. "Yes, sorry Richard. No disrespect intended."

Jules appeared from the alcove and seated himself at the huge Holtkamp pipe organ consol with its massive multiple keyboards and rows of pull-out stops. He adjusted the controls like an astronaut preparing his spaceship for flight, then looked to the rear of the cathedral to insure Princess and Dimitri were there. Only then did he nod to Richard and David who stepped forward to stand before the alter just as Simmie appeared from the alcove dressed in an alter boys robes. David did a double take and said, "Simmie, what the hell are you doing here?"

Richard looked disapprovingly at David. "He's the Vicar who's performing the ceremony."

David frowned in disbelief. "He's what? Simmie, just when and where were you ever ordained?"

Simmie frowned defensively. "I've got a Doctor of Divinity Degree with a gold seal and the whole bit."

David look incredulous. "Where the hell did you get that?"

Simmie's eyes bulged. "From a classified ad in the back of a girlie magazine. I paid the twenty-five bucks, so it's legal."

David frowned at Simmie's attire. "Where'd you get those robes, because they don't fit? You look like the Pillsbury Alter Boy."

Simmie replied huffily, "They're my alter boy robes from when I was a kid, and they do too still fit."

Richard frowned at one and then the other. "Will the two of you stop bickering and let's get on with it?" He nodded toward Jules who began playing *The Bridal Chorus* from Wagner's *Lohengrin*. All eyes turned to watch Dimitri escort Princess down the center aisle in a slow stately pace synchronized to the music.

The three waiters from Aladdin's who stood in front of the other front row pew could be heard gossiping about Princesses skin tight mini-skirted white dress, white hose, and white sequined spike heels. She held a small bouquet of white roses surrounded by baby's breath, and her auburn hair was crowned with a wreath of baby's breath woven through a copper tiara that matched her metallic copper colored eye shadow, a perfect compliment to her natural copper colored complexion.

As Princess and Dimitri passed by the front pew, Jules concluded the music just in time for everyone to hear Julienne whispering to Justine beside her, "My God, she is beautiful!" Princess smiled and her copper complexion glowed from blushing at the compliment as she and Dimitri stopped to face Richard and David at the alter. Smiling at each other, Princess and Richard stepped forward to face Simmie, Richard towering almost a foot taller than Princess and Simmie.

Simmie cleared his throat and began to speak, his normal Irish tenor voice elevated to almost a falsetto pitch because of nervousness. "Dearly beloved, we are here today to join together this man and this..." Simmie's eyes darted nervously back and forth between Princess and Richard, who glared at him. "...this woman in the holy state of matrimony, an honorable state which should not be entered lightly."

225

Julienne opened her mouth as if to speak, then noticed David staring at her sternly, and closed her mouth without saying anything.

Simmie continued. "Richard Rose, repeat after me, I, Richard Rose, take thee, Princess Kowi Anuskasha, to be my lawful wedded wife, to have and to hold from this day forward, for better for worse, for richer for poorer, in sickness and in health, to love and to cherish, till death us do part, according to God's holy ordinance; and thereto I plight thee my troth."

Line for line, Richard solemnly repeated each phrase, stumbling over Princess' Indian name, but making eye contact with her throughout.

Simmie looked amazed that Richard had repeated even her name somewhat correctly, then turned to Princess. "Princess, repeat after me, I, Princess Kowi Anuskasha, take thee, Richard Rose, to be my lawful wedded husband, to have and to hold from this day forward, for better for worse, for richer for poorer, in sickness and in health, to love, cherish, and to obey..."

At this point Princess waved her bouquet in Simmie's face. "Whooah, wait a minute. Scratch that 'obey' shit. If God doesn't instruct him to obey me, then there'll be no such inequity in this ceremony." She looked Richard in the eye. "If your commitment is limited to love and to cherish, then that's all I commit to."

Julienne, Justine, and all the guests murmured their agreement.

Richard looked at Simmie as if it was all his fault. "She's right! Scratch that bloody 'obey' crap."

Simmie rolled his eyes and continued. "...to love and to cherish, till death us do part, according to God's holy ordinance; and thereto I plight thee my troth."

Princess repeated the last phrase with a smile.

Simmie spread out his hands. "By the power vested in me by the publisher's of Gorgeous Girls Galore Magazine, I now pronounce you man and wife. You may now kiss the bride." Richard embraced Princess, lifting her off the ground as he kissed her long and hard. Dimitri had tears in his eyes as he looked from the couple to David. Everyone was smiling and sighing happily.

Suddenly a door slam from the alcove reverberated through the cathedral, followed by the heavy footsteps of a portly man in robes who angrily asked, "Hey! What's going on here?"

Simmie spread his arms to herd everyone down the center aisle toward the front door, hoarsely whispering, "Cheese it, you'se guys. It's Father O'Brien."

As the entourage escaped through the front doors, they could hear Father O'Brien grilling Jules, whose defense was, "I dunno, Father. They asked me something about a wedding rehearsal. I think they just got their churches mixed up."

****

David spoke tenderly. "Did I hurt you?"

Julienne turned on her side and looked at him over her shoulder. "No. At first I thought it would hurt, but then I was pleasantly.......really really pleasantly surprised." She turned completely on her back and looked at him with a big smile. "Didn't you hear my urging you on, and my screaming orgasm?" She looked up and raised her hands to the skylight over the bed. "My God! I never dreamed I would let a man do that to me, and I would never have guessed that I would love it so. No wonder gay males love sodomy."

David lay on his side and made small circles around her areola with his fingertip. "Well, men have a prostate gland which, when stimulated, can produce an orgasm. But women have erotic nerve endings there that lead to the same part of the brain as those in their vagina and their breasts."

She pulled the sheet up to her chin and looked at him. "Do you want me to get a strap-on dildo and do it to you?"

David rolled on his back laughing. "No thank you. That's very generous, and I'm proud of the fact that you've become so liberated." He placed the back of one hand over his eyes. "But, I guess the truth is, I'm still a little bit homophobic, at least enough that I'm not ready for that."

She turned on her side toward him and took his hand away from his face to look in his eyes. "Well, if you ever want me to do that for you, or anything, I will do anything for you, David. " She looked at his lips. "I love you so." Then, with closed eyes, she kissed him as their fingers intertwined. She rolled on her back again and chuckled. "I remember when I was a little girl and I'd eavesdrop on my mother and her friends, and they'd describe that as a form of birth control, but they always acted like they hated it."

David smiled. "Some of them probably did hate it, but those that loved it were afraid to admit it, particularly your mother's generation. The determining factor was probably the quality of their husband's expertise."

She placed one hand on his abdomen and made slow circles. "Well, you are definitely an expert." Her index finger found his belly button and explored it with her fingernail. "So, tell me, Mr. Expert, did you learn that from Aurora?"

He closed his eyes and chuckled. "That's definitely a no win question for me."

She turned on her side to face him again, her hand making circles on his abdomen again. "No, not really. I admit I was a bit jealous when you did that to her, but I was too distracted by her face in my crotch to get too bent out of shape. But I could see you really loved it."

Now he placed his forearm over his eyes. "And the next question is whose ass is prettier, and the answer is her's is very cute, but yours has classic beauty. And the next question is, whose did I enjoy more, and the answer is....," and he turned, placed his hand on her cheek to turn her face to his, and looked in her eyes. "....yours, in part because yours was virginal, but mostly because, more than Aurora or anyone before you, I love you. I truly love you," and he kissed her passionately.

As their lips separated and her eyes opened, she looked at him with a pained smile. He frowned and asked, "What's wrong?"

She shook her head negatively. "Nothing, really. I was just thinking, while we were doing what we were doing ten minutes ago, Richard and Princess were probably doing the same thing."

David mimicked her pained smile. "I hope that wasn't a buzz kill for you."

She smiled. "No, not really. I've never felt uncomfortable about gay sex. It's just that I never experienced it until Aurora, and somehow I don't even think of that as lesbianism, but rather as threesome-ism."

He turned on his back again. "Sounds like you handle it better than me. I've always felt a little awkward trying to dodge and ignore male admirers like Dimitri, and I try to repress the image of Richard and Princess together, probably because of the age disparity rather than the same sex thing."

She turned her head toward him. "None of that ever bothered me; lesbians making passes at me in the gallery, that South American trying to buy me in the gambling den, even the older Englishman with bad teeth and the petite Indian boy with an ass of which any woman would be jealous." She looked up through the skylight. "All I could think of during that ceremony today was how sincere those two people sounded. With Father O'Brian, the Archdiocese of New

Orleans, and all of society against them, they could focus on and commit themselves to their love for each other." She turned her body toward him and stroked his cheek with the back of her hand. "Now don't freak out when I ask you this 'cause I'm not asking you for anything, but I'm just curious. Did you ever think about marriage? Do you see it as a future option? Or are you gonna be one of those gray foxes who're still bagging purple haired widows who swoon around his piano?"

David did not answer immediately, and put the back of his hand back over his closed eyes. Julienne's face froze, and she started to rise and turn away to exit the bed. "Oh God! I'm sorry, David. Please forget I said that."

David gripped her closest hand to prevent her from leaving. "No, stay!" He opened his eyes and turned toward her, taking her hand in both of his. "It's just that your question made me think of Justine and her attempts to label me as a gigolo."

She frowned with regret.and placed her other hand over his. "Oh, David, I don't think of you as a gigolo, and I'm so sorry I asked you that. It's just that I was moved by that ceremony today, and, I don't know..."

David shrugged and patted her hand. "No, you're right to ask it. And the answer is, no, I never thought about marriage....until recently."

Julienne raised one hand and traced one finger over the back of his hand. "Aurora?"

He winced. "No, I tried to convince her and myself that it was real, but I have to admit now that it was mostly pity."

She clasped her hand over the back of his. "That's what she said."

He smiled up at her. "I guess she's a better judge of human nature than I am."

Her brow furrowed. "Not Aurora?"

230

He lay on his back again, pulling her to his side as he kissed the palm of her hand. "For over a year now, I've thought of you and your family as a boxed set. A gold plated bejeweled box. I was intimidated by your father's wealth, and unsure of your interest in me." He inhaled deeply as he entwined her hand in his. "A lot of debutantes have smiled across that railing around my piano. It's sort of a rite of passage to offer up their alleged virginity to some minor celebrity or sex symbol." He looked up at her. "And some of those who smiled at me had very wealthy parents."

She frowned down at him. "After my debutante's ball, the banker's son who escorted me tried to rape me, and I clobbered him with one of his mother's valuable Ming vases, for which she made him pay."

He chuckled. "Luckily, it wasn't me."

She smiled wistfully. "I wasn't ready then, and, when I was, you weren't around. But, lucky me, I eventually found you."

He smiled. "Lucky me, you persevered with my stupidity for over a year, and, lucky me, you finally ripped my pants off."

She lowered her lips to hover over his and, just before she kissed him, said, "Lucky us."

****

Julienne walked down the alley beside the building to the courtyard behind The Voodoo Room. It looked so different in the light of day, just as pretty, but without the romanticism of lanterns and moonlight. She looked up at the balconies of the two higher stories to insure that Valentina Sciciliana and Dimitri Lebedev were not present to see her. She approached the first ground floor courtyard apartment, knowing the second one was used for storage only, and knocked lightly, hoping no one upstairs would hear her.

Zoe answered the door and, when she identified Julienne, partially closed it, her eyes widening and her brow furrowing almost in anger. "What do you want? We don't open for hours!"

Julienne spoke in hushed tones. "I want to ask you some questions, please."

Zoe shook her head negatively. "I'm not the one you should be asking questions of."

Julienne pulled a fifty dollar bill from her purse and extended it to Zoe. "I think you might have some of the answers I need." She looked at the older woman with a pleading expression. "Please!"

Zoe's frown deepened. "I don't want your money! You should ask Valentina Sciciliana your questions," and she closed the door a few more inches.

Julienne sucked in air and said, "I'm afraid of her!" She noticed Zoe looking past her shoulder with fear in her eyes and nearly panicked when she heard Valentina's voice behind her.

"Why would you be afraid of me, child?"

Julienne turned to face Valentina's questioning expression with a look of fear. "I didn't want to bother you. I thought Zoe might be able to answer my questions without disturbing you."

Val looked at Zoe with accusing eyes. "Zoe has said too much already." She stared into Zoe's eyes hypnotically and spoke imperatively. "Zoe should not say another word." Zoe clicked her door closed quietly.

Julienne looked at Val and asked timidly. "Well then, would you answer some of my questions?"

Val closed her eyes and opened them to look at Julienne compassionately. "Ignorance is bliss, child, and I wish you nothing but bliss." Then she turned and ascended the curved staircase and entered her balcony door.

Julienne was about to leave when Zoe's door opened wide and, with a nod of her head, invited her into the tiny apartment. There was a curious odor of cooking herbs and incense and the room was partially illuminated by two votive candles before a tiny alter surmounted by a printed portrait of Mary, mother of Jesus, which was flanked by two period photos of beautiful young brunette haired women. Julienne identified one as a young Valentina Siciliana, and guessed, from the resemblance, the other to be Zoe's mother. At one end of the room was an ornate shiny brass bed with a hand painted ceramic chamber pot beneath it. Beside the bed was a carved wood washstand with a ceramic wash bowl and pitcher that matched the chamber pot. At the other end of the room was a door to a tiny bathroom and a kitchenette screened off by a beaded curtain. On a beautiful elaborate Persian rug beside the door was an easy chair with a carved wood end table beside it. On the end table was a Tiffany lamp illuminating a photo scrapbook with a note clipped to its outer cover. Zoe looked at Julienne, tapped the cover of the scrapbook three times, then exited the apartment.

Julienne sat down and retrieved the note, which read, "I cannot say another word. Do not remove this book from this room. Do not be here when I return from the grocery in one hour. Do not mention this day to anyone."

As if in a trance, she opened the book which began with period photos of Zoe as a young girl and her mother, who also appeared over the alter. These were followed by pictures of Val as a young adult, some together with a handsome Scottish looking man. These were followed by various photos that appeared to be employees and patrons of a bar. One of them appeared to be Zoe and Justine arm in arm in their youthful prime. Another showed Val and the Scotsman behind a bar surmounted by a sign that read 'The Mariner's Club.' She looked closer at some of the group photos, and, in one, she thought she identified her father in his youth among a group of customers at the bar. Another photo showed her father shaking the hand of the Scotsman in front of a 1920's truck bearing the sign 'MacDonald Clock Company' parked in front of one of her father's early banks. Finally, there was a picture of Zoe and Val as young adults holding a basinette with a baby in it.

Julienne closed the book and wondered who she might ask if Zoe or Val had ever had a baby, and if that baby was fathered by anyone in these pictures. There was only one other person in these pictures whom she could identify and of whom she could ask such questions. She closed the book, placed it on the table, and exited the apartment, tiptoeing down the alley in hopes of avoiding Valentina Sciciliana.

Chapter Sixteen
REVELATIONS

The nameplate on the desk read "Miss Livinia Dubuisson, New Orleans Times Picayune Archive Librarian." Her desk in front of the stacks of ledger size books was an island of cleanliness, neatness, and propriety in a sea of dusty molding yellowing copies of newsprint in a day that pre-dated modern methods of archiving printed materials. The bun on the back of her head imprisoned long luxurious black hair which, when freed in the privacy of her bedroom at night, traveled down past her narrow hips to barely cover a well shaped derriere. Her oversize horn rimmed glasses magnified exotic looking almond eyes with long eyelashes. A widows peak surmounted an elongated heart shaped face with high cheekbones and a heart shaped mouth whose full lips begged in vain for the luster of lipstick. The high necked ill fitting floral printed dress could not entirely hide a trim athletic figure for which most women would thank God and their parents genes, but which Livinia had kept chaste throughout a life now into her early forties.

Julienne spoke in those hushed tones we use in libraries, hearing her words echoing through the wooden floors and walls and shelves of the room. "Here's my request card. I'm looking for the names DeVille, Siciliana, and MacDonald circa 1920's and 1930's."

Livinia's eyes widened as she looked at the card. "That's a very wide time span. Can't you narrow it?"

Julienne bit her lip. "How about 1925 to 1935?"

Still looking at the card, Livinia rose and headed to a row of cardfile drawers in front of the book stacks. "I'll start with 1925 and you start with 1930. Pull the cards with the names you want and I'll bring the books out to the reading table for you."

Fifteen minutes later Julienne was poring over the newspaper sized pages of the first book as Livinia brought the second one and dropped it noisily beside the first. "Is there some particular event you're looking for? I've been told I'm a walking encyclopedia of New Orleans history and I might be able to help."

Julienne looked up at her hopefully. "I'm looking for information about The Mariner's Club, The MacDonald Clock Company, and the earliest DeVille Banks."

Livinia's eyes lit up. "Oh, yes!" And she began to flip through pages of the book in front of her. "That all came to light with the beginning of the stock market crash in late October of 1929. MacDonald had owned The Mariner's Club which operated in defiance of Prohibition since its inception in 1919. He owned The MacDonald Trucking Company which illegally transported liquor from the Port of New Orleans throughout the nation. He also owned The MacDonald Clock Company which manufactured illegal slot machines which they transported, along with the liquor, throughout the nation." She stopped on one page of the book and tapped the headline story with her finger. "Here it is! 'Bootlegger Tied To Gambling Syndicate.'"

Julienne began to read the story which included a photo of MacDonald beside one of Al Capone, even though Capone was largely unrelated to the story. "Is there any mention of the names DeVille or Sciciliana?"

Livinia looked doubtful. "I don't recall those names being mentioned relative to that story." She wrinkled her nose. "If you mean DeVille the banker, I don't think he or any of his firms could have been involved in that scandal."

Julienne traced lines of the story with her finger. "It says here that The Mariner's Club was also a brothel." She looked up at Livinia. "Do you recall any stories from that period about brothels, stories that may contain names or pictures?"

Livinia returned to the card catalog. "We have a ton of stories about the earlier pre-World War One Storyville era, but the Prohibition era, let me see." She pulled one card out and, before heading toward the stacks, said, "I'll bring you this one that ran a year after the Stock Market Crash about destitute women turning to prostitution," and she disappeared among the shelves, returning with a third book and opening it at the story mentioned.

Julienne looked at the photo accompanying the story. "Do you have a magnifying lens I could borrow?" Livinia handed her the magnifier and Julienne examined the row of faces in a group photo of women standing before the same bar and Mariner's Club bar sign she saw in Zoe's scrapbook. The caption read, "Photo captured in raid on brothel showing destitute women turning to prostitution at beginning of The Great Depression." Julienne recognized young Zoe and Justine in provocative attire probably photographed a decade before the story ran, and a young Valentina in conservative dress standing behind and centered beneath the sign as a madame might appear behind her stable of 'working girls.'

Livinia sighed. "Sad, isn't it, that circumstances can force a woman to submit to a fate worse than death."

Julienne looked at Livinia's very attractive face and figure, from her sensible shoes to her bun crowned head, and silently thought, "If you'd worked for Valentina Sciciliana, you'd probably have made enough to own a large part of the company you now work for." Instead she said, "Thank you Miss Dubuisson, you've been extremely helpful."

****

David and Dimitri had rarely ever crossed over Canal Street to South Rampart Street, other than during Mardi Gras when, even in 1950's segregated New Orleans, the entire city was integrated by a hedonistic hysteria of food, fun, and fantasy. As they walked down the street that more resembled one in Port Au Prince, Haiti, than a major American city, they were aware they were the only white pedestrians and they were conscious of the covert stares they were receiving from the one hundred percent black population. David pulled Dimitri along when he was distracted by 'The Apostolic Pentecostal Ethiopian Church of the Messiah Haile Selassie,' a store front church with a larger than life size exterior painting of a black Jesus crucified on a cross who closely resembled the Ethiopian Emperor Haile Selassie. Dimitri's next distraction was 'Madame LaVau's Herb Shop' whose windows displayed antique apothecary jars containing dried bats wings, dried snake skins, and a variety of exotic herbs whose scents emanated from the beaded curtain doorway, one of which was reminiscent of cannabis.

The scents of the herb shop were immediately and totally erased by the enticing aroma of heavenly high cholesterol cooking the instant they entered "Raymond's Righteous Ribs Restaurant" and spotted Alex and Gabriel at a rear table. As they exchanged greetings, a young obese black woman with a baby face and a floral printed apron approached the table and frowned at David and Dimitri. Gabriel looked at the woman and said, "Thass'alright, Leticia, if the cops come, we'll tell them they's jus' dishwashers."

Leticia continued to frown for a few seconds until Gabriel and Alex started to chuckle, then she broke up into smiles and laughter. As she placed napkins in front of all four, she looked at David and Dimitri with raised eyebrows. "But he not jokin'. If the po-leese come, you gots to git in de kitchen and start scrubbing pots and pans."

David nodded agreement. "Yes, Ma'm, we understand. Could we have some menus, please?"

She pointed over her head to a huge blackboard on the wall with a menu listed in multi-colored chalk: green for seafood, red for red meats, orange for chicken, tan for side dishes, yellow for deserts, and blue for beverages. She smiled sweetly at him and exited through the kitchen swinging doors with porthole looking windows.

David inhaled deeply. "This place smells devine!"

Gabriel slapped his hand on the table. "Dese are de bess' ribs you gonna fine outside of Kansas City."

Dimitri looked doubtful. "Alex, is all the chicken lethally hot, or can they tone it down a little for me?"

Alex chuckled. "They can tone it down for you. This is soul food, not Cajun."

Gabriel looked at Dimitri with surprise. "When I was in Berlin in forty-five, dose Russkie guys had cast iron stomachs. They could drink vodka day and night, and still kill a dozen Nazis before dey slept."

Dimitri's face tightened into a pained smile. "Yes, well, that's because they were Bolsheviks; cast iron stomachs, cast iron brains, cast iron hearts. They killed my parents before my eyes because my parents had been domestic servants to a rich family."

Gabriel's jaw dropped in shock, and he responded apologetically. "I'm sorry, son. I didn't know."

Alex rolled his eyes. "Yes, well, the world is filled with injustices. In your case, Dimitri, those experiences led to elements in your book upon which this musical is based."

Dimitri sighed. "You mean my marionette show, very little of which remains after everyone else's input."

Alex looked at Dimitri compassionately. "Well, I think the best elements of your original play remain, and I think

239

everyone's contribution has helped broaden the audience base for your original work."

Dimitri looked at Alex with lowered eyelids. "I guess being a choreographer is akin to being a public relations expert. You learn to dance around sensitive issues and how to deal with divas."

Alex raised his eyebrows and said, "Perhaps?" He was relieved when Leticia arrived, took their orders, and retreated. Alex retrieved a stack of papers from a briefcase and placed them on the table. "At this point we have enough material to make a presentation, so the next step is having enough money to make the presentation so, in turn, we can interest backers with enough money to produce the show."

David asked, "How much money do we need and where do we get it?"

Alex blinked. "How much? A lot! Where do we get it? Anywhere we can."

David raised one eyebrow. "That's not exactly the definitive answer I was looking for."

Alex raised both hands and looked down at the papers. "Sorry." He looked up and surveyed the faces of the three men before him. "Whoever invests money from the start is buying a proportionate piece of any ultimate profits. I have contracts here for initial investors offering percentages based on the size of their investment, and the tentative budget breakdown for the entire show. These percentages may appear very small, but one percent of a potential million dollar profit is ten thousand dollars, and some shows make multiple millions for multiple years."

Dimitri narrowed his eyes as he looked at Alex. "You're asking us to invest in our own show?"

Alex started rifling through the paperwork. "Yes, and, if you have anything to invest or not, perhaps you have friends, family, and associates who could invest." He stopped going through the papers and looked at the three men. "I have already selected seven or eight people in New York who we need for the presentation. Even though I'm only offering them a tiny stipend for a few days rehearsal and a promise of casting in the show, we still have to rent a hall for those rehearsals and the presentation, rent a piano, and fly all of you who appear in the presentation up to New York, and house and feed you, etcetera, etcetera."

David asked, "How much?"

Alex looked stoic. "Minimum, ten thousand."

David bit his lip. "I can pay my own fare and housing in New York, but I have no money to contribute beyond that."

Dimitri shook his head negatively. "I'm the same. My fare and housing, but I'm no money bags."

Gabriel looked sad. "I don' have no savings, Alex, but maybe we could mortgage yo' mama's house?"

Alex stacked the papers in front of him. "Let's wait on that, Gabriel. In the meantime, how do each of you feel about your approaching or my approaching your friends, family, and employers? David, you know some well heeled ladies; Valentina Sciciliana, Julienne DeVille, and that woman Justine who lives with those two rich boys. I'll talk to them if you don't want to."

David leaned slightly forward and spoke assertively. "Absolutely not! That would jeopardize my job, my relationship with Julienne, and make Justine more of a pain in the ass than she is already!"

Dimitri lowered his head and looked at Alex suspiciously. "Sorry, that ain't gonna happen with my boss or my friends. I guess we can just consider all our work wasted motion and forget about the whole thing."

Leticia arrived with their food and Alex moved his chair back to make room for her to serve. "No way! The show shall

241

go on! I will find a way, even if I have to mug somebody or peddle my ass on Broadway."

Leticia set the last plate down, put her hands on her hips, and confronted Alex. "As much as I'd like to take a piece of that action, you shut yo' mouf, Alex Pienas. Chile, you'll find a way to do whatever you godda do and still keep yo' fine prissy ass clean," and she waddled back into the kitchen.

Alex pulled his chair closer to the table, started to cut the mountain of ribs on his plate, and whispered hoarsely, "Don't worry, I'll manage to raise the money...and keep my prissy ass clean in the process."

****

The waiter set the plate of crawfish bisque in front of Julienne and the plate of shrimp etouffe in front of David, then rubbed his hands on his white apron leaving streaks of red from the crawfish bisque sauce. Despite the chandeliers and the great food, Galatoires on North Rampart Street was not as fancy or as pricey as Antoines or Arnauds in the heart of the Quarter. Julienne picked up a crawfish shell by the tail and sucked the stuffing contents out of it, making every bit as much noise as David did blowing on a hot spoonful of etouffe and slurping it into his mouth. "David, you know Tommy Griffith at The New Orleans Item. Do you think he could give you any information about my father's possible association with Valentina or Justine?"

David wiped his mouth with the napkin. "For one, I don't know Tommy Griffith. I just pitched a publicity story to him once and, after writing the blurb in his column, he probably forgot my name. For two, he's a close friend of Val and anything said to him would definitely be shared with her, so I'd advise against mining that source. Why do you ask? What are you looking for?"

Her fork clinked as she set it down on her plate. "Well, little details that have come to light have led me on a search that I haven't mentioned because you probably wouldn't approve, you might even consider prying."

His eyebrows raised. "Julienne, you can ask me anything. I thought you knew that."

She closed her eyes, bit her lip, then looked at him. "Did you know that Valentina was once the madame of a brothel named The Mariner's Club and that Zoe and Justine were two of her working girls?"

He shrugged. "I've heard unverified rumors to that affect."

She sat up with interest. "May I ask the source of those rumors?"

His brow furrowed. "It was more like conclusions I drew from nebulous things all three had said over a period of time."

She picked up her fork again. "Well I've verified that with twenty year old newspaper stories. But I haven't been able to clarify what connection my father had with that whole affair. I suspect my father financed some illegal activities during Prohibition, but managed to avoid involvement in the eyes of the police or the press." She stabbed a crawfish aggressively with her fork. "Probably bought his way out of the scandal."

He dug his spoon into his etouffe. "From my conversations with your father and Val that night in the courtyard, I'm convinced they definitely have a shared past."

She swallowed a mouthful of bisque, then looked at him intently. "I think my father may have had a child with either Valentina or Zoe!" She leaned back in her chair. "I may have a half brother or half sister out there somewhere."

He tried not to frown. "What makes you think that?"

She leaned forward and picked up her fork again. "I saw a photo of Valentina and Zoe with an infant. I also saw a photo of my father among customers at The Mariner's Club."

He could not restrain the frown. "Were these photos in the old newspaper story?"

She traced her fork through the sauce looking for remaining crawfish. "No, and I'd rather not yet mention their source because I don't want to get anyone in trouble."

He scooped up a spoonful of etouffe. "I understand. Believe me, I understand."

Her eyes widened as she discovered a crawfish. "I've tried to query Justine on the subject, but she's not talking." She sucked the contents out of the crawfish shell and looked at him. "My father said you 'consort' with Justine, whatever that word implies to him, but maybe you're closer to her than I am and she'll tell you things she refuses to tell me."

He leaned back and sighed. "Keep in mind that Justine has a thing for young men and has been chasing me for quite some time."

She held her full fork halfway between plate and mouth and looked at him questioningly. "Did she ever catch you?"

He closed his eyes and scrunched his face into a painful expression. "Rest assured that any contact between Justine and I was extremely brief, meaningless, and initiated solely by her."

She frowned. "Does that mean she kissed you under the mistletoe at Christmas, or something else? My God, she's old enough to be your mother!"

He opened his eyes widely. "Tell that to Armand and Jules!"

She pulled the empty fork out of her mouth and swallowed. "I guess, after Aurora, I can't throw stones at a menage a'trois who live in a glass house, but their whole La Boheme thing kinda felt weird to me."

He tilted his head. "Let sleeping dogs..."

Julienne frowned and nodded her head up and down. "Yeah, yeah, yeah! Let sleeping dogs lie together." Then she

244

narrowed her eyes as she stared at him. "But, in the future, if you ever lie with that bitch, you'll never lie with me again!"

David straightened his head and nodded affirmatively. "Agreed!"

****

Mrs. Saucier looked through her window disapprovingly as David, Julienne, Princess, and Richard mounted the narrow hollow sounding wood stairs to David's loft. David and Richard gathered the mismatched chairs around the table as Julienne removed a bottle of chablis from her straw bag and rummaged around to find four champagne glasses, reluctant to use the heavy bottomed water glasses. As David filled their glasses at the table, he looked at Richard and asked, "Okay, what's so important or secretive that I have to reveal my impoverished abode to you."

Richard looked around. "My God, man, this is a bloody palace compared to my humble rat's nest, and I bloody well don't have a grand piano or a view overlooking the cathedral's spires."

Princess sipped her wine and smiled. "He has no windows, so he's covered most of the walls with Moroccan rugs and tapestries. It's like *A Thousand And One Arabian Nights*."

Richard smiled at her lovingly. "And you, my love, are my Scheherazade."

David gave Richard a condescending smile. "And you, my friend, are testing my patience ever since you said you have something you wanted to give me in private."

Richard sniffed his wine, then took a big sip. "Well, not only in private, but I figured at your place we'd have the use of a phonograph."

245

David's eyes narrowed and he looked at him suspiciously. "Why would we need a phonograph?"

Richard looked at him questioningly. "David, have you received any mail from Aurora since she returned to Hollywood?"

David was almost glaring at Richard. "No!"

Richard retrieved a large Kraft envelope from his pocket and started to open it. "That's strange, because this came in the mail addressed to you, but care of Lenny Levine, who gave it to me to deliver to you. Inside was a folded envelope with your street address and cancelled stamps on it."

David sat back and sipped his wine. "I instructed the postman to return any mail that came from Aurora." Julienne looked at him in surprise.

Richard wiggled his eyebrows. "I kinda guessed that might be the reason for the cancelled envelope, but the real surprise in the envelope addressed to Lenny was this," and Richard held up a 45rpm record with a Blue Tunes label.

David looked angry. "I don't need more copies of the song she stole from me."

Richard smiled mischievously. "But it's not."

Julienne snatched the record out of Richard's hand and read the label out loud. "It's titled, *Forgive*. Vocals and guitar by Aurora Alonzo. Music based on the public domain property titled *La Paloma*. English lyrics by David Wales." Julienne looked at David in amazement as he straightened up and snatched the record from her hand.

David squinted to read the fine print on the label. "I didn't write this! What kind of trick is she trying to pull?"

Richard raised his eyebrows. "Maybe you should listen to it and find out."

David looked at him suspiciously. "You've already listened to it."

Richard pursed his lips. "Wouldn't you have? Go ahead and listen. You may be surprised."

David snapped the little 45rpm adapter disc in the single record and put it on the turntable. Everyone watched eagerly as he lowered the phonograph arm into the first groove, producing a loud hiss before the music began. Auorora's impressive classical guitar provided an elaborate fanfare before the lyrics began.

Forgive
Is a word that sings from my heart to you.
Forgive
All of the words I uttered that were untrue.

Regret
Is the word that weighs in my heart each night.
Regret
Mistakes I made that caused you to take flight.

    So please hear my song
    and tell me that you forgive,
    Forgive all my faults
    so that I can go on and live,
    Let this white dove
    bring to you peace at last,
    Let this white dove
    erase all the sins of the past.

Forgive
And tomorrow we'll smile and sing new songs.
Return
To my heart to my arms where you belong.

As the instrumental second chorus continued, David looked at Richard. "Not bad. I almost wish I had written it."

Princess spoke pleadingly. "She's trying to apologize to you, David."

Julienne smiled wistfully. "And trying to get back into your good graces."

They all listened to the second vocal chorus, then, as it ended and David removed the phonograph arm from the disc, Princess spoke in a timorous voice. "David, did Aurora tell you much about her past?"

David closed his eyes and nodded his head affirmatively. "Yes, Princess, she did."

Princess looked at the others, then turned to David. "Her past was a lot like mine. When my mother's drinking got bad, they put me in an Indian orphanage. In those days, that's where people went to obtain free slave children; children to work on their farms, to work as domestics, and, some, to use as sex slaves. The man who adopted me sexually abused his own children until they were old enough to run away. Then he adopted me to take their place and be used as a daily sex object. I was so young, that it became a way of life to me. Survival meant compliance, and taking advantage of whatever opportunity came along." She looked at Julienne and Richard who sat with bowed heads and eyes glimmering with restrained tears. "I know Aurora did you wrong, but it was probably instinct for her, to seize an opportunity, to be compliant to Julian's authority. I'm not suggesting that you forget, but to forgive would help you as well as Aurora."

David gave her a pained smile. "How'd you get so wise, despite your history?"

Princess shrugged. "If I have any wisdom, it's not despite, but because of my history."

****

Julienne looked through the cut glass framed door and saw Nettie approaching down the hall. Then her father exited the study and stopped Nettie, after which Nettie retreated down the hall as her father approached. He opened the door, but stood barring her entrance. She looked at him in surprise. "Daddy, am I no longer welcome in the house where I was raised?"

DeVille blinked. "Your mother certainly expects you to attend dinner on holidays and special occasions. But, to be honest, Julienne, the company you chose to keep could make you a liability to a banker or his wife, given the social standing your mother has enjoyed until now in the community."

Her brow furrowed. "Perhaps you're referring to the fact that I've been seen talking to a woman who once operated a brothel, or in the company of two women who worked as prostitutes in that brothel." DeVille's eyes widened. "Would I be tainted by sharing the company of a man who frequented that brothel, such as the man who stands before me now?"

DeVille's jaw dropped. Then he glared at her and said, "Julienne, you're meddling in things that have nothing to do with you. Leave the past in the past, and build a better future for yourself by sharing that future with better company than that you're now keeping."

Julienne smiled facetiously. "Perhaps I could share my future with my half brother or half sister." DeVille looked at her confused. "Which is it, Daddy? Was the child you fathered by one of those ladies at The Mariner's Club a boy or a girl?" DeVille's lower jaw started to quiver as he partially shut the door. Julienne moved closer to the door. "And while we're at it, Daddy, did your mother or one of your grandmothers have an Anglo Saxon lover, perhaps one with red hair?"

249

DeVille closed the door to a narrow opening. "My God, they must be feeding you drugs in that cesspool you've been swimming in. Please, Julienne, I'll pay for you to go to a sanitarium where you can get well. Just step away from those libertines in the Quarter, and please stay away from the house until you do, for your mother's sake, if not mine," and he shut and locked the door, the glass coming close to pressing against Julienne's face.

DeVille retreated down the hall and into the study door. Julienne closed her eyes and took a deep breath, trying to get her heart to stop racing so wildly. When she opened her eyes, she saw her mother stick her head around the living room door, look toward the study door to assure the coast was clear, then tiptoe to the front door, her finger to her lips to insure Julienne's silence. Her mother silently unlocked the door and motioned Julienne to follow her into the living room, shutting the living room door after they entered.

Her mother looked at her with an apologetic smile. "Julienne, dear sweet child, please forgive your father. He is just trying to protect you. The truth is, I am to blame for this mess." and a single tear escaped down her mother's cheek.

Julienne gripped her mother's hands. "Oh, Mother, I am so very sorry. I didn't mean for you to hear about Daddy's infidelities."

Angelina DeVille bit her lip and looked away. "Oh, Sweetheart, your father wasn't unfaithful." She released Julienne's hands and walked over to sit in the love seat beside the fireplace. "At least, I don't think he was, not that I'd have blamed him if he did that."

Julienne sat in the Morris chair opposite the love seat. "Mother, how can you say that?"

Angelina pulled a handkerchief out of her sleeve and dabbed her eyes. "Truth is, I was not the most passionate of brides when your father and I first married, and the fact that I appeared to be barren did not help either of us in the passion department."

Julienne looked confused. "Barren. But you couldn't be barren. After all, you had me!"

Angelina bit her lip, looked down at the handkerchief she kept twirling nervously in her hands, then up in Julienne's eyes. "That just it, darlling. I didn't have you. You were adopted."

Julienne looked stunned. "I was adopted? What? Through an agency? Through an orphanage?"

Angelina tilted her head and look off into space again. "You have to realize what it was like in those days. For a man or woman in society, being barren or impotent was degrading. Adopting from an agency or orphanage would have left a paper trail and complicated both our lives and your life. Children can be cruel if they discover one of their peers is adopted.

Julienne surveyed the collection of family portraits on the walls around her. "So I was adopted from an unwed mother?"

Looking down at her hands, Mrs. DeVille nodded her head. "Yes."

Julienne looked steadily at her mother. "Was I born to Valentina Sciciliana?"

Mrs. DeVille shook her head sideways. "No."

Julienne hesitated. "Was I born to a prostitute named Zoe?"

Mrs. DeVille shook her head sideways again. "No."

Julienne inhaled deeply and exhaled. "Am I the daughter of a prostitute named Justine?"

Mrs. DeVille looked up defiantly and swallowed before speaking. "You are no one's daughter but mine! I raised you! I made you the fine talented young woman you are!" She looked down again and broke into sobs. "That wretched creature only gave birth to you, and then abandoned you."

251

Julienne moved swiftly to sit beside her mother and hold her in her arms. "I know you are, and I am so grateful you are my mother." Her mother sobbed in her arms for almost a minute before Julienne spoke again. "Mother, I have to ask. Is Daddy my biological father?"

Angelina moved out of Julienne's embrace and again dried her eyes. "Your father has sworn up and down that he has never slept with Justine. I know him well and can tell when he's lying, and I believe him. But, whoever your biological father was, he also abandoned you."

They were both startled by DeVille's voice as he stood in the doorway, his eyes brimming with tears. "There's one thing your mother hasn't told you. She is not to blame in all this. She was not barren. It was me. I just blamed her for the first few years of our marriage."

Julienne looked afraid as she asked, "How do you know?"

Then she turned abruptly as she heard her mother speak. "Because, after you were born and your father hadn't touched me in years, I had an affair, became pregnant, and had a miscarriage."

DeVille added, "And I had a medical test that determined it was me who was impotent. Not your mother." He took one step toward the women and extended his hands in appeal. "Julienne, whatever flaws your mother and I have confessed to you pale compared to your friends in the quarter who treated you as garbage and a commodity when you were an infant, and who, now that you're an adult, treat you like a cash cow I beg of you, now that you've had your walk on the wild side, please come home and return to a life of decency with appropriate people who can help you pursue a happy and positive life."

Julienne swallowed hard and turned to her mother, who looked at her hopefully.

DeVille moved his jaw sideways a couple times, then said, "Now do you understand why I tried to keep you away from those people, why I warned you about David and Justine?"

Julienne's eyes widened in realization. "David and Justine! Oh, my God!" She stood up abruptly and headed for the door. "Forgive me. We can talk more later. There's something I have to do!!" And she bolted out the front door.

Forgive

from the trilogy "The Piano Lover"

lyrics by William Karl Thomas

"La Paloma" public domain music originally by Sebastián Iradier

255

Chapter Seventeen
ANGELS AND DEVILS

Justine's eyes widened as she leaned across the marble topped table to hiss into David's face, "It doesn't matter how I found out. You guys need the money desperately, and I have it."

David noticed that the longshoremen and farmers that frequented The Morning Call Coffee Shop were admiring Justine's tight pants as she leaned towards him, her breasts almost touching the two cups of café au lait and order of beignets on the table. Two blocks North of Café duMonde on the triangular corner bordered by Decatur and North Peters Streets, The Morning Call was the haunt of the working class who populated The French Market, a pavilion of open air stalls where the local population procured their fresh produce, meats, and seafood. It was also around the corner from where Justine lived with Jules and Armand, and, David hoped, the least likely place he would be seen with her. He inhaled deeply and said, "All I want to know is, did Alex approach you for the money?"

She smiled like a Wiley cat. "What'sa matter, David, afraid I might have some leverage over you? You wouldn't be the first person to sleep their way to the top in show business."

David sipped his coffee. "I guess you would know, even though you didn't even sleep your way to the middle of show business."

She picked up a beignet and tapped off the excess powdered sugar. "Don't try to swap insults with me, David. I've had every one you can imagine bounce off me and into my dictionary of international curses, insults, and sarcasms."

David sighed. "Yes, I know you are a walking encyclopedia of vitriol and bitterness, but, really Justine, we're only talking about seed money, a small fraction of the overall budget for a musical. You'd be lucky if that got you laid by any of the few straight boys in the chorus. So why don't you back off and stay away from anything to do with this production."

She swallowed a bite of beignet. "You should be proud that I have enough faith in your talent to invest Armand's money in it."

He closed his eyes and shook his head sideways. "I am not proud of any association I've had with you, which is why I want no future association with you." He opened his eyes with a startled expression at the sound of Julienne's voice.

Julienne stood glaring at the two of them. "Well, that's reassuring to hear, that a girl's worst nightmare, one that didn't include mistletoe, wont be repeated in the future."

Justine smiled maliciously. "How deliciously awkward. David's latest piece of fluff," and she looked at David disapprovingly, "the only one that I like or approve of, incidentally," then she looked back at Julienne cattily. "Come to scratch the eyes out of the lioness in her lair. How in the world did you find us?"

Julienne frowned at her. "I went to your apartment to discuss something of mutual interest, and Jules said you were here."

Justine's eyes widened. "Of mutual interest, such as David, perhaps?"

Julienne looked at David sadly. "Among other things."

Justine tilted her head. "What other things?"

Julienne turned her sad look to Justine. "Oh, I think you know."

Justine looked perplexed. "No, actually, I don't. What the hell are you talking about?"

David's puzzled look suddenly morphed into realization. He stood up and, putting his arm around Julienne, began to herd her out of the coffee shop. Justine shouted behind them, "Stop, David. She was talking to me, not you."

Julienne tried to resist David. "Wait! I want to confront her. I want her to know I know who the infant in that picture was."

David continued to force her out of the swinging door to the coffee shop. When they were safely outside and out of earshot, Julienne forced herself free of his arms and confronted him, poking his chest with her finger as she spat words at him angrily. "You knew! She knew! The two of you let me make a fool of myself! It wasn't kinky enough to seduce me into a threesome with Aurora, you have to sleep with my biological mother as well!"

David's eyes flared. "My God, Julienne, I had no idea she was your biological mother. She accosted me when I was drunk long before you and I connected, and I've avoided her predatory advances like the plague ever since."

Julienne's lip quivered and her eyes brimmed with tears. "But you knew about the brothel and their association with it."

David closed and opened his eyes as he turned his palms up in appeal. "All I knew was Justine's admission that she worked as a prostitute for Val at The Mariner's Club, and that she had to leave there when she became pregnant with a child that she abandoned. Val never told her what happened to the child and I never even knew the sex of the child. Neither of us could have known that child was you. Justine still doesn't know."

They both turned at the sound of Justine's voice. "She knows now." Justine stood ten feet from them, clenching her fists at her sides, a look of pained regret on her face as she stared at Julienne. She spoke in a hesitant unsure voice. "Julienne? Are you my daughter?"

259

Julienne stood up straight and, after wiping the tears from her eyes, spoke assertively. "No! I am the daughter of Angelina deVille. She held me in her arms, sang lullabies to me, loved and nurtured me throughout childhood and all my life." She looked at Justine from head to toe and back into her eyes, a look of disgust on her face. "You're just the wretched creature who gave birth to me and abandoned me."

David looked disapprovingly at Justine, then compassionately at Julienne as he extended his hand to her.

Julienne did not extend her hand to him and looked him in the eye with bitter disappointment. "And you're the wretched creature who slept with her," and she walked away without looking back, leaving David staring angrily at Justine who was frozen with a stunned expression on her face.

****

Princess ran up to David and Alex inside the door of the air terminal and squeaked desperately, "Please take my bags away from Richard. He was so insulted when the porter asked to carry his 'daughters' bags that he insisted on carrying them himself."

As the two younger men pulled two of the three bags away from Richard, his heavy breathing slowed enough to complain bitterly. "Cheeky bastards! How presumptuous to assume she's my daughter! And did you see the way they leered at her? Should be some law against ogling a woman like that!"

David dropped the bag at the ticket counter next to the one Alex had deposited. "Consider it flattery that they find her so attractive, and a testimony to your male magnetism that you're married to such a hot looking young chick."

Richard dropped the bag he carried next to the other two. "Flattery my bloody ass! Rather a testimony to how crass the world's become." He leaned closer to David and spoke conspiratorially. "Now listen, David. Inasmuch as I'm not free to travel with her to New York, I'm counting on you to chaperone her. Keep those bloody little chorus boys off of her. The ones here in New Orleans know that I know where they live. But I worry about New York."

David patted Richard's shoulder. "Don't worry. Princess is a lady, and Alex and I will be her body guards ever at her side until she returns."

Richard hugged David briefly. "Bless you, David." Then he lifted Princess off the ground in a bear hug, kissing her noisily before depositing her gently on the floor. "I've got the cab waiting and I'm late for work. Be good, my Princess, I love you so very very much!" He waved to the trio as he left. "Bon voyage, and great good luck with the presentation. I know it'll be a smashing success," and he waved down the impatient cabbie who was about to leave.

Alex looked at his wristwatch. "I hope Dimitri makes it so we can share a cab from La Guardia to the hotel." He smiled sadly as he watched David looking anxiously at the front doors. "Go ahead, David. There's a phone over there. I know you want to make one last call, and I hope she answers this time."

David touched his arm lightly in gratitude and walked swiftly over to the phone booth, closing the folding door as he seated himself inside. Alex and Princess looked at each other sadly, Princess shaking her head sideways. Alex wrinkled his nose. "I know. She's not going to answer. But he has to keep trying."

She stared at David in the phone booth. "Hope is the life preserver that keeps up afloat until we see a ship or a shore or a shark."

Dimitri appeared with a battered leather suitcase emblazoned with various European stickers. "Where's David?"

261

Alex looked toward the phone booth. "Still trying to reach Julienne."

Dimitri looked sadly toward David. "Poor thing." Then he looked at Alex. "Where's Gabriel?"

Alex sighed. "I still couldn't talk him into flying. He's taking the train and I'll pick him up at Penn Station tomorrow in time for rehearsals." He wrinkled his nose. "In addition to fear of flying, I think he gets free passage with his old Porter's Union connections."

David joined them with a sad expression on his face. "No luck. I guess I'll try again from New York."

Alex and Dimitri turned together. "Dimitri and I are gonna wait at the gate."

As David turned to join them, Princess put her hand on his shoulder to stop him. She looked up at him with a timid expression. "Now don't be mad at me, David. There's someone who wants to say goodbye." David looked over his shoulder to see Aurora, dressed all in white, staring anxiously at him from twenty feet away. David started to turn toward the gate, but Princess stopped him again with her fingers on his cheek. "David, please, give her a chance to apologize. I would consider it a personal favor to me. Please."

Princess turned toward the gate as David turned and approached Aurora, stopping eight feet from her with his hands folded in front of him and a stoic expression on his face. Aurora cleared her throat and said, "I won bodder you, David. I here to do a benefit concert por Caesar Chavez add de Municipal Auditorium." She took one step forward and extended the Kraft envelope she held in her hand toward him. "Dis is fo' you, David."

He kept his hands folded as he looked at the envelope. "What is it?"

262

She waved the envelope twice. "I was afrait to give BMI you address, afrait you send everyting back. Dis is de checks fo you *Forgive* song."

David did not move. "It's your song."

Aurora lowered her arm, then raised the envelope to him again, looking up at him. "No, id's your song. Id ees de bess I can do to make it up to you, whad Julian made me do, whad I did." She tilted her head to one side and wrinkled her brow. "Dad song ees you worts. I read many dictionarios an' tort how you say dose tings. I see de worts come oudda you mout as I escrito. Id's you song, David. An four udder top artists tort it good enough to record after I record."

David looked at the envelope for five seconds, then reached out and took it from her. "It's a very good song, Aurora."

She lowered her hand and her eyebrows rose as the corners of her mouth trembled with the hint of a smile. "Tank you, David. Tank you for dad." She inhaled deeply and looked down at his shoes. "David, I take classes een business and entertainment law, learn how be independent o' Julian." She looked up at him with a hint of pride. "I ged de Copyride fo' you song in you name myself." She looked down at his hands. "El Gato, Julian, dey good por mi sometimes, sometimes dey muy mallo por me." She looked up into his eyes. "You always good por me, David. Always!"

David swallowed and said, "I'm glad you think so, Aurora."

She looked down at his shoes again. "And, David, if you ever wan me, por show beezness, por la musica, por sex," she looked up into his eyes, "wid o widout Julienne, por un poco tiempo o mucho tiempo, any way, anywhere, anytime.....I dere fo you." She licked her lips, looked at his hands, then back into his eyes. "I love you, David!" She stepped close to him, stood on her tiptoes, kissed his mouth hungrily with closed eyes, then turned and walked swiftly out of the terminal.

****

Alex walked over to greet the three older men and one older woman who entered the rehearsal hall wearing coats. They shook hands and he ushered them to the two library tables closest to the doors. He helped the woman remove her coat as the men removed theirs and draped them over the backs of the folding chairs at the tables. All four appeared to be in their early to late sixties, the woman with artificially red hair, the youngest portly man with salt and pepper hair, and the two thinner men with white hair, the shorter thinner of the two with a Van Dyke goatee. Alex retreated to chairs in the corner where he joined a nervous looking Dimitri. Black drapes covered the huge windows facing Union Square in Manhattan and two overhead lamps illuminated the library tables, leaving the far end of the room in darkness.

David sat in the darkness together with Gabriel at a nightclub table beside a shiny black grand piano. Behind them six chorus boys, a tall brunette female dancer, and Princess in a platinum blonde wig sat at tables on two levels of risers. The chorus boys were dressed as waiters and the women were in skin tight mini-skirted metallic colored sheaths and spike heels. David looked at Gabriel and whispered, "What do you think?"

Gabriel frowned. "I've never played to a smaller or tougher looking audience."

The overhead lights went out and David moved to stand in the curve of the piano. A single overhead spotlight starkly illuminated him as he raised his head and began to sing, fondling the edge of the piano as he moved towards the keyboard.

264

Her contours possess style and grace
Her presence elevates the place
As if we were a ship in space
Approaching heaven's gates.

Her skin an alabaster white
Her hair black as the darkest night
Against her lure I cannot fight
She is indeed my fate.

David sat on the piano bench and played a musical phrase after each line.

With trembling hands I touch her
As she responds with sighs
And deep bass undertones
That bring tears to my eyes."

David began to accompany himself during the final two stanzas of the song.

Together we will sing our songs
Telling tales of right and wrong
Together is where we belong
My life depends on her.

We both decide where life shall go
We both decide on yes or no
For she is my piano
And I am her lover.

Full colored stage lighting came up abruptly as the chorus boys and two female dancers sprang into their dance positions. The ensemble danced around and on the risers and tables, both women singing to David in a brassy sexy manner. They sang the first two phrases in unison, the first two lines of the bridge by the brunette, the second two lines of the bridge by Princess, then the first three lines of the final phrase in unison, and the last line by Princess as she ends up on the piano bench with her arms around David.

Piano lover please be kind
When you place your hands on me
Make every note every stroke
Bring me ecstacy

Your fingers tease but they please
The strings within my heart
So fill me up fill my cup
With love right from the start

> *And I will cling to you I'll sing to you*
> *Whatever you desire*
> *My lips will bring to you a ring to you*
> *That sets your soul on fire*

For I am yours my every part
Created by a plan
Made just for you for you for you
Piano lover man.

The set went dark again, and when the stage lights came up, the girls were gone and David was sitting with Gabriel while the chorus boys were idly stacking chairs on tables and sweeping the floor as if a nightclub has just closed. Gabriel raised a battered cornet to his lips and played an impressive eight bars of jazz fanfare.

David looked impressed and said, "Mr. Gabriel, I am truly impressed with your talents, but, truth is, we already got a quartet, and that's all the management needs or can afford. After all, this is just a funky gay bar in the New Orleans French Quarter, not Broadway."

The red headed woman and the portly man chuckled, while the two grey haired men tried to repress their smiles.

Gabriel bled the sweat from his horn. "Well, truth is, you need me. You need me more than you know!"

David gave him a pained smile. "Even if a piano, drums, bass, and guitar quartet made accommodations for a horn, the boss wont pay for another instrument."

Gabriel sat up straight. "Oh, you don' have to pay me. I'm jus' here fo' de cause."

David frowned. "The cause?" He rolled his eyes. "Look, Gabriel, if you're a gay activist, you should know that the four of us musicians are the only straight guys in this club, with the possible exception of the bass player who probably fried his gonads along with his brains from too much drugs."

Gabriel shook his head negatively. "No. I mean 'cause you don' know who you love. 'Cause you wasting yo' God given talent to put the de message out dere. And 'cause de world is self destructing in 98,346 days. You gotta make up yo' mine who you love an' dat God gave you a talent fo' a reason."

David looked at Gabriel with suspicion. "Gabriel, do you smoke the same stuff the bass player smokes?"

Gabriel rocked back and forth. "No! I know all dis stuff 'cause I'm an angel. I was sent here to set you straight, to recruit you fo' God's work. God's got plans for you, son!"

David smiled smugly. "Ohhhhhh, I see. Okay, Gabriel. If you're an angel, tell me something. Is God white, or is God black?"

Gabriel's eyes widened with surprise. "Dat's a silly question, son. What color is God? If you must know, she's blue!"

The stage lights suddenly brightened as the chorus boys suddenly froze into position for their next number and sang with an imperative, forceful, and sometimes pleading tone, shouting the first line.

SHE'S BLUE!
Wouldn't you be too
If you had to see
What your world's come to?

IT'S TRUE!
We're a motley crew
Lots of warring nations
Rotten through and through.

    Tortured bodies, tortured souls,
    Our history from days of old,
    We are compelled to dominate,
    To foster misery and hate.

BUT WAIT!
Before it's too late
And self destruction
Is our only fate.

LET GO!
Of your petty egos
Of your lust for power
Of your lust for gold.

    Listen people to our plea,

We can save humanity,
Before we all hear earth's death knell,
Before we turn earth into hell.

LET'S STOP!
Thinking we're on top
When what's beneath us
Is about to drop.

LET'S CEASE!
Seeking golden fleece
When our only answer
Is in seeking peace.

> *We can save humanity,*
> *But only if our minds are free,*
> *It must start somewhere don't you see,*
> *(Slower and softer past this point.)*
> *Start here and now with you and me.*

IT'S TRUE!
That God is blue,
And she's unhappy
With the things we do.

SO STOP!
Making her blue.

David stared in amazement as the chorus of waiters froze after delivering the last line of the song, then returned to stacking tables as they had before the song began. He looked fearfully at Gabriel. "How do you make them do that, and do they know they're doing it?"

Gabriel shrugged. "Mortals all have the potential to become angels. I just deputized them to emphasize what I'm trying to tell you. And, no, they don't know they're speaking for me, but, someday, when their time comes, they'll remember."

David frowned at Gabriel and said, "Really? That song was a message from you? You think I can turn the tide of humanity's self destruction?"

Gabriel raised his eyebrows and looked at him wide eyed. "S'gotta start somewhere. Wan'na keep the mountain from falling, gotta start with the rubble at the bottom, and tha's you!"

David snorted. "I think your efforts would be better invested with the guys at the top, the presidents and potentates that declare wars and turn blind eyes to the atrocities their troops commit."

Gabriel snorted. "Presidents and potentates don't do zilch, unless we tell 'em to. You tell them you want lower gas prices, they'll go invade whoever's got the most oil and the least defenses. You tell 'em you'd rather ride a bike and wait for an electric car powered by solar electric generators, they'll keep their toy soldiers at home looking for drug smugglers. They'll also be more inclined to subsidize electric cars and solar electric sources."

David frowned. "You telling me I gotta ride a bicycle up to the White House and join some picket line?"

Gabriel looked at him accusingly. "I'm telling you you gotta decide on your priorities and make them known to your leaders. You wanna drive your gas guzzeling behemoth of a car in the hopes that the ladies think that whatever's between your legs is as big, even if the progeny from whatever's between your legs die from the results of auto pollution. Or do you wanna ride that bicycle to the White House and show the

270

ladies that what's between your ears is bigger and more important that what's between your legs."

David stuck his tongue in his cheek and then said, "The ladies have been satisfied with both ends of my anatomy, thank you. But I don't see why me, the little guy with no lobbyists or loot or cash or clout, why should I save the rich man's seaside castle from going under the water when the oceans rise?"

Gabriel smiled at him smugly. "Because Mother Nature's wrath will not distinguish between the rich man or poor man, his children or chattel, his house or health. Polluted air blows through Pasadena and Pomona without distinction, Flood waters do not stop at the guarded gates of rich secluded communities, but inundate Westwood as readily as Watts. Not asking you to save the rich man, son. Asking you to save your own ass, save humanity, save the world."

David sighed. "You're asking a sinner, a non-believer. How smart does that make you?"

Gabriel rolled his eyes. "I once knew a man named Thomas. We called him the 'Doubting Thomas.' He doubted all the trappings and rhetoric of the leaders of his day. But he was smart enough to recognize what was in his own best interest, and he ended up doing God's work, even though he claimed he didn't believe in her. If God sends you messages like floods and volcanic eruptions, kinda silly to stand around arguing about who sent the message."

Suddenly the waiters became a chorus of dancers again, shouting their first line.

LET'S STOP!
Thinking we're on top
When what's beneath us
Is about to drop.

LET'S CEASE!
Seeking golden fleece
When our only answer
Is in seeking peace.

We can save humanity,
But only if our minds are free,
It must start somewhere don't you see,
(Slower and softer past this point.)
Start here and now with you and me.

IT'S TRUE!
That God is blue,
And she's unhappy
With the things we do.

SO STOP!
Making her blue.

The stage lights went out, plunging the room into darkness for ten seconds before the room lights came up again. The chorus boys and Gabriel sat at the tables and chairs on the improvised set as David walked forward to stand before the investors seated at the two library tables. They were all talking to each other in low voices, their quizzical and sometimes frowning expressions not revealing their reaction to the presentation. David cleared his throat to get their attention, then said, "I realize a producer or director might make changes to parts of the book and some of the songs, but I would want to lock in a few things. One, the guarantee that Alex Pienas would be the choreographer." He noted with relief that they all smiled, some of them nodding their heads affirmatively to each other. "Two, the guarantee that Gabriel would be cast as the trumpet playing angel." With this they looked at each other doubtfully, one of them shrugging. "Three, as one of the two copyright holders of the book and as the composer and lyricist of the completed song list, I expect top billing for both writers, and for myself as composer and lyricist." Again shrugs and blinks. "But, even though some of the music and lyrics might be edited, dropped, or rewritten, the two songs in this presentation must be locked in, which also locks in the concept that God is a woman."

The three men looked toward the one woman, who stared at David almost malevolently, then with only a hint of a smile. The oldest tallest steely faced white haired man narrowed his eyes at David, leaned forward slightly, and asked in a menacing voice, "Are there any other demands you'd like to make, young man?"

The one woman glared at the white haired man and said threateningly, "Angus?" Angus turned to glare back at the woman.

David responded, "No, sir."

The fat pig faced man turned to David and asked condescendingly, "Now refresh my memory Mr. ...," he looked down at the printed presentation before him, "Mr. Wales." He wrinkled his nose. "You've never written a Broadway play before, never even wrote material for one. Am I right?"

David kept a straight face, lowered and raised his eyelids, and answered, "That's correct. I've written special material for nightclub acts for ten years in New Orleans, but never for Broadway."

The thin man with a goatee and spectacles looked at him suspiciously. "How many Broadway shows have you actually seen, if you don't mind my asking?"

David tried to restrain a smile. "Broadway is a long way from New Orleans, but I've visited New York a half dozen times and seen a dozen Broadway shows. Like most of America, however, I've seen dozens of Broadway shows in

273

movies and, like most of America, understand the concept of a musical. Additionally, I've seen dozens of operas."

The woman turned to the thin man, raised one eyebrow, and said sarcastically, "Well, that a few dozen more operas than you've seen, Harry, because your eyes were closed throughout the one and only opera I saw you attend."

The fat man turned to the woman and spoke argumentatively. "It's a reasonable question, Henrietta. Did you see how nebulous the budget breakdown at the end of this presentation is?" And he slapped a pudgy hand on the paperwork several times.

Henrietta narrowed her eyes at him. "Broadway shows are always nebulous, Angelo. And what do you know about budgeting Broadway shows?"

The fat man's eyes bulged. "I know I don't attempt to build a skyscraper without estimating the steel and concrete and labor."

Angus cleared his throat noisily and glared at the woman. "Oh, come on, Henrietta. Let's stop wasting our time and these young people's time."

Just then a phone rang in the hallway, catching everyone's attention. A voice mumbled a few words, then an elderly stagehand appeared through the hall doorway, struggling to unsnarl a long phone cord in order to bring a phone to the library tables. He held the phone cradle and waved the handset back and forth seeking someone at the table to accept it. Angus waved toward the woman. "Oh, for God's sake, Henrietta, take it and see what they want." With that, Angus stood up, removed his folded overcoat from the back of the chair, and started to put it on. David, Alex, and Gabriel looked at each other doubtfully.

Henrietta accepted the phone and, shielding the mouthpiece with her hand, mumbled inaudibly with the caller, turning to look at David intermittently with a suspicious expression. She motioned the three men to huddle with her. The only line David could hear from what appeared to be an argument was when Henrietta raised her voice at Angus to say, "Well, are you in or out?" This started to lift David's hopes until he saw Angus turn to look at him angrily. After haggling for almost a minute, she finally said something into the pone and hung the handset back on the cradle the stagehand was dutifully holding.

Henrietta turned back to face David as the three men sat down with doubtful expressions. She looked at David and asked, "Mr. Wales, do you know what an 'angel' is in theater terms, and I don't mean one with a trumpet?"

David stood up, cleared his throat, swallowed, and said, "Hopefully, I think it would refer to the four of you."

Henrietta gave a brief chuckle. "Well, actually, Mr. Wales, the four of us were going to be your devils. With three misogynists and an atheist, you didn't have much of a chance. But, in addition to your trumpeting angel, you appear to have one who owns a phone. Actually, the theater term 'angel' refers to a show backer who remains anonymous, so I can't tell you who made that phone call, but they agreed to back whatever part of the shows funding the four of us didn't. That was enough to make three greedy misogynists and one smart atheist decide to buy into your musical. We, however, intend to protect our behinds by picking the best producer/director team we can find. *The Piano Lover* has found a home on Broadway. Let's hope he stays in residence long enough to make our investment pay off."

As Henrietta rose, Alex rushed to help her with her coat as David and Dimitri advanced timidly to say goodbye. The four older people obviously shared a friendship with Alex and were more cordial with him than the other two young men. Angus glared at David as he adjusted the fur lined collar of his overcoat. "You see *South Pacific*, young man?"

David felt compelled to ingratiate himself to these people. "Yes sir. Did you like it?"

Angus snorted. "Damn right! I made a lot of money on that one." Then he stared at David, spacing his words out threateningly. "Didn't lose one...thin...dime!"

The man with the goatee smiled questioningly at Dimitri. "Lebedev? That's Russian for 'swan.' Are you the white swan or the black swan?"

Dimitri's brow furrowed as he looked at Alex and then the man. "I'm the confused swan." The man hesitated, then chuckled nervously.

The portly man held the paperwork in his hand and tapped Alex's chest with it three times. "I'll have my accountant contact your accountant," then he moved toward the door.

Everyone stopped as Henrietta turned to face the three young men and the cast in the background with raised hands. "Thank you everyone for a wonderful performance. If there is a God, may She bless this show!" Then she lowered her hands and her smile hardened. "And if, as I believe, there is no God, I expect you all to work your asses off to make a success of this production," and she turned and exited with the three older men.

The instant they were out the door, Alex picked up the phone that was still on the library table and dialed frantically. David and Dimitri looked at him wide eyed and he answered their unspoken question. "I'm calling Marvin, my lawyer, now to find out who the angel is. All Henrietta would tell me is that it was a financial entity called TGC incorporated." Alex put one finger to his free ear as a voice was heard on the line. "Hello, Marvin? Yes! TGC ink! Yes! That's all we know. Okay, I'll hold." Alex swivelled the mouthpiece away from his lips. "He's checking on the other line."

Princess and Gabriel joined them around the table. David looked at Gabriel. "I don't know of any company or personal name with the initials 'T' or 'G' or 'C,' other than you, Gabriel. Are you part of a corporation?"

Gabriel's eyes bulged in surprise. "No. Never had no assets to incorporate." He looked towards Alex. "Those initials don't even fit Alex's newfound grandparents, an' he din' wan' to mortgage his mama's house."

Dimitri winced. "We're talking a lot more money than that to offer to back a Broadway show."

Alex spoke into the mouthpiece excitedly. "Yes! Yes!" Then his raised eyebrows dropped. "Is that all? Okay. Thanks for trying." He hung up the phone and looked at the circle around him. "TGC ink applied for a corporate charter two days ago in Louisiana. Until all the paperwork is completed, we wont be able to get details on them. All we know is that their underwriting is sufficient to back the offer they made."

Princess surveyed the questioning faces around her, and displayed her characteristic optimism as she said, "God moves in mysterious ways. We know she's female. We know she's blue. And we know she sent us an angel. If she wants the identity of that angel to be a mystery, who are we to question her?"

Piano Lover

from the musical "The Piano Lover"

words and music by William Karl Thomas

279

28 Dmin7   G7   C   Caug   Dmin   G7

love right from the start And I will cling to you I'll sing to you what ev - er you de - sire my lips will

31 A   Bflat7   Dmin   G7 \   Aflat   Cmin

bring to you a ring to you that sets your soul on fire For I am yours my ev - ery part cre -

34 Dmin   G7   F   Dmin   Dmin   Ddim   C

a - ted by a plan made just for you for you for Pi - an - no Lo - ver Man

She's Blue

fom the musical "The Piano Lover"

words and music by William Karl Thomas

281

We can save hu - man - i - ty but on - ly if our minds are free It

must start some where don't you see start here and now with you and me IT'S

TRUE! that God is blue and she's un-hap py with the things we do SO STOP! mak ing her blue.

2

Chapter Eighteen
T.G.C., INC.

Three days before the *The Piano Lover* presentation in New York and immediately after Julienne angrily left David and Justine in front of The Morning Call coffee shop, she debated whether or not to return to her parents home and lick her wounds, or consider some other less embarrassing alternative. A couple blocks away, across from Café duMonde, she entered the gates of Jackson Square and sat on an empty iron bench near a Civil War cannon. She looked at St. Louis Cathedral, flanked by the Cabildo Buildings, and thought that many would chose to enter that house of worship in order to meditate and sort things out, possibly appealing for guidance to the living clergy or the ghosts of saints whose statues lined the walls.

As she stared at the Cathedral, she noticed two petite female figures exit the central doors and head toward the Square as they were absorbed in conversation. She felt mesmerized by the two figures, something about them surprising her, until they got close enough and she recognized Princess talking to Aurora. She felt a momentary panic to run, but surprise paralyzed her until they were standing before her, their eye contact expressing equal, but happier, surprise.

Princess beamed with a genuine smile. "Julienne! What a pleasant surprise!"

Aurora spoke in a hoarse whisper. "Julienne, mi amor."

Julienne's brow furrowed. "Aurora, what are you doing here?"

Aurora sat beside her. "I'm performing a benefit por Caesar Chavez add de Auditorium Municipal."

Princess sat on Julienne's other side. "I was showing Aurora where Richard and I got married, then we were going to Café duMonde. Do you want to join us?"

Julienne looked down at her clenched fists. "No thanks. I've just had a horrible fight with David, and I don't want to go anywhere I might run into him."

Julienne flinched as Aurora put her arms around her and leaned her forehead to touch Julienne's. "Mi amor pobre. Lo siento por tu."

Princess looked sad and waved a limp wrist at Julienne saying, "Whatever she said, me too." She shrugged her shoulders. "Men! You can't live with 'em. They can't live without us."

Julienne shifted her weight to escape from Aurora's embrace. "You mean, men, you can't live with 'em, you can't live without 'em."

Princess shook her head sideways and said innocently, "Oh, I can live without 'em." Then she smiled at the other two women and wrinkled her nose. "Life's just more fun with 'em."

Julienne sniffled and accepted the handkerchief Aurora proffered, dabbing her eyes before she said, "Not always it isn't."

Princess leaned toward her with a concerned look and tone. "He didn't hit you, did he? Don't let 'em do that! You're not twelve years old anymore and you don't have to stick around for that!"

Julienne stared at the iron lace balconies on The Pontalba Buildings across the street. "No, I don't think I'd ever have to worry about that with David."

Princess's eyes followed Julienne's as she scanned the balconies. "So, he didn't hit you, and I didn't think David drank much, or did drugs, or gambled."

After several seconds of silence and no eye contact, Julienne looked down at the handkerchief in her hand and spat out her words in exasperation. "Okay! He slept with another woman."

The other two women gasped in surprise, then Aurora looked at Julienne twirled her finger in a small horizontal circle, and asked softly, "You mean togedder," then she reversed the circle, "or nod togedder?"

Julienne rolled her eyes. "Not together?"

Princess looked back at the balconies and tried to sound casual. "Anybody we know?"

Julienne fidgeted with the handkerchief. "He slept with my mother."

Both women gasped again.

Julienne looked from one to the other, then back at the handkerchief. "But he didn't know she was my mother. I didn't know she was my mother. I didn't know I was adopted until a few hours ago."

Both women turned to her, Aurora again putting her arms around her and saying, "Mi pobre nino." This time Julienne did not flinch, but joined the embrace of the other two as she broke into sobs and the others consoled her. As her sobs subsided, Aurora broke the embrace and threw her hands up. "Eeef nod Café duMonde, less go lonch someplace else."

Julienne dried her tears. "Someplace we wont run into anyone we know."

Princess's eyes widened. "Let's cross Canal Street. People from the Quarter never cross Canal Street."

Aurora looked excited. "Less go a la cafeteria I lake. Id have Spanish decor, senoritas en los balconies, twinkling estrellas en de ceiling."

Julienne's eyes lit up. "Oh, you mean Morrison's Cafeteria. I loved to go there when I was a child. It was like visiting another country."

Julienne explained the revelations she discovered about her origins on their long walk to Morrison's. As the black waiters unloaded their food from trays to table, Princess removed a dime from her purse, then noticed the other two putting quarters on the trays, so she traded the dime for a quarter from her purse and thanked the waiter as she placed the quarter on his tray. As she sat down, she said, "I always thought Justine was a lot scarier than Valentina. You're lucky she gave you her beauty genes, and luckier that she did not have the opportunity to raise you to be as bitchy as she is, if you'll forgive my saying so."

Julienne looked down at her perfectly garnished trout almondine. "You're absolutely right. I won the mommy lottery when I was adopted by my mother. And if Justine has any assets, it's her body. I always felt competitive and jealous when guys would admire her ass every time she went up to David's piano."

Princess smiled at her plate of macaroni and cheese. "And I believe David when he said she jumped his bones and it was only once. I saw her trying to get her claws into him several times, and he dodged her like a bullfighter dancing with a red cape."

Julienne squeezed lemon over her fish and looked concerned. "I know, I know. It was her fault, it was before he and I connected, and he had no way of knowing." She stabbed a piece of almondine on her fork and looked at Princess. "It's just that it seems so weird!"

Princess held a fork full of macaroni and cheese in mid air and looked at Julienne with a stoic expression. "Julienne, I'm a drag queen who married an aging English lush in an illegal bootleg gay ceremony presided over by a night club barker who got his divinity degree from a classified ad in the back of a girlie magazine, while a giant pipe organ marched us down the aisle, all this in a world famous cathedral that houses the arch diocese of the Catholic Church in New Orleans. You think your problem's weird? What's weird is that I haven't been struck with lightening by now!"

Julienne waved her fork full of fish in a circle. "Okay! Duly noted. Little rich girl complains excessively about slight irregularities in her love life relationships."

Aurora picked up a bottle of Tabasco from the center of the table and pointed to her plate. "Dese tamale no ees authentico, pero ees muy bueno." She opened the bottle and squirted a generous amount of hot sauce on her food, then smiled. "Now ees mas bueno!" She savored her first bite, swallowed, then waved her fork toward the other two. "Diga mi a la David's moosical, que dice, 'Lo Pianista.' You read id?"

Princess's eyes widened. "Read it? I'm in it! It's wonderful, so empowering for women." She turned to Julienne. "Did you read it, Julienne?"

Now Julienne's eyes lit up. "Yes! I love it!" She touched Aurora's wrist. "Aurora, you'll love it. In it, God is a woman!"

Aurora spoke with her mouth full. "Of course, God ees a woman. All women know dad!"

Julienne shook her head rapidly from side to side. "But men don't! And that's what the musical is about. Men discovering that God is a woman, and she is therefore in part of them and they better damn well wake up and discover that before they blow the world up with their war toys."

Aurora beamed with approval. "I lake id! When id open on Broadway?"

Julienne gave a pained smile. "It isn't even funded yet. They had a tough time trying to raise enough money to present it to the backers. They're leaving tomorrow to go beg before some money people in a rented rehearsal hall with a cast of ten, including David, Gabriel, and Princess."

287

Princess giggled. "I wear a blonde wig and wiggle around like Marilyn Monroe. I think I'm playing you."

Aurora looked confused and Julienne looked embarrassed, then said, "Actually, Dimitri wrote the original book for his marionette show. In it he fantasized his attraction to David and draws a parallel between David's attraction to you and me, which he portrays in the musical as *The Piano Lover* being attracted to both a rich female customer and a beautiful drag queen who works at the same club where he plays the piano."

Aurora looked slightly stunned as she looked at Princess. "So David ees makin' me into you, and makin' you into Marilyn."

Julienne shook her head sideways. "No! Dimitri wrote the book. Alex is the primary producer. David is writing the songs and lyrics, and adding some input into the story along the way. David was not happy when he learned what Dimitri had done, but Alex liked the drag queen character and kept it in, and also changed some characters such as recasting the angel with his de facto stepfather, Gabriel."

A smile returned to Aurora's face. "Oooooooh. I lake Gabriel." She tilted her head to one side. "Okay. De story's weird. Princess's life ees weird. You relationship wid David ees juss a liddle weird. We can live wid dat!" She wiped her mouth with the napkin. "Now, wad we do to make dis hoppon on Broadway?"

Julienne looked surprised. "What do you mean? Either they get the money from the backers or they don't. How can we influence that?"

Aurora stared at Julienne intently. "I god money. You god money. All God's dotters god money. We pud our monies togedder and make David's moosical hoppon!"

Julienne looked doubtful. "I don't know how much money you have, Aurora, but I certainly don't have that much, and

288

I'm not about to approach my parents on David's behalf. My father hates him."

Aurora looked at Julienne defiantly. "Quando dinero por la moosical?"

Julienne looked at the table and ground her teeth. "I don't know. A quarter, a half, maybe a million dollars." She looked at Aurora and wrinkled her nose. "I've never produced a Broadway musical. I don't know."

Aurora smiled at Julienne intently. "Bud you creade a galleria. Each pintura sur la wall en la galleria ees una producion., un poco que you comission." She spread her hands. "I creade records. Un poco tiempo, I creade uno label nuevo por los records. I creade concerts. All God's dotters creade; creade paintings, gallerias, records, concerts, even babies and Broadway moosicals."

Julienne shrugged. "You're talking co-op, a coalition, a consortium. But none of us really know anything about creating a musical."

Aurora's eyebrows wiggled. "Bud Alex and Dimitri and David do, an all we godda do is make de money hoppon, an we done even have to have de money to make de money hoppon."

Julienne looked confused. "What do you mean, we don't have to have the money?"

Aurora signaled the waiter. "Tengan usted, una flan?"

The waiter looked confused until Julienne said, "Do you have one of those upside down custards with the caramel on top?"

The waiter smiled with recognition. "Oh, yes m'am."

Julienne looked to Princess for approval, then told the waiter, "Three, please."

Aurora leaned forward. "I take business classes een Hollywood. Por una corporation, o por uno projecto, no ees necessito todo el dinero. Solamente promesa el dinero. Diga

289

'underwriting.' Eeef you made de money before, de banks gamble you gonna make de money again. You god uno abogodo, a lawyer?"

Julienne's brow furrowed. "My lawyer is too close to my father and I wouldn't trust him not to tell my father or share my father's opinions about such investments."

Princess smiled broadly. "I know someone who has a great lawyer, and I bet she believes that God is a woman, and I bet she believes in David and Dimitri, even if she doesn't know Alex."

The other two looked at her suspiciously as the waiter set down the three flans.

Princess looked at their skepticism defiantly. "Yeah! Dimitri's told me a lot about Valentina Sciciliana, and I think she's a good and fair woman at heart, and she damn sure knows about money." Princess looked compassionately at Julienne. "And she didn't do too bad picking some good parents for you, Julienne." She picked up her flan spoon. "I don't have no money to put in the pot, but I'm putting my ass on the line going to New York for the presentation. So, if you're willing to talk to her, I wanna be there when we meet with Valentina," and she scooped up a spoonful of flan and held it up like a toast, smiling broader as the other two did likewise.

****

Six hours after lunching at Morrison's, the three women stood in Valentina's living room waiting for her. Only Julienne was aware of how expensive the Persian rugs and French tapestries were, or the many porcelain and pewter figurines, the genuine Degas painting in an elaborate gold leaf frame, and dozens of sterling silver picture frames filled with photos of famous people. Although the two younger women

290

recognized such names as a youthful Frank Sinatra and Tony Bennett, only Julienne recognized some of the names as world famous opera, ballet, and foreign film stars. Aurora gasped as she read the inscription on one picture. "She mus' have bin una chica muy caliente. Leesten to dis, 'Tanks fo' de bess nide 'o mi life,' and dis wan, 'Bless you for makin' mi dreams come true,' and anudder, 'You bring mi fantasies to life.'" Aurora looked at Julienne with widened eyes. "She mus' have bin la tigresa een bed!"

Julienne shook her head sideways. "I don't think those praises were as much for her as for the young ladies she employed."

Aurora's eyes widened even more and she spoke in a whisper. "She una senora de casa de putas?"

Julienne answered in a stage whisper. "Twenty-five years ago. Not recently."

Princess looked at the two others sternly. "She's a very nice lady with a very good heart, otherwise she wouldn't have agreed to see us."

They all three turned with startled expressions upon hearing Valentina say, "Thank you for that vote of confidence, young lady." She stood inside her front door in her trademark black skirt, hose, high heels, and sweater that covered a white blouse with a black string bow tie. Her shiny black hair and dark eye makeup was reminiscent of cartoonist Charles Adams macabre character, Morticia. "I see Zoe let you in." She looked at Princess. "You work with Dimitri, don't you? What is your name, dear?"

Princess blinked. "Princess. It's my stage name, Princess Pocahontas. My real name's too hard for everyone to pronounce, so everyone just calls me Princess."

Valentina looked at her from head to toe and back again. "Very well.....Princess, and Miss Julienne deVille, and Miss...," she closed her eyes and tapped her temple, "La Lune,

291

La Lune," then opened her eyes, "Ah yes, Miss Aurora Alonzo. Am I right?"

Aurora looked at her with a tentative smile. "Si, ees mi nombre, Aurora Alonzo, pero I no work add La Lune no mas."

Valentina walked over to a regal looking chair that commanded the entire room. "Please, let's all be seated." From a table beside her chair, she picked up her black rimmed glasses and some paperwork, putting on the glasses and shuffling through the papers as she read. "Miss deVille, my lawyer's tentative research indicates your and Miss Alonzo's assets are verifiable in the approximate amounts you stated. You will receive copies of the corporate papers he files which provide verification of the necessary amounts of my assets required." She set the papers down, removed her glasses, and looked at the three women seated around her. "Based on a one million dollar startup, I propose the following distribution with proportionate voting rights to the three principals necessary to apply for a corporate charter, said three principals providing proportionate capital or collateral; 16% each for myself, Miss deVille, and Miss Alonzo. As minor investors requiring no capital or collateral investment, 2% each to my assistant, Miss Zoe Sellier, and Miss Princess. That gives us 52%, controlling interest, with 48% for future investors who will buy in at a considerably higher rate." She leaned forward slightly. "If that's agreeable to everyone, I'll have the papers drawn up and an offer made to the New York lawyer representing Dimitri, David, and their friend Alex."

The three young women looked at each other, nodding agreement. Princess looked surprised. "I didn't expect anything for me, really!"

Valentina smiled at her. "Zoe Sellier will act as my proxy when I'm not available and when travel to New York is required. You, Princess, as a performer in New York, can act as a proxy for your two friends whose careers do not allow them to be in New York during the run of the show. You can also be the eyes and ears of this Consortium and report back to us anything you think we need to know, or anything we ask you to look into. So you and Zoe will earn your percentages. Let's just hope these percentages prove to be worth anything."

Aurora smiled warmly at Valentina. "I lake you. I takin' business law class een Hollywood, an' I lake talk wit you about business, about women in business. I see you la tigre een business."

Valentina smiled condescendingly at Aurora. "You ladies have named your new corporation The Goddess Consortium. As such, let me tell you this. In life, you need doctors, lawyers, and Indian Chiefs, Indian Chiefs being a euphemism for politicians. Most of them are men. Whenever possible, have a female doctor if you can find a really good one. When it comes to lawyers and politicians, most of the well connected ones are men. I picked my male lawyer by reviewing all my female peers whose sons were lawyers. I picked the best lawyer whose mother was my good friend. If he screws me in business, he'll have to answer to his mother. That's where the Goddess aspect comes in. Among the men in your life, somewhere in their lives is a woman who can be your ally. Identify her. Befriend her. Keep the balance of power in The Goddess Consortium."

The three young women smiled at each other, impressed with Valentina's logic. Aurora's eyes blazed at Valentina. "Dere's sometin' you wan dad I god. Sometin' Mehicana, sometin' show beeznez, something dad make you lake me so you tell me all dese tings I need to know."

Valentina closed and opened her eyes slowly. "We'll see. Time will tell."

Princess looked delighted. "See! I told you! You guys are talking Goddess. Now you've met one!"

293

Valentina blinked. "All women are Goddesses, Princess. It just remains dormant inside most of them until some emergency calls it forth." She stood up. "Now, if you don't mind, I'd like to talk to Miss deVille in private. Zoe has just opened the bar downstairs and you two ladies are invited to go down and order whatever complimentary drinks you'd like." She headed for the bedroom door and looked at Julienne. "Miss deVille, would you, please?" And she opened and entered the door.

Julienne shut the door behind her as she entered the bedroom dominated by a four poster bed. The large front windows looked out on St. Louis Street and the room was, like the living room, filled with expensive paintings, figurines, and many elaborately framed photos. Valentina gestured to one of two gilded chairs that flanked a marble table filled with framed pictures. As they sat, Julienne identified some of the photos on the table as pictures of herself in various stages of her childhood. Valentina noted her recognition of the photos and said, "Now that you know part of the story, I can tell you. You weren't aware of us, but Zoe and I attended every communion, every graduation, every significant event of your childhood. For the first six months of your life, you were our precious baby. The child that neither of us could have on our own. Before the age of birth control, primitive abortions often rendered women barren. Neither Zoe nor I ever had children for that reason. Everyone thought we were lesbians, but, truth was, we were simply the only survivors without children."

Julienne's jaw dropped. "So, you adopted me first?"

Valentina looked out the window with a pained expression. "Sort of, I guess." Her brow furrowed as she looked out the window. "But, in fairness to myself and Justine, let me explain some things you don't know. During the Italian revolution of 1884, my mother was a teenager in the vanquished Southern part of Italy. Though desperately poor,

294

she was pretty enough to attract a wealthy married man, but, when she was pregnant, he chose to get rid of the inconvenience by buying her a steerage class ticket to America."

Valentina looked at a crucifix on the wall next to her bed flanked by a print of The Virgin Mary and an antique photo of a woman Julienne suspected was Valentina's mother. Valentina continued. "My mother was rejected at Ellis Island for an eye infection, and could not pay the return passage to Italy. As sometimes happened with steerage class passengers, as the boat continued to New Orleans before returning to Europe, they sold my mother to Mississippi River pirates before reaching New Orleans. Eventually she was resold to a madame who ran a bordello in Storyville."

Julienne gasped and stared at Valentina horrified. Valentina sighed. "I was raised in that bordello until I was thirteen, at which time, as was the custom in Storyville bordellos, my virginity was auctioned to a select group of affluent patrons." Valentina smiled at Julienne. "Fortunately for me, a man named Michael McGreagor won the auction, and the next morning, he negotiated with my mother and the madame to purchase me as his personal property." Valentina picked up a framed photo of a handsome Scotsman and handed it to Julienne. "He was a talented, enterprising, and a very kind man, and he treated me as his wife and business partner. When I was nineteen, he created The Mariner's Club as my personal enterprise legally in my name. And he was your father."

Julienne looked puzzled. "But, how..?"

Valentina raised a finger. "Let me explain. A French girl showed up at The Mariner's Club looking for work. Her sad story was that she had run away from her farmer parents in Provence, France, to explore the exciting night life of Paris, but her father tracked her down, returned her to the farm, and beat her for her rebellion. She ran away again to Marseilles, a Mediterranean seaport where two Italian sailors convinced her they could provide her passage to America as a stowaway. While the two men took turns collecting sexual payments from her in the rat infested cargo hold, the ship languished for two weeks in various Caribbean ports before its first American port of New Orleans. True to their word, they delivered her safe and sound, but penniless and sexually exhausted, on the ballast stone docks of New Orleans. She begged for another two weeks before taking the advice of a waitress on Decatur Street to apply for work at The Mariner's Club."

Julienne asked, "Justine?"

Valentina closed and opened her eyes, nodding her head affirmatively. "Yes. Justine cleaned up to become a striking beauty, and she affected a sophistication and false claim to have been a celebrated chanteuse in Paris. Her breathy singing voice did not impress most professional musicians, but it, and the suggestive lyrics she sang, incited sensual fantasies in the minds of her audience. It also incited a gleam in Mack's eye, and, within six months of her employment, Justine was pregnant with Mack's child. I suspected, but did not know for sure until Justine began to show. She and Mack moved out of The Mariner's Club together. After you were born, Mack brought you to me because Justine wanted to sell you to a rival brothel. They used to raise girl children as servants and prostitute them when they came of age. Mack begged me to take you, find good parents for you, and give you a better life."

Julienne spoke almost in a whisper. "Why did you decide on my mother and father? Because they were rich?"

Valentina looked at her and smiled. "Rene was not rich then. He was born dirt poor. Your mother's family had the money, and she only inherited it a decade after they were married." She looked back out the window. "But, to his credit, he compounded your mother's fortune by being a silent partner in Mack's illegal businesses. Sometime after Mack left you with me, Rene proposed adopting you." Valentina closed her eyes. "I think it was the pain in your mother's eyes, the hope that you might help save their marriage, as much as Zoe's and my realization that raising you in a brothel would not be fair to you, that led us to give you up."

Julienne looked at the picture of McGreagor. "My father confessed that it wasn't my mother that was barren, but him."

Valentina raised one eyebrow. "We all knew that. Working girls know. We could look at Angelina and know she was fertile. And none of the girls ever got pregnant with Rene."

Julienne set the photo down. "So he did...?"

Valentina closed her eyes briefly and shook her head sideways. "Only after he had convinced himself that Angelina was barren."

Julienne frowned questioningly. "Did he and Justine ever... ?"

Valentina gave a slight snort. "Oh no! Rene did not like strong women. He liked them cutesy and compliant. Tough and sophisticated scared the hell out of him."

Julienne chuckled. "No wonder he didn't want me coming to The Voodoo Room. You must have scared the holy hell out of him!"

Valentina echoed her chuckle. "He still comes to me when he needs contacts or advice. But, because of my past, he treats me like a social leper, making clandestine appointments, sneaking into the patio after hours with his hat brim pulled down and his collar pulled up."

Julienne set the framed picture of Michael McGreagor on the table, staring at it. "What happened to my biological father?"

Valentina closed her eyes and raised her eyebrows. "Eventually, Justine was unfaithful to him, he left her and

297

married a wealthy widow in California, and passed away a few years ago." She opened her eyes. "Justine came back and attempted to renew her association with me, but I had lost The Mariner's Club and opened The Voodoo Room. I had noting to do with her and refused to let her know your fate in order to protect you."

Julienne looked at Valentina sadly. "I owe you so much."

Valentina looked at Julienne warmly. "It has been such a joy for Zoe and me that you discovered The Voodoo Room. I was even grateful that David seemed to stimulate your attendance, even though I questioned whether he was good for you in the long run. As much as I like David and believe in his talent, I was ambivalent when Rene tried to bribe him to disappear."

Julienne's brow furrowed. "Well, just like his musical, that relationship is an iffy work in progress."

Valentina stood up. "Well, regardless of what happens. Please, Julienne, don't stop coming to The Voodoo Room. I promise that, in public, Zoe and I will remain professional and aloof, and we'll leave the private choices entirely up to you." As Julienne stood, Valentina extended her arms. "Please, child, may I hug you?" As Julienne moved into her arms, Valentina embraced her tightly for five seconds, then held her face as she kissed each cheek, then held her at arms length as she said, "And, Julienne, would you please give Zoe a hug on your way out." Valentina dropped her arms. "You know, Zoe was also pregnant when you were born. She was your wet nurse. After Rene and Angelina took you, Zoe had a miscarriage and could never have children afterward. Whether you like it or not, you have two foster mothers who will always love you."

Julienne's eyes brimmed with tears as she impulsively hugged Valentina a second time, then turned and exited the door.

****

Two days after the *The Piano Lover* presentation, David poured coffee in the four mismatched mugs on the bare table which was mismatched with the other sparse furnishings of the Bleeker Street loft in Greenwich Village. Alex looked around as he raised his coffee mug. "I see you've decorated in an early Salvation Army motif."

David sat and added sugar and milk to his coffee. "Well, the BMI checks covered the lease on this loft, but very little else. If Dimitri, Gabriel, and I are going to use it in our new bi-coastal lifestyle, " he looked at Dimitri and Gabriel across the table, "I'm hoping the two of you can chip in when the monthly bills arrive." He sipped his coffee. "Speaking of which, Dimitri and I have to leave this afternoon if we're going to keep our jobs in New Orleans."

Dimitri rolled his eyes. "Yes! Now that my *The Piano Lover* story is committed on Broadway, I have to write a whole new show for Aladdin's in New Orleans."

Gabriel frowned at Alex. "Alex, did you get the skinny on de angel backer?"

Alex reached behind him and unzipped his thin briefcase. "Yeah, Marvin put a rush on the papers filed in Louisiana. Here they are. Lemme see. The letterhead on the letter of intent says, 'TGC, Inc.,' sub-titled, 'The Goddess Consortium, Incorporated.'" He looked at the others. "Almost sounds like they were created specifically for our project." He looked back at the papers. "Let's see, whereas and wherefore, bullshit, bullshit. Oh, here in the margin. 'Chairman of the Board: Valentina Sicililana.'" Alex looked at David in shock.

Dimitri smiled delightedly. "Bless her black cast iron Sicilian heart! Boys, she's richer than Midas, and, if she believes in us, you better believe we're gonna succeed!"

Alex looked back at the papers. "'Members of the Board: Julienne deVille.'" Everyone looked at David, who looked stunned. Alex continued. "'Aurora Alonzo.'" Again, everyone looked at David, whose jaw dropped. Alex continued. "'Members at large: Zoe Sellier, Princess Kowi Anuskasha Rose.'" Alex frowned at the others. "That little witch! It's a good thing she already flew back to New Orleans. If she were here, I'd turn her across my knee and spank her gorgeous butt until it was as red as a cooked crawfish!"

Dimitri shrugged. "I'm not surprised. Princess always admired Val's strength and independence. And I'd think twice about tangling with Princess. I've seen her kick butt when someone got too fresh at the club."

Alex returned his attention to the papers. "Well, it looks like Val's lawyer is craftier than my friends on Broadway. TGC, Inc. owns 52% of the show and calls the shots all the way down the line." He looked up at the others with an admiring smile. "And they did it with less actual cash than my Broadway friends who had to buy in at an inflated price." He chuckled. "That must've made Angus grumpier than usual."

Gabriel raised his eyebrows questioningly as he asked David, "You think this means Julienne has forgiven you?"

Dimitri looked at his coffee mug and shook his head sideways. "Wow! That's a double whammy with Julienne's and Aurora's names united."

David gritted his teeth. "I dunno. All this went down before Aurora spoke to me at Moissant Airport, but, just like Princess, they didn't mention any of it." He sighed deeply. "I guess I wont know until I go back to work for the Chairman of the Board tomorrow."

****

300

The crank phone in the corner rang and Zoe answered it like an actress in a long running play delivering the opening line for the evenings performance. "She's on her way down." As Zoe lit the table candles and Pete opened the front doors, David sat at the piano awaiting Valentina's usual entrance. He knew she would behave just like Zoe did when he arrived that evening, just like nothing had ever happened. Sure enough, Valentina stepped through the patio doors and delivered her line perfectly. "Let the games begin," and never looked once in his direction as David began to play *South Rampart Street Parade*.

David mused, The French Quarter is like that, a time/space warp vortex. People come from England, France, Mexico, New York, Hollywood, the planet Mars, and they fall into a centuries old romantic period where what happened in more recent times and places falls away, and you're enveloped in the aroma of rum drinks, the golden glow of candlelight, and the moon's silvery beams slithering across the banana trees in the patio.

When he had performed in the New York presentation, he was aware that it was a fantasy, that they were creating an emotional response with lights and words and music and dance. Now he had the curious feeling that his life in the French Quarter was a sort of fantasy. If he were to write it as a non-fiction biographical narrative, it would be as unbelievable as Gabriel being a trumpet playing angel from God, or the piano before him being a woman he was making love to. He heard himself playing music and saw customers strolling in from St. Louis Street, but he had the strange feeling he was observing it all from somewhere above, watching himself play a role, one which, if he were not careful, others would write for him.

He watched Lenny and Louie arrive. Though not blood related, they were like brothers, arguing about such petty things as whether Dixie Beer or Jax Beer was best, but comfortable enough with each other to hug when they agreed or ruffle each other's hair if they lost an argument. They were too homely and alcohol impaired to be attractive to women, but, sooner or later, some woman would be desperate enough to settle for one of them, ensnare them with better food and sex than they were used to, and attempt to reform them. Once domesticated, the first to marry would make the other follow.

Richard Rose came in, as he sometimes did before starting work at the same time David quit work. He waited until David could take a break and join him at an empty back table, one David chose that was a comfortable distance from Valentina. Richard patted the sleeve of David's forearm and said, "I'm very grateful to you and Dimitri for watching over Princess." David waved his hand to indicate no thanks were necessary. Richard took a swig from his beer bottle, then looked at David with a slight frown. "Did she talk to either of you about me?" He raised his eyebrows. "Maybe about snoring, or ranting about Nazis," he paused, "or drinking or something?"

David shrugged. "No. With so little time for rehearsals and eating and cabbing back and forth, we didn't have any time to socialize. Why do you ask?"

Richard looked at his beer and set it down forcefully. "Oh, she's beginning to talk more and more about cutting me alcohol consumption, eating right, and even got some brochures for some sanatorium somewhere that passes itself off as a resort." He sighed. "I weigh twice as much and am almost twice as tall as my little Princess, but she's beginning to sound like she's me bloody mum!"

David's brow furrowed. "She cares about you, Richard. And she's a smart young lady who deserves to be listened to with an open mind. Maybe the two of you should talk to a doctor together to put both your minds at ease. She may learn that all of her fears are not necessary. You may learn some ways to stay around longer so the two of you can enjoy more years together."

Richard stared at the beer bottle. "So you think I'm a lush, too."

David sighed. "Oh, everyone knows you're an alcoholic, Richard, but everyone likes you too much to say it to your face. You're the only one who uses those words in reference to yourself. The problem is, you think you're joking. You don't believe your own words. And you're reluctant to do anything about it for Princess's sake, much less your own." David patted Richard's sleeve. "I love you, buddy, but I've got to go back to work," and he returned to the piano as Richard pushed the unfinished beer away and left without a word.

On his next break, David hoped to avoid Valentina by weaving his way through the tables of some of his fans with a line of banter. "How ARE you." "So good to see you." "So glad you liked it, I love *South Pacific* too." "Thank GOD you like Schubert, because, honestly, sometimes Chopin is just too damn hard to play!" He found himself ending up at the front end of the bar with Lenny, Louie, and Jules. Jules looked at him almost malevolently. "Good evening, Jules."

Jules was very cool. "I wish I could say it was a good evening, but I don't think there will be many good evenings for me for quite some time."

David sat on the stool next to him, facing away from the bar so Pete wouldn't think he was a new customer. "Why, Jules? What's wrong?"

Jules narrowed his eyes at him. "As if you didn't know. You and that Svengali of a boss of yours."

David blinked. "I'm sorry, Jules. I've been out of town for a few days. I don't know what you're talking about."

Jules looked at him in disbelief. "You don't know that the two loves of my life have been lost to me forever?"

303

David's eyes widened in surprise. "Are you talking about Justine and Armand? Did something happen to them? Are they all right?"

Jules anger subsided somewhat and he tilted his head to one side. "Well, nothing happened in the sense of a car crash or a train wreck or a boat sinking. But they're gone."

David's eyes bulged. "Dead?"

Jules' eyes bulged. "Oh God, no! She's Svengali, not Lucretia Borgia." He turned to look at his drink and shook his head sideways. "Although I wouldn't put that past her, really, I wouldn't."

David turned toward him. "Jules, what did you mean when you said they're gone?"

Jules sighed. "They're gone to Paris so Armand can attend the Sorbonne, and they'll be gone for at least four years."

David looked relieved. "Okay. They're alive, and well, and living it up in Paris. Thank God! You had me going for a minute there, Jules."

Jules looked at David out of the corner of his eye. "You really didn't know? I assumed she did it for you and Julienne, and I assumed you at least knew, even if you didn't put her up to it."

David looked at him questioningly. "Put her up to what?"

Jules turned to him and inhaled deeply. "Your employer is a Svengali with strings on a lot of important people in this town, including Armand's fabulously rich father."

David nodded his head up and down. "I can believe that."

Jules looked toward the far end of the bar where Valentina was absorbed in her newspaper. "She played upon their weaknesses, Justine's and Armand's. Oh, I love them both dearly, but Justine is a mercenary and Armand is a puppet. Your Svengali twisted Armand's father's arm to renegotiate the allowance in exchange for good school grades. He threatened to cut them off unless Armand attended the

Sorbonne and they moved to Paris. He even upped the allowance." Jules turned back to his drink. "But, of course, it didn't include any provisions for me."

David frowned. "They didn't juggle things to make any accommodation for you?"

Jules looked at him with raised eyebrows. "I was extra baggage, dropped me like extra baggage full of hot potatoes." He turned to face David. "You know, Armand and I were a couple before Justine showed up. When she learned how rich his father was, she turned him into a bisexual. I went along and participated in the bisexual thing, but I think she was always looking to dump me." He looked at Valentina again. "And, now, thanks to your Svengali, Justine's succeeded."

David looked at Valentiina. "How can you be sure it's Val?"

Jules sighed. "Because Val knows Justine's past, Amand's father's business connections with Mack and tawdry social connections with The Mariner's Club." He looked at David. "Do you really need me to draw dirty pictures for you?"

David pursed his lips. "Noooooo! I think you've painted a convincingly bawdy enough picture with your words." He slid off the stool and looked at Jules sadly. "Would you like me to play something for you?"

Jules eyebrows raised hopefully. "Oh, would you play *Willow Weep For Me*? And could I come sit by the piano while you sing it to me?" David's eyes rolled skyward, and Jules held one hand up as if pledging. "I promise I wont hit on you, like Justine always did. But, maybe some nice looking man would see how sad I look and take pity on me."

David headed to the piano. "Be my guest." Jules took his drink to a table beside the piano and looked up adoringly at David as he adjusted the boom mike a little closer and began to sing the sad song of unrequited love.

As David looked at the tears streaming down Jules sad face, Zoe appeared with two drinks, placing one before David and saying, "The young man at that table over there said your song was beautiful, David." She placed the second drink in front of Jules and said, "He also said you looked like you needed this," and she left with a sad smile on her face.

David and Jules looked over at the handsome well dressed young man at the table who raised his glass to them. Jules looked at David and said, "Excuse me, David, but I have to go thank someone for their generosity, and their compassion." He turned a hidden smile to David. "And for looking so absolutely gorgeous!" Then he resumed his sad expression as he strolled over to sit with the young man.

David looked over to the rear corner to see Valentina staring at him, but she quickly returned her eyes to her newspaper.

Chapter Nineteen
THE FAR EAST

David slipped into the theater seat next to Alex at the rear of the theater. The two stared at the stage fifty feet in front of them where director Max VonDeutsch was screaming at the confused cast who looked sheepishly at each other, avoiding the glaring stare of the director. In his mid fifties, six foot one inch tall pot bellied bald headed Max looked like an angry general haranguing his troops. "Sie alle Idioten sind! Sie kann nicht tanzen, sie kann nicht singen, sie haben kein talent! Sie zweitklassig kantoren aus einer dritten rate synqgogue sind! Gehen Sie zurück zu den Catskills und trug jüdischen publikum, die es nicht besser wissen."

Alex turned to David with a worried look. "Did he just call my carefully chosen cast a bunch of idiots?"

David rolled his eyes and frowned at the stage. "A little more than that. He told them they can't dance or sing, have no talent, are second rate cantors from a third rate synagogue, and should go back to the Catskills and bore Jewish audiences who don't know better."

Alex looked at the stage fearfully. "Henrietta and Angus have saddled me with a for real Nazi, anti-semitism and all." He unzipped his briefcase, removed some sketches, and handed them to David. "Look at these new costumes he wants. They look to me like some eighteen nineties Parisian can can dancers or something."

David's frown deepened as he shuffled through the sketches. "More like some nineteen thirties Berlin cabaret dancers to me. There was a lot of this garter belt and black stocking kinkiness in nineteen thirties German movies and nightclubs." He handed the drawings back to Alex. "He's probably reliving his youth at the expense of our musical."

Alex exchanged the sketches for another set he handed David. "Would that explain these set design sketches he wants built?"

David eyes widened as he shuffled through the set designs. "My God! He's turned the French Quarter into *The Cabinet of Doctor Caligari*."

Alex's brow furrowed questioningly. "The cabinet of who?"

David sucked in air through his teeth as he handed the designs back to Alex. "*The Cabinet of Doctor Caligari*. It's a classic old German silent movie, the prototype of the modern horror movie, and the sets were all designed with weird abstract angles indicating the insane perspective of the film's monster."

Alex returned the designs to his briefcase and slumped down into his seat. "Oh dear God! I've got an insane Nazi turning my first shot at a musical into a kinky Berlin cabaret horror movie. What's next? Is he going to replace Princess with Hitler in drag?"

A tall man rose from the front row, put on a fur collared overcoat, and strode forcefully up the aisle toward them. They didn't recognize Angus in the darkness until he stopped in front of them. "Alex, David, Max wants to have a meeting with you regarding some recasting and some terms and phraseology he wants injected into the song lyrics."

Alex rose to an erect seated position and his worried look evolved into a strong assertive expression. "Angus, do you really think Max is a good fit for this project?"

Angus smiled condescendingly at Alex. "Alex, Max was the principal cinematographer for Leni Riefenstahl on such landmark films as *Triumph of the Will*."

Alex look unimpressed. "I never heard of it."

David stared at Angus. "It was a Nazi propaganda film, landmark in its film technique, devastating in its success as Nazi propaganda."

Angus closed and opened his eyes. "He has worked with every major German film star in the last three decades." He leaned forward a little and spoke in a hushed tone. "He told me he slept with every major female film star Hitler had slept with; Leni Riefenstahl, Marlene Dietrich, Anna May Wong, all of them."

David's brow furrowed. "Was Max a member of the Nazi party?"

Angus stood erect and now smiled at David condescendingly. "Oh David, in the thirties, everyone in Germany was a member of the Nazi party, and all of Scandinavia, half of Ireland, and a few Scots were sympathetic to the Nazis. What's past is past."

Alex looked at Angus doubtfully. "Then, is he anti-Semitic?"

Angus hesitated, bit his lip, then said, "Let's just say that when you two meet with him, don't bring Dimitri with you."

Alex looked at David. "Dimitri's Russian. He's not Jewish, is he?"

David shrugged. "I don't know," then looked at Angus, "and I don't care."

Angus began to button his coat and avoided eye contact. "Well, Max knows, and he cares."

Alex frowned at Angus. "Does Max know that I'm half black?"

Angus smiled brightly at him. "Oh, he's fine with that. He said he greatly admired Jesse Owen when he photographed him at the nineteen thirty-nine Olympics in Berlin."

David suppressed a chuckle as he looked at Alex with a pained smile. "Oh Alex, that must be very reassuring to you."

309

Angus began to put on leather gloves. "But if you're uncomfortable with anything, Max can just meet with David.." He smiled broadly at David. "After all, David, it was your blonde hair and blue eyes that helped me get Max on board with this musical. When he saw your picture, he became very enthusiastic about the project."

Now Alex suppressed a chuckle as he looked at David with a pained smile. "Oh David, that must be very reassuring to you."

****

Zoe's eyes bulged in surprise at the sight of David as she exited the rear door of the the Voodoo Room carrying a case of empty beer bottles. "Mon Dieu, David, you scared me. What are you doing here thirty minutes before opening? Usually you're lucky to be here thirty seconds before."

David reached out and gripped the sides of the beer case, offering to carry it to the stacks under the staircase leading to the upper apartments. "As an employee of the Goddess Consortium, I hoped to discuss some things that are going on with the show with one of the Board members."

Zoe wrenched the case out of his grip and headed toward the stacks. "Well you're talking to the wrong Board member. My little two percent carries no weight." The empty glass bottles tinkled as she dropped the case on the top of a stack, leaned on it, and turned to look at him. "And you damn well better be very successful with that show so Princess and I can at least buy a cup of coffee with our shares."

David gave her one of his most professional smiles. "Actually, I was hoping you'd tell me if Val has met or communicated with any of the New York investors, or with the Director they've hired."

Zoe turned more toward him and put her other hand on her hip. "Remember what I told you when you asked me about Justine's gossip? You can save that seductive smile for tonight's customers and consider yourself lucky that I don't tell Val you've been snooping around behind her back."

David gritted his teeth. "Well, she's hardly talked to me since the Goddess Consortium was incorporated, and there's some things going on in New York that she might want to know about."

Zoe shrugged one shoulder. "So, tell her."

David rolled his eyes. "Zoe, you know I'm scared to death of her. Besides, now I got two jobs to lose if I piss her off."

Zoe looked at him compassionately. "Okay, David. If there's something you think the board should know, tell Princess."

David sighed. "Princess just clams up if we ask her anything about the Consortium."

Zoe pushed away from the stacks and headed back to the Voodoo Room. "So, don't discuss the Consortium. Just tell her what you think the Consortium should know."

As Zoe entered the rear door, David looked skyward and pondered the wisdom of her words.

Later that night, just before closing, Julienne appeared beside the piano with a hesitant smile on her face. "David, if you're free and if you're comfortable with it, I'd like to buy you a meal, a drink, a coffee, or all three."

His smile was equally hesitant. "Is this a command performance from a member of the board, or an invitation from the lady who, until recently, was the love of my life?"

She sighed. "This is an invitation from a friend, one who, like quite a few people around here, loves you." David looked into the corner to see Valentina looking at the couple with a blank expression, and then she exited through the patio doors to leave Zoe and Pete to lock up. David looked at Julienne.

311

"Let's go to Café duMonde. I hear that general area has recently been divested of pests and vermin."

She looked perplexed. "Okay. If you say so. I'll wait for you by the door."

As they walked the familiar walk to the outdoor coffee shop, both were silent for the first few blocks. Then David spoke. "Did Aurora tell you that she came to say goodbye at the airport?"

Julienne skipped over a wide crack in the ballast stone sidewalk. "Yes, she kind of asked my permission to do that. Not that she had to, or that I would ever claim the right to deny anyone access to you."

He nodded his head. "I'm pleased to know that the two of you have an amicable relationship."

She rolled her eyes. "We all seem to have an amicable relationship, amicable, but awkward."

He looked sideways at her. "So the two of you haven't....?"

Her eyebrows rose as she continued to look for uneven stones in the sidewalk. "Well she's interested, but there hasn't been the time or opportunity to discuss things......or think things out." She chuckled. "I wonder, in a divorce, are there legal papers about who gets the dog, and who gets the friends, and who gets the third wheel on a tricycle?"

Alphonse greeted them as they sat at the corner table. "Evening Miss Julienne, Mr. David. The usual; two café au lait and one order of beignets?"

David smiled weakly at him. "Yes, thank you, Alphonse." David looked at Julienne and tilted his head. "Is that what we're doing? Getting a divorce, dissolving a union that was never formally established?"

She grimaced. "I don't know. When you asked about Aurora, the image of a tricycle popped into my head and I was just rambling."

He opened his napkin. "Well, you'll have plenty of time to sort things out. I'll be in New York three days a week for the next six to twelve weeks until the show's ready to preview in Boston.. I hope you don't mind if I continue to use that piano until the score's completed."

She looked at him with a pained expression as Alphonse set their order in front of them, his furrowed brow expressing empathy for her distress. She sounded pleading. "Oh, please, David. I gave that to you as a gift." She inhaled deeply and tried to look calm. "Let's decide now, if and when we break up, you get the piano, you get the dog, you can even have the tricycle. All I want is joint custody of the friends."

He looked at his coffee glumly as he stirred it. "What am I going to do with a tricycle that has only two wheels?"

She threw two sugar cubes into her coffee with a plopping sound and looked at him sternly. "You're a clever fellow. You'll figure something out."

David sighed and leaned back in his chair. "Let's start over. Hi, Miss deVille! Why don't you take me to coffee. I promise I wont be factitious. Maybe, over coffee, I could apologize to you for anything I've done in the romance department to offend you. I assure you, it was never my intention to hurt you in any way. You are the one person in my life for whom I would make romantic concessions. Please don't let your father or your friends convince you otherwise."

Julienne held her coffee cup in mid air, then set it down without drinking, her eyes glistening. "Oh, David. My parents and friends have no say in this, and I know you are not at fault. I cherish all my memories with you, even those with Aurora. It's that one image that was conjured by what came before, the one of you and Justine. I don't blame you, but, for now, I can't erase the image." She stood up, removed a bill from her purse and put it on the table, then stooped down and kissed his lips, whispering in his ear, "Please, give me time." Then she

313

walked swiftly to the curb and hailed a cab as David turned to watch her leave, his own eyes glistening in a saddened face.

****

Alex shook his head sideways. "I know this schedule's tough, David. But, now that the production's funded, they're paying your weekly airfare, and maybe I can ask Marvin about them paying for your lodgings here on Bleeker Street."

David shook his head sideways. "It's not so much that. The BMI checks are getting larger and can cover that enough that I haven't even bugged Dimitri and Gabriel to chip in. It's just that, with so little New Orleans time, things aren't going well with Julienne. In fact, things aren't going at all with Julienne."

Alex picked up the music manuscript from the table littered with coffee mugs and put it in his thin briefcase. "I'm sorry about that, David, but, speaking of BMI, your *Forgive* song getting on *The Hit Parade* radio show has earned you a lotta new respect from the backers. The musical's publicist wants to exploit your professional music association with Aurora to feed off her growing celebrity. The publicist's name is Ling Wan Park and she'll be at the rehearsal this afternoon to talk to you about it."

David wrinkled his nose as he collected the coffee mugs and wiped the table with a dishtowel. "Ling Wan Park. What kind of name is that?"

Alex zippered his briefcase and rose to leave. "She's Asian, Korean, I think. Used to be an editor at Random House and branched out into journalism and publicity. She handled publicity on some of the shows I've worked on. I like her. I think she's smart as a whip." He opened the door to the stairwell and raised one eyebrow. "It always amazes me that people like you and her manage to be so smart and talented,

314

and not be gay." He shut the door just in time to avoid the wet towel David threw at him.

****

As Julienne, Princess, and Dimitri sat in the wire chairs in the patio, Princess admired the life size statue of three girls in Grecian robes dancing in a circle. "Ohhhhh, are those the sisters?"

Julienne smiled. "This restaurant's named Court of the Two Sisters after the original owners of this property, but that's actually a copy of a famous statue called The Three Muses. They just use it as decor because it comes close to their theme."

Princess continued to admire the statue. "I like statues like that. I love that life size bronze one of the Goddess Diana with her bow and arrow and little dog. It's in the garden beside the Aquarium in Audubon Park."

Julienne smiled warmly at Princess. "I should take you to DelGado Museum in City Park. There's a lot of beautiful things in there I think you'd appreciate."

Princess's eyebrows raised. "Oh, I'd love that. I love parks, even though I haven't been to many museums. Dimitri took me to Hubert's Museum in New York." Her eyes widened. "Do you know that Dr. Hubert has an entire circus of trained fleas. We saw them under a magnifying lens actually pulling chariots and building human pyramids." She shrugged. "Well, actually, they were flea pyramids. But it was really amazing."

Julienne smiled at Dimitri. "Glad to see you guys have the time to enjoy the cultural sights of New York during your rehearsals there."

Princess opened her menu. "Yeah, but most of Dimitri's writing work is completed and they wont have all my numbers choreographed for a while, so they're saving on airfare by not flying us there as often as David. Fortunately for David, this is the Summer off-season in New Orleans and Valentina's willing to let him have three, sometimes four days a week off when they need him in New York."

Julienne looked at her menu. "Which explains why he hasn't been around much, lately."

Dimitri folded his menu and put it down, looking at Julienne with a phoney smile. "Which explains why we're invited to a fancy lunch with a board member."

Princess lowered her menu and glared at him. "Dimitri! Of course she wants to hear about David, and this is a pleasant way to mix business with pleasure. Besides, it's TWO board members, and one sarcastic employee."

Julienne looked from Princess to Dimitri with a pained smile. "Why don't we all order something special that we'd like, and maybe some cocktails for starters?"

The waiter came, took their orders, and left. Julienne looked at the floral centerpiece and nodded her head up and down. "Yes, I'd appreciate hearing about David and how the show's progressing. All I know is what I read in the papers and see in the pictures of him with Aurora when she's broadcasting from New York occasionally. Her and that Asian girl that's sometimes in the pictures with him, or the three of them."

Dimitri gave Julienne another phoney smile. "So, who are you concerned about? Aurora or Ling?"

Princess glared at him again. "Dimitri!" She looked at Julienne consolingly. "We really don't know, Julienne. We're not there often enough. That Chinese girl..."

Dimitri corrected her. "Korean."

Princess shot him a dirty look. "She's just the publicist, all business. She orders photographers and people around like Alex when he's choreographing the waiters at Aladdin's. And

316

I don't think Aurora's there very often because she has to fly back and forth between Hollywood and New York when she has broadcasts there." She licked her lips, looked at the floral arrangement, then back at Julienne. "Have you contacted him? I think he's put a phone in the Bleeker Street loft and I can get that number for you. He lets me and Dimitri and Gabriel stay there when we're in town."

Dimitri narrowed his eyes at Princess. "You should ask David about giving out his number, Princess. Besides, Julienne apparently hasn't bothered to use postal mail or telegrams or pony express to contact him."

The waiter mercifully arrived with their drinks at that moment. Julienne said, "Don't bother about the phone number, Princess." She looked at Dimitri. "I have no intention of invading anyone's privacy." She lifted her glass. "Let's just relax and enjoy our lunch, shall we?" The other's lifted their glasses and clinked them against hers.

****

Dimitri scowled at Ling. "I don't see why you need to include me in this pre-publicity. David and Alex have changed at least fifty percent of my original story, so it's not accurate to hold me up at the author of the book."

Ling half sat on the edge of the desk close to Dimitri so she could look down at him from a commanding position. "Listen carefully, Dimitri, and don't interrupt me. One, you are the ORIGINAL author of a book that now bears both your and David's names, and both of you must therefore be in these interviews as collaborators, not competitor's harboring sour grapes."

Dimitri raised his finger and opened his mouth, but Ling raised her hand and continued before he could interrupt. "Second, you have a Russian name and accent, and you spent

317

the first twelve years of your life in Russia. The press is going to want to know if you're a Communist whose musical espouses Communist propaganda, or if you're a loyal American who is militant only about the rights of women and gays."

Dimitri jumped in before she could stop him. "Are you North Korean or South Korean?"

Ling raised one eyebrow and glared angrily at him. "I was raped by a North Korean soldier when I was thirteen, and my mother had been kidnapped and forced into sexual slavery by the Japanese as a so-called 'Comfort Woman.' The Korean males of my generation had learned to be misogynists from the Japanese and South Korean women had little rights when North Korea invaded. You better damn well believe I am one hundred percent American and anti-communist!"

Dimitri looked at her defiantly. "Did I tell you that the Bolsheviks shot my parents in front of my eyes when I was twelve and my uncle had to pay a ransom to rescue me to England?"

Ling lowered her eyebrow, but continued to look at him impassively. "How fortunate for you. If you'd been a few years older, you probably would have been raped before your uncle bought your freedom. I bought my freedom by shooting the man who raped me with his own gun and defending myself from other attackers with a broken machete. But we're both citizens of the United States now, with the freedom to advocate for our respective causes, and supporting this musical with interviews in which we say the right things is the best way to do that."

Dimitri smiled facetiously. "You win! Your story has more pity points than mine has."

Ling frowned and began to speak. "Dimitri..."

Just then David knocked lightly on the class panel in the open office door. "I'm sorry I'm late."

As David sat down, Dimitri, still staring at Ling sarcastically, said, "Tell them you're anti-Communist, David, and that your undershorts are patterned with red white and blue stars and stripes."

Ling looked at David placidly. "David, if asked, are you comfortable saying that you are anti-Communist, pro-American, and are only militant about the civil rights of women and gays?"

David's brow furrowed. "I don't like to say I'm anti anything. Can't I simply say that I do not support Communism and that I am proud to be an American?"

Ling stared at him and hesitated a moment, then said, "I guess that would be sufficient. Also, if asked if you are gay, are you comfortable stating for the record that you are heterosexual?"

Dimitri looked at her suspiciously. "Why do you assume he's heterosexual?"

Ling ignored Dimitri as David looked amused at his question, then looked at Ling and said, "I'm fine with that, and, if it's a female journalist, is it okay if I feign making a pass at her?"

Ling smiled and shrugged. "If it's done in good taste, it might be cute, but I don't think you'll find many female journalists among the New York press." She stood up, moved behind the desk, and put on black rimmed glasses as she sat down. "Now, David, if they ask about your association with Aurora, she would like to keep that publicly on a professional level until and unless the musical is a success, at which time you can both decide if it's in your best interests to expand that public image. Do you agree?"

David looked at Dimitri frowning at him. "Agreed."

Ling shuffled through papers without looking up. "And Dimitri, if you're asked about your gender orientation, what do you want to say about that?" Ling looked up at Dimitri as she tapped a pencil on the papers on her desk. "Incidentally, Alex doesn't want anyone to claim any personal or intimate association with him. He's very private about things like that."

Dimitri glared at her and inhaled deeply. "So am I!"

Ling returned to looking at and shuffling papers. "Fine. Just say that, but tactfully, and with a smile."

Dimitri turned to David as his stare morphed into an excessively phoney smile.

David's brow furrowed as he asked , "Ling, will we be interviewed together with Max?"

Dimitri looked at Ling angrily. "Yes, who in the hell decided that some kinky Nazi should be directing this musical?"

Ling removed her glasses and looked from one man to the other. "Max VonDeutsch, was a highly respected film director in Germany and has directed two Broadway musicals. He is a personal friend of two of the backers, Henrietta and Angus, and they got Alex to agree to have Max sign on to protect their interests. Both his prior musicals have been very successful."

Dimitri frowned at her. "He's a kinky Nazi who thinks all gays are freaks, and he's the biggest freak of them all!"

David looked from Dimitri to Ling with a pained expression. "He is trying to turn *The Piano Lover**
from a lovable group of French Quarter gays into a nineteen thirties Berlin cabaret show replete with garter belts, high hats, and a German accent. He even suggested some German and Yiddish words and phrases he wants me to work into new lyrics, with which I expressed my disagreement. I think he has a Semitic thing going as well as the Berlin thing."

Ling looked down at her papers and bit her lower lip before looking up to respond. "Perhaps you two should try to talk to some of the other backers about that. I can arrange that you two aren't interviewed at the same time as VonDeutsch, but I can't control whatever he'll be saying in his interviews." She pushed away from the desk and stood up. "Is there anything else on your minds regarding publicity at this time?"

The two men stood up as Dimitri asked, "Will Princess be interviewed with us or...."

Ling nodded her head affirmatively. "Princess will be interviewed with several of the other principals in the cast. If all goes well, all of you will be individually interviewed again the day after the opening."

David looked at her seriously. "Ling, may I assume that what we discuss here about Max or any other personnel concerns is confidential and wont be repeated to Max, Henrietta, Angus,or anyone else?"

Ling closed and opened her eyes, nodding her head again. "Yes, strictly confidential."

****

Julienne sat as the waiter pushed her chair forward. "Mother, isn't The Blue Room at The Roosevelt Hotel rather overkill for lunch?"

Angelina deVille opened her napkin and looked around the sparsely populated room as the sound of clinking china and high heeled footsteps reverberated between the hardwood dance floor and multiple crystal chandeliers in the ceiling. "You used to love it when we brought you here during the evenings they broadcast over WWL. You'd put your little shoes on top of your father's shoes and dance with him all evening, right out there on that dance floor."

Julienne shrugged. "Yes, I remember it fondly. I just thought, lunch, maybe a coffee shop in the Quarter, a tearoom on St. Charles."

Angelina flipped her menu open noisily. "Oh, Julienne, let me affect some degree of generosity or control. With your father I'm just a classy piece of furniture in the shadows. It's only with my female friends and in my charity work that I'm in charge and can call the shots." She lowered her menu and stared at her daughter with an indulgent smile. "And I say we're having a fancy lunch at the most expensive place I could think of."

Julienne lowered her menu with an amused smile. "I'd have thought that would be Antoine's or Arnaud's in the Quarter."

Angelina signaled for the waiter. "Oh, you know I can't go into the Quarter. Renee would be haranguing me about the risks of being shanghaied into the white slave trade."

Julienne shook her head sideways. "I don't think too many ladies your age have been shanghaied into the white slave trade recently."

Angelina focused on re-aligning her place setting. "The gardener and pool boy still admire my figure when I'm lounging beside the pool."

Julienne looked up as the waiter arrived. "Well Daddy better not catch them admiring you, or you'll lose your fan club quick."

Angelina looked up at the waiter with a commanding expression. "I want Beluga Caviar on toast and a Russian spinach salad on the side." She looked at Julienne, then back at the waiter as an afterthought. "Oh, yes, and a bottle of French Chablis. None of that California swill."

The waiter spoke very softly. "Oui, Madame. And you, Mademoiselle?"

Julienne looked at him. "I'll have a B-L-T and a glass of that Chablis."

Angelina sounded shocked. "Oh, darling, please! Have something more indulgent. Don't leave me here looking ostentatious with my caviar." She leaned forward and spoke

322

conspiratorially. "Have something you wouldn't normally get for yourself. Something forbidden, outlandish, exorbitant!"

Julienne rolled her eyes as she pondered her choices, then asked. "Scratch the B-L-T. Do you have escargot at this hour?"

"Oui, Mademoiselle."

Julienne frowned. "I don't like them served in the shell. Do you have one of those little dishes with recesses for the snail and garlic butter."

"Oui, Mademoiselle. They come six on a plate."

Angelina waved at the waiter. "Make that two plates." She looked at her daughter's frown. "What? I may want a taste or two."

Julienne looked back at the waiter. "And Melba toast, and a Tabooli salad, do you have that?"

The waiter smiled at her as if he were proud of her choices. "Oui, Mademoiselle. Two orders of escargot, Tabooli salad, Melba toast, and French Chablis. Oui?"

Julienne wiggled her eyebrows at her mother. "Oui."

Angelina smiled as the waiter left. "Oh goody! The day is looking up."

Julienne looked at her mother questioningly. "Mother, do you agree with Daddy's disapproval of my lifestyle."

Angelina's smile faded. "I just said today's looking up. What are you trying to do, child? Rain on my Beluga caviar?"

Julienne looked at her out of the corner of her eye. "Mother, I invited you to lunch to discuss these things."

Angelina began rearranging her silverware again. "No, you called me, and I invited you to lunch, to a fancy extravagant happy lunch."

Julienne stared at her mother. "Answer the question, Mother. Do you think that, in the long run, I will regret fighting for the things that make me happy?"

Angelina started rearranging the floral centerpiece. "Nobody has a crystal ball, Baby. Valentina Sciciliana may look like a fortune teller, but we all just work with what we got and hope that fate will be kind."

Julienne looked at her mother's hands rearranging the flowers. "Do you think, like he does, that I shouldn't associate with entertainers, that I should look for more stable friends among New Orleans gentry?"

Angelina plucked a single flower and smelled it with closed eyes, then looked at Julienne. "I knew someone who was kinda like in show business. The man I had an affair with." She looked at the flower. "He was a preacher, not of our religion, not of our race, not of our social class."

Julienne looked astounded and almost impressed with her mother. "Not of our race? You had an affair with a black man?"

Angelina stared at the flower as she twirled it. "Oh God, no! Rene would have probably shot us both. I meant, he wasn't Creole. He was Anglo Saxon, a Baptist minister, not exactly a red neck, mind you, but one of those who rants and raves in a tent that goes from town to town."

Julienne smiled sadly. "Mother, don't tell me that you found God in a tent?"

Angelina smiled and almost chuckled. "Nooooo! God and I have our private conversations, and I think I sometimes hear him laughing at all the priests and preachers in their tents and cathedrals." She smelled the flower again with closed eyes. "No. A friend dragged me to the tent in the course of their own search, and, by happenstance, I met a man there, who just happened to be a preacher." She opened her eyes and looked at the flower. "A man with golden hair, piercing blue eyes, and a dimpled smile that melted my heart."

Julienne was stunned as her mother's words conjured the image of David in her mind.

324

Angelina placed the flower back into the floral arrangement. "My heart had become stone cold at that point. Renee was convinced that I was barren, and without an heir my father would not bequeath his fortune to me. I had never experienced an orgasm with Renee, and he retreated further from me and into the arms of those harlots in the Quarter." She looked down at the handkerchief she retrieved from her sleeve. "And I retreated into the arms of a charismatic man who made me feel like a woman for the first time in my life."

Julienne watched her mother dab one eye and the side of her nose with the handkerchief. "Why didn't you run away with him? Was he married?"

Angelina looked up at one of the chandeliers. "No, he wasn't married, but I was. When I became pregnant, he offered me marriage if I would divorce Renee, but, before I could decide, I had a miscarriage." She looked down at the handkerchief. "To be honest, I liked my privileged life, the benefits of my father's fortune."

Julienne asked sadly. "What happened to him?"

Angelina smiled up at the chandelier again. "Oh, he was so handsome, and there were so many women who admired him." She smiled at Julienne. "And then you came into my life."

The waiter arrived with their food. The two women began eating in silence. Then Julienne asked, "I am not concerned about money, like Daddy is, because both David and I have excellent odds for success. And I have no doubt that David's intelligence, sexual, and cultural compatibility are far above that of any man I've known."

Angelina put some caviar on her toast point with the little seashell spoon that avoided any metallic taste. "Put sex on the top of the list. Economic stability second, and notice I said 'stability.' Wealth is not the point, but avoiding being poor enough to fight over money is." She furrowed her brow and waggled her head. "Intelligence, culture, those are very subjective, and certainly not as important as the first two."

Julienne skewed a snail on her tiny fish fork and gestured with it as she spoke. "My main concern is fidelity. David's not a womanizer. He doesn't have to chase women, because they chase him, like your preacher. But he's introduced me to a casual sex lifestyle and I don't know if I can handle that indefinitely."

Angelina looked at her daughter intently. "I'm afraid to ask what you mean by a 'casual sex lifestyle,' but I can assure you, once you have children, that wont work."

Julienne stabbed green leaves in her salad. "I'm not sure I want to have children."

Angelina dropped her salad fork with a clatter. "Whaaaaaaat? What do you mean, you're not sure about having children? What, in God's name, do you think marriage is for? How in heaven can I have grandchildren until you have children?"?

Julienne blinked. "Calm down, mother. Lots of people don't have children. Lots of people live together and don't get married."

Angelina looked shocked. "Not proper people! Not God fearing people!"

Julienne looked confused. "You just told me that you and God laugh together about some religious conventions. If you don't buy church dogma, why are you so locked into marriage and children?"

Angelina raised both hands in supplication. "Because that's what life's all about, to perpetuate the species in the best possible form. Children are the ultimate motivation, children are all you've got to push forward."

Julienne's brow furrowed. "Daddy's motivation to have a child was to seal the inheritance deal with your father. Your motivation to have a child was to save a failed marriage.

That's a lot of pressure to put on such a small person. Maybe you came to appreciate and enjoy and care about my welfare in the course of seeing me grow up, and I am eternally grateful for the wonderful privileged life you've provided me, but I'm not planning my life according to the design of dogma or Darwin."

Angelina's angry stare morphed into a frightened expression as she lowered her eyes to her plate. She spoke in a hesitant frightened voice. "Very well, Julienne. You live your life as you see fit. The door is open if you want to come home. The door is open if you need assistance like a psychiatrist or a sanatarium. Or you can just come to dinner on holidays and we can have lunch together from time to time." She looked up into Julienne's eyes pleadingly. "Just, please, Julienne, don't tell your father about our lunch today, and don't say to your father the things you just said to me. I love you both. I don't want to see you lose each other. And, Julienne, I don't want to lose you."

Julienne touched her mother's forearm and looked at her with a sad smile. "You are my mother, who I dearly love, and you will never lose me, nor would I ever want to lose you."

Angelina smiled wanly as she looked down and dipped her little seashell spoon into her Beluga caviar.

****

Aurora started to unbutton David's shirt, then spread her hands and heard his heartbeat as she rested her face on his chest. "You sure you wan do dis, David?" She felt his chest rise and fall faster beneath her cheek. "I love you. I love Julienne. And dis chica chino ees muy caliente." She looked up into his face. "Bud I done wan hurd no one."

Just then Ling stepped out of the bathroom and stood in front of the floor to ceiling windows facing Bleeker Street, her trim figure hidden only by one of David's silk shirts she had

327

found drying in the bathroom. Aurora turned her head enough to see Ling's body silhouetted against the moonlight, the bluish light not completely washing away the golden hue of her long legs, narrow well turned buttocks barely visible below the hem of the shirt, and perky almost flat breasts barely peeking out of the unbuttoned shirt. Ling's large almond eyes were luminous beneath the bangs of her short gamin haircut as she moved the hair away from one side of her face to look at them anxiously and hungrily.

David waggled his jaw from side to side and said, "Can't ride a tricycle with only two wheels."

Aurora frowned and said, "Whaaaaaad? You sound drunk, David. Maybe you no can...," then she felt something against her abdomen and continued, "...o' maybe si." She looked up at him again. "Can I tase furse, David?"

David started to unbutton his own shirt. "Whatever turns you on, baby."

Aurora moved towards Ling like a toreador, stopping in stages to remove first her blouse, then her bra, then her high heeled shoes and pants. Ling backed away from her until the back of her knees were caught by the seat edge of the only upholstered chair in the loft, causing her to fall backward into the chair while the shirt flared open on both sides. Aurora dropped to her knees a few feet from the chair and crawled toward Ling like a tigress stalking prey. She lifted Ling's legs up and over the overstuffed arms of the chair while David walked over to stand beside the chair naked, close to Ling's face. Ling looked up at him with an expression cross between excitement and fear, then, as Aurora lowered her head to Ling's neatly trimmed delta of pubic hair and made contact, Ling's head arched back, her eyes closed, and her mouth opened and emitted a long eerie wail that was soon silenced.

328

Chapter Twenty
PAST IMPERFECT

"Princess? What kind of name is that?" DeVille stared fascinated at Princess's tightly mini-skirted figure as she examined a larger than life size Egyptian statue while visitor's footsteps echoed through the large rooms of The Delgado Museum.

Julienne found her father's admiration of Princess's figure revealing, and in contrast to his obvious disapproval of her as a French Quarter entertainer, and she knew he would have been shocked to discover Princess was a male transvestite. "She told you, it's her stage name as opposed to her difficult to pronounce real name. Consider it a nickname."

He continued to stare at Princess as he spoke, his eyes traveling up and down her figure. "It's a child's name. I used to call you that until you were ten and asked me to stop."

She rolled her eyes. "I remember."

He couldn't take his eyes off of Princess. "Why is her name un-pronounceable? Is she from India, South America, Asia? She's obviously not white or black."

Julienne blinked. "She's more American than you or me, Daddy. Everything in this world is not black and white." Her voice became irritated. "Daddy, look at me. You said you wanted to drop something off for me."

He tore his gaze away from Princess and handed Julienne a large Kraft envelope. "Yes, well, it seems your accountant inadvertently picked up some of your mail when he was sorting out your bills at the gallery. When you didn't get back to your mother and me since the last time we saw you, I took the opportunity of returning your mail in order to see you."

She removed a smaller white envelope from the large envelope. "Daddy, there's only one envelope in here, it's from David, and it's been opened."

He looked at the envelopes in her hand. "Your accountant did that before he realized his mistake."

She looked at him accusingly. "Why did my accountant contact you instead of me?"

He blinked and looked toward the Egyptian statue to discover Princess was gone. "You'd have to ask him that." He looked around searching for Princess in vain, then back at Julienne. "Tell me, Julienne, what is The Goddess Consortium?"

Her eyes narrowed. "Daddy, do you know an accountant or lawyer in this town that I could hire who's not beholden to you?"

He reached out and held her free hand. "Julienne, dear child, please come visit your mother. Consider moving back home. We've leveled with you about the past. Give us the credit of having done our best for you, and let us help you get back on your feet, find new friends, and rebuild your life."

She removed her hand from his and walked in the direction of the Egyptian statue. "Inasmuch as my accountant seems to tell you everything, you're well aware that I am on solid economic footing, and I am very happy with my current friends, thank you." She stopped and turned to face him with the statue looming behind her, pointing to him with the opened envelope. "Let's see if you can be honest with me about one single thing, Daddy. Did you read this private letter from David?"

He lifted his hand toward her, saw her lean slightly backward, and lowered his hand to his side. "Trust me, Julienne, everything I've ever done regarding you has been in your best interest."

Julienne closed her eyes and slowly opened them. "Perhaps from your perspective. But trust you, when your spy network monitors my every move, you bribe my accountant and my lawyer to be party to that, when you open my private correspondence and violate the privacy of words written between lovers? Trust must be earned, and I cannot trust you until you learn to respect me, my privacy, and my choices in life."

DeVille's eyes glistened. "Julienne, I..."

She turned to leave, then turned back and raised the envelope to silence him. "Oh yes, tell my accountant and lawyer they're fired," and she turned and left him standing beneath the fierce stare of the Egyptian God of the Underworld..

****

The waiter held the chair for Princess as she sat down, surveying the old paneled walls and tiled floors of Tujague's Restaurant with both surprise and awe. "I never ate here before, Julienne. I know it's a very famous restaurant, but, somehow, I thought it would be fancier. You know, like the chandeliers and statuary you see through the stained glass windows of places like Antoine's and Arnaud's."

Julienne opened her menu. "Tujague's started off a century ago serving the farmers and longshoreman from The French Market across the street. They're more famous for their good food and their longevity than for fancy decor."

Princess squinted at the menu, as if that would help her translate the French terminology it used. "They say a lot of famous people have eaten here."

Julienne folded her menu and looked for the waiter. "That could be said of a lot of French Quarter establishments. But, yes, a lot of presidents and movie stars have eaten here, in small part because of Madison Street."

Princess folded her menu. "You mean that street on the corner that's only one block long."

Julienne nodded her head. "Yes. Because of its seclusion, a number of celebrities have owned houses or apartments there, and eaten here because it's so close and private for them."

Princess's eyes widened. "Have you ever seen any celebrities here?"

Julienne chuckled. "Yes, well, do you know of the stage and screen actor, Jose Ferrer, and his wife, Rosemary Clooney, the singer?"

Princess's smiled. "Ohhhh, I love *Come On-A My House*! I use it in one of my acts."

Julienne waved her hand in the direction of Madison Street. "Well, they have an apartment on Madison Street and bought some paintings from my gallery, even asked me to come over and hang the paintings for them, and even took me to lunch here at Tujague's in appreciation."

Princess's eyes widened. "You had lunch with Rosemary Clooney and her husband here? Where? What table?"

Julienne smiled at Princess's enthusiasm. "Over there, at that rear corner table. They were always trying to keep a low profile."

Princess stared longingly at the corner table, then turned to Julienne. "It must be wonderful to have rich and famous friends like Rosemary Clooney."

Julienne motioned to the waiter. "We're not friends, not even acquaintances. I was just their art dealer and picture hanger. After all, you know a rising recording artist, Aurora, and, if the musical succeeds, you may well become rich and famous yourself."

Princess looked demure. "Oh, I'm afraid to even think about that. I know I survive on stage because I just want to please people and make them like me. Fame and success are scary things that seem way over my head. I'm just grateful for people like Dimitri and Alex and David who help me look and perform my best and make the audience like me....love me, if I'm lucky."

Julienne looked at Princess with admiration. "Oh, Princess, you're so much more than you give yourself credit for. You've shown surprising moments of insight, and I think your connecting us with Valentina was as important as Aurora's idea of a co-op in creating The Goddess Consortium. You are loved and admired much more than you realize."

Princess looked embarrassed, and somewhat relieved when the waiter arrived. "Julienne, I can't read the menu. You know this kinda food better than me. Why don't you order for me, and excuse me while I go to the little girl's room," and she exited to the rear of the restaurant.

Julienne re-opened the menu. "We'll have two Shrimp Remoulade Cocktails, two orders of Stuffed Crabs, two iced teas, and we'll look at the pastry menu afterwards." Julienne set down the menu, picked up her purse, and removed the envelope containing the unread letter from David. She closed her eyes, inhaled deeply, and clutched the envelope so tightly she almost crumpled it. Then she removed the letter, opened it up, and read:

Dear Julienne,

I don't know where to start. I guess I should explain the enclosed check to reimburse you for the piano. I know you said it was a gift, and I don't want my reimbursing you to be interpreted as a conclusion or closure in any way. It's just that my BMI checks have increased enough to enable me to repay you, and because, every so often when I look at it, I can hear your father's accusations that I'm exploiting you.

But then, I'm sure he'll interpret The Goddess Consortium as just that. As if the investment of my own time, effort, and money were not enough pressure to succeed, now I have the minor concern of your father's accusations and the major concern of your risking your gallery and your personal nest egg. I know that Val and Aurora can afford the risk, but you're not (better say not yet) as rich as your father. Additionally, you've invested in someone about whom you have serious doubts, who you now see in a totally different light, and who you may not want to see again.

In addition to the apologies I've already expressed, let me add here my vow to repay you any material losses you suffer at my expense. Whatever choices you make, whatever direction in which our respective lives go, I will always cherish you and what we have shared. Having not heard from you since our last meeting, and if it makes things feel less awkward for you, do not feel obliged to respond to this letter unless you want to. You asked me to give you time, but time does not stand still. Life goes on, and I hope your life is eventually filled with joy and happiness. If I am not part of that future happiness, hopefully you will sometimes remember the past happiness we've shared.

Love,
David

Julienne's heart was racing very fast, and she hurriedly stuffed the letter and envelope into her purse so she could use her napkin to dry her tears. She could see Princess approaching from the rear of the restaurant and took a couple of deep breaths to try to compose herself.

Princess sat down with an irritated frown. "I'm sorry I took so long, but that woman just wouldn't let me alone."

Julienne blinked. "What woman?"

Princess re-arranged her napkin. "Normally I don't have problems in ladies rest rooms, especially if they have doors on the stalls."

Julienne's eyebrows rose. "Oh, I never thought about that. Did she, I mean, were you...?"

Princess moved back as the waiter set their shrimp cocktails before them. "I would've been okay if I hadn't forgotten to latch the stall door. This humongous woman barged in on me."

Julienne nodded a 'thank you' to the waiter, then asked Princess, "Did she...see anything?"

Princess inspected the three forks in her place setting until Julienne pointed to the tiny one with three tongs. "No, thank God. She just loved my dress and thought I was so beautiful and wished she could lose weight so she could look like me. Bless her poor hippopotamus soul, her bones weigh more than me. Really! Of all the times and places to pay someone compliments." She tasted her first shrimp and smiled. "Oooooh, tangy. What's in this?"

Julienne swallowed her first bite. "Remoulade sauce. It's a New Orleans recipe. So, how did you get rid of her?"

Princess shrugged. "I told her what I tell fresh guys at the club, 'I'll respect your privacy if you respect mine.' Then I added, 'Please shut the door.'"

Julienne sipped her tea. "Yes, privacy can be a delicate thing. I'm dying to ask you about David, but I'm trying to respect his privacy and not put you in the middle."

Princess swirled her fish fork in the empty bottom of the shrimp cocktail cup. "Yeah, I know what you mean. It's tricky when you love everyone concerned, and everyone concerned doesn't seem to be communicating with each other." She set her fork down and looked at Julienne. "So I'll tell you what I told David. Don't tell me anything you don't want others to know, because I don't want the pain of keeping secrets from people I love."

Julienne linked her fingers in a prayer-like fashion as the waiter removed the empty dishes. "Damn, Princess, see how wise you are. So, what did David tell you?"

Princess stared at her glumly. "Practically nothing."

Julienne raised one eyebrow. "Your lips say nothing, Princess, but your eyes say more."

Princess sighed and looked at the stuffed crabs set before her. "My eyes are seeing Aurora visiting New York more frequently for broadcast and recording sessions, and she and that Chinese publicist girl leaving rehearsals with David more frequently." She hesitated over the remaining two forks, then impulsively picked up the correct dinner fork, her eyes focused on her food. "They may be just going to business lunches. Some of the conversations I heard involve David possibly writing more songs for Aurora, but that will be on hold until *The Piano Lover* score is finished in two or three more weeks." They ate in silence for almost a minute, then Princess set her fork down and looked at Julienne. "Julienne, have you tried to contact David when he's in New Orleans during the latter part of the week?"

Julienne looked away as she finished chewing and swallowing, then inhaled deeply and looked at her plate. "I've headed toward The Voodoo Room several times, but always chickened out. I'm haunted by the revelation of Justine." She spread her hands and looked around the room. "Even sitting here in what was formerly one of my favorite restaurants, all I can think about is that she lives a few short blocks away."

Princess's eyes bulged. "I don't think so. David said she moved to Paris with Armand weeks ago. They dumped Jules, and maybe he still lives there. David said that Jules said he thinks Valentina coerced Armand's father to send them to Paris for four years."

Julienne looked shocked. "Valentina didn't say anything to me! David didn't say anything to me!"

Princess nodded her head affirmatively. "That's what I said, none of you guys communicate with each other." She speared another fork full of stuffed crab. "But Valentina, she don't tell anyone anything anyhow. She's like this silent power working behind the scenes, kinda like Dimitri pulling the strings of those dolls of his, and we just see the drama on the stage."

Julienne leaned slightly forward. "You say Jules is still living there?"

Princess swallowed. "I'm not sure. I guess so."

Julienne started rummaging through her purse. "Princess, I really enjoyed showing Delgado Museum to you, and lunch, and I'd like to do more outings like this with you. But would you forgive me if I left you here. Here's money for the bill and enough for a cab." She dropped two large bills in front of Princess's plate and looked at her with a pained expression. "Right now I'm desperate to find Jules, to verify what you heard, to talk to a fellow victim of Justine. I hope you understand."

Princess smiled, closed her eyes briefly, and waved Julienne away with her hand. "Go, misery loves company, and I hope you find it therapeutic." As Julienne left, the waiter approached to remove her plates, prompting Princess to say,

"Whoa, there! " As she put the two large bills in her purse, she spoke imperiously. "After you've put all that uneaten food in a doggie bag for me, you can bring me the pastry menu, please."

Julienne walked swiftly the two blocks to Betty's Bar, then crossed over to the paint chipped door of the stairway leading to Jule's apartment, finding an 'Eviction' notice tacked to the door. She rang the doorbell button repeatedly, fearful that Jules was no longer in residence. Finally she heard a slurred voice from above and turned to look up and see Jule's in a bathrobe leaning shakily over the balcony railing. "For God's sakes, are you trying to split my head open with that Goddam doorbell?" He looked at her with bloodshot eyes and shook his head slowly sideways. "If you split my head open, then you'll have to help me pick up all my squishy brains and sad memories that fall out. Now, you don't wanna do that, do you, whoever you are?"

Julienne shaded her eyes with one hand. "Jules, it's Julienne! Julienne deVille. Let me in. I need to talk to you."

Jules tried to stand erect and raised one finger skyward. "Julienne! Svengali's motivation to destroy my pathetic life."

Julienne's brow wrinkled in confusion. "Jules, press the button so I can come up and talk to you."

Jules looked down at her imperiously. "Do you have any wine?"

Julienne rolled her eyes, shrugged, and then said, "Yes, I have wine for you. Press the button."

When she entered the apartment at the top of the stairs, Jules inspected her with disapproval. "You don't have any wine. You're a faker and a fraud, one of Svengali's minions come to finish me off, put me out of my misery."

Julienne hastily put her purse down and grabbed Jules by his upper arm before he could fall, guiding him to one of the two sofas that flanked a long coffee table. "Jules, sit, before

338

you fall. There, doesn't that feel better, doesn't it help keep the room from spinning?"

Jules waved his hands in front of him. "Spin, spin, spin. The world keeps spinning. It never stands still. Time never stands still." He grabbed both of Julienne's arms and pulled her down to sit beside him, a desperate frowning look on his face. "Make the world stop spinning, Julienne. Make time stop, make it stop before they left, before we met Justine. Do that for me, please, Julienne."

She held him by the shoulders until he stopped weaving. "Poor baby, I would if I could, believe me. I could use a little of that time stopping magic, too." She stood up, looked around for the kitchenette at one end of the room, then started to prepare some coffee. "So tell me, Jules, how long have they been gone?"

Jules kept looking into space and blinking. "Since a couple days after I last saw you. Remember, you came looking for her with that frightened look on your face."

She lit the gas burner under the water kettle and started putting coffee grounds in the drip coffee pot. "Oh I remember. A day that will live in infamy!"

Jules tried to rise, then fell back on the sofa. "So it was. It was my Pearl Harbor, the destruction of my ship of dreams, all my ships of dreams." He turned and pointed at her angrily. "And it was all because of you! Svengali did it for you! She sent that Hitler bitch to invade Paris to get her out of your and David's hair." He leaned back and looked at the spotted ceiling. "And I was poor Poland getting trampled in the process."

As Jules drifted off to sleep, Julienne finished the coffee and poured herself a cup, carrying it through the apartment to discover all the 'La Boheme' details David had described. There were various canvases on the walls, some signed by Jules that she looked at with interest, obvious exercises in abstract, cubism, and a couple odes to Salvador Dali. In the hall to the rear bedroom, a mural started on one wall and continued into the bedroom to cover all four walls, plus the floor and ceiling. The unsalvageable mural was probably one of the best works of art in the apartment.

She found some of Jules clean clothes, some wash cloths and a towel, then, using water from the water kettle, proceeded to give the unconscious young man a sponge bath, removing traces of caked on vomit from his legs, and struggling to get him into shirt, pants, shoes, and socks. By the time he woke up hours later, she had a hot cup of coffee on the table before him.

Jules looked suspiciously through narrow slitted eyes in all directions, then at the clothes he wore. "Was I a bad boy? Did I say things I shouldn't?"

Julienne sat on the sofa on the other side of the coffee table across from him, and sipped her coffee. "A lot!" She set her coffee down. "But, don't worry, Jules. It all had to be said. It was all for the best." She leaned back and let her arms rest limply at her sides. "There's no one to blame here. You and David and I are just collateral damage in Justine's war with the unfortunate world into which she was born." She looked up at the spotted ceiling. "What my parents did, what Armand's father did, what Valentina Sciciliana did were all well intentioned efforts to help Armand and me, to protect us from Justine. You and David were just caught in the line of fire." She smiled sadly at him. "Sorry about that."

Jules avoided eye contact. "Did I do anything I should apologize for?"

She smiled, closed and opened her eyes, and said, "No, Jules, you're okay."

He sipped his coffee and shook his head sideways. "Not really. I'm being evicted. My job as organist at St. Louis

Cathedral only pays a small stipend. I have no skills. I even lost a job as a bus boy working with Armand."

She leaned forward and picked up her coffee. "You have skills. You know how to stretch canvases. You know how to clean paintings. You know how to frame and mount them. And you have a cultured vocabulary and manners. You can work for me at my gallery. It would just be as a flunky and gopher, but it would pay a minimal living wage and have potentials for you, if you don't screw up." She sipped her coffee. "Interested?"

His eyebrows raised in surprise while his face smiled with relief. "You're the devil of my downfall and the angel of my redemption. Dear sweet Julienne, if I wasn't gay, I'd propose to you here and now!"

She looked at her coffee. "Don't bother. I don't think marriage is in the cards for me."

His brow furrowed as he looked at her sympathetically. "Dirty dealings in the David department?"

She sipped her coffee and set it down. "I may have waited too long, and he may have fixed his tricycle."

He looked confused. "Me thinks thou dost blather incoherently."

She stood up and picked up her purse. "I'd have thought you, of all people, would know about tricycles." She pulled her checkbook and a pen from her purse. "How much rent do you owe?"

He looked down, shamefaced. "I'm in arrears two months, a hundred dollars."

She scribbled a check, tore it off, and handed it to him. "Here's a check for one hundred and fifty dollars. We'll take ten dollars a week out of your paycheck until it's repaid." She lowered her purse and waited until he made eye contact with her. "I've never noticed you to have the symptoms of an alcoholic, Jules, and assume this binge was a temporary

341

reaction to a life changing event. If I see any further traces of this behavior, you wont have a job. Understood?"

Jules rose, stood at attention, and gave her a military salute. "Yes, M'am, General, Sir!"

Julienne smiled, waved him a casual salute, and headed down the stairs as she said, "Carry on!"

****

Zoe turned the key to let David into Dimitri's living room, whispering, "He's probably asleep, but it will please him to find you waiting by his bedside." She turned to leave, stopped, tapped her chest, and looked at David. "This consumption thing, it gets to him every three years or so. He looks very bad, but he always pulls through in a few weeks. I think it's just stress."

David gave a pained smile. "Well, his work on the musical's book is pretty much finished, so maybe that'll reduce the stress."

Zoe mirrored his pained smile. "I think your visit will do him a lot of good. The worst thing for him is fearing that his absence will lose him his job at Aladdin's."

David chuckled. "If the musical is a success, I don't think he'll have to worry about that. He should be asking them for a substantial raise with the increase in business his celebrity will cause."

Zoe's eyes widened. "That's what Val told him."

David smiled approval. "Good! I'll stay with him 'till he wakes."

Zoe started down the courtyard stairs as she said, "I'll bring his lunch a little later." She stopped again and looked at him questioningly. "Would you like me to bring you something?"

David smiled gratefully. "No thanks, Zoe. I just came from lunch." Zoe continued down the steps.

David walked quietly to the rear bedroom where Dimitri lay as if in state, his pajama clad arms spread symmetrically as he lay straight as a board in the exact center of the four poster bed. David watched Dimitri's eyelids flutter as his audible breathes coated the inside of the clear plastic oxygen mask with moisture after each exhalation, which immediately disappeared after each labored inhalation. Contrary to the labored sound of his breathing, his pale face looked blissfully relaxed.

David strolled around the room admiring the ballet posters and framed photographs of Dimitri looking adoringly at Russian ballet stars while posing with them in the lobbies of performance halls in New Orleans, New York, Paris, and London. Although the furnishings were few, David recognized that the ornate gilded and brocade upholstered pieces were very expensive and probably reflective of Dimitri's childhood in the palatial homes of his parent's Nobel employers. Like Val's apartment, the master bedroom was at the front of the building with windows facing St. Louis Street, then a narrow hall to the living room at the rear and an exterior door to a balcony and stairway leading to the rear courtyard.. There were three doors in the hall; an open one to a bath next to the master bedroom, a partially open one to a small kitchen at the rear closest to the living room, and a third closed one in the middle, presumably a second bedroom. Curious, David opened it.

David found himself in what was obviously Dimitri's workshop. A long workbench on one wall was cluttered with woodworking tools and unfinished heads and limbs of marionettes in progress. On the wall, hanging between portraits clipped from magazines and posters, were the finished dolls of his many characters who were caricatures of the portraits; Churchill, the Jester, David, and others. The room was windowless and illuminated by several work lights on swinging arms over the workbench, and the whole place smelled like the various woods from which the dolls were carved.

The wall opposite the workbench reminded David of his own apartment, in that it had a full length floor to ceiling mural. This mural, however, was seen through a painted arched portico, beyond which was the skyline of St. Petersburg in Russia with all it's spires, terrazo inlaid walls, and gilded domes of mosques and synagogues. The mural was lit by three ceiling lights focused on the wall. In the darkness in front of the wall, David could barely perceive what appeared to be a hospital gurney with several drawers beneath its top surface. The cloth that covered the top surface appeared to be covering something on top of the gurney and, as David's eyes adjusted to the darkness, the shape of what was beneath the covering made David gasp.

David approached what appeared to be a body lying on a gurney and covered with a floral printed sheet. With a feeling of shock and apprehension, David slowly pulled back the sheet to discover what appeared to be a life size beautiful male nude body, the head of which looked familiar, until he remembered the bedroom photo of Dimitri staring adoringly at ballet star Rudolph Nuriev. David's hand shook slightly as he reached out slowly to touch the surface of the body and, as his eyebrows rose, close his hand into a fist to tap the surface three times with his knuckles, the beginnings of a smile starting at the corners of his mouth as he heard the hollow sound of wood. Dimitri has built himself a lifelike life size wooden replica of a nude Rudolph Nuriev, complete with genitalia.

David was shocked to hear Zoe's voice. "Sorry! I thought this door was locked."

David closed his eyes and raised his hands. "No, no! I'm sorry. I guess I just succumbed to natural curiosity."

Zoe set the tray of food on the workbench and came to stand beside David . "You know what this is?"

David inhaled deeply. "I think so."

Zoe placed her hands on the chest of the wooden figure. "It's called a 'merkin' or a 'Dutch wife.' This is the best one I ever saw."

David looked at her puzzled. "Dutch Wife? But, it's male."

Zoe made a fist and knocked the wooden chest of the doll. "Well, all I know is what I learned from the sailors at The Mariner's Club. The Dutch were the greatest ship builders in recent centuries, and they made life size wooden female dolls for the sailors to have sex with during months at sea. In Asia, they made them out of rubber."

David's brow wrinkled. "But it's male."

Zoe looked at him condescendingly. "You do know Dimitri's gay, don't you?" And with that she reached down, gripped the doll's phallus, and pulled it up on its wooden hinge until it snapped into position bolt upright."

David looked directly down at it in surprise. "Oh!"

Zoe pointed to indentations in the pad beneath the doll, two indentations on each side of the doll's hips. "Those were made by his knees and toes."

David rolled his eyes. "Oh!"

Zoe moved up and placed her hands on the head of the doll. "Maybe you should know this, too. But first, you gotta promise you'll never tell Dimitri that you were in here or know anything about this."

David closed his eyes and nodded his head up and down affirmatively. "Ohhhhhh, yes! That's for sure. You can take my word on that."

Zoe said, "Look," as she gripped the doll's head with both hands and said, "Sorry, Rudy," then turned it slightly pulled the head off the doll to reveal it was mounted via a wooden peg with a bayonet base. Then she pulled open a drawer under the gurney's top surface, placed the head in it, removed another head and installed it on the doll.

David opened his eyes, looked down, and gasped, "Oh, my God!" He stared horrified at a replica of his own head.

Zoe stared at him mischievously as she switch the heads back to Nuriev. "Okay, enough of playing with dolls. Let's go give Dimitri his lunch. Only, this time, I'm not gonna forget to lock this door."

After locking the door, Zoe set the food on a wooden breakfast tray with pockets on both sides to hold a newspaper and a small vase with one rose in it. Dimitri woke as she moved the breakfast tray into position for him, straddling his hips, and said, "Look whose here to visit," then left down the hallway.

Dimitri's voice cracked a little as he removed the oxygen mask and said, "Thank you, Zoe," then turned to smile at David. "So good to see you, David. Are they all mad at me in New York?"

David pulled the gilded chair beside the bed. "Oh, don't worry about them. Besides, you completed all that Alex had requested of you before you left."

Dimitri lifted the crystal goblet of orange juice and took a long drink. "Well he requested precious little of me. It's like you two rewrote the whole thing, and, if you hadn't, I suspect Max would have rewritten the whole thing into a 1920's German S.M. show, the fucking Nazi."

David blinked. "Oh, that's right! You left before the big blowup."

Dimitri buttered his rye toast. "What blowup?"

346

David leaned forward and smiled broadly. "There was an investor's meeting over complaint's about Max's proposed changes to the book. Dimitri, you would have been so proud of Princess. She acted as a two percent shareholder and as proxy for the others fifty percent. She stood up to Henrietta, Angus, Harry, and Angelo and their minority forty-eight percent, and she thoroughly reamed them out."

Dimitri frowned as he dropped the butter knife on the plate with a clatter. "Oh, damn, and I had to miss that! It would have been so delicious to watch her bite their dinosaur ass's."

David shrugged. "Well, Alex and I would have missed it if Princess hadn't insisted we be present at the meeting. I think she wanted us for moral support, among other things."

Dimitri waved his buttered toast in the air and wiggled his shoulders as he smiled mischievously. "Tell me! Tell me all about it! What did she do?"

David said, "Well, I can 't do Princess justice," then he proceeded to attempt an imitation of Princess that sounded more like Shirley Temple singing *The Good Ship Lollipop*. "'Henrietta, didn't you describe yourselves as three misogynists and an atheist who would be our devils and deny funding until The Goddess Consortium put up the majority funding. Speaking as proxy for that majority funding, we propose that Max VonDeutsch be discharged as Director of *The Piano Lover* and Alex Pienas be appointed to replace him.'"

Next David started doing a bad imitation of a Scotsman. "Then Angus started sputtering, 'But, but, but, we like Alex, but he's never directed a Broadway show before.'"

Then David switched back to Shirley Temple. "To which Princess replied, 'But he was the Choreographer on four Broadway shows, two of which were nominated for a Tony. And didn't you brag to us that Max's very first film won the top German film award back in the Stone Ages? Maybe Alex's first time out as a director will be a winner!'"

Switching gears, David attempted to impersonate Henrietta, which sounded like a bad Sophie Tucker. "Then Henrietta was sputtering, 'Now see here, young lady, atheist or not, I have a right to protect my investment.'"

David switched back to Shirley Temple. "To which Princess replied, 'Well, see here, old lady, you've only invested twelve percent, and you're outvoted, Max is outdated, and Alex is in!'"

Dimitri was coughing intermittently between laughing hysterically. "Oh, David, forgive me, but you are such a bad impersonator that you're hilarious. You could make a great act out of doing bad impersonations."

David smiled at him warmly. "Anything to make you smile, Dimitri."

Dimitri's laughing subsided and he stared at his plate. "You want some of this, David? I can't finish the rest of it."

David smile diminished. "No thanks, I had lunch just before I came."

Dimitri continued to stare at his plate. "Remember that day in Ling's office when we first complained about Max?"

David leaned back in the chair. "Yes."

Dimitri sighed. "Ling and I had some heated words before you arrived."

David nodded his head. "I kinda sensed that. That's why I knocked."

Dimitri rolled his eyes. "She told me she had been raped by a North Korean soldier when she was thirteen."

David closed his eyes. "Yes, she had told me that previously."

Dimitri coughed and put the oxygen mask back on his face and inhaled three times before removing it again.. "I told her about the Bolsheviks shooting my parents and that she won because she had more pity points, but I lied."

David knew he was supposed to ask the question. "How so?"

Dimitri closed his eyes. "When they entered our servant's quarters, first they shot my parents with their rifles, then, because they were not completely dead from the gunshots, they bayoneted them multiple times."

David sighed and looked at Dimitri's breakfast tray. "I'm sorry, Dimitri."

Dimitri opened his eyes and stared down the hallway. "And then they started raping my fourteen year old sister...," and he paused before continuing, "...and me repeatedly. I remember the first one choking me with his phallus down my throat, then actually pinching my nose so I couldn't breath. I think he actually wanted to kill me with his thing in my throat, kill a twelve year old boy because the two children had lace on their collar and cuffs when the man broke into the room." He looked at David. "We were peasants, just like them, peasants recruited to be house servants. Does that make any sense?"

David felt compelled to make eye contact. "Of course not."

Dimitri looked down the hallway again. "They raped my sister again and again, and she died, I don't know, after the second or third day of being continually raped." His eyes slowly moved down to the plate before him as his head shook sideways. "I was unaware of her death at that time, because by then my anal sphincter had been torn and I was incontinent until I had surgery months later in England." He smiled painfully at David. "I remember the English Officer who brought the ransom money, and how shocked he was that I continually soiled myself."

Though Dimitri's eyes were dry, David fought back the tears in his own eyes. "Dimitri, people like Julienne, who had

349

an idyllic childhood, and myself, whose only complaint was being poor and hungry, when we learn about the early life of people like you and Princess and Ling, we are amazed by, not just your ability to survive, but to do so with such exceptional talent and strength of character.

Dimitri looked at David expectantly. "So, do I have more pity points than Ling?"

David was surprised by Dimitri's sarcasm and, as he wiped away the tears that ran down his cheeks, he smiled, chuckled, and said, "Yes! Oh my God, yes! You are the grand champion of pity points."

Dimitri closed his eyes tightly, clenched his fists, and smiled. "Yes, yes, yes! I win!" Then he sighed and looked at David. "I had to win, because I'm jealous of Ling. She has you, and I don't."

David smiled sadly and shook his head sideways. "Oh no. She doesn't have me. She's had some parts of me on some rare occasions, but she doesn't have me."

Dimitri wrinkled his nose. "But that's still more than I have of you."

David walked over to the bedside and took one of Dimitri's hands in both of his. He looked at Dimitri fondly and continued to shake his head sideways. "Oh no. You have much more of me than she does. More respect for your greater talent, and, for whatever it is worth, a deeper, longer, and more enduring friendship."

Finally, tears flowed from Dimitri's eyes and ran down to drip onto the oxygen mask hanging on his chest. "Thank you, David. That's worth a lot to me."

David patted his hand. "Enough to make you promise you'll get well and come to the opening?"

Dimitri smiled. "Yes, David, I promise."

****

350

David, Dimitri, Princess, and Gabriel scrambled to get the dishes off the table top before Alex threw the newspapers down. While caricatures of theater and film greats stared down from the wall behind their booth in Sardi's Restaurant on 44th Street, they pored over the reviews of *The Piano Man* on it's opening night. After tearing through pages and mumbling among themselves, Alex started to rise from his seat holding a folded newspaper in his trembling hand. "Listen, listen, listen! 'The most unique show to come along in many years champions the civil rights of blacks, gays, and women, and does so with soaring lyrics and gut breaking comedy that should make its profound statements palatable to the most jaded theatergoer.'"

David stood up with another paper. "I like this one. '*The Piano Lover* makes the claim that all women have always known and all misogynists have always feared; God is a woman, and she's pissed! Fortunately, she can sing and dance and deliver comedy better than anything Broadway's seen in years.'"

Dimitri had to push the two taller men aside in order to stand up and read the next review. "Look, look! They even spelled my name right. 'First time playwrights Dimitri Lebedev and David Wales have scored a hit with *The Piano Lover*, turning French Quarter licentious libertines into social crusaders.' And look, Princess, they really liked you. 'Another Russian with an unpronounceable name was the actress who is almost too beautiful to play a male transvestite, but nailed the character of Patrice with classy choreography, stylish vocals, and impeccable comedy timing.' This guy even likes you, Gabriel. 'Kudos to the makeup team that turned the amazing musician who played The Angel Gabriel into a totally convincing Louis Armstrong look alike.'"

Gabriel looked perplexed. "The makeup people didn't do nothin' to me."

Princess raised her voice. "And why'd he call me Russian. Where's Ling? Didn't she tell them I'm Choctaw Indian?"

Alex sat back and put his arms around Gabriel and Princess. "Hey, Gabriel, you're an 'amazing musician," and Princess, you're 'too beautiful' to play yourself. Don't look a gift compliment in the mouth. You are the stars of a hit musical. Thank God for what she's done for us tonight."

They all raised their drinks and toasted together. "Thank God!"

Ling arrived with a stack of newspapers and a big smile. "Oh, I see you already got the papers. Did you read those reviews?" They all responded affirmatively. "Honest, I've worked on all the musicals that Alex has been in, and I never saw better reviews than this. You definitely have a hit, and probably have a shot at The Antoinette Perry Award."

Dimitri's nose wrinkled. "The what?"

Alex looked at him. "The 'Tony' Award. It's for excellence in the theater. A couple of the musicals I've worked on were nominated, but none ever actually got one." He smiled broadly at all around. "Maybe the third time's the charm."

Ling gestured to Gabriel and Princess. "Princess, Gabriel, I have some press photographer's in the lobby, if you don't mind. I'll be reading a statement, and all you have to do is pose pretty. Okay?" As Princess and Gabriel squeezed their way out of the booth, Ling turned to Dimitri and David. "David, Dimitri, don't go anywhere. I'll be back for you in a little bit. It's just pictures. I'll be giving them a prepared statement. Okay."

They both nodded as Ling escorted Princess and Gabriel away. As David watched them receding to the front of the restaurant, he saw a familiar face in the distance headed

352

toward him. He excused himself from the table and walked briskly toward Julienne with a smile on his face. "Well! This is a fabulously pleasant surprise! Did you see the show?"

Julienne looked stunning in a black silk sheath, black stiletto heels, and a single strand of pearls. "Yes! It was fabulous!"

David's brow was questioning. "Why didn't you come backstage?"

She returned his warm smile. "I did, but you guys were swamped with admirers."

David escorted her to the booth, Alex and Dimitri seeing them and exiting the booth before they arrived. He waited for her to be seated. "Did anyone come with you?"

She put her pearl bejeweled clutch purse on the table. "Valentina couldn't come, but Zoe did. The two of us spoke to Princess and Gabriel backstage, then Zoe went back to the hotel. I figured you might be here."

He smiled as his eyes darted over her face, her hair, her bare shoulders, and back to her eyes. "I'm so glad you did." He tried to hail a waiter with no success. "I was hoping I'd see you at The Voodoo Room, or maybe at some of our haunts."

She ran her hand through her hair and looked around the restaurant. "I had a lot of loose ends to tie up. Perhaps more than I should have bothered with." She turned and smiled at him playfully. "But it's not like you didn't have company."

He stared at the haphazard stack of newspapers for several seconds. "Yes, well, Aurora's been in and out of town, recording sessions, radio broadcasts."

Julienne looked around the restaurant. "Is she here tonight?"

David continued to stare at the papers. "No, she's in Hollywood trying to establish her own recording label. She's asked me to write all new songs for her premier album on the new label."

Julienne reached out and patted the back of his hand. "That's wonderful, David, and with the success of this musical, your career is firmly established."

He exhaled noisily and turned to smile at her. "And one thing that insures is that your investment, and all The Goddess Consortium investments, are safe."

She closed and opened her eyes while slowly shaking her head side to side. "I was never worried about that, David."

He raised both eyebrows and shook his head up and down. "Well, I was. Oh, I know you never pressured me once about any of that, but I couldn't help but feel the sting of your father's accusations, and I wasn't really sure whether Val trusted me, either."

Julienne bit her lip. "Oh, I think Val trusted you about material things. I just think she had doubts about your being husband material."

He suppressed a chuckle. "I don't blame her. I don't know if I'm husband material myself."

She smiled. "Despite the way your musical, *The Piano Lover*, ends......"

He looked at her abruptly. "By the way, Alex said you should never tell anyone how it ends, that way they have to see the musical to find out."

Her smile broadened. "Despite the way your musical, or any musical or play or movie or book or fairytale ends, I've learned that, in reality, there are no absolutes, no perfect endings, no fading into the sunset. Until we draw our last breath, things can change, promises can be broken, unexpected joys can be discovered." He turned and looked at her seriously as she continued. "I certainly never expected you in my life, or any of the adventures I've shared with you. I regret nothing. Experiencing the best of them was certainly worth suffering the worst of them."

Just then Ling appeared. "David, the photographer's are ready for you."

As David rose, Julienne followed him until she was standing a few feet from Ling, staring at her. "So this is Ling."

David gestured from one woman to the other. "Ling Park, this is Julienne deVille."

Ling's eyes widened and her nostrils flared. "Ohhhhh. You're Julienne. You are as beautiful as Aurora told me."

David looked furtively from one woman to the other, then cleared his throat.

Ling looked from David to Julienne, extended her hand to Julienne, and said, "It is really a pleasure to meet you, Julienne." Julienne hesitated, then extended her hand and the two women barely touched palms together. Then Ling looked at David. "I'll wait for you with the photographers, David," and she exited toward the front of the restaurant.

David looked at Julienne's blank expression with his mouth partly open, then blinked.

Julienne sighed, then looked at David with a Mona Lisa smile. "I see you've fixed your tricycle."

He buttoned one button on his coat and pulled his coat sleeves down to remove any wrinkles. "Some vehicles have spare tires."

She gave him a pained smile. "Well, I don't want to keep your public waiting."

David turned to go, stopped, turned partially back and looked at Julienne sideways. "Julienne, I don't know what your capacity for adventure and discovery is, but I would like you to stay, I invite you to stay, and, if you chose not to, I will understand," and he turned and exited toward the front of the restaurant.

Julienne watched him go until he was out of sight, then began to walk slowly toward the front of the restaurant. Halfway there, she stopped, surveyed the front one hundred and eighty degrees of the restaurant, then turned around and surveyed the rear one hundred and eighty degrees of the restaurant. She walked back to the booth, sat down and pulled one of the newspapers toward her.

A waiter stopped in front of the booth and asked, "Can I get you anything, Miss?"

She looked up absently and said, "I'd like a tri....." Then she shut her eyes tightly, shook her head sideways, and said, "I'm sorry." She opened her eyes, sighed, looked at the waiter and said, "I'd like a grasshopper, please."

THE END

YOU ARE INVITED

to review this book on amazon.com. Simply enter the title in Amazon's search window and, once on the title page, click on "Customer Reviews," then click on "Write a Review."

You are also invited to offer the author feedback or ask any questions you may have about this book or any of his books that you've read. You may communicate with him directly through the following e-mail address:

williamkarlthomas@gmail.com

THE PIANO LOVER

The book you have just read is available from Amazon.com in an E-edition for your Kindle, Nook, I-pad, or other E-reader, or read it on your computer by downloading Amazon's free E-reader application.
ISBN 978-1-62768-005-9 Softcover $14.95
ISBN 978-1-62768-006-6 digital E-edition $4.99

PIANO LOVER THE MUSICAL

The second novel of *The Piano Lover* trilogy includes the script and score of an entire original musical stage production. Follow the careers of the talented alumni from New Orleans French Quarter who helped create the 1950's and 1960's counter culture.
ISBN 978-1-62768-011-0 Softcover $14.95
ISBN 978-1-62768-012-7 digital E-edition $4.99

PIANO LOVER THE MOVIE

In the third novel of the trilogy, the musical is made into a movie. The entourage experience professional and romantic adventures in Hollywood, San Francisco, Santa Barbara, Malibu, New York, New Orleans, Matzatland, and Jamaica West Indies with their famous and celebrated show biz peers.
ISBN 978-1-62768-013-4 Softcover $14.95
ISBN 978-1-62768-014-1 digital E-edition $4.99

OTHER BOOKS BY
WILLIAM KARL THOMAS

All books are available in print and digital editions from
Amazon.com or from any bookseller by their ISBN number.
Details and excerpts online at http://www.mediamaestro.net.
Order autographed copies from Media Maestro - Book
Division, P.O. Box 50672, Tucson, AZ 85703.

LENNY BRUCE: THE MAKING OF A PROPHET

William Karl Thomas' intimate and poignant memoir of his ten year collaboration with the most controversial comedian of the 20th century, a martyr to First Amendment rights. The book begins before Bruce's rise to international fame and continues through the night Bruce died. A Japanese language edition is available from DHC in Tokyo, Japan.

ISBN 978-0-9799477-0-4 Hardcover: $24.95
ISBN 978-1-62768-003-5 Softcover $9.95
ISBN 978-0-9799477-4-2 digital E-edition: $2.99

THE CANDY BUTCHER

The amazing biography of screenwriter, film producer, playwright, actor, nightclub comedian Frank Ray Perilli, creator of such notable films as *The Doberman Gang, Harlow* and such cult films as *Dracula's Dog, Little Cigars, Fairytales, Cinderella, The End of the World, Alligator,* and more than two dozen offbeat films and plays.

ISBN 978-1-62768-019-6 Softcover $9.95
ISBN 978-1-62768-020-2 digital E-edition $2.99

HOLLYWOOD TALES FROM THE OUTER FRINGE

William Karl Thomas' career brought him in contact with 'A' list celebrities and the armies of 'little people' who served them. This anthology of twelve short stories reveals the intimate relationship between the two set against a historically accurate 1950-60's background.

ISBN 978-0-9799477-3-5 Softcover: $9.95
ISBN 978-0-9799477-7-3 digital E-edition $2.99

THE JOSAN AND THE JEE

A novel about three women who survived massacres and rape during The Korean War, and their intimate relationship with an American GI dealing with his own demons, from his failed marriage to his unfaithful stateside wife to his contentious relationship with his bigoted military boss.

ISBN 978-1-62768-001-1 Softcover $9.95
ISBN 978-0-9799477-5-9 digital E-edition $2.99

CLEO

A novel about a beautiful and talented black female journalist who is an intimate friend of black entertainment and political celebrities during the turbulent civil rights era in the 1950's and 1960's. Her professional and private life takes a quantum leap when she crosses paths with a cynical but equally talented white male publicist.

ISBN 978-1-62768-002-8 Softcover $9.95
ISBN 978-0-9799477-6-6 digital E-edition $2.99

THE GENTEEL POOR

A memoir telling the story of four generations of the author's colorful and talented family spanning the Civil War, World War I, the Great Depression, and World War II. This coming of age memoir deals with the social and ethnic evolution of the New Orleans/Gulf Coast area a century before it was devastated by Hurricane Katrina.

ISBN 978-1-59663-565-4 Hardcover: $29.95
ISBN 978-1-62768-000-4 Softcover $9.95
ISBN 978-0-9799477-9-7 digital E-edition $2.99

A PLACE FOR US

The biography of Wendy Wolf who entered an iron lung at the age of four and emerged a polio survivor whose life illustrates the challenges of opportunity and acceptance people with disabilities face and the triumphs and successes this extraordinary woman achieved. An inspiration for every disabled person and every single mother.

ISBN 978-0-9799477-2-8 Hardcover $29.95
ISBN 978-1-62768-004-2 Softcover $9.95
ISBN 978-0-9799477-8-0 digital E-edition $2.99

IMMORTAL: a science fiction trilogy

A millennium into the future, three alien archeologists attempt to determine how humanity self destructed themselves and their planet. Their discovery of a dormant android guarding a human gene bank on a Saturnian moon leads to a conflict among them regarding humanity's potential future. Share the alien archeologist's discovery of human evolution and the turning points that shaped earth's civilizations in the first book of this trilogy.

ISBN 978-1-62768-007-3 Softcover $9.95
ISBN 978-1-62768-008-0 digital E-edition $2.99

IMMORTAL: RESURRECTION

In the second novel of the trilogy, the alien female allies with the android's desperate attempt to resurrect humanity while alien forces mount an expedition to rid the universe of human dysfunctional behavior that threatens the universe.

ISBN 978-1-62768-015-8 Softcover $9.95
ISBN 978-1-62768-016-5 digital E-edition $2.99

IMMORTAL: ARMAGEDDON

In the third novel of the trilogy, a small band of newly created humans defend the survival of the human race against an alien expedition determined to rid the universe of future human folly, and the origin and mission of the android is revealed.

ISBN 978-1-62768-017-2 Softcover $9.95
ISBN 978-1-62768-018-9 digital E-edition $2.99

ABOUT THE AUTHOR

 William Karl Thomas was born 1/25/33 in Bay St. Louis, Mississippi, a small Gulf Coast town in which Tennessee Williams lived and wrote about in his works. In 1951 Thomas married his former high school teacher and was divorced after a four year childless marriage. His checkered background includes being a cocktail pianist in New Orleans French Quarter, serving a year of combat in the Air Force during the Korean War, being a photographer, a journalist, a feature/documentary cinematographer, a screen writer, an industrial film producer, a public relations executive, and a book author. He has worked for and with such notables as Frank Sinatra, the Rat Pack, Lenny Bruce, and others.. In the course of various assignments, Thomas has lived or worked in Oxford England, Paris France, Japan, Korea, Jamaica, Mexico, Canada, and various parts of the United States.

The Manchester Guardian has stated, "He superbly evokes the seedy atmosphere of the cheap Hollywood clubs and coffeehouses," and "His work sometimes reads like a Bogart script." Kirkus refers to, "His historically astute depiction of the country and era" and "(He) aptly conveys the heights and depths of human capability," and refers to *The Josan and the Jee* as "An emotionally challenging but rewarding war novel." Readers reviews say " One of the best books I have ever read; maybe the best," and "This story will make you sad and happy at the same time. It is difficult to put the book down."